*By Stuart Johnstone*

Out in the Cold

Into the Dark

# INTO THE DARK

## STUART JOHNSTONE

Allison & Busby Limited
11 Wardour Mews
London W1F 8AN
*allisonandbusby.com*

First published in Great Britain by Allison & Busby in 2021.
This paperback edition published by Allison & Busby in 2022.

A CIP catalogue record for this book is available from
the British Library.

10 9 8 7 6 5 4 3 2 1

ISBN 978-0-7490-2653-0

Typeset in 10.5/15.5 pt Sabon LT Pro by
Allison & Busby Ltd

FSC
www.fsc.org
MIX
Paper from
responsible sources
FSC® C171272

Printed and bound by
CPI Group (UK) Ltd, Croydon, CR0 4YY

*For Rose Winifred Johnstone*

# CHAPTER ONE

## Mr Beeswax

'Hello, emergency service operator, which service? . . . Emergency service operator, do you require fire, police, or ambulance? . . . Hello? . . . Is there someone there? . . . How can I help you? . . . Hello, is there—'

'Aye, aye. I'm here.'

'Hello, sir. What is the nature of your emergency? . . . Sir? I need you to tell me—'

'Well, if you'd just shut up for a minute maybe I would tell you, wouldn't I?'

'Angie, I think it's Mr Beeswax.'

'What's that? Who're you talkin' to there?'

'Nothing, Mr . . . uh, sir. I was just consulting my colleague. How can I help you tonight?'

'I'll tell you how you can help me . . . I just, eh. What is it now?'

'Sir, could I start by taking your name please?'

'Don't interrupt me. Ach, I've gone and lost my train of . . . Didn't your mother teach you not to interrupt people? It's rude. Ach, where was I now?'

'Sorry, sir. But your name please? I need to log the call and I need your—'

'My name? I'll tell you what my name is, it's none of your bloody beeswax, that's what my name is.'

'Thank you, sir. I'll log that for you. Now what is it we can do for you tonight? You have something you'd like to report I assume?'

'Are you laughing? I can hear you laughing. Your little pal beside you, too.'

'No, no. Not laughing, sir. We'd never do that. What is it you'd like to report Mr Bees . . . eh, sir?'

'You *are* laughin'. I can hear ye and whoever it is you're with. I can hear them an' all.'

'Sir, I can assure you, there is nobody laughing here. Now what is it today, sir? Theft of a yeti, perhaps? Has another monster been assaulted?'

'You *are* takin' the piss. I bloody knew it. And what do ye mean again? I've never called you before in my life, ya cheeky wee—'

'Now, now sir. No need for any bad language. What is it to be? Aliens in the park? Armed robbery of a—'

'He's butchered him. He's bloody butchered him and dumped him in a damned ditch.'

'. . . Uh . . .'

'Cut his eyes out, so he has. What kind of a monster could . . . Cut his eyes out?'

'Sir, what exactly are we talking about here? . . . Sir, are you still there? . . . Sir, are you still on the line?'

'Cut his eyes—'

'Sir? Hello? No, he's gone.'

'That's it. He just hung up after that. What do you think?' DS Cunningham swept the mouse to the top right of his computer screen and closed the window.

Alyson Kane rubbed at her arm where goosebumps had formed. 'That got pretty dark, pretty quick. What are we listening to?'

'A treble-nine call, obviously. The DCI wants it looked into.'

'It's a bit . . . unprofessional. Don't you think?'

DS Cunningham laughed. 'It is a bit. I'd hate to be the poor sod who handled that call. If he'd thought for a second it was going to be studied in connection to a murder case, he would have stuck to the script, for sure.'

Alyson lifted one of the Starbucks coffees she'd placed on the table in front of them and sipped. Her train had been late this morning, therefore so was she, and rather than run to McNair Street Police Station, she'd allowed a few more minutes of tardy timekeeping to bring her sergeant a placating gesture. Coffee never failed. When he stopped her in the corridor, she thought perhaps this trick had been played one too many times, but he hadn't seemed to have noticed the time and ushered her into his office to play her the recording of the call.

'So, what's the story, boss? Is this to do with the Bradley case?' she asked, pointing at the MP3 file in the folder on the screen.

'I'll tell you in the car. This coming in has reminded the DCI that it's been a while since we updated the family and you and I have drawn the short straw,' he said, standing up.

Alyson's heart sank. If this wasn't the worst part of the job, she didn't ever want to see what beat it. She followed Duncan through the enormous room on the third floor of McNair Police Station, which was empty but for a few lone DCs typing away at terminals. Outside, she dropped herself into the passenger seat of the unmarked Ford, clutching her coffee to her like a safety blanket. She prayed he'd be doing the talking this time. During the last visit he'd left it to her and she'd stumbled over her words and tortured herself by playing a constant loop of it in her mind for days afterwards.

'So, this recording . . .' she prompted him, once they'd joined traffic.

'Right, well, this guy, he's a frequent crank caller. Or maybe not a crank, more confused. Mr Beeswax, as they called him, phones in maybe once every other month. They traced it to a care home out in Edinburgh. He calls in at crazy hours of the night, reporting outlandish things. He's clearly senile. The call handlers are bored to tears at that hour and I suppose they were just have a bit of fun with him. Unprofessional, but harmless, really.'

'Until now. It's the eyes thing, I suppose?'

'That's right.'

'And the DCI wants *me* to look into it?' A jolt of euphoria surged through her, displacing the dread of updating the family and making her feel a little lightheaded.

'She does, yes. But Alyson, don't get excited. The thing

is, that call you listened to is from March.'

'What? You're kidding.'

'I'm afraid not. Three full weeks before Callum's murder.'

The euphoria in Alyson's chest dropped into her stomach, morphing through disappointment into something more resembling irritation. She took a moment before she spoke; counting to ten, her mum called it. 'Then what's the point? I'm assuming Mr Beeswax, or whatever his name is, isn't considered a suspect, or even a witness. Why this? Why me?'

She could hear the petulance in her voice, despite her best intentions. But Duncan Cunningham was one of the good ones; he was three years before his retirement and so had long since given up on any career advancement. In Alyson's experience, you remove ambition from a gaffer and you end up with a level-headed one. They're the ones you can rely on to help you with your career. There's no competition, no games. Along with the ladder-climbing, he'd also given up on his appearance a bit. He had no problem wearing the same shirt and tie combination four days in a row. He was bald across the majority of his head, with a Caesar's laurel of hair remaining which he allowed to grow, bucking the middle-aged shave-it-all trend and so making him look older than his fifty-eight years.

He was silent as he negotiated a roundabout, then took the exit for Rickerburn, before addressing her again: 'It's desperation, that's what it is. The DCI's feeling the pressure and you know as well as I do that shit rolls downhill. Twelve weeks with no tangible leads, suspects or witnesses and she's getting . . . creative . . . in the face of some tricky questions from above. That's what I think.'

'But this could be looked into by anyone. It'll take all of an afternoon. Why not get uniform on it?' Alyson unfolded her arms, conscious of how much like a sulking teenager she must look.

Duncan turned to her, exhaling. 'You want some advice?'

'That's rhetorical, right?'

'Of course it is. Look, just go with it, and do it with a grateful smile on your face. You remember what the incident room looked like last month?'

'It was going like a fair.'

'Every spare detective, pro-active team member and a small army of uniform all queueing to get five minutes on a computer terminal. Now you have your pick from dozens. They're scaling this back big time, but for the moment, you're still involved. Don't give them an excuse to send you back to interviewing plebs for housebreakings. Go do this and don't rush back. Get some local help and stay involved.'

He had a point. A good one. The day after a dog walker had discovered the mutilated remains of ten-year-old Callum Bradley – his body dumped at the side of an old open-cast mine, his eyes . . . God, Alyson never wanted to see *those* photographs again – they had set up the dedicated Major Incident room. The day she'd entered, it had seemed small and ridiculously crowded. Alyson had been rescued from a housebreaking team to which she'd been seconded to for three months, but which had stretched into a tedious seven months. What was she complaining about? All the things she'd been tasked with had been pretty mundane. Collect CCTV here, log productions there; but now she was working a murder.

'OK,' she said. 'Where is this old weirdo?'

'North Edinburgh. I'll email you the details. You know anyone out there?'

Alyson laughed humourlessly. 'Actually, I do. A community sergeant who works out that way. And he owes me. Owes me big.'

They pulled up to the house and Alyson drew a long breath before she pushed the car door open and stepped onto the kerb.

It was Mrs Bradley who answered when they knocked, though she barely looked to see who she was opening the door to. She was in the same semi-catatonic state she'd been in each time Alyson had seen her. Mrs Bradley shuffled back along the hall. Alyson allowed Duncan to go ahead of her.

Mr Bradley sat at the kitchen table. His beard was new, his trembling hands were not, as he reached out to shake Duncan's hand. Alyson felt wretched about the initial weeks of the investigation when he had been treated as a suspect, though mercifully ruled out after an air-tight alibi, and from prints and DNA samples he freely gave.

Alyson stood in the corner of the kitchen while Duncan uttered phrases they all had come to know so well and said nothing: 'Investigation is ongoing', 'pursuing several leads', 'working around the clock.' She faced the floor and willed it to be over.

Mrs Bradley was sobbing in another room.

# CHAPTER TWO

## Morgan's Case

'I'm really sorry about this, Sarge.'

'Don't apologise, Cathy. Listen, I've worked with plenty of officers who'd go off sick if their budgie sneezed, and you're not one of them. You've a chronic problem and you need to look after yourself. You hear me?'

Cathy sniffed on the other end of the line and confirmed she understood, her voice breaking with emotion.

'Thanks for ringing me, but you didn't need to do that. Now call the HR line to let them know and then you rest up. I'll manage your cases. Give my best to that family of yours.'

'Thanks, Sarge. Really.'

I felt bad for her. Cathy was the senior constable on my small team and a good cop. It wasn't unexpected, not really. I'd been watching her throw back pills like smarties for weeks and had once watched her from the first-floor window as she tried to exit her police vehicle. It had taken her two attempts in as many minutes.

I was well aware of her back issues. It was a smash a few years ago during a pursuit when she was with the Traffic Unit. A lesser officer would have pursued a claim against Police Scotland, if not for compensation, then at least for early retirement with full benefits. Not Cathy. She loved the job, even after twenty-something years. Her enthusiasm was as obvious as it was infectious, which made her an ideal tutor constable. Joining the Community Policing Team was supposed to be a way of easing her back into service. I'd immediately taken to her when I'd joined the team three months ago.

I laid down the phone and walked through to the canteen which consisted of a table large enough to sit eight, a few armchairs and a TV/DVD combination job in the corner. A small bookshelf sat beside it, devoted almost exclusively to Stephen King paperbacks and movies. Cathy's shiny new probationer was sitting at the table, at work and ready to go half an hour early, as I expected. He was clicking away at his mechanical pencil, trying to find the right length of nib to, no doubt, faithfully record that he was 'on duty' in his notebook. Which reminded me, I hadn't even opened my own in over a week. I'd find time to go back over it and fill in the days missed: day and date, time on duty, time off duty. A bit silly, but we all knew of at least one officer who had been requested to hand over their notebook to a procurator fiscal depute at court after a bad showing in the box. It's a disciplinary offence to have holes in the recording of your notebook. Probationers tend to it like a sick pet, whereas those with service, more like a distant relative. Seriously, walk into a waiting room in any court in the land and you'll find a clutch of cops frantically back-filling months of non-entries; especially the ones who wear suits and generally live in pads of witness-statement paper rather than their little black books.

'Morgan.'

'Sarge,' he said, dropping his pencil on the table. He chased after it and knocked his notebook onto the floor. He reached for it with a long, thin arm.

'You're with me today.'

'Yes, Sarge.'

'It's all right, relax. Sit down and finish your drink. Muster in twenty minutes.'

The boy was on his feet, it was difficult to think of him as anything else. He was twenty-four, I knew from his file, but he was still filling out. His body armour gave the false impression of some bulk, but you could see from his long, thin limbs that he could benefit with putting on a few pounds. He was fidgeting and trying to stuff his notebook away, almost toppling over his can of Fanta. Was I as awkward and nervous when I started? Probably.

At 2 p.m. my small team assembled in my office. The shift officers mustered in the canteen, but with just the five of us – four, now that Cathy was off – it didn't seem necessary.

Vikram and Mandy had been working together for over a year and I didn't see any point in breaking that up. They cleared their cases and produced a decent amount of pro-active work and that reflected well on the department as a whole. *If it ain't broke* . . . So, I decided I'd work with Morgan, at least for today. Besides, it was about time. I'd never worked a full shift with him and his evaluation was due in a few months' time. Good opportunity to see what he was made of.

'Two car break-ins were reported overnight in Pilton. Day shift were apparently too busy to deal with it, so I'm afraid it's dropped to us. Or rather – to you,' I said and handed over the printout to Mandy. She had eighteen years' service, Vikram just nine, which put Mandy in charge. An unwritten rule in policing. Strictly speaking all constables are the same rank, but that's not how it works in practical terms. Ask lanky, fresh-out-the-box Morgan here to give Mandy an order and just see what happens.

'This is happening just a wee bit too often, Sarge. The shift dumping stuff on us, I mean,' said Vikram.

'Agreed. I'm going to have a word with their sergeant, but you know what it's like, how they view us community officers.' There was a grumble of agreement. 'And if you get a chance, could you get out by Muirhouse, by the golf course, been a few complaints about off-road bikes.'

'Will do, Sarge,' said Mandy, and she and Vikram set off.

'So, what would Cathy have had you doing today?' I asked Morgan.

'Actually, we were going to follow up on a fraud case. It's a bit of a mess, so it is.' Morgan was from Northern Ireland and had a thick accent. The 'so it is' came out as a single word – *soadis*.

'You can explain on the way. I forget, have you had your driving course yet?'

'Not yet, Sarge, no.'

*Bollocks*, I thought. I was never fond of driving for an entire shift. It drained the energy from you. Even though you need to have a full driving licence to even apply to the police, they wouldn't let you near the wheel of a police vehicle until you'd passed a week-long driving course. A torturous week that I wouldn't fully describe to the lad. No point in scaring him, he'd just have to find out for himself.

It was a fine afternoon. That is to say, it wasn't raining. I pulled the car out of the Drylaw office and turned left while Morgan fished through his notebook for details of this case he was working on.

North Edinburgh, our beat, took in very contrasting corners of the city. The northern border was easily delineated by the Firth of Forth and confined areas such as Granton and Newhaven. Not particularly affluent areas of the city, but not the worst. The East border was Leith and was a whole thing in itself. However, we were headed west. Cramond lies at the north-west edge of the city. Its distance from the city centre should logically mean a more achievable house price than areas within, but its proximity to the water and relatively easy access to arterial routes back into town meant that it was reserved largely for those with serious wealth. I wouldn't be putting a down-payment on a three bed here anytime soon.

'Is Cathy all right?' Morgan asked, a little sheepishly as if he wasn't sure it was OK to do so.

'Not really. She's going to be off for a while, so we might need to find you another tutor to help you complete your probation. How long do you have to go?'

'Nine months.'

'How are you finding it all? Any problems?'

'No problems, Sarge. Not as such. Just all takes a bit of getting used to is all.'

'It gets easier every day. In a few years you'll have forgotten all this stress.'

'I hope so. And I hope whoever's taking over from Cathy has the same patience. Sometimes takes a few goes for something to sink in with me, you know? Come off here, Sarge, take a left at the lights.'

'I'm sure you're doing fine, Morgan.'

'Sarge, you mentioned at muster how the shift officers view us community lot. How'd you mean?'

'I'm sure you're getting a sense of it. The shift responds to calls, they're the front line. Us, well we're more about preventative work, public reassurance. The happy smiley face of Police Scotland, right?'

'I suppose. At least that's what I thought when I got posted, but . . .'

'But it doesn't really work that way?'

'Well, yeah.'

'The police budget is tight. Once upon a time, community departments did all that public reassurance stuff, but the reality is we're just another layer of call handling and since we're second to the table with these calls, we tend to get the scraps. The icky end bits nobody else wants; often the protracted nonsense that takes loads of man hours to bottom out and with little chance of a collar.'

'Take a right up here, Sarge, then go right to the end.'

'What is it we're heading to again?'

'It's a fraud and theft. We're still debating over whether it's a housebreaking or not.'

'Sounds complicated. And a good example of what I'm talking about. Let me guess, it was left to you by some backshift or something that didn't like the smell of it?'

'I suppose. Cathy wasn't happy about it anyway. I might need a bit of help with it. It's the house at the end of this row, number fifty-seven.'

It was a nice street. Detached homes with large mono-block driveways set behind coiffured hedges. I pulled up at the very last house in the cul de sac and reached for my radio. 'Control from three-four, over.'

'Go ahead three-four.'

'Can you mark us at fifty-seven Duchess Park, over.'

'Roger three-four.'

'So, what's the story?' I asked.

Morgan patted at his pocket and produced his notebook. He scratched at his jaw, his skin raw from shaving too close, and some acne just below his ear. 'It's an elderly couple stay here. Some fella turned up, offered to cut down a tree in the back garden. They agree a price of fifty quid but then he starts giving the old "more complicated than we first thought" thing. This goes on for over a week with various, dodgy lookin' lads comin' and goin' like. In the end they get strong-armed into handing over two thousand pounds. The main fella even drives the old boy to a cashpoint. Not only that, but a few days later they notice jewellery and some cash missing from their bedroom. Real bunch of bastards.'

'Sounds it. Where are you at with it?'

'I've taken statements. Done some door to door, though not the whole street yet.'

'What about CCTV at the cashpoint?'

'Uh . . . well. I don't know if maybe Cathy was . . .'

'Relax. I'm not testing you. You get the precise cashpoint in your statement?'

'Uh, hold on, let me see.'

He flicked through his notebook, searching for the entry. I stepped out of the car and stretched my back and shoulder. The injury I'd received during the events back in Stratharder had healed well, according to the doctors. I'd be lying if I said I'd been doing the exercises the occupational therapist had given me religiously, but I *had* been doing them. They were helping too. Most of the strength had returned, though the range of movement, the therapist's words, wasn't quite there.

Morgan's door closed and he stepped around the car. 'Uh, I'm sorry, Sarge. I just noted that they drove him into town. I *did* get a description of the vehicle though. But uh, not a reg plate or that. I'm sorry.'

'It's fine, Morgan. I said relax. That's why we're here, right? Dot the I's cross the T's?' As I pushed the gate to the front garden a man squinted and then waved from under a rose bush.

'Hello, Mr White. Do you remember me?' said Morgan.

'Uh?' the man said and struggled to his feet. He pushed his glasses nearer his eyes, but still looked confused.

'I'm Morgan Finney, sir.'

The old man stared blankly across his bowling-green lawn.

'I was here last week, we talked about those bad fellas and your tree and the money and all that?'

'Oh, you're the police?' he said, seemingly now able to see us sufficiently.

'Uh, yes sir.'

'Maybe lead with that one next time,' I said softly.

'I do remember you, son. Hello.'

The man, easily into his eighties, took off his gardening gloves and dropped the secateurs onto the lawn. He approached and shook both of our hands. The skin of the back of his hand was like paper.

'I wondered if I could go back over a few points?'

'Of course, aye. Come away in.'

We followed the old man, single file up the garden path at a snail's pace and onto the doorstep.

'Control to three-four,' my radio crackled.

'Why don't you go ahead, I'll be right there,' I said.

Morgan nodded and then followed Mr White into the house, ducking as he did. The probationer was tall, six-foot-three, I'd have guessed.

'Go ahead, three-four.'

'Sergeant Colyear, I have a message for you from a DC Kane,' the female voice said.

DC Kane? Alyson. 'Go ahead with your message,' I said.

'Roger . . . and I'm quoting here. "Don, check your damned phone." Over.'

I fished into my pocket and unlocked my phone. Four messages and two missed calls. All Alyson.

'Three-four, all received, thanks.'

I clicked on Alyson's number. She picked up immediately.

'The fuck have you been?' she said.

'Hi Aly, nice to speak to you, too.'

'Yeah, yeah. Where are you?'

'Where am I? I'm at work.'

'I know you're at work, dipshit. I mean where are you right now?'

'I'm – I'm at a call. Well, not a call, just following up on something for . . . What's this about?'

'I'm at your desk twiddling my thumbs. Need you to come pick me up.'

'Me? You're in Edinburgh? What's . . . Hey, I thought we weren't talking?'

'Yeah, well it's my turn to do the whole only-get-in-touch-when-I-need-a-favour thing.'

A sore point, but a fair one. Last year she'd done me a hell of a favour and I'd left her somewhat in the shit afterwards. This wasn't something I could refuse her. Besides, I was curious.

'OK, Aly. I'll be about an hour I think, judging by the pace of our—'

'The fuck you will, Colyear. Get your skinny arse back here and pick me up. This office is depressing as shit and I don't know the area well enough to take masel' a walk.'

I smiled. I couldn't help myself. Her brash manner delivered in her broad Glaswegian accent. I missed both. Edinburgh can be tough, don't get me wrong, but it wouldn't stand a chance in a fight with Glasgow – there wouldn't even be one. Edinburgh would about turn and run like fuck just from the smack talk.

'OK, Aly. I'll be right there.'

'Bring coffee,' she said and hung up.

'Aly Kane,' I breathed, and went to give Morgan the bad news that he was walking back to the office once he'd finished here.

# CHAPTER THREE

## Martin

She didn't say anything as I entered, but she knew I was there. We were in my office and there she was, a subordinate constable, in my chair, her grey suit jacket slung over the back rest, at my computer, failing to even acknowledge my presence and . . . *oh for God's sake*. She held a hand out across the desk, continuing to type with the other, still without so much as glance in my direction. I pushed the venti cappuccino, with extra shot, into her palm. I sat on the edge of the desk and appraised her while she finished her email, or crime report.

So, the short hair was for keeps then? I wasn't sure what had changed, but somehow it now worked for her. I recalled seeing her last year when she had surreptitiously smuggled myself and Rowan Forbes into a very busy Glasgow police office. It was the first I'd seen her in a long while and the first

I'd seen her without the shoulder-length, brown wavy hair. At the time I'd thought this pixie cut, exposing her strong jawline, was somehow harsh on her, but I didn't think so now. She was a powerful woman, figuratively and literally; six feet tall and broad-shouldered. Men were intimidated by her stature, her words, and perhaps she had, whether by design or by way of her subconscious, been trying to hide it. Joining CID had maybe given her the confidence to wear it on the outside and why not. She was into cross-fit, whatever that was. Some multi-discipline thing that satisfied her obsession with the gym. She won the fitness prize at the Tulliallan training college we graduated from together when we first joined. I was never in contention, I was happy to coast along in the middle of the intake, not standing out for good reasons or ill. Tulliallan was a special torture you just had to get through, in my mind.

'Thanks . . . for . . . the . . . coffee,' she said, hitting a key with each word and slamming the return with the last. 'Hey, check you out. You look, you know, normal.'

'As opposed to?'

'Last time I saw you, Colyear, you looked like a toothpick in a suit. Good to see you've found your way to a few good meals. Watch you don't overdo it though,' she said, her eyes glancing at my stomach as I peeled off my body armour and dumped it in the corner of the room.

'You're never happy, Aly. I see you're still your petite, demure self.' She stayed seated but made a motion with her hands to imitate a curtsy. 'So, am I getting a hug or what?'

She stood, letting the chair wheel away behind her and approached me. Her face was granite. She prodded a finger into the space between my chest and shoulder. It hurt, but I tried not to show. 'You, left me with a shit storm.'

'I did. I'm so—'

'They had to draft in public order units to quell that wee riot you left in your wake.'

'Really? Shit. I am sorry, Ally. I was up to my neck in—'

'Stop.' She clamped her hands to her ears. 'Whatever it was you were up to your neck in, I don't need to hear about. Just tell me it's all in the past.'

'Fair enough. And yes, it is.'

She gently placed a hand on each of my shoulders and drew me in for hug. My chin found her shoulder and I rubbed at her back. We mutually patted to signal that the embrace had been long enough.

'Seriously though, you're all right? How's the shoulder?'

'I'm fine. Not perfect, but it doesn't bother me too much.'

'So, you've chosen semi-retirement?'

'What do you mean?'

'Edinburgh. I thought you'd be itching to get back to the action.'

'Edinburgh sees plenty of action, don't you worry about that. Anyway, are you going to tell me what you're doing in my city, or what?' I said, to change the subject more than anything else. If she'd pursued why I'd elected a beat in Edinburgh I wouldn't have lied to her, I'd have to have told her it was all about my living arrangements with Dad.

Alyson's eyes narrowed slightly and she breathed out, then her hands found her hips. 'Close the door,' she said.

I did, and went back to perch on the edge of the desk

while Ally sank back into my chair.

'I'm here about the case I'm assigned to.'

'The Callum Bradley murder.'

Her eyes narrowed even further. 'How did you know?'

'Same way you knew I was working in Edinburgh. We're cops – we're nosy bastards. Besides, Aly, we'd all like to be on that case. Everyone in the force will have taken an interest in the murder. It's no secret who's working it.'

'Suppose, aye. Well, it turns out I could use your help to bottom out a lead.'

'Really?'

My face must have lit up, because Aly said: 'Don't get excited. It's almost certainly bullshit, but it's something that needs looking at all the same.'

'All right. What do you need from me?'

'Company really. And just in case, some corroboration.'

'To what?'

'To this.' She reached for her jacket on the chair and pulled her phone from a pocket. She looked pointedly at the door.

'It's closed, Aly. Do you want me to lock it?'

'Yeah, would you?'

*What the hell's going on?* I thought. I gave the latch an extra push, clicking the lock into place. Aly had placed her phone on the desk. I stood, hands gripping the edge as I listened to a confused old man being teased by a call handler. When it ended, I waited for something more, but Aly put the phone back into her pocket.

'That's it? What's it have to do with the Callum Bradley murder?'

'Almost certainly nothing. Especially since it was recorded three weeks before the murder happened. It's just something the old man says that throws up a tenuous link.'

I replayed what I just heard in my head. What had been said that might instigate an enquiry? 'The thing about the eyes?' I said.

Aly reduced the distance between us and lowered her voice. 'Don, you can't repeat this. Not to anyone.'

'What?'

'Promise.'

'Fine, I promise.'

'The decision to withhold certain information to the press was made right at the beginning.'

'Oh no . . .' I said.

'Yeah. When his body was found, his eyes had been put out by a blade. Not a soul outside the enquiry team knows about this recording.'

I wasn't familiar with the nursing home. It wasn't one I'd visited, and I'd visited a fair few – it being a large part of my role as community sergeant. I didn't mind the visits to the old folk's homes. They had the best biscuits and you were always made to feel like a minor celebrity, despite the occasional geriatric grope. One of the few privileges of being old, you can get away with almost anything.

The nursing home was in Muirhouse, the most challenging area in my beat. It was a large housing estate really, a bit of a rat-run with high density housing and comparable to some of the areas I'd covered in Glasgow, though it wasn't going to feature in any 'Top Five Shittest

Scottish Neighbourhoods' list. It had some tough characters, though, and I'd steadily been getting to know them.

'Well, this is Pennywell Court. Has to be here somewhere. Maybe that's it?' I said. The place was barely discernible from the houses on the rest of the street, but a small road round the side of the last building opened into a parking area. There was a zone sectioned off by yellow markings to be kept clear for ambulances. Four other cars were parked. The sign above the door invited you to 'PENNYWELL ARsE HOLE', the 'PENNYWELL CARE HOME' altered by a marker pen.

There were laminated warnings against leaving the door open and to not allow anyone to follow you in or out of the building. To the right of the door was a silver box with a black button. Alyson pressed and held it for a moment. It let off an electric buzz and somewhere inside I could hear a similar sound. We waited for a minute and Alyson raised a finger to try again when a face appeared at the glass-fronted door. A white-haired woman stared out. I might have jumped back had Alyson not been there. I thought for a moment that the old woman was talking to us and that the glass was too thick to hear her, but then we heard the buzz of the intercom and a younger female voice came from behind her.

'Come on now, Mimi. Stand away from the door.'

The old woman continued to open and close her toothless mouth. Now it seemed more like the action of a goldfish rather than talking. A blonde lady, her straight hair pulled back into a tight ponytail, cupped her hand to the glass to get a look at us. The midday sun hitting the pane must have made it difficult to see. She spotted my uniform and smiled. I raised a hand in salutation.

She ushered the old lady around and directed her off down the corridor. Now the old woman *was* talking, a long, high-pitched and ceaseless babble as she shuffled along, her feet never quite clearing the carpet. 'Abuckin-telt-ye-here-no-here-buckin-polis-here-some-pissin-buckin-shite-bam,' she squeaked and faded away down the hall.

'She's a charmer,' I said as the door opened.

The lady held it, then locked it behind us.

'She sounds like a horror, but it's just how she communicates. Believe it or not, I can tell what she wants from the particular tone of her swearing.' The lady laughed.

'I'm Sergeant Colyear, I work out of Drylaw station. I'm the community sergeant for Muirhouse. This is DC Kane, she's looking into an incident and we thought perhaps you might be able to help us, uh . . .' I glanced at the name badge pinned to her light blue shirt, 'Vicky?'

Alyson and Vicky smiled at one another and Vicky looked down at the warrant card Alyson wore around her neck.

'Of course. What do you need?'

'Is there an office or something we could go to? What we're looking into is of a sensitive nature,' said Alyson.

Vicky's eyes widened slightly at this. 'Uh, yeah. We share an office, but I'm pretty sure it's clear at the minute. This way.'

She led us to the right, the opposite direction of the shuffling Mimi. We passed a common room on our left, which had a bunch of large armchairs all pointed at a television with the volume turned way up. The corridor had that grey, hard-wearing carpet you always saw in places like this. Pennywell was little more run-down than the other care homes I'd seen. Nothing drastic, just little details I noticed, like the furniture being a bit tatty and the tired watercolours on the wall not sitting square in their frames.

We followed Vicky into her office and she closed the door behind us. There were three desks, all pretty disorganised. A large calendar dominated the main wall and featured a staff rota, as well as various fluorescent reminders. A breeze from the open carpark-facing window was fluttering the bloom of post-it notes.

Vicky stood with her arms folded, waiting for whatever had prompted our visit. Alyson got right to it. She produced her phone from her pocket.

'Vicky, I'm going to play you an excerpt from a telephone conversation. It's a call to the treble-nine system. Our records show that the call came from this building.'

'From here? When?' her eyebrows furrowed, incredulous.

'It was a while back and has only recently been brought to my attention. All I want to know is if you can identify who the voice belongs to. Well, that and which phone it came from.' Alyson tapped at the screen on her phone and clicked at the volume button. The now-familiar conversation grew into the room. Alyson played a section from the beginning, before anything important was said. Then she tapped the screen again and left Vicky to think in silence.

'Could you play that one more time?' she said.

Alyson did, but it only played for a few seconds before

Vicky began talking over it.

'That's Martin. Yeah, definitely that's Martin talking.'

'One of your residents?' I said.

'Yes. He's been with us about eighteen months. I know because he was one of the first new residents after I joined.'

Alyson began taking notes. 'What's Martin's second name?' she asked.

I expected Vicky to go searching for a file, but there was no need. 'Simmons,' she said without a second's thought.

'He's still here? And he's here right now?' said Alyson.

'Aye, yeah. He's on the first floor. I think . . .' Vicky leaned over to look at the wall calendar. 'Yeah, he'll be with Jackie at the minute. Can I ask what this is about?'

'It's . . . uh . . . Well, it's probably nothing, but we do need to have a wee word with him. Figure out how he's been making these calls and why,' said Alyson.

'I think I can solve that mystery for you. Do you want to come up, then?'

We followed Vicky out of the room and to a flight of stairs.

'Does he have any family?' I asked as we climbed.

'A son. Though I've never met him. Lives in America some place. Not exactly involved, if you know what I mean.'

'That's sad. Is it common?' asked Alyson.

'Not *un*common. It sounds cruel, but I guess that's just how it goes sometimes.' Vicky opened a door to another corridor and we were met with a strong smell of ammonia. We followed her through. 'We all like to think we'll be there for our folks when the time comes, but the reality is people have their own lives, jobs and kids of their own. So while some residents get a daily visit, most get a once-a-week drop in, you know? And then there's folk like Martin who just don't have anyone. Here's where your call came from.'

Halfway along the corridor a payphone hung on the wall, complete with domed plastic privacy guard. Alyson lifted the receiver to reveal the phone's number underneath. She checked it against her notebook, then looked at me and nodded.

'I'm sorry if this is about nuisance calls. If we could remove the function to dial nine-nine-nine we would, but there's regulations and all that.'

'I understand,' said Alyson.

'Martin should be in here, but I should warn you, it's likely you'll not get any sense out of him. Or anything at all, really.' Vicky cautioned as she led us along. We reached another common room. The chairs had all been pushed to one side and a plastic sheet had been laid on the floor. In the centre was a chair and a man sat upon it, getting his hair cut, I assumed by Jackie.

'Hiya Martin. Listen, you've got a few visitors today. Are you up to saying hello?' Vicky brushed a strand of cut hair from his nose.

The old man didn't look up or react to Vicky in any way. He stared straight ahead, his mouth open a little.

'We're pretty much done here, I can give you some peace,' Jackie said, her name badge glinting in the light as she removed the towel from Martin's neck and used it to brush fallen hair from his shoulders, before gathering her bottles and scissors. She seemed a little taken aback by the uniforms.

'There's a staff room on this floor. I'll wait there until you're done,' said Vicky as she and Jackie made their way out, leaving us with Martin.

He hadn't moved at all. He sat on the chair in his white vest looking at nothing in particular.

'Maybe we could get him over to one of the comfy chairs?' I suggested.

We guided Martin onto his feet and he soon got the idea. He shuffled forward and Aly and I took an arm each to lower him into the chair. Alyson sat in front of him, lowering her head to his eye level.

'Martin, my name is Alyson Kane, I'm with the police. I was hoping I could ask you a few questions. Would that be all right?' There was no response. She tried again and still he stared blankly ahead. Then she snapped her fingers in his face.

'Aly, for chrissake!' I hissed and looked around, but we weren't being watched.

'Ach, this is bloody pointless. I knew this was a waste of time. Give the woman the shitty errand. Let her fanny around in Edinburgh while we do the real work in Glasgow,' she said and then muttered, 'Not that there *is* any real work.' She folded her arms and sat back in the chair.

'Investigation's not going well then?'

'Well look at the leads we're following up,' she gestured at Martin. 'What do *you* think? We've got nothing, Don. Sod all,' she said in a whisper.

'I'd heard you had DNA, fibres?'

'We do. A fingerprint too, but no suspect to tie it to. These things are all very well if you have someone to check for a match or a profile already on the system. We've nothing. Now here I am trying to interrogate a cucumber.'

'Aly.'

'Sorry.' She stood and placed a hand on Martin's shoulder. 'I'm sorry, Martin. You're probably a lovely person, but this is a lot of nonsense.' She started towards the door. 'C'mon.'

I hesitated, not sure if it was all right to leave this man on his own, but he wasn't going anywhere fast.

We found Vicky in the staff room, scribbling at a clipboard.

'All done? Did he say anything to you at all?'

'Not a word. I'm guessing he's in decline? On the recording of the call, he was pretty animated,' said Alyson.

Vicky put down her clipboard and shook her head slowly. 'Dementia's as mysterious as it is devastating. I'm sorry it's this Martin you met today. When I first met him, days like these were few and far between. Now they're more common than the good ones. It's the hardest part of the job seeing that decline and just being completely helpless. Honestly, you should hear him talk when he's within himself, he's a fascinating man. D'you know, he's a professor? Or was.'

This took me by surprise. 'That man in there?'

'Mm-hmm. It's like, Social Sciences. I forget what exactly, but you should hear him talk. Sharp and funny, charming even.'

'That's not what I heard on that tape,' said Alyson.

'No. Like I said, dementia is such a mystery. That Martin you hear on the tape only comes out now and again, some kind of in-between state. Confused and upset, sometimes angry.'

'Is he . . . capable of leaving the building?'

'Oh God, no. Not anymore.'

'Even when he's lucid?' I said.

'Well . . . I suppose, but he's not really around for long. Lucid Martin's not going to get very far, and he's never tried, as far as I'm aware.'

Alyson looked over at me. 'Is there CCTV here?' she said.

'Just a camera at both entrances, but nothing inside the building.'

'How long is it backed up?'

'I think it's about six months. It's a pretty new system. One of the few things that actually works in this place,' Vicky muttered, then looked embarrassed to have done so.

'Can we take a look through?' said Alyson.

'Sure you can. Listen, I'm not allowed to ask what this is all about, am I?'

Alyson chewed on this for a moment. Vicky had been nothing but kind and accommodating after all. 'I'm sorry, I really can't say. I will tell you this, though. There's nothing to worry about. Once we have a look at what those cameras have recorded, I don't think we'll need anything else.'

It didn't take long to find what we were looking for. Or rather, not find. The day before Callum Bradley's murder to the day after on both cameras. It took a little over an hour to speed through the footage and pause to examine everyone coming in and out of the building. Our Martin was, unsurprisingly, nowhere to be seen.

'I'll submit a copy of this anyway. Justifies my existence at least,' Alyson sighed. She highlighted the appropriate time frame and selected 'Record'.

Vicky left while we prepared the disc.

'That's it then?' I said.

Alyson shrugged and finished the tea Vicky had brought us. 'I'd liked to have taken a statement from our boy, just to round it off nicely, but who knows how long that might take to get. It'd be like fishing, just sitting around and waiting for a bite that might never come. Hardly good use of tax-payer money. I'm sure the bosses will be all right with this.' She ejected the DVD from the machine and I signed a production label, confirming I witnessed the recording.

'Well, how about I get that statement for you?' I said. I was a little surprised to hear the words coming out of my mouth.

'You'd do that? It could take forever. I mean, I know you community lot aren't exactly rushed off your feet, but this would be a bit . . . above and beyond.'

'It would be neither. It would be us square. I feel bad about last year and this pays that debt, right?'

'Aye, I suppose. Plus a drink some time. But yeah, that would be us square.'

# CHAPTER FOUR

## New Town

It took fifteen minutes to find a parking space. That's one infuriating thing about Edinburgh's New Town. If you return home after 6 p.m. you're left touring the cobbled roads trying to find a space within your designated permit area. If you get fed up and drop it into a street with the wrong code, there's bound to be a present tucked under your wiper the next morning, *that'll be sixty quid, thank you very much*. I eventually returned to a space I'd already deemed too small, but I was getting tired and frustrated. I left centimetres on each side between a Freelander and an Audi. They'd both be furious trying to get out in the morning without damaging the paintwork.

'Faither, you in?' I yelled into the dark hall. It was still light outside and would be until nearly 10 p.m., such is summer as far north as Edinburgh, but this basement flat wasn't blessed with great through-light. I hung my coat and dropped my keys into the bowl on the hall table with a clatter. No reply. I checked my watch, 6.20 p.m. He was in the pub already. It had been getting earlier and earlier these days, though I suspect he actually adjusted his behaviour when I first moved in, to hide some bad habits. Like his inability to wash a dish. I gathered two bowls, one plate, three glasses and a loaded ashtray from his room. I made his bed and opened a window to try to shift some of the tobacco smell.

I loaded the dishwasher and took a beer out to the garden. *This was why he bought the place*, I reminded myself. A private garden in central Edinburgh, not bad. The previous owner of the flat hadn't done much with this little outdoor space, but Dad had been busy. A little patio area at the far side and a series of vegetable planters. He'd made himself a lovely spot and it was the only part of the house, other than the kitchen, that we shared.

He made a pretty good housemate, actually. As much as I worried about him shutting himself away in that one room, it meant I didn't feel like I was intruding. Plus, it was his idea I move in. I was struggling a bit with my shoulder and had been somewhat rudderless after the events in Stratharder last year. There were a few moments when I'd opened my laptop to start drafting an email – my resignation – but it hadn't happened. I'd stay at dad's until I figured out my next step, I thought. Well, the next step had been to come back off a career break and request a posting in Edinburgh.

*   *   *

When I woke the next morning at eight, Dad's door was closed over. I hadn't heard him come in. Judging by the debris in the kitchen, it had been a heavy night. The butter was melting away on the countertop, the jam jar open and a buttery knife lying within. I hoped he'd had more than toast for his dinner.

It was a rest day and I had no plans. I headed down into Stockbridge where the market bustled and smells of different fast foods battled for supremacy. I listened to some rock mix in my earbuds while I walked until I felt thirsty. By the time I'd found a supermarket I realised I'd been wandering in the general direction of Muirhouse. *Ah, what the hell*, I thought. *I'll pop in and see if Martin is in a talkative mood.*

I approached Muirhouse from a direction I'd never previously taken and was soon a little lost. I stopped when I wasn't sure whether to turn left or right at the end of a street. I considered checking the maps function on my phone, but I was in no particular rush and so took the left option along a tight avenue. I walked past a block of flats and became increasingly aware of voices somewhere up ahead. I pocketed my phone just as I caught a glimpse of where the noise was coming from. A group of five or six lads were gathered around one of the large concrete supports under the building. A strong smell of cannabis was in the air. My eyes met with theirs briefly and I kept walking. I was hoping there was some exit to the street and I wouldn't have to undertake an embarrassing double-back now that there was an audience. As the voices went quiet, it happened. My stomach cramped as if it made a fist inside of me. My right hand went to my knee to stop me doubling over. I kept walking, keeping my pace even. 'Fuck,' I said to myself as I heard the rattle of bicycle pedals. My stomach pitched again. *Yes, I've got it*, I thought, *message received*. This thing that happens to me, some extension of intuition, hadn't happened once since I took my post in Edinburgh and some small part of me wondered if this thing had gone for good, hoped maybe. God knows it wasn't always useful. A bike passed me on the left. A blue BMX ridden by a thin lad in a maroon hoodie. Then a bike to my right. A yellow mountain bike, the rider pulling a long wheelie as he passed. I knew they'd engage me at some point, so I decided to walk on until it happened. The bikes ahead criss-crossed and then stopped, marking the point the encounter was to happen.

'Got a fag?' yellow mountain biker said.

'No, sorry. I don't smoke,' I said. I made to walk around, but BMX boy pushed back on the ground and wheeled in front of me.

'How about twenty quid then?' he said.

'Excuse me?' I said with an incredulous laugh.

'You don't smoke, eh? Smokes ur 'spenive. Mean's you're loaded. So, gee-us twenty quid and we'll make sure you get home safe, eh?'

'Thanks, but I think I'll manage just . . .' I tailed off as I heard footsteps.

*Here we go*, I thought. The rest of the group had caught up. If there had been any plan to run, it was too late now. My guts continued to churn like the drum of a washing machine.

Another two passed me from behind and another lingered to my rear. A cloud of reeking weed smoke was sent into my face by the tallest of the new arrivals; he was in his early twenties and the most physically capable of the small crowd of street rats. I was guessing this was the leader.

'Much ye ask him fur?' this one asked BMX boy.

'Twenty.'

'Twenty? Nah, he's good fur fifty.'

'Nobody carries cash anymore. I've nothin' on me. Not that you'd be getting fuck all if I had,' I said. I tried to look calm and I wasn't overly worried until this leader showed up. Taller than me by three or four inches, his black hair was plastered to his head in some product. A miserable attempt at a moustache on his top lip. He leaned back as he spoke with his eyes pulled into slits as if getting a measure of me, a fat joint held shoulder high between two fingers.

'That's awrite. 'Ere's a cash machine in the Co-op. We'll come with ye.'

I had a think about how much cash I did have on me. Maybe fifteen and some coins? It didn't matter, this would only ever stop if they emptied my account. If I hit this guy hard, maybe square in the throat, there might be a chance I could get to a main road before the rest of them swarmed me, but which way was the main road? And what if I missed? Or just didn't put him down. Too risky. Then what?

I looked behind me for options, then saw something. 'How you gettin' on Mikey? Is your mum's leg better?'

The lad looked like I'd just asked him to solve an algebra equation. Mikey Denholm's face screwed up in confusion until I physically saw him make the connection. His eyes widened and he took his black baseball cap off to scratch at his head.

'Fuck's he talkin' about?' the leader asked.

'He's fuckin' polis, eh.'

I'd run into Mikey a few times. Last one was a shoplifting. He'd been cornered by security staff at Morrisons for trying to leave with three bottles of wine. He was only fifteen, so I'd had to charge him in front of a parent. His mother was a nice lady. Mikey was the eldest of four boys and she had her hands full trying to keep them all out of trouble; she was doing her best, especially as she was on crutches after an operation on her ankle. I forgot why, exactly.

The lad on the BMX took off. Warrant out for him, probably. His reaction inspired enough doubt for me to change things up.

'Get your bike out my way before I lock you up, ya fuckin' idiot,' I said to mountain biker. I heard the west in my voice intensify, as it did whenever I resorted to this sort of language. It carries a threat that can't be matched elsewhere in Scotland, perhaps anywhere at all. He smirked, but he moved. I thought that was it, but my stomach had not settled and then I felt why as I moved. The moustachioed leader took a grip of my shoulder.

'Unless he's plain clothes, he's no a cop right now. Twenty quid. Then you can go.'

It may not have been the wisest move but having the little shit's fingers on me sent a surge of adrenalin shooting through me. I slammed both palms into his chest. He didn't expect it. He fell on his backside, his joint exploding into sparks. I knew he'd get up and try to save face, so I kept going. I stood over him, my fists balled.

'I think you're on your own, son. If you want tae have a go, then fine. Up you pop and we'll go.' At least I hoped he was on his own. This kid looked like he could fight, but if it was just him and me, then I was prepared. If anyone else joined in, even wee Mikey over there, it could get very messy.

'That's assault!' the leader shouted, and I didn't need the noise in my stomach settling to tell me it was over. He got to his feet and walked off. He waited until he was fully fifty yards clear before the insults started flying: 'Polis bastard!' etc., etc.

As Vicky opened the door to the care home, her face told me she hadn't recognised me straight away in my civvies. She smiled awkwardly; her bottom lip was swollen.

'What happened to your lip?' I said.

'Just a wee accident. Happens all the time when you're moving residents around, you know? Are you here to see Martin again?'

'Is he the same as yesterday?' I asked.

'Afraid so, but listen, we're just getting organised for lunch—'

'Oh, I'm sorry, I could come back later. It's my fault for just turning up unannounced.'

'No, I was just going to say, why don't you join us?'

'Are you sure? I wouldn't want to be getting in the way.'

'Are you the policeman who was here yesterday?' said a voice behind me. I turned to see a lady, about thirty or so with long dark hair. She was looking me up and down.

'Eh, yes. That would be me.'

'You didnae say he was a looker, Vic. How come you've no got the uniform on? Ye cannae beat a man in uniform, eh, Vic?'

Vicky was laughing, probably at the look on my face.

'Leave him alone you. This is Sergeant . . . Oh I'm sorry, I've forgotten . . .'

'Colyear, but just call me Don. Especially since I don't have the uniform on.'

'This is Michelle, she's just getting first floor organised for coming down to lunch. She can show you to Martin's room and maybe you can bring him down for us?'

'That sounds fine,' I said.

I followed Michelle upstairs and she opened the door to Martin's room. He was sitting in a chair by the bed looking out of the window, or at least he was pointed at it. There was a musty smell about the place. Along one wall was a wardrobe and a set of shelves. Some popular novels stood there, but it was mostly thick academic volumes. On the bedside table a radio played softly.

'How are you Martin? Are you ready for your lunch? That's good,' said Michelle, as if he'd answered her. She guided him to his feet and brought him slowly out of the room. Once in the hall she gave me his arm. He walked slowly, but steadily. Without thinking I was guiding him towards the stairs, but then there was some resistance in his arm. He knew where he was going. Instead of left we went right to a lift. Once inside he turned around on his own.

It reminded me of being on holiday when I was kid. I

might have been five or six and we'd gone to see an aunt in England. Not a close relative and I don't remember visiting them again, but they'd lived near Blackpool. We spent a day on the Pleasure Beach and someone thought I would love a ride on the donkeys they have traipsing up and down the sand. I was duly seated upon one of the beasts. There were other kids on other donkeys and they were being led by people to a certain distance and then turned around. Only I was left on my own. For a moment I thought there had been some mistake, that the thing might carry me off into the sunset, but no. At some invisible line in the sand, the donkey stopped and turned of its own volition and brought me back to my parents. The poor creature, having done this for so many years, had the distance burned into its DNA.

Martin was like that. In his fugue state, some part of his mind had the building mapped.

A soft ding sounded and the doors opened. Martin began to move and I simply held his arm and followed him to a large dining hall. Once there I sensed him giving his arm back to me. I looked up and Vicky, who was busy seating Mimi, was waving me towards a vacant table to the left. Once the seat was by his knee, Martin sat himself.

I approached Vicky, not quite sure what I was supposed to be doing.

'Do you mind feeding him? Just lift the fork to his mouth, he'll do the rest,' she said.

'Buckin-polis-bam-shit-fucked-bam-ur-day,' squeaked Mimi. There was a smear of mashed potato on her cheek.

'That's right, Mimi. This is the police officer who came to see us yesterday. One of the staff will come to take your order. You can choose for Martin and yourself, the options are on the board.'

'Me? Oh, I wouldn't want to—'

'Of course you would. There's plenty and we all eat with the residents.'

Vicky went back to settling the ever-fidgeting Mimi and I returned to Martin.

'Let's see, Martin. We have a choice between lamb with all the trimmings, or it's mac 'n' cheese,' I said, reading from a large whiteboard on the wall nearest to us. At the latter option, Martin moved. It took me by surprise. His hand lifted from his knee a few inches and fell back again. I looked to see if Vicky had spotted this, but her attention was still with her friend with the Tourette's. 'Mac 'n' cheese?' I said. 'Are you sure you wouldn't rather have the roast?' Martin coughed. One sharp exhale and his eyes moved to me, then back to middle distance. 'OK, if you're sure. I'll have the lamb and if you change your mind we can swap.'

Within a few minutes a tall lad came over. Somewhere in his twenties, burly, with massive hands and equally enormous smile through his thick, well-trained beard. He took our order, introducing himself as Mathew and returning with plates and a pot of tea.

Martin ate the pasta greedily. I could barely get a fresh forkful loaded before he let his mouth hang open for the next bite. I then ate my own lunch which, while being south of restaurant quality, wasn't half bad. After lunch, staff took Martin for a shower and bathroom necessities and I had a chance to chat again with Vicky. It was interesting to see her work with her colleagues. She was around forty and had a soft way about her, and although a lot of her workmates were older, they all seemed to respect her authority. There was a solid community amongst the staff and she was at the centre of it.

'Can I ask you something?' she said as the other staff were preparing a changeover. The late shift had come in and were getting into scrubs. Vicky was putting her outdoor coat on.

'Sure.'

'Martin, he's not in any trouble, is he? I mean, I don't mind you being here, not at all, but if I thought that he was . . . well, I don't know. I just mean is there something I should call his son about? Also, I have my own bosses I should probably—'

'He's not in any trouble, Vicky. I promise you. There has been the silliest link to an investigation we're looking at and all we're trying to do is cross it off. I'm just hoping to get Martin in one of these lucid states and then we can put it to bed.'

'OK. Well, in that case, you're welcome to visit anytime and stay as long as you like. It's lovely that he has a visitor. Who knows how long he has left and I'm not sure if his son will even see him before . . . Well, not to dwell, eh?'

'You've been very kind, Vicky. I wonder if I could ask one more favour though. If he comes back to himself and I'm not here, would you call me?'

'Aye, sure.' She took her phone from her purse and tapped away then handed it to me with a fresh contact page open. 'Don-police', it read. I typed my number and handed it back.

'If it's all right, I might just sit with him in his room for a while before I go?'

'Absolutely. I think he'd really like that. He might not seem like he appreciates it, but some part of him does,' she said and opened the door to leave.

'Do you really believe that?'

She stopped in the doorway, her eyes searching the ceiling. 'Actually, yes. I do. Have a nice night.'

Martin was put into bed by one of the staff, afternoon naps being standard in the place. I sat in his chair and looked out of the window. To the left you could just make out the three bridges spanning the Firth of Forth. The iconic red rail bridge, then the old road bridge, now put out to pasture with the gleaming sails of the new Queensferry Crossing fanning and posturing in its face like a flamboyant bird.

I pulled a book from the shelf, *Economics for the Common Good* by Jean Tirole. The cover explained that the author had won a Nobel Prize in economics and so I was curious. I read the introduction and then gave up; my head couldn't quite grasp what I was reading. By then Martin was gently snoring. His arms lay above the covers and I took his hand. I thought about my own father with our slightly strained relationship, and I wondered how often I would visit him if he were Martin. The radio played sedate orchestral music and Martin's breathing seemed to follow the beat.

I woke with a start as my head fell forward and my chin hit my chest. I must have clasped my hand tight as I came to as Martin snorted into life too.

'I'm sorry,' I said. 'I must have nodded off.' I lowered his hand to the sheet and stood to stretch my back. I'd had a strange dream, one of those where you're flying, but you don't have full control of your direction. I glided above a silver-grey mist. Short tendrils reached up from the surface as if to take my hand, but my fingers slid through without resistance. It was illuminated by the moon overhead. The tops of buildings were just about visible through it. I had woken as my focus, which had been straight down at the hidden town beneath the cloud, was suddenly captured by a church spire I hadn't seen coming and I would have flown directly into it.

'I better get going, Martin, but I'll come back if that's OK with you?' I gathered myself and pulled the door open.

'Huukay,' breathed Martin. I looked over at him, but he was already snoring once more.

# CHAPTER FIVE

## Mea Culpa

'Jesus, where the hell have you been?'

'Sorry, Sarge. Train again, but I brought you a—'

'Get rid of those. The DCI has something for us, she's on the warpath.' DS Cunningham spoke in a growled whisper. He took both cups of coffee from Alyson and began looking for somewhere to ditch them. 'Listen, if the DCI asks—'

'Heads up. Here she comes,' Alyson whispered back. She checked the front for her blouse and pushed at her hair. The DS was still trying to lose the cups as DCI Kate Templeton strode purposefully towards them along the corridor. 'Ma'am,' Alyson greeted.

'There you are. You're feeling better then?' DCI Templeton spoke with a clear, educated English accent that never failed to intimidate. It cut with precision; a scalpel of a voice.

'Ma'am?' Alyson's eyes flicked to DS Cunningham.

His eyes were wide, *Go with it*, they said.

'Ah, yes, ma'am. Much better. Just a bit of . . . um.'

'Well, I hardly think coffee is what the woman needs, Duncan. A touch of the shits is likely to turn into a full-blown dysentery if you throw caffeine at it. Come with me, both of you.' DCI Templeton snatched one of the cups out of Duncan's hand and sniffed at it before taking a sip. She marched back towards her office. The DCI was about the same height as Alyson, which made her at least an inch taller than Cunningham, and his short legs scuttled to keep up.

'Touch of the shits?' Alyson said, from the corner of her mouth.

'Had to tell her something. What you want me to say? Ah, just late as usual, boss. Nah – said you nipped out to get pills for your stomach.'

'Close the door, please.' Alyson did while the DS took a seat. 'Get up, Duncan, this won't take long. You're to go to Govan Police Station. There you will interview a man proclaiming to be responsible for our murder.'

'What? Really? When did this happen?' said Duncan.

DCI Templeton looked at the clock on the wall behind them. 'Twenty . . . four minutes ago. He has not yet requested a solicitor, so I want you to speak to him before he changes his mind. Organise a marked escort and get over there now. There's no time for strategy, just use what you know and get this confession on tape ASAP.'

'Uh, yes, ma'am. Do we know—'

'Duncan, are you listening? You should be halfway there by now. Now bloody well move. Report back to me once you're done.'

They didn't bother with the escort. Instead, they poured themselves into the back seats of a traffic patrol vehicle and were soon doing somewhere close to seventy through the town centre, maintaining the insane speed throughout Glasgow. They tried their best to discuss the case, but it was next to impossible over the siren. In less than six minutes they'd pulled up to the secure gates of the Govan station, which slid away to allow them entry. The driver dropped them at the door. Someone must have been watching from the camera, because the door buzzed just as they reached it. They pushed it open and an officer Alyson had never met before handed her a folder and told her to follow him. He was dressed in a dark blue suit and she'd only caught the rank on his ID, another detective sergeant.

He led them through corridors, flanked by two other officers with expectant faces. It seemed everyone was aware of why they were there. They stopped outside a door and the Govan DS gestured to it. 'I'll bring him up. The room's all set. Good luck.'

'Thanks,' Duncan replied, and pushed the door open to the interview room. Alyson felt dizzy and even a little nauseous, partly from the fairground ride of a journey here and partly from the enormity of what was about to happen.

This room was the same as countless others she'd used. This room, and all the others like it, *were* the job now. Before, it was uniform, handcuffs and baton. Now, it was strategy and a tape recorder, only there was 'no time for strategy' here. The DCI's posh voice echoed in her head.

'How do you want to play this, Sarge? You lead, I'll follow?'

'No, I want you to lead. I'll come in where I think it's required. This is your show.'

The nausea changed gear. 'You sure?'

'You'll be fine. You know this case inside and out. Take your time. Let all this rush just fade away. Take a breath.' Duncan separated three plastic cups and filled them from a water jug that had been left for them on the table.

Alyson did as she was advised. She drew air in through her nose, held it, then exhaled out through her mouth. Just like the gym. She felt herself settle, the giddiness lifting. She opened the folder to find the case files she was familiar with. Or at least, a neat-printed copy of them. Instead of the glossy photographs, she held high-res paper prints, but they were all there, as well as the crime report. She lifted her head to the ceiling to check where the camera was and made a mental note.

There was a rattle from the door and the sound of voices. The door opened and Alyson made to stand, but felt Duncan's hand on her forearm and she sat back.

'Please take a seat,' Duncan said to the man being shown in by the Govan DS.

'Press the buzzer if you need anything,' the DS said, and left.

The man pulled the chair opposite them away from the table slowly, his eyes were fixed on the file in front of Alyson on the table. Everything about him was forgettable.

Average height, average build. His hair a blonde-brown mix and not really styled in any particular way. He wore brown cords and a grey T-shirt that bore no logo or design. He was an investigative nightmare. You could have dinner with this guy and still struggle to pick him out at a VIPER parade.

Duncan sat across the table and to the left of the man, nearest the wall. He removed the two cassettes that were left for them from their cases and loaded them into the recorder. The man looked up and opened his mouth to speak, but he was silenced by the high-pitched whine from the machine as the tapes ran clear and began to record.

Alyson began talking before he could say a word; anxious to get his caution on tape before he uttered anything.

'The time is fourteen-thirty-two hours on Tuesday the twenty-seventh of July. I am Detective Constable Alyson Kane of Police Scotland. We are in interview room two of Govan Police Station in Glasgow. I will ask the others present to identify themselves.'

'Detective Sergeant Duncan Cunningham of Police Scotland.'

'And you, sir. Would you please identify yourself for the recording.'

'Uh, my name is David. David Ellis.' The man seemed unsure if he should be talking to Alyson, or at the tape machine or to the camera above the door.

Alyson continued: 'Before we start, I should state for the purpose of the recording that you have attended voluntarily. Is that correct?'

'Yes. That's correct.'

'And you have elected at this stage to waive legal representation?'

'I just want to tell you—'

'Sorry David, but can you please just confirm for the recording that this is the case,' said Duncan.

'Yes. I don't need a lawyer.' He brought his hands up on to the table, one turning over the other, gripping the knuckles of each. He was still struggling to make eye contact.

'At this stage, David, it's only right and proper that I advise you that you are going to be asked questions into and about the death of Callum Bradley. Before I do, I must caution you that you are not obliged to say anything in response to these questions, and anything you do say will be noted, visually and audibly recorded and may be used in evidence. Do you understand?' Alyson had to say this, the evidence could easily be regarded as inadmissible if she didn't, but she understood how they might frighten a person into changing their mind about a confession.

'I do understand, yes. I just want to tell my side of it.'

'OK, David. In your own time,' Alyson said, sitting back in her chair and inviting David to proceed. In normal circumstances she would have offered a hot drink, perhaps something to eat, but David here wanted to talk and she was going to let him.

David stayed quiet for a minute, perhaps choosing his words. Then, for the first time, he looked directly at her. 'Uh, OK. Well, I wanted to come here today to hand myself in. See, the boy, Callum, I killed him,' he said. His hands rubbed at his chin, then mouth.

Alyson was about to ask a question but Duncan tapped a knuckle on her knee. *Say nothing*, it meant.

Another minute passed. David's hands went from his mouth to his eyes. He began sobbing. Alyson looked at Duncan, his face told her again to let this happen. She searched her pockets and found a packet of hankies. She pushed them across the table.

'Thanks,' David snorted. He blew his nose and wiped his eyes with the back of a hand. 'I'd been thinking about it for a while, you know? Like a . . . I dunno, like an addiction or something. Most of the time it's easy to push it away, distract myself with work or whatever. But that night, I cracked.' A fresh wave of tears came. This time he didn't seem so keen to pick up the story.

'What kind of work is it you do, David?' Alyson asked.

'Warehouse work. I do shifts. Forklift mostly.' He pulled another hanky from the packet.

'You like it?'

'Not really,' he said with a laugh. 'Pays the bills and usually keeps me out of mischief.'

'But not the evening we're talking about?'

'My work's fault.'

Alyson let some time pass, but he didn't seem to want to elaborate on this point. 'It's your work's fault that you killed Callum Bradley?'

'Aye. Well, no, I mean not really. Look, I live on my own. I don't get paid a lot, but they make you take annual leave. My boss was telling me I had to take it. I said to him, just pay me the hours and he said can't do it. Union. So, I'm at home for three weeks and these urges come back and . . . I mean three weeks. I couldn't stop it.'

'Tell us about that evening. Why Callum?'

David shrugged and looked up with raw eyes. 'Just bad luck. I had been driving around for . . . hours. Trying to make myself go home. Either that or trying to find the courage to actually do it. Who knows? I remember, I parked up on this street. Musta been around teatime. I had the wheel in my hands and it was like I was speaking to it, saying *go home, go home, go home* and then I look up and there's this kid in a blue jumper. He's sat on a kerb trying to fix his bike. The second I notice he's there, he looks up at me. He looks at me and he . . . he smiles.'

It was nearly three minutes before he composed himself again, but eventually the tears stopped.

'What were you driving, David?'

'My van? It's a wee Vauxhall Combo. I use it to keep my tools in. I do odd bits, small carpentry jobs and repairs when I'm not at the warehouse.'

Alyson's heart leapt in her chest. Her fingers curled into her palm in excitement.

'What colour is your van, David?' she said.

'Red. Dark red, like maroon.'

The excitement waned a little. 'What street was this where you came across Callum?'

'Honestly, I don't know. I live in Paisley, but I'd been driving around for hours, like I said. I had come into this wee town, Rickerburn. I've never even been there before. Between Edinburgh and Glasgow. I don't know the place, but there I was.'

'Then what happened?'

'I don't even want to say it out loud.' His face was screwing up again. Tears forming fresh pools.

'That's why you came here today, David,' Alyson said softly and evenly. 'You need this. To get it out. Now's your chance. Just take your time,' Alyson pushed one of the cups in front of him.

He took a deep breath and drained the whole thing. 'Like I said, he was sitting there. This wee boy and I told myself – *just drive away*. But then my door was open, almost like someone else had done it, but I'm stepping out and now I'm thinking, *right, if he starts to walk away, just get back in the van and go.* But he didn't move. He was on the kerb by his bike and there's not a soul in sight and now I'm telling myself, *stop walking*, but I don't and before I know it, I'm down on my haunches and the boy is still smiling. "Hiya," I said. You know what he says?'

Alyson could feel a tension through her neck and down through her spine. She said nothing.

'He says, "The chain's come off my bike. Can you help me fix it?" There's no fear in him and so it was like a sign. Then . . .'

'Go on, David. It's OK,' said Duncan.

'I said I'd make a deal with him. I'd help him with his bike, if he could show me how to walk up into the bing. You know these shale bings out there in Rickerburn. Like three big man-made hills of red dirt. He says: "It's easy, there's a path." I tell him I'll fix his chain if he will take me over. At this point I'm sure he'll get scared and that will be the end of it, but he agreed. I . . . fixed his chain and then . . . I took that boy.'

'*Where* did you take him?' said Duncan.

'I just looked for somewhere quiet, you know? We walked up to this path and I urged him to go a little further and then a little further.'

'What happened in the bings, David?'

'I . . . I can't. I don't want to even . . .'

Alyson wanted to reach across the table and hit this miserable little man, crying into his hands. She wanted to hit him until the information poured out of him in red torrents. Instead, she gripped the hem of her skirt under the table until she felt her knuckles crack.

'Did you kill Callum Bradley, David?' said Duncan.

'For the purpose of the recording, the suspect David Ellis is nodding,' added Alyson.

'Thank you, David. I know how difficult this must be. But I need you to tell me some more about how that happened. Can you do that?'

'For the purpose of the recording, the suspect David Ellis is nodding,' she said again.

'What do you need?' said David. The eye contact was gone. He was picking at a finger that looked red and angry from self-abuse.

'How did you do it?' said Alyson. The question came easily from her mouth but in the back of her mind she wondered at the absurdity of it. Not *why* did you do it, the question any normal, compassionate person might ask; the question that would be paramount above all others, but *how*. This question, in the eyes of an investigation was far more important.

'I, uh . . . I strangled him.'

Now she could ask the question. 'Why did you strangle Callum Bradley, David?'

'I didn't mean to. It's not what I had planned, I—'

'What did you plan to do?' said Duncan.

'I . . . I didn't have a plan. It just happened. I had him by the hand and we were on this small track. By then he was getting upset. I wanted to take him further but he was clearly scared. I . . . I took out my, you know, penis and then he just started screaming. I panicked. I pulled up my trousers and put my hand over his mouth but he wouldn't stop. I didn't even know my hands had slipped to his neck . . . not until it was too late. Then he was quiet and . . . he was just . . . gone.'

Alyson and Duncan sat in silence. They waited for the most important part. Now Alyson had both hands on her skirt, pulling, twisting. Her face, however, was like the surface of a pond. A full minute passed. Now David was looking at them. His eyebrows furrowed in confusion.

*Come on*, Alyson thought and fought against her lips forming the words.

Duncan was the next to talk. 'What did you do next?'

'I got out of there. What do you think? I left him on the path and I ran back to the van. I was sure I'd come across someone and that I'd be seen. I got in the van, turned and I drove. I didn't stop until I was home. Over the next few days, I was sure the police were going to come to my door. I sat and stared at it. I was due to go back to work, but I called in sick and I just waited. After about a month had passed and nobody came I—'

'Go back a step, David. You've strangled Callum

Bradley. The boy is still in your hands. What did you do then?' said Alyson.

David looked at them blankly.

*Fuck, fucking bastard*, she thought.

'I, uh, I dunno. I can't remember if I laid him down or if I dropped him, but I let him go and I—'

'Did you do anything with the body, David?' said Duncan.

'Do? Like what?'

'You tell us. Did you attempt to hide it? Did you do anything sexually? Did you mark the body?'

'No. I just got the hell out of there.'

He looked disgusted at the question and that was all they needed. The look on Duncan's face as he stood and made for the door surely mirrored her own as Alyson took her notebook from her pocket and began writing.

'What? What's going on? What did I say?'

The door closed behind Duncan.

*It's not what you said. It's what you couldn't say, you little fucker*, Alyson thought. And if their conversation were not being recorded, she would have. Instead, she began reading from her notebook.

'David Ellis. I am about to prefer a charge against you, but before I do so I must caution you that you are not obliged to say anything in response to the charge and that anything you do say will be noted, visually and audibly recorded and may be used in evidence. Do you understand?'

'Where's the other guy gone? What's going on?'

'The charge against you is that on the twenty-seventh of July, at Govan Police Station you did falsely confess to the murder of Callum Bradley, compelling officers to investigate said confession and thereby waste the time of the police—'

'What? No, wait—'

'That is contrary to the—'

'I did. I killed that boy. You need to lock me up. Please, just listen.'

'. . . Criminal Law Act 1967. Do you understand the charge?'

'Please . . .'

'Do you understand the charge that has been read to you, Mr Ellis?'

'Look. I do have these thoughts. They're evil. Please. You need to lock me up.'

'Interview terminated at fifteen-twelve hours.' Alyson ejected the tapes and removed them from the machine. She calmly signed her name on the labels and pushed hers and Duncan's chairs back into place. Only then did she address David again.

'You'll be getting locked up all right. But only long enough to take prints and DNA. After that, if I ever see you again . . .' *Breathe*, she told herself. The camera over her shoulder was still recording. *Just breathe.*

This time they were urged to sit in DCI Templeton's office, though she didn't seem like she intended to sit herself.

'Definitely not our man? You're sure?' she said. She stood in the corner of her room at a bookshelf. The shelves were white and clinical but they were home to an assortment of colourful pictures and nick-nacks. The pictures were of children, two blonde kids with DCI

Templeton's prominent nose.

'I'm certain, ma'am. I'm sorry. We've taken swabs and prints, of course, but it's not our fella. Everything he knew he learned from the papers. He had nothing beyond that,' said Duncan.

'By that you mean the wounds to the eyes?'

'Yes, ma'am. That and the fact that he claims the murder happened at the locus.' This being another thing withheld from the press, that the boy had been dumped where he was found, but forensic examination of the crime scene confirmed he had not been killed there.

'Bastard. I really thought this was it. What possesses these fucking people?'

It had been agreed on the drive back that Duncan would field all questions, that the boss was bound to be furious, but this question was asked at Alyson.

'I, uh . . . Who knows, ma'am? He admitted to some pretty ugly thoughts and maybe he wanted himself put away before he does actually act on them. But I suspect it's more about the attention. Some narcissistic urge you'd have to ask a psychologist about.'

'You charged him with fucking about, I take it?'

There was something comical about DCI Templeton's propensity for swearing. Her plummy accent seemed somehow absurdly contradictory.

'Of course, ma'am.'

'So, Duncan. Where does this leave us?'

'It, uh, leaves us exactly where we were at the morning meeting, ma'am. We're no further forward, I'm afraid.'

Now she was sitting. She looked out through the

window as she spoke. 'I don't need to tell you that the detective super is up my arse like a barbed-wire enema on this, Duncan. We need something soon. You hear me?' she turned to face them. Her stare reminded Alyson of that old film. The one with Medusa and the Greek soldiers turned to stone.

'We're doing everything, ma'am. I assure you.'

'Maybe time to start thinking out of the box, Duncan. What about you? What's with this geriatric fuckwit on the phone?'

Alyson looked at Duncan. Though she couldn't say why, he wasn't going to help her. 'It's probably a dead end, ma'am.'

'Probably? I didn't send you out there to gauge its probability, I sent you there to follow up or write off, which is it?'

'Uh . . . Write off. Most likely.'

The DCI laid her hands on the desk and leaned towards Alyson. She was not happy. 'What is the fucking situation?'

'It's in hand, ma'am. We, eh, I, identified the person making the call. An old man. CCTV confirms he didn't leave the building the date of the murder. It's just that he's in and out of lucidity. I wanted to get a statement from him, just to tie a bow on it, but I'll have to wait until he can provide one. I have a colleague keeping an eye on—'

'Colleague? No, fuck that. I want you on this until it's done. I asked you to do this, so bloody well get it done.'

'Yes, ma'am.'

'And the next time you take it upon yourself to delegate a task I have personally assigned to you, you can go ahead and reassign yourself back to whatever tin-pot task force you came from.'

'Yes, ma'am.'

Her attention turned back to Duncan, thank God. 'Where are we with the van?'

'Again, no further forward. Our timewaster today mentioned he had a van, and we will get it checked,' he added urgently. 'But it's not the right colour and it's as much a red herring as the rest of his bullshit.'

Alyson was aware that a white van had been seen by a witness in the vicinity of the locus on the night in question, this being the reason she'd become excited during the interview, but she wasn't sure what the strategy was for this line of enquiry.

'How many white vans matching the description came back on the PNC check?'

'Thousands, ma'am. It's impossible with the information we have. The witness has been interviewed twice. Without even a partial reg it's a non-starter. We've asked traffic and patrol to be a wee bit . . . liberal with stop-searches in the area, but I wouldn't hold your breath on that one. That leaves our forensics, and you know better than I do where we're at with that.'

'Yes, fucking nowhere. All right. We need to widen the net on perverts.'

'Ma'am?' said Duncan.

'By now we've interviewed every sex offender we have registered. I think we need to start looking at anyone who's been identified as a suspect at any time within, say . . . fifty miles of the locus.'

'Ma'am, I'm not sure that's entirely—'

'Legal? Well, interviews will be held on a voluntary basis, at least to begin with. But Duncan, don't be soft with this. Make it clear if they don't speak to us and provide details of their whereabouts then it doesn't look good for them. Understood?'

'Ma'am.'

The two shuffled from the room like chastised school children.

Alyson waited until they were well clear before she breathed, 'Desperate.'

'Desperate doesn't come fucking close,' Duncan breathed back.

# CHAPTER SIX

## Awake

I was pulled out of a dream so fast that I woke with the sound of my own yelling in my ears.

I jolted upright as Dad had come crashing into my room. I didn't catch the first thing he said as I was still in some in-between state.

'What's going on?' I said.

'Your phone. It's been going off. You left it in the kitchen. Did you no hear me calling?'

'What?'

'It might be your work. I don't know if it's important. Here.'

He tossed the phone onto the bed. I lifted it with one hand and rubbed at my eyes with the other. 'Thanks.'

'Sorry to have given you a fright. I'll put the kettle on,' he said and left.

I dragged another pillow behind my head and tried to focus on the screen. It told me it was a little after seven. *What's he doing up so early?* There were three missed calls, all within the last ten minutes. I tapped the screen to return the call.

'Hi, Vicky?'

'Hi Don. I'm sorry to phone you so early, but you said to call if Martin came back to himself.'

'Yeah, it's no problem. There's been some improvement then?'

'I'll say. He's full of stories this morning. If you wanted to speak to him, now would be your chance.'

'Thanks for letting me know. I'll just get myself together and come over.'

'I wouldn't leave it too long if I were you. We never know how long he'll be around.'

I pulled on yesterday's clothes and wandered into the kitchen, still a bit bleary-eyed. The back door was open and there was a cup of tea prepared for me on the countertop. I figured I could spare a few minutes. I quickly tapped a text to Alyson and joined Dad in the garden.

It wasn't yet warm, but it was bright and looked like it would soon be a lovely day. I said as much to Dad as I sat opposite him at the little round table he'd recovered from the doorway of one of the many charity shops in Stockbridge and restored. The shop had been closed and he'd been on his way home from the pub, he'd explained, and someone had just dumped a load of stuff in front of the shop, convincing themselves that it was an act of charity rather than the fly-tipping it actually was.

'It was a work thing, right enough?'

'Sort of, yes,' I said.

He folded his paper and swapped it for his coffee. The smell of it was inviting. There was another smell, something floral. Something he'd planted maybe. 'Must be important if they're calling you on a day off?'

'It's a favour I'm doing for a friend. You've heard me mention Alyson in the past?'

'Aye, I think so. She's the big, brawny detective?'

'I'm not sure that's how I described her, but yes.'

'You should invite her round. You never have anyone round. Not since the redhead. Who, by the way, was out of your league, boy. Why you dumped her, I have no clue.'

'Mhairi and me just weren't a good fit, Dad.' It was strange that he should mention her, I felt that she had been part of a dream. Though whenever Dad and I talked in recent weeks, this was something that would continually come up.

'The hell with fit. She was a wee stunner. You think your mum and I fitted together like jigsaw pieces? Not on your life. No, we had to work at it. You have to work at it, Donald. Relationships don't drive themselves, takes two sets of hands on the wheel.'

'Well, it's done. I don't regret it,' I said, and I meant it. Mostly. 'I better get going. How come you're up so early anyway?'

'I'm always up early,' he said and went back for his paper.

'Away, you've not seen 7 a.m. since I moved in here.'

'Well, I'm meeting a friend for breakfast, or brunch or whatever.'

His face was now hidden back behind the paper. I pushed my finger over the top and lowered it. As I did the floral smell hit me again. 'Are you wearing aftershave?' I said.

'What if I am? I mean I shaved, so I put some on, after.'

'So you have.' His full white beard had been trimmed back like one of his bushes. His neck was now clean. His hair, which he'd been letting grow long was pulled back into a small ponytail. White strands that were not quite long enough to be tethered hung and framed his face.

'Stop staring at me, for chrissake.'

He tried to pull the paper back up, but I wouldn't let him. 'You're blushing,' I laughed. 'What's going on?'

'Away, I'm no blushing.'

'You are so. Who are you meeting, exactly?'

'I told you, a friend.'

'What friend? It's clearly not one of the barflies.'

'Heather. All right? Now can I get back to the news, please?'

'Heather? Who's Heather? Faither, come on. What's the story?'

'For God's sake,' he said and folded the paper once more. 'It's not a big deal, all right. She works at the cafe I go to. We got chatting. Turns out she has a wee allotment and I sometimes help to dig out.'

'I bet you do.'

'Don't be depraved.'

I laughed and stood. 'Dad, you've nothing to be embarrassed about. I think it's great. Especially if it means a healthier lifestyle. When will I get to meet her?'

His eyes rose and his mouth twisted as he thought.

'What day is today? . . . and then I've got that thing next week, so . . . bloody never. She's just a friend all right?'

'OK, Dad. OK.'

I checked my phone as I collected my keys from the hall. There was a message from Alyson:

ON MY WAY, BUT GET A STATEMENT ANYWAY

I drove to the care home and was met at the door by Vicky. She explained that she'd gone into Martin's room first thing and had found him been sitting at the window with a book in his hand.

'Where is he now?' I asked.

'He's in the garden. I'll show you.'

Vicky wore a broad smile on her face, a face that was wearing a lot of makeup, I noted. I guessed something like this, a little bit of good news, must mean a lot in a care home. The windows and doors had all been flung open as the temperature rose. A refreshing breeze flowed through the corridor. I followed her to a door at the far end of the dining hall. I stepped out into a little garden area I hadn't previously been aware of. It wasn't a large space and there was nothing elaborate about it, but it was pleasant nonetheless. A small, paved path in a square enclosed a patch of grass with a few shrubberies dotted around, and the roses planted within them hung a lovely scent in the air. Martin sat at a bench on the far side. There were a few other residents, but they weren't bothering the man who was scribbling into a pad of paper. I turned to look at Vicky, shocked at what I was seeing.

'Come on,' she said and practically skipped around the path. 'Martin, someone has come to see you. I'll let you two talk.' She gave one last smile before she left us.

'Thanks, Vicky,' I said after her, and then to Martin, 'May I?'

He looked up at me through glasses I hadn't been aware that he wore. He took them from his face and let them rest against his chest on a cord around his neck.

'Please,' he said and moved along the bench a little. As I sat I saw the man taking me in, top to bottom. 'I remember you from a dream,' he said.

'You do?'

'I remember your face. You have a kind face. I'm told I've been something of a nuisance when I've not been quite myself. If I've caused any trouble, please accept my apology.'

I must have been staring at him – his face was a wonder. It was the same man, the one whose mouth I shovelled food into a few days before and yet this was a man who was made younger, firmer and charming by his lucid presence. Where his features previously hung in docile abandon, they now stood proud and strong on his handsome face. 'It's . . . really, it's nothing to worry about.'

'My name is Martin Simmons, though you already know that.' He put out his hand and I shook it. His grip was steady and firm. 'And you are Sergeant Colyear. Though not dressed like a policeman. It's nice to meet you.'

'It's nice to meet you too, Martin. I hope you don't mind the plain clothes. I do have ID in my—'

'That's not necessary. Victoria has told me who you are,

and that is fine with me.'

'Vicky has been telling you about my previous visits?'

'She has. She also informed me of some late-night calls I made and how they have necessitated these visits. Again, I am sorry.'

'Thank you, but it really is nothing to worry about. Not your fault, I'm told.'

'It's like waking from a heavy, drunken night. You don't remember what happened and you worry that someone is about to tell you about all of the naughty things you've been up to. I asked Victoria what it was I said on the phone to cause the police to get involved, but she was either unable to tell me, or following your instructions not to.'

'The former, I assure you. I'm looking into a sensitive case, or at least I'm helping out while others do. I really should do this in a more official capacity, if it's all right with you, Martin?'

'Certainly.'

I patted at my pockets and a sudden dread washed over me.

'Something wrong?' Martin said.

'I was in such a rush to get here that I forgot my notebook.'

'Would this do?' He picked up his pad and pen and held them out to me.

'I suppose so,' I said. I figured we could transpose the statement into Alyson's notebook when she arrived.

It was an A4 pad and he had not been writing, but drawing. It was an admirable sketch of the lady sitting at the other end of the garden. It captured her looking out at distance, her hands folded on her lap. To the bottom-right of the drawing he had written '*Penny for your thoughts*'.

'This is lovely, Martin. Do you know the lady?' I said, gesturing at the woman on the bench.

'No, I don't think I do. I'd introduce myself, she looks lonely, but there really is no point. Anyway. Shall we get down to business?'

I took a fresh page and noted Martin's details. It took him a while to remember his date of birth and he was less than certain he'd got it right. I'd check with Vicky later. 'Martin, this will sound silly, but I wouldn't be doing my job if I didn't give you a common-law caution before I ask you any questions. Do you mind?'

'Mind? Not at all. It's like television. Please, go right ahead.'

'OK, Martin, I'm going to ask you questions. You're not obliged to make any comment to these questions and anything you do say will be noted and may be used in evidence. Do you understand?'

'I do indeed.'

I marked out the caution on the pad and wrote the first question before asking it. 'All right,' I began and looked around. I read with my voice lowered a little. 'In the early hours of the seventeenth of March, a telephone call was made to the treble-nine system from this care home. Are you aware of this telephone call?'

'Only what I've been told.'

I copied his answer and penned the next question. 'Do you recall making a telephone call at that time?'

'No, I'm sorry, I don't.'

I looked around again, hoping to see Alyson arriving. I thought the best thing to do at this juncture would be to play Martin the recording, but I was on my own for the time being. I continued with what I had. 'I've heard the telephone call and I can tell you that the voice sounds very much like you, albeit agitated and not as eloquent. Do you accept that you made this call?'

'I don't doubt it. But alas I can't confirm.'

'That's fair, Martin,' I said and noted the answer. Then continued: 'The person making the call became very upset and began talking about the mutilation of a person. Does this mean anything to you?'

'Oh, dear God. What was I saying?'

'You, or the person calling, made reference to . . . injuries to eyes.'

I watched Martin's own eyes rise and then drift off to the left. 'Injuries to eyes?'

'More specifically it was regarding "Cutting eyes out". That's what was said. Can you tell me why you would say something like that?'

'I said that?'

I nodded as I wrote. There was a pause as I copied out the next question: 'This is the sensitive part, Martin. You see, we are investigating the death of a child. The details of the injuries to this child are known only to a very few. This reference you make to eyes is pertinent and I wanted to know if there was any way you could know anything about the death of this child?'

'Well, that's disturbing. I . . . I don't see how I could possibly know anything about . . . But. . .' Martin looked to be in a mild state of shock. His hand trembled lightly as it rubbed at his chin. His eyes now met mine and he said. 'Was it a boy? Was the child a boy?'

I hesitated. As warm as it was, I could feel the hairs on my arm standing. I wasn't sure whether or not to confirm. The pen in my hand was poised over the pad, but I wrote nothing. This was Alyson's case. She should be making this decision. Again, I looked behind me on the off-chance she was walking into the garden, but no. 'Can you tell me how you know it was a boy?'

'I don't know. I'm sorry, it's just that I seem to remember some kind of awful dream. I don't even know when I might have had this dream. You don't think that *I* had anything to do with what happened to—'

'No, Martin, not for a minute. I'm sure it's just some morbid coincidence. Are you all right? You've gone quite pale. I'd like to ask you more about this dream, but maybe I should get you some water?'

'Thank you, yes. That would help, I think.'

I laid down the pad and pen and made my way inside. Rather than asking a member of staff I went to the kitchen and let the tap run until the water ran nice and cold. The smells of lunch spilled from the large ovens. One lady, dressed in industrial whites smiled at me, though her face wore a look of *what are you doing in my kitchen?* I filled a plastic cup and returned to Martin. He now sat cross-legged and faced away from me at a tree in the corner.

'Here you are, Martin. Are you feeling OK?'

'Huh?' He seemed startled as he turned on the bench. 'Oh. Ha.' He laughed and took the cup from me. He took a long sip and handed the cup back. 'Thank you. You're a good boy, Alan.' He turned back to the tree.

'Martin, it's Donald. Sergeant Colyear.' I placed a hand on his arm, urging him to turn back to me. Again, he got a fright as if not aware that I was sitting right next to him.'

'What's wrong?' he said. 'What's the matter, Alan?'

'It's not Alan,' I said. A frustrated laugh left my mouth. 'Look, Martin, if we could just finish up this interview. I have more . . . Martin, please, just sit down.'

'Alan,' he said, now on his feet and trying to walk towards the tree. I kept hold of his arm and tried to direct back towards the bench. He became rigid and his face took on a stony look of rage. 'You're not my Alan.' His fingers dug painfully into the back of my hand as he tried to peel me off of him. 'You're not my boy,' he shouted.

'Please, Martin. Just sit down.'

'Help!' he yelled. 'Help!' and he began beating at my hands with his free arm. His eyes were wide and spit flew from his bottom lip. 'Help!'

'Hey, hey, hey!' Vicky was running across the lawn. As she reached us, I let go of him. 'It's all right, Martin, it's all right.'

'Not my boy,' Martin said. 'Boy' stretched out as he began to cry. His knees threatened to give way under him and I wasn't sure if I should help, but another member of staff, the big lad, arrived. They each took an arm and began walking him inside.

'I'm sorry,' I said to Vicky as she passed.

'It's all right. I'll get him back to his room,' she said softly. That's when I noticed Alyson. She moved out of the doorway to allow Martin and his helpers through. I sat back on the bench and waited for her to join me.

'Always drama with you. I think you're cursed,' she said and sat.

'It's crossed my mind too.'

'I got here too late then?'

''Fraid so.'

'At least tell me you got a statement? My boss is being a total dick about this.'

'Sort of. I forgot to grab my notebook as I left the house, but I have this.' I picked up the pad from the ground where it had fallen in the excitement and handed it to her. 'Oh wait, there was a bit more, but I forgot to write it down. Aly, he was talking about having seen something in a dream. He knew it was a boy. Somehow, he seemed to know something. Let me just try to remember exactly what was said.'

'This is fine, Don. Never mind the crap about dreams. You've stopped here where he says he can't possibly have had anything to do with it and he has no knowledge of anything. This is perfect.'

'But Aly—'

'Yeah, yeah. Spooky dreams, but let's not, eh? Come on, I just drove here at a thousand miles an hour and without breakfast. Show me to a cafe.'

# CHAPTER SEVEN

## Dropping In

'Sarge, do you have a minute?'

'For you, Morgan, I have a full ninety seconds. What's up?'

I couldn't help but think of this lanky lad as a boy. At thirty-five I was pretty young myself, especially for someone promoted, but the sheer lack of confidence in Morgan Finney gave him the demeanour of a kid on their first day at high school. He wore a ubiquitous expression of fear and confusion. He hovered awkwardly, stooping under the doorframe of my office. He looked equally expectant to receive either an invitation to enter or a punch in the face.

'Well, come in,' I urged, and he did, shaking his head at himself. He handed me an envelope folder and sat. 'What's this?'

'It's the case I told you about. I took your advice and

made some enquiries with the bank and it turns out they do have CCTV at the cashpoint. This is what I got from it.'

I pulled several sheets of paper from the folder. Upon each was a printed capture from the footage. Most of the frame was taken up by the face of the poor bugger who'd been marched to the bank to withdraw the cash, but at the edges there were some interesting details.

'In the third one, Sarge, if you look just past the auld-boy's chin there . . .' In his accent 'there' came out as 'thur'. I looked thur and right enough, another face, though not very clear. 'I spoke to our fella and he confirms this is the guy who drove him, the same guy he'd been dealing with all the way through the debacle.'

The blurred face was of a prototypical thug; big, bald and brutish. He faced side on as if keeping a look out, or perhaps just bored. Looking at the time stamp in the top corner, it had taken over eight minutes for the victim to make the transaction. As the pictures progressed, our bald thug disappeared as a small queue formed behind the dithering old man. Then the victim was gone, replaced by a dark-haired woman. There were a few sheets with her.

'What's with these?' I asked. 'You hoping to track this woman down as a witness?'

'No. Just look at the top left corner of those stills.'

I looked once at the seven sheets with the lady in front of the camera, then put the sheets together and flicked the pages. The edge of a white van ran like an old movie, reversing into the view of the camera and then taking off. On two of the sheets the corner of the reg plate was visible. We had a partial plate.

'Morgan. This is really good work.' I didn't mean to sound so surprised, but I couldn't stop the pitch of my voice rising.

The lad instantly flushed red. 'Well, it was your idea,' he said.

'Irrespective, this is really good. I'd probably have missed the van. It's something to work with. Really good, Morgan. Circulate the picture of the driver – if we get lucky someone will recognise him, but don't hold your breath.'

'Will do, Sarge.' He stood to leave.

'Hey, I'm sorry I've not been around the past week to keep an eye on things, been a bit preoccupied with an enquiry. What do you have on today?' I asked.

'Not a lot. I need to do some door to door for a vandalism the day shift didn't get around to.'

'Again? This has got to stop. Where is it?'

'Another car got trashed in Pilton over the weekend.'

'All right, I'll come with you. We'll get it done quick and then see if we can find something more interesting to do.'


The weather had taken a turn. A week of rain had levelled what previously had teased at becoming an exceptional Scottish summer. Today, though cool and overcast, was dry, so we walked.

Three times I had to tell Morgan to slow his pace. First off, we didn't have a lot on, so why rush around north Edinburgh? And second, I felt like I was jogging to keep up with his long legs.

'Sarge, who's your boss then?' he asked as we crossed Ferry Road.

'What do you mean?'

'Well, you're my boss, I report to you. But who do you report to? Who gives you instruction?'

'Ah, OK. Well in theory, that would be Inspector Reynolds.'

'In theory?'

'Inspector Reynolds is in charge of all community teams in the Edinburgh and Lothians area.'

'I don't think I've ever met him.'

'Well, that's where the "theory" part comes in. See, Inspector Reynolds is doing the job that four or five inspectors used to. Thanks to budget cuts he has the impossible task of overseeing a ridiculously large area and workforce. So, my job, as I see it, is to stay off his radar altogether. If I don't ruffle any feathers or allow any of my team to screw up too badly, he leaves us be, and he's just grateful he doesn't have to get involved. With a bit of luck, you'll never have to meet him.'

We continued walking north into the housing estates of Pilton.

'What are your ambitions in the police, Morgan? Where do you see yourself?'

'Oh, I don't know, Sarge. Honestly, I'm just hoping to make it through my probation period. I'm a bit worried I'm not going to make it, if I'm perfectly honest.'

'Really? Why so?'

He shrugged his thin shoulders. 'I really struggled at Tulliallan. I was borderline for the written exams and I was shocking with the fitness.'

'You look pretty fit, what happened?' I remembered my

time at the Police training college. Eleven weeks in my first year and another six in the second. I forced the memory out of my head. It was not a fond one.

'The running was fine, like. It was all the bloody press-ups and that. I tried my best but I'm just not naturally good with that stuff. I swear one of the training sergeants had it in for me, wanted to fail me. I came back to division with a letter.'

'What does that mean? A letter?'

'Sort of a warning, like. I only mentioned it because I assumed you'd know all about it.'

'It'll likely be on your file, Morgan. But I'm kind of a take-everyone-on-their-own-merits sort of guy. God knows I've had my own issues with bosses and colleagues. Keep going the way you are and we'll get you through your probation, don't worry.'

We completed the door to door, getting nothing from neighbours and leaving calling cards for the few houses where there was no reply. This was the fourth car to have its windows smashed in the past two months – just the sort of thing that would ping on Inspector Reynold's radar if I didn't get on top of it fast.

The whole time we were performing our fruitless task, I thought about how we were only ten minutes from Pennywell. I'd meant to call after leaving Vicky with Martin so distressed, but I hadn't gotten around to it and now nearly two weeks had passed. A phone call just didn't seem appropriate.

'I've got a little job that needs doing,' I told Morgan. 'Fancy tagging along?'

The improvement in the weather wasn't to last. A light drizzle fell and was gaining momentum by the time we reached the care home. We ducked down the side road just as a crack of thunder sounded and the drizzle turned to rain. The growl of an exhaust pipe could be heard as we pulled into the car park. We got out of the car and I rang the buzzer. While I waited for a response, I eyed a blue Subaru, complete with large rear spoiler, idling in the space reserved for an ambulance. A man sat in the driver's seat having a heated conversation on his phone. He did a double take when he saw us. Our eyes met for a moment before he turned on his stereo and a muffled blast of dance music erupted, only to be drowned out by the exhaust as he drove off.

'Hellooooo?' came a voice from the intercom. The voice had clearly been calling for a while, but I could only now hear it.

'Hi, is that you, Vicky? It's Don Colyear. I was in the area and hoped it would be all right to stop by.' I was half yelling as the noise of the rain grew, pattering off the glass covering above the front door. I pulled Morgan under it as he was getting soaked, probably too nervous to squeeze in next to me. The response on the intercom came after a lengthy delay.

'I'll be right there.'

The door unlocked and we ducked inside, shaking the water off us. I assumed it had been Vicky who'd opened the door for us, but I now saw it was her colleague, Michelle. She was looking at us like we were lunch, just delivered.

'All right, boys. D'you need some help getting out of

those wet things?'

'Yeah, actually, is there anywhere we can hang some of this up?' I said.

'Aye, there's a long radiator in the office. C'mon.'

'Is Vicky around?' I asked as we followed Michelle along the corridor.

'She's around. Just busy with the residents.'

'I was hoping to have a quick word.'

'I'll see what I can do. There y'are. Take off whatever you like.'

I peeled off my armour and hooked it around the radiator, which was burning hot. This place was always so warm. Morgan did the same while Michelle eyed him.

'And what's your name? You look awfully young to be a copper.'

'I, uh . . . M'name's Morgan.'

'Morgan?' Michelle repeated, her face screwed up.

'Yeah. You know, capital M, small organ,' he laughed.

'Well, that's a shame,' said Michelle, her hands on her hips, her eyes on the lad's crotch. 'Still, it's not the size of the carrot, it's the crunch in the bite. Am I right?' she said to me and laughed.

'That's what I've heard.' I laughed back. Morgan's face was beginning to glow, but I couldn't help myself.

'Are you looking to see Martin while you're here?' she said, once she'd composed herself.

'I suppose. What kind of state is he in?'

'In his quiet state. He's in his room if you want to come up?'

'Better bring a radio,' I said to Morgan as we left our

things behind. He unclipped his radio from the armour and we followed Michelle upstairs.

Martin was in his window seat, staring ahead – perhaps looking out at the rain, perhaps not.

'I'll see about getting Vic, give you lot a few minutes, eh?'

'Thanks, Michelle,' I said, and sat on the bed beside Martin and placed my hand on his.

'Is this your da?' Morgan said, a deep and soft sympathy in his voice.

'My dad? No. I wish my dad was this quiet,' I laughed and instantly regretted the joke. 'No, this is Martin. I only met him recently. He's been helping us with an enquiry.'

Morgan's face squeezed in confusion for a second. I decided against enlightening him.

'There's a spare chair behind the door. Bring it over.' He did and sat. 'Michelle's clearly got a thing for you,' I mocked.

'Ah . . . yeah, she's a riot, like.'

'Want me to put in a good word?'

'Oh, no. Thanks. No. I'm fine, like.'

'You have a significant other, Morgan?'

'No, not currently. Got enough on my plate with the job an'all. Happy as I am.'

Martin breathed softly in and out through his nose. If he knew we were there, he made no indication.

'You're from Northern Ireland, right?' I said.

'From Coleraine, yeah.'

'What brought you over to Scotland?'

'Uni. I got a place at Napier here in Edinburgh.'

'Ah, you're a graduate? A scholar like our Martin here?'

'No, not really. I dropped out in my third year,' he said, looking over the books on Martin's shelf.

'What happened? If it's OK to ask?'

The question seemed to make him uncomfortable. He folded his legs and then his arms. 'I just, I sort of decided it wasn't for me. The first year was grand. Second year, things started to get a bit on top of me. Third year I barely got going before my grades started to drop and I ended up off with a bit of stress.'

'Sorry to hear that. I'm sure it's pretty common. What did your parents think?'

'Well, they were worried, naturally. Wanted me to come home. But I'm really fond of the city, you know? I didn't really give Edinburgh a lot of thought before I got here but I really took to it. It's only wee, but every corner is full of all sorts.'

He was right, the city was a pretty special place. At any time, there was something to do. Tourists snapping at the buildings, a labyrinth of cobbled closes, and if that wasn't fairy tale enough, there was always the castle on a giant rock right at the centre of it all.

'Why the police?'

At this he shrugged. 'The honest answer, Sarge, is they were hiring. Of course, that's not quite what I said at the interview. "Lifelong ambition", I think I described it as. Oh God, I don't know why I'm telling you this.'

I laughed. 'It's fine, Morgan. I joined for the same reason. I had bills to pay.'

The door opened and a smiling Vicky walked through. She wore more makeup this time, though not enough to conceal the bruising around her right eye.

'How's our professor?' she said.

'In a pensive mood today. I think he's considering the rain,' I said.

'I do that too when it rains,' she said. 'I consider moving to Spain. Do you want to come down and get some tea? We'll leave Martin to his thoughts for a while.'

Michelle offered to arrange the tea while we took a table in the empty dining hall. We'd gathered our things from the office, damp and hot, and reassembled ourselves.

'I'm really sorry about my last visit, Vicky. I got him into a spiral and I wasn't sure what to do. I didn't mean to upset him.'

'Don't worry about it. It's not your fault he went into the dark.'

'Into to the dark?' I said.

'That's how I think of it. It's like he comes into the light when he's himself. You can see it in his face, this light. You can hear it in his voice.'

I thought about that version of Martin in the garden. She was right. It was as if some inner glow radiated through him.

'But he doesn't stay long in the light, you just have to enjoy him while you can. 'Cause all too soon he falls away again, into the dark. I wish there was some magical way to reach in there and pull him out, but . . .' She shrugged and gave a small shake of the head.

Michelle's appearance was announced by a chorus of

rattling crockery. She set a tray down and began to pour for everyone.

'A wee word of advice,' said Vicky. 'When you're dealing with people suffering from dementia, it's better just to go with what they're saying. If they think you're some other relative, it's best not to correct them. Just play along.'

'Is that not a bit . . . I dunno, cruel? Or disrespectful?' said Morgan, giving a voice to my own thought.

'Maybe on some level. But if you consider it entirely on their wellbeing, then no. There's no point in upsetting them, which is what confrontation will do. You have to think about the fact that you're not going to teach them something. They're not going to take your correction and do better next time. It's kinder to leave them comfortable in their reality.'

'Oor Mimi thinks I'm her daughter most of the time. I spend half the day updating her on the adventures of her grandkids. It makes her happy. A wee white lie,' said Michelle.

'I suppose that makes sense. If it happens in the future, I'll try to remember that. Was Martin agitated for a long time after I left?'

'He was, yes. He was up half the night ranting and raving. He must have remembered something about you being there as he kept asking for the police. And he was yelling about hearing God, which isn't like him.'

'He's not religious?'

'Not at all. When you get him in a lucid state, he's pretty vocal about not having any time for the Church or any organised religion.'

'Sorry again. Good news is I won't be back to bother him. Alyson was happy with what we got, so there's no need to bother him further.'

'Aw, well you can still stop by any time you like. It's nice to see police walking around. You never do any more.' Michelle said this to Morgan, not to me.

'She's right. Stop in any time,' said Vicky as I took a last sip of my tea and stood. There was a better light in this room and the blue-green around her eye was more prominent.

'What happened here?' I asked and leant over to get a better look at the swelling.

'Och, just another accident. Happened while I was getting one of our residents out of the bath. It happens. Right, Michelle?'

'Aye. Happens all the time,' Michelle said with a smile. A smile that was not genuine.

# CHAPTER EIGHT

## Nan

Her name was Josephine, though almost everyone who knew her had either forgotten that, or had never known it in the first place. She was 'Mum' to Aileen, otherwise she was 'Nan'. She rarely even thought of herself as anything else. Now and again at the bank or post office, she'd be standing in line and pull her card or cheque book from her bag and there was her given name, a name that had belonged to a younger version of herself but had been put in a drawer somewhere, at some time.

She sat across the table from Poppy and thought about this. She'd hidden her surprise and dislike when Aileen had told her that she'd picked the name Poppy for her first, and since Aileen was, what? Forty-two? No, forty-three – probably only grandchild. But it had grown on her. Now, looking at that jam-smeared face, she couldn't be anything else but Poppy. She wondered if she would be Poppy all her days, or whether that name would give way to its own age-earned alternative and find a place in its own drawer.

Aileen dropped Poppy off early on a Wednesday so that she could get to her one fitness class of the week before work. Not that it was a problem for Nan. Even on a Wednesday she'd have been up and breakfasted for an hour or two before they arrived. It also meant that Nan had an extra hour with Poppy before they walked to school, and so the girl could eat her breakfast sitting down, rather than clenching a piece of toast between her teeth while her jacket was pulled over her head and before she was dragged down the garden path to make the fifteen-minute walk to school in ten.

'All finished?' said Nan. Poppy nodded and held her hands wide to be cleaned after dropping the bread onto her plate, aware she'd stick to anything she might come into contact with. Nan ran a cloth over the girl's fingers, folded it, then wiped her face before planting a kiss on the now-clean mouth.

Nan got Poppy ready, making sure her feet were snuggly in the end of her wellies and that her coat hood was firmly pulled over her head before stepping out into the morning drizzle. She snapped open her umbrella and took the girl by the hand. Poppy was singing something to herself, a tune Nan was not familiar with, perhaps she'd heard it in the car on the way over. Her mum was a keen singer, always had been. She'd have liked Aileen to have another. Nan suspected she was a better grandmother than she'd ever been a mother; sometimes these maternal instincts set in later in life, she considered. She regretted not taking more interest in Aileen's schooling, wished she'd encouraged her to go to university, to see more of the world. Aileen had lived for a couple of years in Fife, not exactly spreading her wings, but at least out of Edinburgh. She'd hoped it would be the start of something for her daughter. The start of what, she wasn't sure; but when she'd announced she was pregnant and that she and Andrew had broken up in the same breath, she knew all that was gone.

She'd helped Aileen buy her own flat with what little savings she had. A small place in Lochend, walkable to Nan's own place in Leith, though not on a school day when Aileen had to get all the way out to her work in Portobello. An 8 a.m. start meant the easiest thing to do was to drop Poppy and let Nan get her to school and pick her up after.

'Morning, Nan,' said Jessica's mum. Nan wasn't sure of the woman's own name, just that her girl was in the same class as Poppy. And there it was, Nan thought, as she returned the greeting and planted one last kiss on Poppy's head before letting her run inside with her classmate; that's when it starts, when you have children. 'Jessica's mum'. 'Mum' to Jessica, and perhaps also to her husband when Jessica was around, her own name starting its slide into that drawer.

Nan checked her watch. She was running a little late, though it wouldn't be a problem.

She reached the manse and knocked as she entered, making a show of jangling her set of keys loudly as she did. Then she called her arrival into the hall to alert Father McCauley in case he was in a state of mid-dress, which had happened more than once. If it happened again, her suspicion that it was not just down to bad luck would be confirmed. She wondered how late he slept on the days she wasn't there to clean.

There was no reply, so she walked straight to the kitchen expecting the mess she ordinarily encountered, already mouthing her complaint. However, all she found was a half-finished cup of tea next to the sink. No plates, no ashtrays, no wineglass stained and reeking from last night's tipple. Had he finally gotten the message?

She washed the cup then opened the cleaning cupboard in the hall and set about her routine of dusting and vacuuming. She worked from the bottom up as usual, leaving the bedroom until last. At one time, she had been told, three priests would have lived in this grand old house, yards from the chapel. As it was, Father McCauley was left to rattle around on his own. He was Nan's second priest in her time cleaning for St Mary Star of the Sea Church. He was messier than Father Kaminski, but at least he was full of cheer and chat. She always felt like she was intruding with Father Kaminski.

Nan ignored the unused bedrooms, they only needed cleaning once a month at most, and moved on to Father McCauley's. She chapped on the closed door, though assumed he had already left for the morning. Unusual, though not unheard of. With no reply she pushed the door and stepped into the dark room. The curtains were closed and as she pulled them wide the spilling light revealed a made bed. This *was* a first. She instantly felt pleased as she dusted the bedside cabinet, then guilt set in. It had been something of a routine between the pair of them; Nan asking Father McCauley if he'd ever heard of such a thing on God's green earth as a coaster, or was there some commandment: 'Thou shall not lift a finger to clean up after thou-self', always met with a mumble of amused dismissal or a none-too subtle eye roll. Clearly, though, something had dropped and now she wasn't sure how to feel about it. She had felt a little redundant cleaning up after the fastidious Father Kaminski, like she spent most of her time hunting dust rather than being in any way useful. Maybe she'd speak to Father McCauley, make it clear she'd only been complaining in jest.

Nan tidied away the vacuum and set the washing machine. The cycle would be done by the time she'd finished cleaning the church itself. She crossed the courtyard to the back door of the church and pulled at the door, but found it locked. *Strange*, she thought, *maybe he's gone on an errand?* She pushed her shoulder into the door as she turned the key, a muscle-memory motion she'd learned over the past fourteen years which saved punishing your wrist on the sticky lock. She felt the familiarly satisfying clunk of the lock giving.

She entered and pulled the door closed behind her. The smell of incense hung thick in the air. Catholics didn't use it every week, she'd learned, but when they did, it filled every corner of the building. She liked the smell, though it made the back of your throat dry to be around it for too long. She set the hot tap running in the utility area and filled the mop bucket, then wheeled it through the swing doors into the church aisle. The smell of pine disinfectant displaced the incense as she sloshed the mop in the bucket. She had just pushed the mop forward on the floor when she stopped. Something was lying at the far end of the aisle. She pushed her glasses a little further up her nose and tried to focus. Whatever it was seemed to glisten in the morning light. Nan took a few steps and stopped again, leaning the shaft of the mop against a pew. Something made her hesitate. The colour. She tried to take in what she was seeing. It was spherical and a deep red. It looked like a watermelon if somehow you managed to remove all of the skin and leave the round flesh intact. Nan was beginning to convince herself that's exactly what it was, wet and crimson, as she began walking towards it once more.

Nan was halfway down the aisle when she saw that the thing was not just a ball, it was in fact attached to something. Three more steps and she saw that it was attached to the shoulders of Father McCauley.

# CHAPTER NINE

## Forensic Strategy

Alyson reached across the coffee table to accept the mug being passed to her. Her mother eyed her arm as she did. Aly should have known better than to wear a sleeveless blouse.

'You need to lay off those weights, Alyson. How are you going to get a man if you've bigger muscles than they have? It's intimidating.'

How long since she last played this broken record; three, maybe four weeks? 'Mum, I couldn't give a shit if men are intimidated.' Alyson selected a chocolate finger from the plate of biscuits; maybe because she just fancied one, or maybe because they were her mother's favourite.

'You *should* give a shit. You should give a very big shit indeed.' Her mother turned back towards the television where some woman was silently trying to sell the nation some scented candles. How this home shopping channel quite managed that through a screen, Alyson had no idea. Though looking around the living room at the motley of knick-knacks, glassware and, yes, scented bloody candles, she suspected they were doing a pretty good job.

'You need to get out more, Mum. Less QVC and more fresh air.'

'And turn into a hulking brute like you? I think not.'

'Mum, you're not going grow a pair of biceps by going for an hour's walk once a day.'

'I get my exercise, stop fussing.'

'What exercise?'

Her mother shifted in her seat, irritably. 'I meet with the girls twice a week and I have my book club at Ailsa's on a Thursday. I walk there.'

'Mum, Ailsa lives three streets away and you walk because the pair of you get through three bottles of pinot while you're discussing the book none of you have read. And meeting the girls for coffee and cake is not the same as getting some proper—'

'I'll start jogging when you stop pumping iron and scaring the boys away. Look at that, I can see the veins in your arm. It's not right. It's not . . . feminine.'

Alyson's phone buzzed and beeped from her jacket pocket to rescue her. She lifted the jacket and took it through to the kitchen before she answered, leaning her back against the fridge. It was Duncan.

'What's going on, boss? Don't tell me I've got my shift wrong? I'm not supposed to be in until three.' She checked the time on the microwave: 12.22.

'Where are you?' he said. His voice was hurried, though not angry.

'I'm at my . . . I'm not late, am I? I'm sure I was on a back shift.'

'You're not late. Something's come up. How quickly can you get to Edinburgh?'

'Edinburgh? Again? Is it this old fucker again?'

'Alyson, be quiet and answer the question. How long before you can get there?'

'I . . . I dunno. An hour and a half at least. I'm in Ardrossan, at my mum's. I'll leave right now. Where am I going?'

'We're meeting at Leith Police Station. Be as quick as you can.'

It was an hour and a half before Alyson even reached the outskirts of Edinburgh. Her phone, propped on her dash, told her it was another twenty-eight minutes to Leith and once there she couldn't figure out where to park; everything was metered. She abandoned her car, knowing she'd be returning to a ticket and ran inside, explaining to the desk sergeant who she was. She could feel her blouse sticking to her back with sweat. She was directed to the first floor and the last office at the end of the corridor. She could hear there was animated conversation within the room from halfway along the corridor, and it was only as she turned the handle and pushed the door open that she realised just how badly she needed to pee.

When she stepped through the door, she was met with silence. Blood rushed to her cheeks and her voice failed in her throat. There were at least a dozen people sat around a table, maybe fifteen, staring at her. At first she didn't think she knew a single face, that maybe she'd just made a complete dick of herself by barging into the wrong meeting, but then, someone in the corner cleared their throat. Duncan. He beckoned her with a flick of the head. She closed the door and was relieved as the chatter started up once more.

She ducked her head and started towards Duncan. There were many voices trying to be heard at once, but only one winner: DCI Kate Templeton. Alyson hadn't seen her when she entered, but now she was unmistakeable. She wasn't on her feet, but sat with her back perfectly straight, which was enough to have her looking down on most heads. 'As I was—*AS I was saying*,' she barked to hush the others. 'A current and ongoing investigation supersedes a new inquiry. Not that—would you let me fucking *speak*, thank you. Not that this is a new inquiry, simply a development of our own.'

'What the hell's going on?' Alyson whispered to Duncan as she drew up a chair next to him. A man she didn't know moved to the side to allow her to squeeze in, but did not look happy about it. Another DS, she saw from the warrant card around his neck.

'Right now, it's a pissing contest. I'll explain everything later, but a body was discovered this morning. An initial examination has linked it to our inquiry.'

'Shit, here in Edinburgh? Another child?'

'Obviously here in Edinburgh. No, not a kid,' said Duncan.

A tall, balding man sitting opposite DCI Templeton was responding to her declaration, his finger slamming into the table for emphasis. 'You were invited here out of professional courtesy. That you have an open inquiry does not detract from the fact that a murder occurred in *my* city, bloody yards from where we're sitting, and if you think I'm about to step aside and let you lot waltz in here like you own the bloody place—'

'I'm sorry, does your pay cheque read something different to mine? Is yours in some fucking time warp and come headed 'Lothian and Borders'? No, I think fucking not. This is Police Scotland. This case is attached to my inquiry and I am the senior investigating officer,' Templeton replied.

'Just typical. Just bloody typical of you people,' said another officer. Unlike DCI Templeton, he was in dress uniform. Alyson strained to get a look at his shoulders, then saw that he was a superintendent, effectively Templeton's superior.

DCI Templeton sat back in her chair and crossed her arms, before releasing one to gesture across the room. 'Do you want to tell us all what you mean by that comment?'

'You know exactly what I mean,' the superintendent replied.

'Actually, you'll have to excuse my ignorance. I have no idea what you're alluding to. Please enlighten me.'

Alyson had an idea of what he was getting at, which probably meant Templeton knew, fine and well. There was a pause while the superintendent chewed it over. It seemed like he'd thought better of it when it suddenly spilled from his mouth. 'You fucking Strathclyde lot. You haven't the first clue what it means to collaborate, only to take over. The whole lot of you are nothing but playground bullies. If you think I'm going to let you fucking Glaswegians run roughshod over my inquiry, you're in for shock, lady.'

There it was. It was an old complaint, probably running prior to the amalgamation of the Scottish police forces in 2013, but since then it was a tangible resentment that would rear its head whenever events spilled over old borders. The general opinion was that during the amalgamation there was little in the way of merging and more that everyone else was brought under the banner of Strathclyde, the largest of the forces. In Alyson's experience, most officers who'd joined prior to 2003 still very much saw themselves as fighting under different, obsolete flags.

'I think you'll find that this is *my* inquiry. It is your job to investigate on my behalf. Don't ever lose sight of that. It is my ball and I will decide who gets to play with it. Understood?' said an older lad in plain clothes.

There was an instant 'Yes, ma'am' from both DCI Templeton and the superintendent without a hint of gripe or sarcasm, making Alyson wonder who this woman was.

'That's the PF,' Duncan said, maybe seeing the question on Alyson's face.

The procurator fiscal now stood. She was a short woman, with a bob of red hair and square-framed glasses. There was something of a librarian about her. She removed her glasses and rubbed at her eyes, before replacing them and leafing through the papers in front of her.

'How certain are we that this is the same suspect as the

Bradley case?' she said.

'We can be absolutely certain. The prints from the knife are nice and clear. They've been checked and they're a match for prints found on the body in the Bradley case,' Templeton replied.

'You agree with this?' The PF was talking to a man at the far end of the table, a few seats down from Alyson. He stood and confirmed that they were in the ninety-ninth percentile, then sat again.

'In that case, the Bradley team will head up this inquiry, too. I want this air-tight and I can't see anything but confusion and the doubling of workload if we separate this into two teams. Superintendent Hadley, you will make every resource available to DCI Templeton, won't you?'

'Yes, ma'am,' he said, a hint of exasperation in his voice. The superintendent stood, which prompted a chorus of chair scraping as half the room did likewise, and moved to leave. Alyson stifled a laugh when she saw DCI Templeton wink at him as he gathered his hat from the table.

Once the door was closed over the PF addressed the room, though Alyson felt she was probably addressing her directly, due to her being late.

'For those of you who missed introductions, I'll quickly go around the table once more. I am Patricia Ewing, Procurator Fiscal for Edinburgh. Senior investigating officer, as we just dramatically established, is Detective Chief Inspector Kate Templeton and her team.'

DCI Templeton, reading from papers in front of her, didn't look up, rather just waved a hand in their general direction. 'DS Cunningham, who is the designated crime scene manager, and DC Kane.'

'Thank you. From Edinburgh University Chemistry department is Doctor Simon Fischer. He'll be liaising with our CSM DS Cunningham, and our representative from Scenes of Crime, Derek McEwan.' The men raised a hand as their names were announced.

'I'm going to pass on to DCI Templeton, who will give us some insights into the previous crime scene and what we might expect from today. Kate.'

'Thank you, ma'am,' said Templeton and stood, taking one last look at the sheet she was holding then laying it in front of her. 'If our first crime scene is any indication of what we can expect, then we are looking at an absolute playground of evidence. The decision was made, earlier today, to do an initial sweep of the locus. While that may well have fucked with my scene to a degree, I have to say I accept and endorse that decision. The weapon which is likely to have been used was found at the locus and since we had no way of knowing if we had some madman on the loose, that knife was recovered and prints taken, which is how we find ourselves in your fair city. The rest of the scene is as found by our witness, Josephine Wilson.

'The victim is Father Brian McAuley, a seventy-one-year-old Catholic priest. Pronounced dead at 10.12 a.m. this morning. As it stands, there have been seven persons entering the crime scene, which is seven more than is ideal. Our witness, two beat officers, one detective, two paramedics and a police surgeon. I'm passing around sketches of our locus. A common path will be set up through the rear entrance of the church, this being the entry point of the witness and therefore our best hope to preserve as much of the scene as possible.'

Alyson took a copy of the sheets passing around and handed the rest on. A floor plan, sketched in black pen, showed the church on Constitution Street, it really was right around the corner from where they were sitting.

'As you can see,' Templeton continued, 'the main section of the church is wide and we're looking at a pretty complicated internal due to the pews and whatnot, so we'll take it slowly and methodically. The one major drawback to the discovery of our victim, is our witness was cleaning as she entered, and has likely obliterated some seriously fucking important evidence. Specifically the sink area marked on your sheets, which was scrubbed clean before she entered the main section. Can't be helped, but very fucking frustrating.

'Now, one last thing before we head out. I don't know many of you. My team works predominantly in the Glasgow area, so I'm sorry if this is patronising, but I'll say it anyway. The scene you're about to enter has been described as particularly disturbing. No one will blame you if you need to step out to take a breath. OK. I'll now hand control over to Crime Scene Manager DS Cunningham.'

It wasn't Alyson's first crime scene. It wasn't even her first murder – but she was nervous as the van pulled up to the blue and white tape. It seemed pointless driving to the church. It would have been quicker to walk since they had to negotiate a bizarre system around the roadworks extending Edinburgh's 'fucking tram system', as the detective sitting next to her on the short journey over had described it, the same guy who'd sat next to her in the forensic strategy meeting. He and one other officer had been begrudgingly assigned by the superintendent to assist with the inquiry, providing local knowledge and likely doubling as spies in the camp. The unmarked vehicles they travelled in were also given over after more grumbling and some cajoling from the PF. A bitter little exchange at the rear yard of the Leith police office ensued. At the end of which DCI Templeton had suggested to the superintendent, out of earshot of most, though not Alyson and Duncan, that they might go ahead and play a quick game of Fuck Off, and that he, the superintendent, should go first. Time would tell if she would get away with that one.

They were let through the cordon by a fresh-faced uniformed officer and down a tight alleyway at the side of the church which led to a pleasant courtyard at the rear; a square piece of ground, shielded from the noises of the city. A statue of Christ, his arms open wide, stood behind a trimmed hedge and in front of another building. The three vans pulled into a small parking area clear of both buildings.

Alyson stepped out of the van into warm sunshine. She allowed herself a second to present her face, eyes closed, to the warm light, considering it in some way inappropriate in the face of what they were about to walk into.

'That's the manse, where the priest lives . . . lived,' said Duncan.

'I know what a manse is,' Alyson said, then opened her eyes to look at it. It was about twenty metres from the rear door of the church. A grey stone building, nearly as impressive as the church itself.

'Right. Well, we'll move on to there after we deal with the locus, though our witness also cleaned inside. Here, you're on camera duty.' Duncan had reached into a box and handed Alyson a small video camera. It seemed to her that Edinburgh had a better budget for gadgets than the west. It was a neat little thing. 'You know how to work it?'

'I'll figure it out. They're all pretty much the same,' she said and powered it up.

Duncan cleared his throat, bringing an end to the various little conversations amongst those present. 'All right everyone, suit up please, including footwear covers, thanks. This outdoor area has already been examined and photographed, but still, try not to disturb anything. DC Kane and I will do an initial sweep and recording. Thereafter we will begin collecting evidence as discussed.'

Alyson opened her pack and stepped into her suit. She applied her gloves, shoe protectors and mask before setting up the camera. With a nod from Duncan she drew a long breath, released it and hit record. Another young, uniformed officer guarded the rear door to the church. She insisted on noting their details before stepping aside. Duncan drew back the door and Alyson raised the camera before entering.

Duncan motioned for Alyson to move to the left and into a small kitchen area. She drew the camera across the surfaces and into the sink, though it all seemed pretty sterile. The smell of disinfectant was strong, even through the mask. She aimed the lens at the floor and around the edge of the a window. Duncan then guided Alyson by the shoulders back into the main area. A long aisle lay in front with a thin, red piece of carpet drawing the eye down to the end where a set of white steps rose up to the altar area. At the foot of the steps, something lay very still. She tried not to look at it, at least not while they made their way down the aisle, keeping to the left of the carpet as they'd discussed at the meeting. Alyson trained the camera at the rows of pews, sweeping left and right; there was a soft swooshing from her paper suit as her elbows brushed her sides, otherwise there was no sound. There was a very churchy smell about the place, nothing unpleasant, as she'd experienced in other crime scenes.

Duncan gave her a tap on the shoulder and pointed to the top of a pew. She drew the camera down and allowed the lens to focus on what he'd found. Three arcs of smeared blood. Duncan motioned to the next pew with similar marks, this time a little heavier and then again and again. Five pews in a row where bloody fingers had been drawn across the top, as if the killer had used them to clean his hands. DCI Templeton was right, it *was* a playground of evidence.

And there was the victim, dressed in white and green priest's robes. He lay face down, diagonally across the floor, his feet pointing at the pews, one outstretched arm reaching towards the steps, as if they might be his rescue. A thick and sickening puddle of crimson pooled around the body from above the head to his lower chest. Alyson could feel her pulse quickening as she bent closer. She started at the feet, at his black shoes, one of which was only just clinging to the foot at the toes. She worked her way up the back of his robe, silver Celtic embroidery around the deep green stripe up the back. Beyond the waist, blood had soaked into the cloth and had been working its way up his flanks. On his outstretched arm, the left one, was a single stab wound, with a circle of blood around the hole at his shoulder. Though this was not what had killed him. You didn't need to be a pathologist or even a lowly DC to know why this man had stopped breathing. Alyson's hand shook a little as she moved the camera to the man's head.

Were it not for the rest of the body, it might have been hard to say exactly what you were looking at. She focused on the view panel of the camera and tried to imagine she was only watching television. The man's silver hair was stained pink. To each side of his head was just a pulp of flesh.

'Jesus,' she said. It came out involuntarily. Unprofessional, and in this place, wholly inappropriate. She rotated around the head, the face buried into the floor. Each side was the same; stab wounds, but *so* many stab wounds in and around each ear that the skin hung from the sides of the skull in tatters.

# CHAPTER TEN

## Your Place Or Dad's?

'Ten quid? Really? I remember when it was a fiver, and that wasn't too long ago,' I said and fished the note from my wallet before stuffing it into the glass Vikram was holding.

'There's only five of us on the team, four if you consider Cathy's going to be out with her back for the foreseeable; but don't worry, the tradition is to put it all into the kitty anyway. You *are* coming tonight? It's Morgan's birthday,' said Vikram.

'Ah, I don't know. I never was one for work nights out,' I said, and it wasn't a lie. I was never that interested, but the fuller truth was that for a long time I was despised on the shift and so invites like this one never came my way.

'Oh, come on, Sarge. The team's too small for no-shows. If you don't come, you'll be leaving me with the two youngsters and Vik here'll piss off home to his bairns before midnight,' said Mandy.

Mandy was in her early forties, divorced and pushing for promotion. She had a kid herself, but was pretty private about it. Vikram on the other hand, despite only having just turned thirty, had four and never missed an opportunity to push his phone into your face to show you one of them with the latest smile or loss of balance, prompting you to feign interest and amusement.

'All right, fine, but I may well be pissing off around the same time as Vikram here.'

Vikram hid the glass of cash as Morgan came into my office, his head buried in his probationer progress folder.

'OK, grab a seat,' I said and propped myself on the edge of my desk to face the three of them. 'As you know, a murder inquiry is under way in Leith. While it doesn't affect us directly, I think we can anticipate some resource back-filling as things progress. It's likely the shifts will be called upon to protect the locus and such and then we'll likely be required to tidy up more calls. This is just fair warning. Meantime, I need to do a monthly report to the inspector, so as much as I hate to have to do this, we need to play Justify-My-Existence.'

There was a groan from Mandy and Vikram. Morgan simply sat there looking confused. I grabbed a pad of paper from the desk. 'So, in the last month, what can you give me? Anything at all.' I looked to Cathy first, though as she worked only with Vikram, she was talking for both of them.

'To be honest, Sarge, we've mainly been doing boring follow up for the shift. There's not an awful lot to report.'

'How about that spate of vandalisms you've all been

doing door to door for, did we get anyone for that?'

'Not that I'm aware of. Someone will just write it off before long,' said Vikram.

I dropped the pad and pen onto my desk. 'Right, screw this. Everyone at the back door,' I pulled on my armour and walked to the front desk, where I grabbed keys for the cell van, something I would normally have to book out in advance, but I was hoping this wouldn't take long. I pulled the van, a modified Transit, up to the back door. Now the other two had the same confused look as Morgan. I rolled down the window and said, 'Mandy, Vikram, in the front with me. Morgan, sorry mate, but you're in the back.'

'What back? There is no back. Just the . . .' It dawned on him, and to his credit he didn't complain, as Vikram opened the door to the cell with a smile and let the lad climb in before slamming the door.

'Are you going to tell us what we're doing here, Sarge?' said Mandy as I slowed up a little after tearing into the housing schemes of Muirhouse. Morgan had rolled around in the back for a while, but had apparently figured out how to brace himself since the thudding had stopped.

'I will, but right now just keep your eyes peeled for any little shits you see on bikes.'

It was four in the afternoon, we were due to finish at six and since it was Morgan's birthday, I didn't want them staying on late. It would risk messing up this night out I was dreading, which meant if this thing was going to happen, it would have to happen soon.

'There,' said Vikram, pointing out to the left.

I slowed the van to a crawl and approached the group.

Two sat on bikes, three or four others on a wall outside an off-licence grocery store, most likely trying to convince passers-by to assist them in a spot of underage drinking. Like a pack of spooked animals, they scattered as we were spotted.

'There he is,' I said and put my foot down. They went in all directions, but I stayed on the little shit on the red bike. He was quick, but pedals are no match for an internal combustion engine. He cut left across a field and I couldn't follow. I drove to the next junction and pulled into a series of tight streets. Again, I slowed. I wound down the windows. I pulled up to an intersection of adjoining residential roads and turned off the engine.

'Vikram,' I whispered. 'Get ready.'

He took off his seat belt just in time, as the sound of a bike chain grew rapidly. The red bike flew out in front of us. The rider clocked us and almost lost it. He skidded to a halt just as Vikram's feet hit the tarmac. The boy struggled to get his feet connected to the pedals and was just about getting the bike back up to speed when Vikram caught up to him.

'Damn, he's fast,' said Mandy.

I drove the short distance to our capture and jumped out to meet him.

'Good evening, Mikey,' I said. Vikram had the lad by the shoulder, his legs were still either side of the bike frame, but he was going nowhere.

'I've no done nothin',' Mikey Denholm said. He looked from me to Vikram and Mandy.

'That right? Then why are you running, Mikey?' I said. I

took his shoulder from Vikram and urged him off the bike.

'Everyone was running, so I just . . . I've no done nothin'.'

'That's not what I've been hearing. I hear that you've been putting bricks through car windows, lots of them. I think I've got you for seven, no – eight, in the past few weeks.' I walked him to the van, pushing him firmly, but not too firmly, against the rear doors. His white tracksuit squirmed under my grip. I had no idea if he was involved in this spate of vandalisms, but it was worth digging around, and the little encounter I had with him and his pals had not slipped into memory by the sounds of what he said next. I just hit gold.

'What? That's no me. Why would I be throwin' bricks through windaes?'

'"That's no me?" So you do know who's been doing it?' I said.

Vikram brought the lad's bike around and Mandy looked on with interest.

Again, the twitchy little fella's eyes darted around from face to face. 'I don't know who's been doin' it. An' I wouldnae tell yous if I did.'

'Ah, Mikey. That's just about the worst answer you could have given, wee man. Listen, I'm sorry about what comes next. Well, not that sorry, obviously, but you've left me no choice. If you tell anyone about this, I'll just deny it. Frankly, I think your mum's more likely to believe me than you anyway. Get the door,' I said to Mandy.

She walked around us and I pulled Mikey off the van. She opened one door wide, then the other. Then she reached for the handle of the cage and pulled. Mikey jumped when he saw Morgan stooped over in there. Mikey tried to back away, but I held him firm.

'Another one for you, Morgan. And listen, this time try not to leave any marks on the face will ye,' I pulled Mikey towards the cage and he immediately went into a panic.

'Noooo!' he squealed.

'Just get in,' I said. 'If you're not gonna talk, then you're goin' in.'

'Please . . . It wisnae me. It wisnae—'

'Then who? You've got one chance or you're goin' in with him. I'm no fuckin' around,' I growled.

'It's . . . There's a few, but I never. Look, I'm no a grass.'

'It's you or them, Mikey. Tell me.' Now his eyes were locked firmly on Morgan. I knew I had him. 'Your tall pal, the one I put on his arse the last time I saw you. Is he one of them?'

'Please. I don't want to say.'

'Look Mikey. This is the situation. Either you give me a statement, or I hope you're tougher than you look.'

What he *did* look was utterly defeated. 'You can't make me.'

'You're right, I can't. But look, this isn't going to see a court room. I'll take you home and get a statement and your pal gets charged, probably a fine. He needn't know you told me, but I need a yes from you right now.'

His eyes were still on Morgan, but he was nodding his head.


'I don't know who was more terrified, the kid or Morgan,' Vikram laughed, and we all joined him, except Morgan.

'I wasn't scared, like. I just didn't know what the hell was goin' on. I honestly thought you *did* want me to beat him up.'

We were conversing at a low yell, which might have been dangerous given the unlawful nature of the topic, but nobody was going to overhear a thing with the music blaring. Morgan had seemed really touched by the birthday card stuffed full of money, until Mandy snatched it from him and went to the bar. We stood at a table in the corner of the bar on Hannover Street. It had been a while since I'd been somewhere that might qualify as trendy, with only the occasional visit to the St Vincent or the Cumberland Bar near to the house since my move to the capital. I had noticed a few things: one, while I wasn't the oldest in the bar at thirty-five, I was in the upper percentile, and two, that birthday present of Morgan's wasn't going to last long with the city centre prices here. It wasn't so bad that I felt uncomfortable, however. There was some DJ opposite our table, mixing the music on a table smaller than ours and it wasn't as terrible as I feared; a mix of dance and some soul classics interwoven with some skill. The interior was dark, but not night-club dark and although it seemed busy for a Thursday, we'd snatched a table without having to hover. All in all, not a bad choice of Mandy's.

'It was just a ploy. Sorry, I should have let you in on it, but honestly I was just making it up as I went along. You're all OK with what happened?'

The three of them were nodding.

'Fuck aye. Seven vandalisms cleared up in an hour and a half? Who cares if you bent a few rules? That was impressive,' said Mandy. I had a sudden sense that maybe she'd been reserving judgement about me, perhaps Vikram too, who stood holding his pint with a big grin on his face. Tonight I reckoned they'd decided I was all right after all. I didn't know if stories of my past had reached them, or if they cared.

'Just leaves getting round to Mikey's pal's house on Monday to charge him. I'll take you along, Morgan, but I'm afraid the pleasure will be all mine,' I said.

'Fair enough.'

'By the way, did you get any response from that picture you circulated of our bald thug at the cashpoint?'

'Just the one. Someone from St Leonard's emailed me, suggesting I might look at some fella.'

'Do you remember the name?' I asked.

Morgan sipped from his pint while he thought. He was drinking cider and the smell always made me gag. 'Colin, something. Mc-something-or-other.'

'McStay?' offered Vikram.

'Aye, maybe. Sounds right.'

'Colander McStay?' said Mandy, almost choking on her own drink.

'Colander?' I asked.

'I never thought about it. It's not a great picture,' Mandy went on. 'But I suppose it could be. Colin McStay's a meathead from out Wester Hailes. Used to work doors and run around as part of a crew. Fancied himself as the biggest, baddest gorilla in the jungle. Right up until he picked a fight with someone better. A knife gets pulled and Colin ends up with enough holes in him to drain pasta. Just don't call him "Colander" to his face.'

'We can check SID when we're back on, see if there's anything on him running a business,' I said. The Scottish Intelligence Database was a handy tool, particularly if you planned on getting involved with someone you hadn't yet encountered. It was an open intelligence gathering format that any officer could access and contribute to. If you were lucky, you could find everything from a new telephone number to someone's most recent relationship, to give you a bit of an advantage.

'Right, enough shop talk,' said Mandy as three people approached us, removing their coats. 'This is Lynsey and her husband Dave. I've known Lynsey since high school, and this is Marcella from my yoga class. I hope you don't mind me inviting a few friends along, I thought a few more faces wouldn't hurt.'

She was right. If her friends hadn't arrived to dilute the conversation, we'd have talked about work for an hour or so and then run out of topics. We sent Morgan to the bar as we said our hellos. I got talking to Dave for some time, learning about his job. He was a contractor for the Ministry of Defence. He operated drones for the army and the air force to shoot down. It was nice not to be the one talking about my job for a change. It was a strange fact that as a police officer, if you are invited to a dinner party, you tend to find that you're the only one whose occupation is mentioned after your name as you go around the table.

As predicted, Vikram, a little shaky on his heels, bid the everyone farewell just after eleven, leaving the rest of us to finish off Morgan's birthday present.

'Where is Morgan anyway?' I asked Mandy as she placed an elbow on my shoulder for support. She was rocking a little herself.

'I was gonna ask you that. I was thinking about setting him up with Marcella. Whaddya think?'

Marcella was talking to Lynsey, sharing a laugh. She was late twenties or early thirties. Her dark hair fell to her shoulders either side of a pretty, round face.

'You might need to find her a stepladder, but aye, she seems really nice.' She was maybe five-three, but only because she was wearing heels.

'Marcie, Marcie, c'mere and meet ma boss,' said Mandy, walking over to take her friend by the forearm. She'd clearly forgotten we had been introduced earlier, though we hadn't really talked. 'Yous stay here while I go find that lanky eejit,' she said and pushed her glass into my chest for me to look after.

'Maybe I should hide this,' I said, and Marcella laughed.

'She'll only go buy a fresh one, and that might be worse.'

'True enough.'

'So, you're Mandy's boss? Does that make you a chief something-or-other? I can't imagine anyone being boss over Mandy.'

'Oh, no, I'm just a lowly sergeant. And you're right, I'm not really sure I see myself as Mandy's boss. My job is really to just let her get on with hers. What do you do yourself?' I said and drank, but then laid both my glass and Mandy's down as I suddenly felt I'd just about had enough.

'I'm in HR,' she said and sucked from her straw. Her eyes watched me. 'I can see you dying a little inside. Don't worry, I get that a lot and I won't bore you with details.'

'No, I'm sure it's . . .' I was glad to see Mandy returning, dragging the boy behind her. I had no idea where I was going next in the conversation.

Mandy unceremoniously pushed between us. 'Marcie, this here is our probationer. Now he doesn't look like much, but he's a good lad and he's . . . how old are you today?'

Morgan, despite any Dutch courage, looked mortified. 'I'm, uh, twenty-five.'

'Right, twenny-five. So, you know, plenty stamina, you know-what-a-mean. Sarge, pint!'

I handed Mandy her glass and she waddled off.

'Happy birthday. Sorry, I didn't catch your name before,' said Marcella.

'Oh, it's Morgan. Morgan Finney.' He pushed out his hand and they exchange an awkward, limp shake. I looked around for an escape route, but there was nothing obvious. *Maybe just head home*, I thought.

'I'm Marcella. Only Mandy gets away with calling me Marcie. Morgan's an unusual name?'

'Oh, yeah. Capital M, small organ,' he laughed. 'Blame me parents.'

'For the small organ?' Marcella sipped again from her straw.

'No, for . . . you know, the name, like.' He had no idea he was being teased and it was like watching a train wreck, frame by frame.

'Right. Well, I'm all out here,' Marcella said, shaking her empty glass. 'I'm going to the bar. Can I get you gents something?'

We both said we were fine. Morgan's face was giving off heat. 'Why do you do that?' I said, as Marcella disappeared into the bar crowd.

'What?'

'That thing you do with your name.'

'Oh, that. Well, I just . . . I dunno, like. I suppose I'm just trying to put people at ease. Open up with a joke, you know?'

'I'm not sure it has the effect you're aiming for. My advice, stop belittling yourself. Have a bit of confidence, or at least pretend you do. Especially if you're being introduced to a woman.'

'Yeah, you're probably right. She is a bit of a ride, isn't she?'

'Uh, not the phrase I might use, Morgan, but if you mean Marcella is attractive? Yeah, I suppose.'

'Right. I'll go for a piss, and when I come back, confidence!'

'Good luck. I'll see you on Monday.'

The lad slunk off and I started digging through the pile of coats under our table for my own.

'You're heading off?'

I nearly bumped my head on the table as I stood. Marcella had returned already.

'You decided against the drink?'

'Yeah, bar's busy and I think I'm about done anyway. Mine is the black one there.'

I lifted her coat and handed it to her. 'Morgan's just gone to the bathroom. He'll only be a minute if you did want to hang around a little longer?'

She wrinkled her nose as she tucked the coat over her arm. 'Thanks, he seems like a nice lad, but I prefer guys with a little more road under the tyres.'

'Ah. Well, I'm sure he'll be disappointed, but he'll get over it. Mandy on the other—'

'I mean you,' she said, and there wasn't a hint of embarrassment. I, on the other hand, must have started shining like Morgan. 'Shall we get out of here?' she said.

'Right, yeah.'

The blaring music was muted instantly by the heavy door closing behind us and a new buzz was in the air. More music and voices drifted down to us from George Street and a mix of smells hung in the still-warm air. Beer, traffic and the ubiquitous scent of yeast from Edinburgh's breweries mixed to form a familiar city centre aroma.

'So, what do you think?' said Marcella.

I was about to answer when she looked both ways along the path before pulling me down to her height for a kiss. Our lips locked hard and there was the smallest clash of teeth before we found a rhythm. She sucked gently on my bottom lip as we separated.

'I'd invite you to mine, but I have the worst flatmate. We can go to yours? Are you far?' she said.

'Uh, I'm actually just down the hill, but I'm not sure it's a good idea. I sort of have the worst flatmate too.'

'That's a shame. I guess it's not meant to be.'

She kissed me again, pressing me against the glass of the pub. I hoped Morgan wasn't standing right on the other side. Her tongue was in my mouth and my hands had found the small of her back around the inside of her coat. 'Maybe . . . If we're really quiet, it might be OK.'

'I can be quiet,' she said.

We walked, making awkward conversation. The type that pretends what happened hadn't just happened and what's going to happen isn't right there in the front of your mind. I wondered if this kind of thing happened in all corners of the world or whether it was a purely British phenomenon. We headed downhill out of the centre and in to New Town, and were at the front door in less than ten minutes. We kissed again before I turned the key and led her into the dark hall. I had intended to take her straight to my room, but a noise caught my ear. Something wasn't right.

'Stay here a minute,' I whispered.

'What's wrong?'

'I don't know. Just give me a minute.'

The sound was coming from the living room. I could feel a breeze from the kitchen. Either a window or the back door was open – or had been forced open. I looked around and had to nudge Marcella to the side to get to the hiking pole Dad left by the coat stand.

'Call the police. Treble-nine,' I said and then pushed open the living room door. A dark mass was writhing in the centre of the room. My heart was thundering in my chest. I hit the light switch and raised the pole to strike. There was a yell and there was a moment where I couldn't look away despite wanting more than anything to do so. My father's pale arse was still jackhammering. Evidently he was too in the moment to realise, and perhaps misinterpreting the yells coming from the woman under him as vocalised pleasure.

'Jesus fuck, Dad!' I said and finally managed to tear my gaze away. I dropped the pole and left the room as I heard my Dad protesting and apologising in the same breath.

'I'm really sorry, Marcella. This isn't going to happen tonight.'

'Yeah, I was just thinking that. Never mind, I'll leave you to whatever that is. Give me a call sometime,' she said and left. I wondered briefly if she knew she hadn't given me her number.

A moment later, a middle-aged woman crept past me in the hall, saying goodnight in a tremulous voice while carrying various items of clothing.

'Goodnight, Heather,' I said and closed the door over. I took a deep breath and went to the kitchen to turn on the kettle and wait for my father to find his underpants before having what would surely be a painful conversation.

# CHAPTER ELEVEN

## The Takeaway

I left the house early next morning, nursing a bit of a hangover. I'd have tried to sleep past it, only that would have risked another run-in with my father.

I walked to the city centre again, even passing the source of the hangover as I went. It was a little after seven and the pavement was wet from an overnight rain, but the sky suggested a bright day ahead. The streets were already busy with yellow-vested workmen finishing off the structures that appeared every August for the Festival. The whole of George Street was full of them and with only two days to go before the celebrations kicked off, it seemed impossible they'd be finished in time. However, I'd seen how incredibly quickly Edinburgh was transformed before, and how quickly it was dissembled to normality the moment September arrived.

Commuters hurried towards Waverley station while

I queued alongside others who had the time to spare for coffee served from a converted VW camper van. I'd also buy a bottle of water, I decided, feeling my mouth tacky and a dry scratch at my throat.

I thought about last night's kitchen conversation, Dad an undulating blend of embarrassment, apology and anger. He was sorry he'd instigated his relations (his words) in the living room, only they'd been out in the garden sharing a bottle of wine, but it had become chilly and when they'd reached the couch, well, things had progressed quicker and further than he'd anticipated. Though had I needed to make such a bloody fuss? His overriding concern being that the whole thing would mean Heather would likely never want to come over, or worse, never see him again.

I pushed the memory out of my head. We'd have another go at a chat tonight; a little more time will have passed and we'd both have the alcohol out of our systems – or at least I would. I saw I had a text from Alyson as I got to within three of the front of the queue. It had arrived some time along my walk.

IN EDINBURGH TODAY, PROBABLY FOR THE FORESEEABLE. YOU ABOUT FOR LUNCH?

Followed by a sandwich emoji. I stepped out of the line and typed.

HOW ABOUT BREAKFAST INSTEAD? WHERE ARE YOU?

I tried to give her directions to Leith Links, but she wasn't getting it, despite the fact she was spitting distance from the collection of fields, footpaths and playparks that served the good people of Leith. I told her to google Tesco and I'd meet her outside there. It took me longer than I expected to get down Leith Walk; not the first time I'd underestimated just how long the street is..I arrived at the supermarket and saw Alyson finishing a cigarette. She mashed the remainder into the top of a bin when she saw me.

'Did I know that you smoked?' I said and kissed her cheek, the tobacco smell making me gag a little.

'Just the odd one when I'm stressed. I'd given up before we started in the police. I had a pretty bad habit before then.'

Alyson and I had joined the police in the same intake. I was pretty unaware of her at Tulliallan, the police training college, but we'd become friends after being stationed together before our professional paths diverged.

'You're working on this murder at the church then?' I asked in a hushed voice, assuming this to be the source of the stress and her reason for being in the capital.

'I am, yeah, but let's wait until we find somewhere a bit quieter.'

We made our way to a cafe just off Leith Walk and then took our selections to a bench at the Links, barely saying a word.

'Explain something to me,' she said as we sat. She waved a hand at the park around us. 'Leith, is it Edinburgh, or is it not?'

I laughed. I needed this explaining to me as well when

I moved to the city. 'Officially, yes. Unofficially, it sort of depends on who you ask. Leith was once a separate town from Edinburgh all together, before it was swallowed up by the "City of Edinburgh". Don't ask me the date, twenties or thirties, I think. But even now, if you ask a resident where they're from they're as likely to describe themselves as a Leither, rather than mention the city. Where Leith starts and ends is beyond me, but locals will happily point you to the very paving slab where you've left its confines. People can still be a bit territorial about it, so be careful.'

'Noted. Rough night?' Alyson asked as I drained my bottle of water.

'You have no idea,' I said and gathered myself before enquiring, 'If you're here, does that mean they think this priest murder is related to the Bradley case?'

She nodded as she bit into a croissant. She washed the mouthful down with a sip of her massive coffee. 'Officially it's still under wraps, but this morning we've been getting calls from journalists, so it looks like the cat is out of the bag, or soon will be. Likely be a press conference this afternoon to try to get in front of it.'

'How do you think they've gotten wind of it?'

Alyson paused as an elderly couple crossed in front of us. 'It's not clear. It might be that some sharp-eyed journo saw me or anyone else from the team here in Leith, but I suspect someone at the station has loose lips. It doesn't really matter. It would have come out soon enough anyway.'

'You think it's the same person? Same killer?'

She nodded again. 'Place is full of prints and fibres. We

even have a decent shoeprint. Not that it does us much good at this stage.'

'Because nothing's on file?'

'Right. The shoeprint helps us lean more heavily on the killer being male. Size eight is the estimate, but other than that we're as we were before, only one more body.'

'Shit. What's the connection between the bodies?'

'That's what we're working on, working *long hours* on. It's also kind of why I wanted to see you.'

'Oh?'

'Thing is, these twelve-hour shifts are hard enough, but then I have an hour commute home. It's killing me. I was wondering how your dad might feel about me crashing through the week. I won't lie, it might be a few months we're talking about.'

'Oh, Aly. Your timing could not be worse,' I said, and relayed the events of the previous evening: Marcella, Dad's arse and the conversation. 'Compose yourself. It's not that funny,' I said. She was heaving laughs, slapping the seat of the bench and trying not to spill her coffee. 'Seriously, I think I might need to move out, so if you find a place to crash, let me know if there's another room.'

I wanted to ask more about the case, but that's just not something you do. If I was to learn more, it would have to come unsolicited and Alyson was making noises about getting back to the office.

'Come around for dinner at least. I'll get you fed before you head back west. You'll also be doing me a favour,' I said.

'In what way?' We were walking back now. We dropped

131

our debris into a bin by the path. There was a chorus of shouting and laughing coming from a primary school at the far end of the fields, kids arriving for the day.

'With you there, Dad won't want to bring up last night.'

She laughed again. 'I don't know, are you cooking?'

'What if I said I'll order takeaway?'

'In that case you're on.' We reached the corner and I could see the marked vehicles parked outside of Leith station. I also saw the joy leave Aly's face. It was as if someone had opened a tap beneath her chin. She really was stressed. 'I might be as late as eight tonight, are you sure that's OK?'

'It's fine,' I said and gave her a hug. I watched her stop at the door of the office and take a breath before going inside.

I took myself to the cinema for a lunchtime showing of Disney's latest attempt to milk every possible penny out of the Star Wars franchise and then found myself walking with yet another coffee. I'd be rattling like Alyson if I didn't knock this on the head.

I was avoiding going home, it occurred to me, when I found myself thinking about what to do next. It was three o'clock and I was standing on Princess Street like a rock in a river as people, predominantly tourists, flowed around me. The faint buzz of bagpipes mixed with the noise of a thousand conversations.

I headed back, chastising myself for being such a child. I'd sit down with Dad and have an adult conversation. I'd tell him how great it was that he'd met someone, that maybe the three of us could go out for lunch and we could push through the embarrassment and that it would all be fine.

When I reached the flat, I called out as I tossed my keys onto the hall table, but there was no response. In the kitchen I found a note. It was succinct.

At Heather's, probably spend the night. See you tomorrow. Dad.

The note was breezy. Maybe he was already over the awkwardness, or perhaps staying at Heather's, wherever the hell that was, was him now avoiding me. Irrespective, I was glad.

I got a text from Alyson at half-past seven alerting me that she would be an hour or so, I responded that it was fine and gave her the address. In fact, it was after nine when the door went.

Aly looked beat as I took her coat. I shook the rain from it and led her into the kitchen.

'Oh, I'm sorry,' she said, seeing the plastic boxes of Chinese food lying on the worktop. 'When did that arrive?'

'Don't worry, we'll just nuke it. Are you hungry?'

'Starving.'

'Glass of wine?' I said pointing at the bottle on the kitchen table where two glasses stood next to it.

'Ach, I'd love one, but I better not, with the car.'

'Oh, that's another thing. Dad's staying at his . . .' I almost said girlfriend, but the word seemed ridiculous somehow. '. . . his new friend's house tonight. So, if you want, you're free to crash. I cleared the crap off the bed in the spare room if you want to just relax.'

'That's really good of you. Um, I didn't bring a change

of clothes . . . Do you know what, fuck it. Gimme that bottle.'

The bottle was done by the time we'd finished off the food at the table and talked about nothing at all important. I suggested we open another and switch to the living room. We carried our glasses through and Alyson stopped before she took a seat. 'Show me where your dad was doing the shagging, I am not sitting there.'

I laughed and pointed her to a safe spot in an armchair. I myself took the opposite end of the couch from the disturbed tryst, now that she'd put that in my head.

'Ugh, I feel better. This is exactly what I've needed,' she said, slinging her legs up over the arm of the chair. She cradled her glass to her chest.

'I'm very glad to hear it,' I said. I was waiting for an opportunity to push the conversation into her investigation, but with it being such sensitive information I didn't want to risk asking and be met with an awkward 'I really can't talk about it.' In the end it took just one more glass of red before she opened up without prompting.

'You remember the PM we attended when we got to the shift?' she asked.

'Of course. I still think about it from time to time.' I don't know if it was some exercise in desensitisation or just that management felt it was worthy experience to gain insight into police procedure, but it was customary to take the brand-new, out-of-the-wrapper recruits, fresh from their Tulliallan torture to a post-mortem within the first few weeks of your arriving to division. For Alyson and me, it just so happened to be on our very first day.

'You remember that I had to step out when the mortician removed the brain? And then again when he pushed all the organs into a bag under the ribcage?'

I gave a small laugh as I recalled her face that day, as devoid of colour as the residents of the morgue. The worst part for me was the smell created by the circular saw as the skull cap was removed. I'd swayed on my feet a little and had saliva flooding my mouth preparing for vomit. I *had* managed to stay upright and to keep my breakfast, but only just.

She sipped from her glass, then went on. 'Since joining CID, I've been to another four, each one easier than the last. Until a few days ago, if you'd asked me if I could still be bothered by a dead body, or a PM, I'd have confidently said no way. But, fuck, Don, you should have seen the state of that priest.' Again, I resisted the temptation to ask any questions and just let her tell me, whatever it was she wanted to get off her chest. After a moment of reflection, she continued. 'I was holding the camera while the pathologist and mortician worked the body. The PF lasted all of three or four minutes, saying she'd read the report instead. Even my boss, and she's a tough lady, was gripping the table. It was like something from a sci-fi movie. He had the body of a frail old man, nothing shocking there, but his head?'

This time she drained her glass and I couldn't resist the question. 'The eyes again?'

She brought her legs back to the floor and leaned forward shaking her head while she swallowed the last mouthful. 'No, his eyes were still there. It was the sides of his head. Do you know . . . no, of course you don't know.

Well, the weapon they found in the church, the knife, the tip was broken off. I watched the pathologist pull that piece of metal out of a hole in his skull. Do you have any idea the force needed to snap the blade of a knife like that? In the end they could only approximate the number of stab wounds. The skull had caved in on one side due to so many punctures, the guy's brain quite clear though the hole. It would have been one thing to stand at the back of the room like the rest, but I had to lean in to get a good shot of everything.'

'That's awful, Aly. I'm sorry. Here, let me top you up.' I leaned forward with the bottle and she held out her glass.

'All of this goes no further you understand?' she said.

'Of course, goes without saying. Still no link between the two victims?'

'No, not yet. My guess is there isn't one. Just two poor bastards in the wrong place at the wrong time. Kate Templeton, my boss, doesn't like that idea. I think it scares her. How do you stop someone who strikes indiscriminately? And how do you track someone down when there's no motive to hang an investigation on?'

'I see your point.'

'Unless something happens soon, I think we're looking at a situation where this guy will only be caught if he gets picked up for something else and bang, we have a print or DNA match. DCI Templeton barely goes home and I get daggers when she sees me leaving. I'm not sure how much more I can take.'

'That doesn't sound fair. It's too much pressure.'

Alyson shrugged. She took one last sip from her glass

before standing, with a wobble, and setting it down on the table. 'It's marginally better than being taken off the case. At least, I think so. What I need is to get to my bed. Do you mind?'

'No, of course not,' I said and stood too, to give her a hug. 'You're end of the hall on the left. I'm on the right if you need anything.'

'Thanks. Goodnight.'

'Night, Aly.' She'd just left the room when I had a thought. 'Hey,' I said. 'When you say he was stabbed on either side of his head, you mean around his ears?'

She pushed her head back through the door. 'Oh, his ears were completely obliterated. Why?'

'No reason. I guess I was just trying to picture it,' I lied.

I finished off my own glass, thinking about something I'd heard.

# CHAPTER TWELVE

## Water Under the Bridge

The Water of Leith Cafe in Cannonmills was the designated spot for peace talks. I was a few minutes early and so ordered two cappuccinos, assuming Dad would be having his usual. I was a little nervous and a little embarrassed about being nervous. I sat, dipping my complimentary piece of shortbread into the chocolate-dusted foam and watching the window. Only one other table was occupied, though not entirely surprising since it was midday on a Monday.

Ten minutes later I reached for his shortbread, figuring it was the least he could do for being late, besides he needn't ever know. Then I spotted him crossing the road; he was with Heather. At least, I assumed it was her. She looked vaguely like the woman who'd rushed past me in the hall a few nights ago. They were holding hands.

I stood as they entered and accepted my father's robust

shake. Then Heather, looking indecisive, kissed me on the cheek. An involuntary 'Oh, OK,' left my lips as she moved to the other cheek. 'I'm sorry, Heather. I didn't realise you were coming or I'd have ordered something for you too. Let me get the chap's attention.'

'No, no. That's OK, really. I just wanted to pop my head in and say hello. Maybe try to give a better impression of myself before leaving you boys to it.'

'Yeah, look. I'm really sorry—'

'Really, there's no need to be. Water under the bridge, eh?' she said and gestured to the window and laughed. The cafe was right on the edge of a bridge spanning the river. I laughed too and hoped it sounded genuine. She then kissed my father, a lingering open-mouthed kiss, and left. I was screwing my face, I suddenly realised, and forced it to relax before he noticed.

'Usually get a wee bit shortbread,' he said, spinning his cup and looking around the saucer, disappointed. 'Must be out.'

'Must be. Listen, Faither, before we get started, I just wanted to say a few things, if that's all right with you?'

'Aye, though I didnae mean for this to be a confrontation or anything. I just thought we should, you know, chat.'

'Good. My thoughts exactly. All I was going to say was . . . Look, I think it's brilliant you've met Heather. She seems nice and she's clearly good for you. Look at you in a clean shirt.'

He smirked and lifted his coffee, already looking more relaxed.

'I can't remember how many times over the years I've

said to a friend or colleague that I wished you'd meet someone. I really mean that. Now, about the other night, I'm sorry I embarrassed you. It wasn't my intention and if I've caused any tension between you two, then I deeply regret it. I was just surprised is all. One minute I think we're being burgled and the next . . . well.'

'It's me should be apologising, acting like a bloody teenager. On the bloody sofa, what was I thinking?'

'Dad, it's your house. You should be able to do as you like. That's why I've been thinking . . .'

'Is that what that smell is?'

'I've been thinking I'll start looking for a place. The only reason I haven't is because I wasn't sure if Edinburgh would be a good fit for me. And after what happened last year, I wasn't sure if staying in the police was on the cards either. But I can honestly say I'm in a much better place, both literally and figuratively. I like Edinburgh, and I like working here, so I think I'll stick around. I can rent at first—'

'Nonsense. If you're hell-bent on moving out then I won't stop you, but you're as welcome to stay now as you were when I first suggested it. I'll no have you moving out into a rented place. That's just pouring good money down the drain. No, if you're goin' tae do it, then at least wait until you find a place to buy. If I can help, I will. Til then, you stay put. Besides, I like it at Heather's. She has a lovely big place out at Inverleith. I reckon I'll be there more than home.'

'Moving in? So soon? Is that not a bit . . .?'

'I'm seventy next birthday, Donald. Caution is an indulgence of the young. She likes me, I like her and we're enjoying each other as you, much too graphically, saw.'

At this I laughed and choked on my coffee. Dad patted me on the back of the shoulder as I coughed and laughed it out.

'OK, Faither. If you're sure? I won't kick the arse out of it. I will start looking.'

'No rush. And I've to invite you to dinner at Heather's sometime soon, she said. I don't know your shifts, but we're happy to work around you.'

'That's kind. It'll be nice to get to know her properly. I'll let you know. I better be getting to work,' I said, seeing the clock behind the waiter at the till. I stood and swallowed the remainder of the coffee. 'Hey,' I said. 'It's really nice of you to let me stay and I don't want to seem like I'm taking advantage, but I wonder if I might ask a wee bit more?'

'Well, you can ask.'

'Alyson, you remember?'

'Aye.'

'She's found herself working in town for a while. She asked if she might stay to save her running back and forth from Glasgow. How'd you feel?'

'It's no bother. Like I say, I'll no really be there. Are you two . . . ?'

'No, nothing like that. Just friends. Thanks, Dad, I'll let her know.'

He stood and shook my hand again. I knew better than to attempt a hug.

At Drylaw station, Mandy was itching to speak to me. I managed to fend her off while we mustered and discussed

141

events in the area over the long weekend off. There wasn't much to catch up on and, miraculously, no smashed car windows. She eventually cornered me in the hall while the others were busy sorting through their kit and printing off crime reports.

'Well?' she asked in a low voice, drawing out the L's into a sordid interrogation.

'Well what?'

'What do you mean what? You and Marcella is what.'

She reminded me of a puppy watching a ball about to be thrown. 'I haven't the slightest clue what you're on about,' I said and moved to walk on.

She skipped around in front of me. 'Oh, no you don't. Marcie pulled that shit and I'm not having it.'

'Excuse me?' I said in mock disgust.

'I'm not having it, Sergeant.'

'Better. But I still have nothing for you.'

'Oh, come on. I know she went home with you. I got that out of her.'

'What else did she say?' I stopped walking, now curious.

'Not a damned thing. No matter how much I badgered her.'

'Look, nothing happened. Not really. Does Morgan know we left together?' I said. Now I was whispering.

'I don't think so. He never mentioned anything. So, are you seeing her again?'

'I . . . Did she say she wanted to see *me* again?'

'No.'

'Wait, did she say she doesn't want to see me again?'

Mandy was now wearing a large, smug smirk. 'No,

142

she just didn't say either way, but you don't need to be a detective to see that you like her.'

I shook my head and started walking again. 'It's a moot point, Mandy. Trust me. Tell her I said hello.'

If Morgan did know I'd left that night with the woman he'd set his sights on, he didn't show any sign of resentment. I took the van out of the station, thinking that it spoke well of Marcella that she hadn't used that night as a source of hilarity. Certainly, there was a good anecdote there. Had she not said anything to be kind to me? Or was she just a bit embarrassed about the whole thing herself?

It suddenly occurred to me that Morgan had been making chat during the short drive over and that I hadn't heard a word; something about football, I think. I'd driven almost on autopilot, but the destination had been on my mind since I'd shared the bottle of wine with Alyson.

'You want me to stay in the van, Sarge?'

'Huh?'

'Should I come with you? Or stay here?' Morgan said.

'Oh. As you like. I won't be long, but there's probably a cup of tea inside.'

Michelle answered the intercom and then opened the door to us. 'Come away in, lads, I hope you've got your dancing shoes on,' she said and then walked off down the hall.

'What is she talking about?' said Morgan. I was about to say I had no idea, but then the sound of music caught my ear. I followed Michelle and the noise grew. I recognised the song, something from my childhood. I couldn't tell you who it was by, but it was sort of a novelty song. I remember my mum doing some kind of dance to it, such an early memory. Michelle opened the door to the dining hall and a loud blast of the song hit us. There were flashing lights and balloons being kicked into the air by the dozen or so gyrating residents being instructed from a small stage that had been erected. A woman stood there, with a ridiculous 80's style pink wig on, flanked by two large sets of disco lights and speakers. She had her arms raised in the air, as did most of those following her as she sang 'Ah-Ga-Doo-Doo-Doo'. Michelle ran into the centre of the room to yell the song back at the woman, hooking her arm around Mimi as she did. As crazy as it was, those taking part seemed to be having a great time. From the far corner I saw Vicky waving, she came skipping over, keeping to the beat.

'Let me guess. You heard the song from outside and just had to come and join in?'

I laughed. 'Actually, it was Morgan here wouldn't take no for an answer. I wondered if I could steal a few minutes of your time, Vicky. It wouldn't take long.'

'Aye sure. Just gimme a sec. Michelle!' she yelled and had to shout again over the music. Michelle came over, still singing. 'I'm just going to have a word with Sergeant Colyear, you're OK with this lot?'

'Course. Hey, you need him an' all?' Michelle nodded at Morgan.

'No, he's all yours,' I said and patted the lad on the shoulder. He glared back but didn't put up much of a fight as Michelle pulled him into the room.

I lowered myself into the office chair and waited for Vicky

to return. She did so after a few minutes with mugs and packet of digestives. I felt a moment's guilt that I had all but promised Morgan this cuppa and instead he was probably performing a 'jump to the left', doing the 'The Time Warp' by now.

'The residents seemed to be enjoying themselves,' I said.

'They love it. Every second Monday Shirley comes in with her mobile disco and has them all up. It's good exercise and a great giggle. She doesn't charge a penny either. Her own mother was cared for here a few years back before she passed and, I suppose, it's a sort of thank you.'

'That's nice of her. I must admit, the thought has come to me lately about what I might do when my own dad gets old. Though to be honest, I could see him outlasting me. My view of what a care home is has changed since I've come to know this place. I suppose the clue is in the name, but you lot really do care for your residents. It's reassuring.'

'Aww, thank you. I have the best team and although it's hard work sometimes, I think we're all pretty happy here. You're here about Martin?'

'Yes,' I said and laid my mug down. 'How is he?'

'Much the same. No outbursts of late but he's dark most of the time.'

'I wanted to ask about his last outburst. You mentioned something and I wondered if you might be able to elaborate on it a little.'

'*I* said something?' Vicky laid her mug down now. 'What was it?'

'I wish I'd written it down, but it was something about hearing God?'

'Yes, I do remember that. He was up all night. I've never seen him so distressed. Between me and Mathew we had to practically hold him down until he fell asleep.'

'Mathew is the tall staff member with the beard?'

'That's right.'

'Do you remember what Martin was saying, exactly?'

'Shouting more like. Um, it was, oh what was it now? "The word of God" I think. "Hearing the word of God". If you want, I could call Mathew? He might remember it better than me.'

'If it's not asking too much?'

She shook her head as she scrolled through her phone. She then laid it on the desk between us and a ring tone sounded through its speaker.

'Vic, everything all right?' came a deep voice. There was a busy noise behind him, voices and crockery.

'Everything's fine. Listen, I'm sorry to call on your day off, it's just that I have Sergeant Colyear here, he had a few questions. Is this a bad time?'

There was a pause as Mathew seemed to be saying something to someone where he was. Then he was back. 'Gimme a second, Vic, hold on.' Then another pause and suddenly the background noise was gone. 'OK, I've come outside, I can hear you better now.'

'Mathew, it's Don Colyear here. Sounds like we've caught you at a bad time. It's not all that important if you're busy?'

'No, it's fine. I'm at a family dinner. Trust me, you're doing me a favour. What's up?'

Vicky leaned forward and spoke. 'Do you remember that

146

night with Martin? He was going off and we had terrible trouble quietening him?'

'Aye, we were up half the night with him.'

'Well, do you remember what it was he was saying? It was something about God, like hearing the word of God, right?'

If I'd thought about it earlier, I'd have asked Vicky not to prompt him. It would be better to hear his thoughts without influence, but I needn't have worried.

'Sort of, aye. But the thing that struck me was he wasn't talking about himself. You remember? He kept going on about "how can *he* hear the word of God?" over and over.'

I felt a wash of dread, or perhaps excitement, flow through my entire body. It must have washed the colour from my face as Vicky was looking at me with concern.

'Is that right, Vicky? Is that what you remember?' I said.

'Uh. Yeah. I think Mathew's right. That's what he was saying. Are you OK?'

'Do you remember anything else, Mathew? Anything at all?'

'Uh, not really. Except he was begging us to call the police. We figured he had his conversation with you in his mind. Right, Vic?'

I spoke again before Vicky could respond. 'Listen, thanks for your time, Mathew. It's a big help.'

He managed to get out 'Aye, no bother', before Vicky ended the call. She was following me down the hall as I went searching for my probationer.

It might have been the only thing in the world that could have made me stop in my tracks at that moment, but

147

the sight of Morgan, in full uniform, doing a pony-spank dance with his hat to the sound of 'Gangnam Style', with a beaming Michelle bent over in front of him was just about too much to handle. Elderly residents stood to either side of him trying to replicate the move.

'Morgan, we're off,' I shouted over the music. He didn't even seem embarrassed; he just came running.

'Is everything OK?' Vicky asked as she opened the front door for us.

'Honestly, I'm not quite sure what's going on. Look, I'll be back. If I can explain I will. Right now, we have to go. Thanks for your help.'

She smiled, though there was more concern than anything else in it.

It took moments to get back to the station. Morgan had been trying to ask me the same question as Vicky, but I had no answers for him. I told him to go work on his probationer progress file and I closed the door to my office. I took a pad of paper from a drawer and called to speak to a supervisor at the call handling unit.

# CHAPTER THIRTEEN

## You Better Sit Down

When I called Alyson, she was pleased to hear that she could move herself in, but when she said she would be going back to her own place to pack some things, that she'd stay as of tomorrow, I insisted that maybe she suffer another night without a change of clothes.

'It's really late, Don. You're lucky to have caught me here at all. I'm practically heading out the door. What's going on?'

'I . . . I'm not sure exactly, but I really do think you should head over to the flat, I'll meet you there.'

There was a pause and a heavy breath before she said 'Fine. I'll probably be half an hour or so.'

I was dog-tired myself when I got in, but was still running on a buzz of adrenalin. It was a little after midnight and I hadn't eaten anything since breakfast. I filled myself with toast and peanut butter while I arranged the paperwork on the dining table and waited for Alyson to arrive. When she did, she dumped her coat in my arms at the door and went rooting around the cutlery drawer for a bottle opener, until I pointed out the bottle of white she brought in with her was a screw top.

'For fuck sake. Honestly, I can barely keep track of the days of the week. And getting through town was a nightmare, every road I know is shut off with the bloody festival. How long is it on for?'

'Just a month.'

'An entire fucking month?'

'Yup. We get the city back in September. Don't be a grouch, it's great. We should do something.'

'I *am* doing something and I've no time for anything else. Now, what's so bloody important?'

I took the bottle from her and filled two glasses. 'Have you eaten?'

'McD's on the way here. Not proud of myself, but it's calories. Now, out with it.' She drained half of her glass, which I refilled and gestured for her to sit. 'What's all this?'

'It's sort of a timeline.'

'For what?'

'Let me just start from the beginning.' This time I gulped from my glass and tried to find a way to explain. 'So, this is about Mr Beeswax, Martin.'

The look on Alyson's face was one of abject frustration. 'I'm way too tired for this, Don. And I'm in no mood to be taking backward steps. Seriously, I don't—'

'Just hear me out. It won't take long. Here,' I said and

planted the bottle next to her glass. 'You drink, I'll talk.'

She sipped and glared at me over the rim of her glass, tapping a fingernail on the neck of the bottle. 'Fine, but if you're still talking by the time I reach the bottom of this, I'm leaving you here and going to bed. Now, go.'

'OK,' I said and searched out my first sheet of paper from the pile in front of me. 'Yes, here. So, I've been doing some digging. This first bit you know. Martin calls treble-nine in the early hours of the seventeenth of March, right?'

'If you say so,' she said and drank, barely engaged.

'Callum Bradley is murdered on the ninth of April. That's twenty-three days. Now, what was the date of the second murder?'

'I'm guessing you already know that, but you're trying to get me involved in your little Columbo moment here?'

'Fine, it was a week ago today, tenth of August. Now, do you remember the date you met me at the care home when I took a statement from Martin?'

'Nope,' she said, bored.

'All right. It was the twelfth of July.'

'Wow. Hey, do you have any peanuts, crisps even? I think that junk I ate has me craving for more salt.'

'Uh, maybe.' I fished around in a cupboard and found a packet of pickled onion Monster Munch. I tossed them to her and for the first time tonight she seemed excited. I continued: 'That same night Martin had a complete meltdown. I thought it was because of me, and, well, maybe it was but then again maybe it wasn't—'

'You're rambling, Colyear.'

'Right. OK, the crux of it is this.' I pushed a piece of

paper across the table. Something I'd handwritten earlier.

Alyson took the sheet, turned it around and squinted at it before shaking her head and reaching into her coat for a set of glasses I wasn't aware she wore. She pushed on the tortoise-shell frames and squinted still, but read it aloud. '"How can he hear the word of God?"' she turned the page over to see if there was more. 'That's shocking,' she said.

'Well, that's what I thought.'

'The *handwriting* is shocking, not the message.' She pushed the paper back across the table.

I was getting a little frustrated with her sarcasm, but I refused to let it get to me. 'This is what Martin was yelling, all night. That and he wanted to call the police. If the staff hadn't been holding him to the bed, that's exactly what would have happened and we'd be looking at another call like the one that started all this.'

'It's a coincidence, and maybe not even that. I see how you're trying to connect the call to the injuries to the priest, but you're stretching at best and at worst you're taking the senile ramblings of a man, probably not far from the end of his time, and trying to force them to fit with a completely unrelated murder. Do you have any idea what would happen if I took this to my boss? When she got done laughing, she'd have me directing traffic in the Outer Hebrides until I retire.'

'Aly, at least try to be a little more open-minded. Those dates I mentioned, between Martin's outburst to the discovery of Father McCauley's body, that's twenty-two days. Almost exactly the same timeframe as the Bradley murder.'

At least this time she took a moment before shooting me down. She swirled the wine in her glass, her eyes on the table while she thought. There was a suggestion of a smile on her face. 'What exactly are you saying? You're suggesting that our old man is somehow involved in these murders? Because if you are, I'd do two things: One, go take the man's prints to prove you're wrong and then, two, we get your head checked, because you're nuts to—'

'I'm not saying he did it. Of course not. He's not capable and has an indisputable alibi. What *am* I suggesting?' I said, a question to myself which I hadn't, until that moment, allowed to be asked, at least not so clearly. 'I don't know. I'm just asking you to listen, that's all for now.'

'All right, Don. Look, I don't want to fall out, I know you're trying to help and God knows I'm grateful to you and your dad for letting me crash, so I'm sorry if I seem less than impressed here. I can see you've gone to some trouble. Maybe we should just drop it? I'm under a lot of pressure and I'm really behind on my sleep. How about a movie and I can watch half before I zonk out on the sofa?'

'I know you're really under it, Aly. And I know this is all a bit out there, but let me just show you what else I found. Please?'

She topped up my glass and then emptied the rest of the bottle into her own. It was a metaphorical hourglass, so I got on with it.

'The call that we connected, rightly or wrongly, to the Bradley murder was not the first time Martin picked up the phone to us. I've spent the day going through call data and then most of the evening going through crime and incident reports. Now you might need to let your mind relax a bit here, try to just listen.'

'Like one of those magic eye illusions? You know, the pictures that are all lines and dots until you relax your eyes and wham, a fucking horse appears?'

'I think you should slow down on the wine, but yeah, sure, like that. Since Martin entered the home, there have been a total of ten calls to treble-nine from the first-floor call box. Of the nine I hadn't heard until today I think we can discount four where he doesn't really say much, or it's just abuse and no content, and one where he's actually just singing down the line. In the remaining five, he does have something to report. I can let you hear the audio files if you like?'

'You're doing just fine there without, Don. Crack on.'

'The first one comes in at the beginning of last October, it's here somewhere.' I pulled out the sheets from the pile and pushed them towards her. She glanced at them, but only picked up her glass. 'That would be around four months after Martin moved in. Like the call you heard, there's a whole preamble and fuss with the call handler, trying to get his name, only to be met with "none of your beeswax". Then there's some abuse and just as the call handler is about to hang up on him, Martin reports the slaying of a monster. "The beast cut down" and why are we, the police, not doing anything about it? I know, I know,' I said looking into Alyson's bored and twisted face. 'Here's the thing; twenty-five days later there's an assault. A Halloween party in Harthill, so not too far from where Bradley's body was discovered. Two guys have a falling out and end up in the street. Guy A is dressed as the Joker from Batman, guy B is in a big furry suit, he's come as Sully from Monsters Inc.'

'Love that movie, cry every time.'

'Yeah, it's a good one. Anyway, on paper you'd fancy the Joker in a fight, but he's getting the shit kicked out of him, so he pulls a knife and plunges poor Sully three times. He does a runner, but it's witnessed by a dozen costumed piss-artists and he's picked up the following day and arrested, they got the knife too and it's nothing to do with our two murders, but still . . .'

'What happened to Sully?'

'Oh, right. He's fine. None of the new holes were fatal.'

'Good, but you're seriously stretching there, Fox Mulder.'

'I know. On their own, they're unremarkable. But, listen, next call that comes in, where something of any note is actually said, is about six weeks later. Martin is all upset about the "wrath of the driver", his words. The call handler tries to get more out of him, but Martin is all over the place, talking about food. This is the first time we see a bit of humour from the handlers as they play with him on the line for a little while before the call ends.'

'Then you trawl through the crime reports for anything that happened twenty-something days later, and you find some spurious connection, right?'

I pulled out the next set of stapled sheets I'd prepared. 'Road rage incident in Portobello. Someone gets cut up at traffic light and then forces the other driver to stop by boxing him in. He gets out and tries to get the other driver to enter into a fight. He's not interested and warns the other guy to get out of his way. He refuses and is subsequently reversed into. Nasty as it turns out, broken arm, ribs and apparently only inches away from having his head under the wheel.'

'You're—'

'Stretching, yes. I know. But the driver was charged with attempted murder, though it later gets pleaded down to assault and no jail time. Interesting note from the court case though, the culprit avoids a driving ban. His brief argues that it would be devastating to his income and therefore his family as his job is driving for a local pizza and kebab place.'

'Donald Colyear,' she said, placing the palms of her hands flat on the table. She spoke in a measured and thoroughly patronising tone. 'I love you. You know that, in a strictly platonic way of course. And I am grateful for you trying to look out for me, but trust me when I say that I think it might be you who really needs a good night's sleep. This is beyond batshit and it's so tenuous that I am, frankly, a little worried about you. Look, any and all avenues of tangible enquiry are well under way. The rest of CID and I know what we're doing. Now, I am going to bed.'

'There's a few more things.'

'Are they any less ropey than what I just heard?'

I thought for a second. No, I'd already played my best hand. Showing her any more only weakened my case. She took my silence as the only answer she needed.

'Good night, Don.' She rose, walked around the table and kissed the top of my head.

'I'll bring you some water,' I said.

# CHAPTER FOURTEEN

## Morning Meeting

Alyson was on time for once. It was a curious thing, walking to work, not something she'd ever before been able to do. It was common for police officers to ensure they lived outwith their beat, never shit where you eat, that sort of thing, but since the inquiry being moved to the capital was likely to be a temporary arrangement, she didn't see the harm in it.

The morning meeting had become a stale and repetitive gesture. New updates that might promise to take the investigation forward were now a rare phenomenon. Perhaps she'd liven things up by getting to her feet and giving them Don's passionate presentation from last night. The thought made her laugh and she chuckled into her hand.

'What's funny?' said Duncan.

'Oh nothing, just a joke I heard.'

'Come on then, I could do with a laugh. Before the DCI gets in.'

Alyson shook her head, she was still laughing. She was picturing Don's face. He'd looked like a cat who'd brought home a dead mouse, proud, excited and entirely incredulous as to why you weren't pleased to see it. 'It was one of those had-to-be-there things,' she said.

The door crashed open and DCI Templeton strode into the room. There was a time when these entrances had made Alyson jump, but now she was all but immune, unlike the two Edinburgh DCs, one of whom, who'd been swinging back on his chair, smacked a hand on the table to stop from toppling.

'We got the toxicology back from the lab; nobody will be shocked that it threw up nothing of any interest. About as much use as tits on a bull,' she said. She hadn't once looked up from the folder in her hand. She found her seat either by peripheral vision, or muscle memory. This first-floor office in Leith Police Station had been their base since moving the operation. There was no separate room for the DCI, instead she worked from this large desk in the back corner which then doubled as the morning meeting venue. The rest of them hot-desked around three smaller tables. From here you had a view of Constitution Street and the sound of constant drilling from the tram-works. You could actually see a corner of the church from the window. DCI Templeton was referring to the blood work of Father McCauley. They all knew and nobody was at all surprised that it failed to help them in any way. His cause of death was one of the more obvious Alyson had encountered, only the decapitated casualty of a motorcycle accident in her second year had it beat.

'Duncan, where are we with congregation interviews?'

The DS looked over at the two Edinburgh DCs. Danny, the older of the two, cleared his throat and said: 'We're getting through them, ma'am, though every time we get one down on paper it throws up another three names. All as useless and loosely connected than the last.'

'Yes. I've read through the ones you've submitted. It's not likely one of his Church crowd is suddenly going to hand us a suspect or even a motive, but it's important to tick these off.'

'We've another three lined up for today,' said Adrian, the other DC. It may not have been in the best interests of group harmony to have these two work together while Alyson and Duncan continued as a team, perpetuating the east-west divide, but she wasn't here to make friends and she liked working with Duncan and so she was relieved.

'Duncan, I need you two to go back to Rickerburn and re-interview Bradley's friend. His parents won't be pleased so be sensitive and take the statement at the house. The first two accounts tell us almost nothing.'

'Will do, though the kid is only eleven and it's a nightmare trying to get his mum to stay out of the way.'

'Do what you can. While you're out there, you might as well bring back some files from the office. I think we're here for the long term. And see if you can get my chair back here too, the furniture in this place is a fucking joke.'

'Do you mind if we swing by my place after? Friend of mine is putting me up in Edinburgh while we're stuck there and

I'd like to grab some things,' said Alyson.

'Lucky you. Nice place?'

Duncan was doing just under sixty on the M8, which would have been infuriating if there had been urgency at all to their day. This interview was the one thing they had to do before heading back to Edinburgh and back to sifting through the same old data, so they decided to stretch it out a little.

'It is, actually. Garden flat in the New Town. My friend's uniform at Drylaw. We joined together.'

'Handy. I'm jealous, this drive back west at the end of every day is getting dull. And yeah, no problem, we can get some lunch after we interview the kid and swing by yours.'

Duncan signalled off at the junction for Harthill and they were soon heading south and west, entering into Rickerburn before long. As they pulled onto the new road, Alyson looked out along into the distance. About a mile away stood the bings. The man-made red-ash hills where Callum was discovered. Rickerburn was a nothing of a place, built up when mining was still a thing, but when the times moved on, the people there had not. Grey, blocky terraced homes made up the majority of the residential buildings. An industrial park and a run-down high street were the only other features. They passed what Alyson knew was the old police station, long since sold off and now an end-of-terrace home. She wondered what it would have been like to be a small-town cop here, knowing every face. Policing had become so centralised now.

'I knew the last cop to work out of there,' said Duncan, as if reading her mind. 'He finished up his career here,

160

bit prematurely actually. The official story is that he got injured, but the truth is he got stopped for drink-driving. He used to go to the pub after every shift, that one there, actually.' Duncan pointed a finger diagonally across the windscreen. A black-and-brown fronted pub stood at the end of the High Street. Mock Tudor panelling on the front, flaking and rotting. 'The Flying Goose' emblazoned above the door. 'He'd get shitfaced and drive home. While he was the merry little town bobby, nobody cared, but then he goes and charges the local big man, some two-bit dealer, for possession of a sad amount of weed. I guess he was getting pressured to get his numbers up. Next thing you know a complaint is called in to the chief constable and he gets pulled over, miles over the limit.'

'Silly bastard.'

'Lucky bastard. I'm not sure it would happen now, in fact I'm pretty sure it wouldn't, but he got pensioned off. Probably down to the fact that he'd been doing this thing in front of the entire town for the best part of a decade, the Force were probably scared that a news story was being readied. Nowadays I reckon Police Scotland would make an example of him. I think this is the street,' said Duncan, pulling into an estate, a little newer than the grim houses at the other side of town, but not much.

'It is. The house is just up here on the left.' It was they who had interviewed the lad the last time, but that was many months ago now.

Duncan pulled up and turned to Alyson as she was opening her door. 'I want you to do the interview this time.'

'OK, why?'

'I'd only be asking the same questions as last time. If there's any chance of getting anything new out of him, a change of angle might be the only way. Go with your gut, see what you can do.'

'All right,' she said and thought, it's *you* who's seeing what I can do. As a young DC, everything was a test and everyone was watching, always.

The scowl on the woman's face as she opened the door confirmed what Alyson already knew. This was going to be long afternoon.

'Mrs Beattie, I'm Alyson Kane, we spoke on the phone this morning?'

The woman didn't reply, but pushed the door wide and stepped aside to let them enter.

The house was as Alyson remembered it. Humble, but tidy. There was a war raging between the smell of cigarettes and the smell of cleaning products. Furniture polish and air freshener did their best to mask the sour reek of the tobacco.

'He's in the living room, end of the hall,' Mrs Beattie said.

Alyson thought about removing her boots, or at least offering to, but then spotted Mrs Beattie was wearing outdoor shoes. She pushed the door at the end of the hall and found Mr Beattie sitting at a dining table. He was reading a newspaper, a hand-rolled cigarette burning between two fingers clutching the pages. He moved the paper aside for a moment to look at them, then returned to his sheets. William Beattie was sitting on a rug watching cartoons and likely oblivious to their arrival.

'David, they'll want to sit at the table. Move that stuff away,' said Mrs Beattie.

The 'stuff' was an ashtray, cigarette papers and a large pouch of tobacco.

'Aye, OK,' he said. 'I'll put the kettle on then?' He folder his paper and gathered up the other items.

'They're just here to speak to Billy, they're not stayin' long. That's right, eh?'

'We'll be as quick as we can, Mrs Beattie. I promise,' said Duncan. This is what Alyson had promised the woman this morning on the phone as well.

'Love, we can at least offer them a cup of—'

'I spoke to Citizen's Advice you know. Billy doesnae have to give a statement, let alone . . . what is it now? Three? It's no good for him. He's had nightmares.'

'Love,' said Mr Beattie, his free hand now on her shoulder. She was red in the face and her eyes glistened. She'd been rehearsing this, Alyson thought, working herself into a bit of a state.

'You're right, Mrs, Beattie,' Alyson said. 'He doesn't have to help us any further. And we're very grateful for the information Billy has provided. But a wee boy is dead.' This she said leaning in towards the irked woman, out of earshot of her son. 'We want to catch the person responsible so that it doesn't happen again. To do that we need a bit of help. We need any witnesses to provide every detail they can, however small, so that we can build up as clear an understanding as we can. Sometimes that takes a few visits. Now, I am very sorry to be coming here again, I hope it will be the last time—'

'It *will* be the last time,' she said and folded her arms across her chest.

'Fair enough. We'll be as quick as we can.' Alyson placed her folder on the table and walked over to Billy who hadn't seemed to have been aware of the exchange. 'What are you watching?' she said.

'Clone Wars,' he said to the screen. He was the image of his mother. Small, slightly upturned nose below round-framed glasses. His reddish-brown hair stuck up in places.

'That's a Star Wars thing, isn't it?'

'Uh-huh.'

'You remember me, Billy?'

This time he did look at her, but only for a moment. 'Police lady.'

'That's right. Would you mind if we pause the show and go have a little talk at the table? Would that be all right?'

'Uh . . .'

He looked over to his mum who looked like she might protest again, but Mr Beattie said, 'It's fine, Billy. 'Mon up to the table, won't take long.'

''Kay,' he said and found the button on the remote.

Alyson produced statement paper and took a brief affirmation from Mr Beattie that he was Billy's legal guardian and that he would be present while Billy gave an account of what happened on the day in question. Then it was down to Billy, sitting at the table, his legs swinging between those of the chair, nervously. Alyson decided it would be pointless to have him go through every single point in minute detail as before. Mrs Beattie loomed somewhere behind her and was likely to pull the plug if things dragged out too long.

Instead, Alyson asked Billy if he would give a quick account and then she'd pick just a few points to focus on.

'I saw Callum at school and we'd said we'd meet up later, on our bikes. So, I got home and got changed and cycled up to the Drummy.'

'This is the old abandoned road at the edge of town. Drumshore Road, but you call it the Drummy?' said Alyson. This she already knew from previous statements, but wanted to clarify for the record.

'Uh-huh. You can cycle dead fast on it, 'cause there's no cars. Loads of glass but, so you sometimes get a puncture.'

'How long were you there?'

'Not sure. Few hours?'

'You went there as soon as you got home from school and after getting changed. You didn't watch TV or play videogames?'

'No, went straight there.'

Billy and Callum's school let out at 4 p.m. on a Thursday, this had been checked. It was a fourteen-minute walk with adult legs, so perhaps eighteen to twenty minutes with kids fooling around on the way. 'What time do you have your dinner?'

'Six. Gets his tea at six,' came Mrs Beattie's voice from behind her.

Alyson turned, 'Thanks Mrs Beattie. I really do need Billy to answer these questions though. His truth might be a little different from yours and that could be important.'

The woman didn't reply to this, but her eyebrows said enough.

'You said previously that you left Callum playing there

because you didn't want to be late for dinner. Do you remember if you were late that day?'

'Don't think so.'

'Mrs Beattie, do you recall if Billy was on time that day?'

Again the eyebrows, seeming to say *Oh, now you want my input?* 'I can't be sure, but I don't remember him being late. He gets a row if he's late, so if he doesn't remember it either, I guess not.'

The boys then had been playing at the Drummy for about one hour and forty minutes as the cycle home took all of six minutes, being largely downhill. 'What do you remember about cycling home that day?' Alyson knew what he saw, but wanted the boy to bring it to mind naturally.

He shrugged. 'Don't remember.'

Alyson breathed out a little frustration. 'Think about it for a minute, Billy. You said goodbye to Callum?'

'He was doing wheelies, but yeah I shouted that I was away home. He waved. I remember he nearly came off his bike when he waved.'

This is the moment Callum Bradley had last been seen alive. 'And then which way did you cycle home? The quickest way is down to Main Street, did you go that way?' She knew that he hadn't, but again she wanted to start to fill his head with these important moments.

'No. Main Street's too busy. Mum doesn't want me cycling on the roads. Came down through Pine Walk, there's a path takes you along past the football fields, but you don't have to cross any roads.'

'Good. Now, tell me about cycling through Pine Walk.'

'Oh, the van? There was a van there.'

*Good lad*, Alyson thought. Pine Grove was the nearest residential street to the Drummy. Every door had been canvassed, but the only person to have seen this van, was Billy Beattie.

'Tell me again about the van, Billy.'

His legs started swinging again. His mouth was twisted to the left, his eyes searching the ceiling to his right. 'Well, I don't know really. It was white, had something on the side?' He shrugged again. Alyson let a moment of silence sit, to see if he might offer anything else, but nothing was forthcoming.

'OK Billy. I wonder if we might try something, sort of like a game.' She didn't mean to, but her eyes searched out Duncan, who was perched on the arm of the sofa, watching. She felt a little silly for doing what she was about to, but she'd seen it work. Duncan was letting her get on with it. 'I want you to picture that little bit of your journey. Imagine it's like a movie. Can you do that?'

'Can I close my eyes?' He seemed quite excited by the idea.

'Sure you can. I want you to start at the point where you come into Pine Walk, then slow it down a little and watch it until you're out of the street again.'

'OK.' His lips were pursed and the fingers of his right hand rubbed at the surface of the table. His eyes were held tightly closed.

'Are you done?'

'Uh-huh.'

'Now I want you to do it again, slow it down even more and this time tell me what you're seeing.'

'Um, I'm cycling. You come off the path onto the road and it goes sorta down hill and to the right. I'm cycling pretty fast, 'cause I don't wanna be late. There's cars parked on the road and I'm peddling and normally you can do like a wee bunny-hop up onto the kerb at the far side of the street where there's another path, but there's this van there, a white van, and I have to slow down. I pull the bike up onto the path and start cycling again.'

'That's good, Billy. Now just rewind a little to where you realise you can't jump your bike onto the path. Can you see if anyone is inside the van?'

'No, I don't know.'

'Take your time. You can rewind or play the movie as much as you like.'

'No, I really don't know, there's a shine off the windows and you can't see inside.'

'All right Billy, that's good. Now, are you going in front of the van, or behind it?'

His eyelids were closed, his eyes were moving beneath them. 'Behind the van, the path is closer to the back.'

'Slow it right down now. As you put your feet down to pull your bike onto the path, what can you smell?'

'Smoke. I can smell smoke.'

'By "smoke", do you mean fumes from the exhaust?'

'Yeah.'

'So, the van is running?'

'I don't know, I suppose so.'

'That's good, Billy. Now one more thing and we can stop. Keep your eyes closed and rewind the movie just a few seconds when you pass the side of the white van. Is there a moment where you can see the side of the van best? Take your time.'

'Yeah. I have to press my breaks pretty hard just as I get to the side.'

'Now, just there, I want you to pause the movie. The point where you can see it best, just hold it there. Now, what's on the side of the van?'

He took his time and again his face twisted up as he really tried. After thirty seconds or so, Alyson was reaching out her hand to place on his shoulder to assure him he'd done well, but they could stop now.

'It's a hammer I think.'

Her hand froze. 'You think you see a hammer on the side of the van?'

'Yeah, like a drawing of one. There's more stuff and it's mostly yellow, but all I can remember is that I think it's a hammer.'

'That's really good, Billy. You can open your eyes now. You did really well.'

# CHAPTER FIFTEEN

## Colander

'There you are Mr White. These gentlemen will drop you back home,' said the civilian staff, a woman around my age with a geniality about her that would have marked her as a civilian even without the ID hanging around her neck. I'd forgotten her name but had bumped into her a couple of times for this very purpose.

'Thank you, dear,' he said.

Morgan stood to allow the old man to sit in the public reception area of St Leonard's station. The lady let go of his elbow and then motioned to me with a sideways nod of the head. I walked with her through the secure door.

'He couldn't pick him out,' she said softly.

'Shit. Well, it was more out of hope than expectation anyway.'

'Are you sure you've got the right guy?'

'Not fully, no, but if he'd picked this guy out, we'd have solid ground to start pushing hard.'

'Well, sorry I couldn't help.'

She'd just turned to walk off when something occurred to me. 'Hey, my probationer's never seen a VIPER parade. I appreciate you're probably run off your feet, but I just wondered . . .'

She smiled and said: 'Sure, it's still loaded up, do you want to bring him down?'

We left Mr White with a cup of tea at reception and followed the civilian staff down to a dark room, the VIPER suite. Three chairs sat around a table, pushed against the wall. On it a large television stood. Nothing else.

'Do you want me to run through the usual spiel as if this is for real?' she said.

'Why not. That way Morgan will get to see what a witness goes through. Stand over here,' I said to Morgan and directed him at the screen.

'All right, Morgan. This is a VIPER presentation. VIPER stands for Video Identification Parade Electronic Recording.' Like so many acronyms, I suspected they'd appended letters, in this case the E and the R, to successfully complete a dramatic moniker. Like the government advice-giving organisation SAGE, the Scientific Advisory Group for Emergencies. 'Emergencies' was a bit redundant, but without it, the name became a lot less wise and a lot more droopy. 'VIPER replaces the need to have real-life suspects and stand-ins attend at a police station and is therefore less intimidating for a witness. You're going to be shown a series of short videos, where a subject will look straight at the camera and then to the left and right, before returning to camera. A number will appear before each is shown. If you see the person responsible for the crime, remember the number but allow the video to play to the end. At that point if you wish to see any or all of the subjects again, we can. You understand?'

'Aye, crack on,' the lad said. He seemed to be enjoying himself. We hadn't been allowed to watch this while Mr White was being shown the reel. It was vital for court purposes that it was done independently, with investigating officers excluded from the process. It was common for an officer to have any number of these parades organised in their career and never actually see one themselves.

The lady lifted a remote and the parade began. I knew it was an automated system, the physical attributes of thousands of volunteer stand-ins catalogued. All you needed to do was list the characteristics of your accused and the computer would produce this reel, with the suspect placed at random amongst them. A series of men, all bald and bullish, appeared in front of an identical grey background, turning this way then that and then on to the next one. I'd seen pictures of Colander McStay just yesterday and still it was hard to pick him from the others.

'That's the end of the parade. Do you think you saw the person in question? If so, can you give me the number?'

'Jeezo, that was tough, like. Honestly, I've got no idea. I've only seen the fella on crappy CCTV,' said Morgan.

'It's number two, I think,' I said, though I was far from certain. If I'd been a witness, she wouldn't have confirmed if I'd been correct, just recorded the results and sent them for processing with the case file, but as this was just for fun, she told me I was right. 'Can you bring Mr McStay up on the screen again for a moment?'

She obliged and now that I knew it was our guy, he seemed to stand out from the stand-ins. A bit bigger and a bit meaner. He did not look pleased to be turning for the camera. Luckily his VIPER image was already on file as there wasn't enough to have had him brought in for capturing. The brute turned first to the left and then to the right. I noticed something I hadn't clocked the first time around. An area of his neck was pixelated. The blurred section moved slightly around that part of his neck as he turned.

'What's going on there?' I said.

She paused the screen and saw what I was referring to. 'Yes, sometimes that's done to cover up an obvious scar, tattoo or perhaps a birth-mark or something. The court wants a witness to recognise the suspect's face, not just some small part.'

We thanked the lady and joined Mr White back at reception before driving him back to his house. He was doing us a favour and so rather than have him make his own way across town, I'd made sure he was collected and returned safely.

'Where does that leave things?' asked Morgan as I pulled out of Mr White's street.

'Back at square one, really. We might get lucky with someone else reporting something similar, but for now it leaves this particular lead dead in the water.'

'Is police work always this frustrating?'

I thought about that for a minute. 'Often, yes. That's why you grab hold of any and all little victories when they come along; you don't know how long it'll be 'til the next one,' I said. Then I began to think. 'Do you have the crime report with you?'

'Somewhere, yeah. Gimme a second.' Morgan reached into the back seat and produced his folder. I had one much like it. I worked out of it for about the first two and a half years of my service, most cops did. It's a bit like buying a new bag and pencil case for the new school year. It'll remain shiny, new and organised for a while then order is abandoned over convenience. Soon the lad would be carrying around scraps of paper and hunting for a working pen like the rest of us. 'Yeah, I have it. What do you need?'

'Did you include McStay as a suspect on the system?'

'I did, yeah.'

'What address did it have for him?'

He flicked through the pages of the report. 'Uh . . . There's a few, but most recent is in Merchiston.'

'Merchiston? Nice. What's the address before that?'

'Let's see, there's one in Dalry, then before that Wester Hailles.'

'He's working his way up. Why don't we go see Mr McStay? See if he's home in Merchiston?'

'We can do that?'

'Of course we can.'

Morgan looked a little nervous at the idea. I asked him to bring up the address on his phone, my own route map through the city still a little vague, particularly as we wanted to avoid anything to do with the city centre and the festival.

We stayed to the west and soon were driving through neighbourhoods. Flats and tight terraced houses were replaced by driveways and detached homes.

'Left here, then the house is about halfway up on the right.' I pulled into the street and was hit by a pang of jealousy. The first thing I noticed was that there were no parked cars on the roadway, not one. It was almost unheard of in Edinburgh. The reason for this became clear; each of the detached homes had its own drive tucked behind iron gates. We found the house and I parked up just beyond. I called in our location to control and we stepped into the drive of number fourteen, where two identical black Range Rovers were parked. Both had private reg plates trying to spell out McStay 1 and 2 but you really had to use your imagination.

'You OK?' I said. Morgan was chewing frantically on his bottom lip.

'I'm fine, yeah.'

'You don't look fine,' I said and pressed the bell next to the large front door, also black. The bell was one of those with a camera and an electrical chime, perhaps alerting a mobile phone somewhere, but there was no answer. I stepped back to get a look at the windows, nothing was moving in the large bay, Georgian panes. The drive continued past the house to our right.

'There must surely be someone home. Unless there's a McStay 3 somewhere. Come on,' I said and followed the drive round to a separate building. A large double garage, newly built but trying to stay in keeping with the rest of the house. I wondered if he'd bothered to get planning permission. There was some knocking and clattering coming from within. The large white garage door was pulled down, but there was a gap underneath which I was just about to reach for when a voice came from back up the drive.

'Can I help you?' a woman said.

I stood from my crouched position and put on my best innocent smile. 'Hello, I'm sorry to bother you, I'm looking for Colin McStay,' I called and started back towards her. She stood with her hands on her hips looking unimpressed.

'You want wi' him?'

'Just a chat. Is he around?'

'Chat about what, exactly?' Her accent was Edinburgh, but not the accent of her neighbours. There was a definite twang of housing scheme. She was around fifty, her hair blonde and straightened within an inch of its life.

'We're looking into something and Colin's name came up. Just wanted a word.'

'Away back inside, hen.' Another voice, again making us turn. Colander McStay walked towards us from the garage, wiping his hands on a rag. My pulse quickened at the sight of him, so I wondered what was going on in Morgan's head. He wore combat shorts and a dark blue vest with the emblem of some gym on the front, but too faded to make out properly. His arms bulged grotesquely.

'You sure? Should I call David?'

'Naw, naw, it's fine. Away inside.' The woman left us. I wondered who 'David' was. Muscular backup? A lawyer perhaps? 'Get you guys a drink?' he asked, tossing the rag on top of his wheelie bin.

'No thanks, Mr McStay, we won't take up too much of

your time,' I said. I was trying to look him in the eye, but it was impossible. I couldn't stop looking at that part of his neck that had been pixelated. He'd been in the sun, a lot it seemed, his skin that angry-bronze colour you get just before burning sets in. At least, most of him was. Below his chin and to the left, was a mess of white lines, you could even see the spots where some heavy-duty stitching had been applied. Someone had really tried to put this guy in the ground. I suspected someday, if it hadn't already come, whoever was responsible would wish they'd tried just that little bit harder.

Further marks peppered his shoulders and one nasty-looking one right in the centre of the left bicep.

'Come on through,' he said, and opened a wooden gate. We followed him though to a garden that was, I thought, the place where taste came to die. There was some grass, but mostly it was decking, multi-coloured paving, faux-alabaster sculptures and yes, it took a moment to see, but there was a hot tub. Again, I wondered about his neighbours; I imagined some petition somewhere, signed by the entire street, but nobody brave enough to post it through the letterbox. 'Sure you don't want a drink? You must be dying in that getup?'

It *was* warm and I felt sticky under the uniform, but again I refused. He motioned at a glass garden table and we sat.

'So, what's this about?' He folded his blocky arms across his massive chest. He looked at me with one eye closed to the overhead sun.

'We're looking into a cowboy operation. Bunch of

177

guys in white vans purporting to be legitimate tradesmen but fleecing unsuspecting pensioners out of . . . well, their pensions.'

'Uh-huh. And how is it you ended up at my door?'

'Your name came up during our investigation,' Morgan said.

The one open eye shifted to the lad. 'And who the fuck mentioned my name?'

'I, uh, I can't really—'

'Clearly that's not something we're going to divulge, Mr McStay, but we're duty-bound to follow up every lead, you understand,' I said.

'Aye, I know how it goes. And I have a record and all that, but I've been legit for some time now. Think it's time for you lot to respect that. You no think?'

'What is it you do these days, Mr McStay?' I said.

'You can cut that shit oot. It's Colin.'

'All right. What line of business are you in, Colin?'

'Consultancy work,' he said.

'Consulting on what?' I said.

He took a moment to answer and in that moment any attempt at convincing me he was in any way 'legit' evaporated.

'Security,' was his reply. Almost as vague as his first answer. It was pointless pursuing it.

'So not landscaping?'

'Landscaping? Does it look like I'm a fucking gardener? I'd have decked over that patch of grass if it wisnae for Dex.'

'Dex?'

'The dog. He won't go on the artificial stuff, so I keep that over there as his piss patch.'

'So, no gardening equipment kicking about then, Mr . . . Sorry, Colander?' Morgan said. It was an accident and you could see in his face he wanted desperately to take it back, but it was out there and there was no putting it back in the bottle. A sinister smile grew on the face of McStay.

'I'm sorry, Mr McStay, I didn't mean any offence,' said Morgan, there was a small waiver in his voice.

'You don't hear me using nasty nicknames, do you? Like, fucking pig bastards. Someone might call you that. That would be a bad one, wouldn't it?'

'Mr McStay, there's no need—' I said.

'Cunts in blue. That's another one.' He was on his feet now and I was getting to mine. I wasn't worried about him attacking us, not really, but his neck seemed to thicken as he spat insults and I was ready to get out of there.

'Come on, Morgan. I think we've taken up enough of the man's time.'

'Aye, that's it, away and fuck off the pair of you.'

I opened the gate to the drive and saw that the garage door was still slightly ajar. It was a futile request, but I asked anyway: 'Don't suppose there's any chance of getting a look inside here?' I said.

'Course you can, just pop back with a fuckin' warrant.'

'Thought not.'

'I wonder if you'll make it back to the road before I introduce you tae Dex. Let's see, will we?'

We didn't meet Dex, though we didn't dawdle on the way back to the car. By the time I pulled out, there were a dozen faces on the street having a good look. Perhaps now one of them would find the courage to deliver that petition?

'I'm so sorry. That was so bloody stupid of me.'

'Relax Morgan, it's not a big deal.'

'I really messed that up.'

'You didn't mess anything up. All that was going to happen is we were going to dance around the issue of him probably being responsible for these scams. The real purpose of the visit was to get a look at where he lives and to let him know we're on to him. Even if we can't get him for these current crimes, it might be enough to make him think twice about continuing.'

My words of reassurance didn't seem to help much. The lad stayed quiet all the way back to Drylaw station. Raising Morgan's confidence was not going to be easy. I left him in the canteen, sulking into his sandwich, and returned to my office where I sank into my chair. I stretched the encounter with Colander out of my arms and back and felt like I could sleep. I reached for my phone, thinking I'd just take a peek before settling into a few hours of checking through the team's crime reports. There was a text message from an unknown number:

DON, THIS IS MICHELLE AT PENNYWELL CARE HOME. VIC GAVE ME YOUR NUMBER, SAID I SHOULD LET YOU KNOW WHEN MARTIN WAS TALKING SENSE. HE'S UP AND ABOUT THIS MORNING. IN CASE IT'S IMPORTANT. X

# CHAPTER SIXTEEN

## Just a Word

Michelle met me at the front door of the care home and took me through to the canteen where the residents were eating lunch. There was a general buzz of conversation and clanking of cutlery and crockery.

'Vicky's not working today?' I asked.

'Backshift. I'm switching with her in about an hour. She'd told me to message you if she was off duty and I found Martin "back in the light" as she calls it. I wasn't sure if you were still interested?' she said.

I wasn't sure either. Alyson's reaction had somewhat knocked the enthusiasm out of me, despite what I found on the force systems. Still, I'd come and hadn't really considered not coming. 'Martin's over by the window. Can I get you something to eat?'

I thanked her, but refused, though she insisted on getting

me some tea. Martin was talking to another gentleman. Both had finished their meals, their empty plates awaiting collection.

'Good afternoon, gents. Lovely day,' I said.

'It is, aye. Hey, if you're here for me you're goin' tae have to use that baton, I'm no comin' without a fight,' the man I didn't know said.

I laughed. 'No danger. I only pick battles I can win.'

He laughed in return and was kind enough to realise I needed to speak to his companion, so made his excuses and left us alone.

'Sergeant, isn't it?' Martin said.

'That's right. How're you doing?'

'Fine, fine. I'm sorry, I don't quite remember your name.'

'It's Don Colyear.'

'That's right. I'm fairly certain you're the first Colyear I've come across.'

'There's a few of us around, but not many. You're keeping well?'

'I'm doing all right, Sergeant, yes. So, have I been back on that damned phone again?'

A staff member arrived with my tea and we sat in awkward silence while he cleared the plates away. 'Are you up to a walk?' I said.

'If you don't mind me taking your arm, a walk would be very pleasant.'

I had meant around the garden, but Martin saw this as an opportunity to get out of the place altogether. Rather than walk around the housing scheme, I suggested we take the short trip to Cramond. Michelle was a little nervous about leaving him in my care, but I agreed to call at the first sign of any problems and that was good enough for an afternoon pass for Martin.

'Have you ever been in one of these before?' I asked as he fixed his seatbelt in place. A few of the staff were having a giggle from the office window and taking photos with their phones as we drove off.

'A police car? Once. I was a bit of a drinker in my thirties, went around with a bunch of rockers, fancied themselves as a gang, but it was nothing so organised. Anyway, we're in a bar in Galashiels of all places and a bunch of scooters arrive in the carpark. It wasn't much of a fight to be honest, but the landlord got a fright. I don't know what he said down the phone but within minutes the place is surrounded by bobbies. I wasn't involved in the fight as such, but I spent a few hours in a cell before they sent me on my way with a flea in my ear.'

'You surprise me, Martin. I thought you scholars were too busy with your noses in books for that sort of thing.'

'Ach, I'm sure even policemen get up to no good when they think nobody is watching.'

'I can neither confirm nor deny.'

He laughed. 'That incident was enough for me to turn something of a corner. By then Angela was pregnant with our Alan and I was starting my PhD in Edinburgh. It was time to do a bit of growing up.'

'Angela was your wife?'

'Yes. Lost her to breast cancer when she was in her fifties. Gosh . . .' he said.

'What?' He was looking away out of the side window, deep in thought.

'I just realised it'll soon be twenty-five years since the horrible disease took her. I remembered I have a big birthday coming in a few weeks and so the maths is easier.'

'So, what? Eighty?'

'Yes, eighty. A fortnight today actually.'

'I hope the staff will be organising something?'

'Most likely, but I'll probably be absent at my own party, so they needn't bother.' His tone had gone glum.

I changed the subject. 'Alan, he's in the States?'

'He works in business analytics. As far as I can tell he's well regarded.'

'That sounds like one of those jobs that I wouldn't really understand even if you explained it to me.'

'I don't know all the ins and outs myself, but as I understand it, companies employ him to take a good look at their practices and he identifies where they could be better. For his large fee they often find they're paying out less on overheads and profitability goes up. That's the theory.'

'He's kept busy then?'

'I'm guessing the staff told you he's not over to see me too often?'

'There was mention,' I said and slowed as the line of traffic in front came to a standstill for no apparent reason.

'I really don't mind. I'd be more concerned if he was wasting his youth sitting at my bed. He's better where he is.'

'Any grandkids?'

'No. It's just never been a priority for him and his partner. Do you have to sit in this traffic like everyone else?

Can't you use the thingymabobs?'

'The lights and siren? We're only supposed to use them in emergency situations, not for skipping queues,' I said. I could see he was disappointed. I thought on it for a moment and then pushed the gear stick into first. 'All right auld-yin, hold on to your hat,' I said and lit the car up. His mouth formed an 'O' as the siren wailed and cars in front began edging to the verge. I cut past the line at sixty, slowing a little for the lights which were the cause of the hold up and cut right towards the coast. 'You OK?' I said and cancelled the emergency functions, bringing the car back to a legal thirty.

'Quite all right,' he said, a wide smile on his face.

I pulled into the little car park at Cramond Beach, which was as busy as I'd expected with the fine weather. I helped Martin to exit and we walked, slowly, down the path to the promenade where dogwalkers and cyclists made way for one another. We drew a few looks with me in uniform, but if Martin noticed he didn't seem to care.

There was a stiff breeze as was almost always the case along the Firth, but the sun overhead made it a welcome one. The tide was out, so a steady stream of bodies could be seen walking the causeway over to Cramond Island.

'I wanted to ask you about a bad night you had a few weeks ago,' I said.

'You might have to narrow it down, not that I'll probably remember anyway.'

'It was the day we talked in the garden. Unfortunately, you slipped off and then had a restless evening, mentioning things about God. About not being able to hear the word of God. By all accounts you were extremely upset. Do you recall any of this?'

He thought on it as we walked. I was aware of people gesturing at us, alerting their own walking companions to the sight of a police officer taking the arm of an old man. I tried to ignore the smiles and one man who'd decided it was worthy of a photograph.

'I'm sorry. I don't think I remember this.'

'That's all right, but you don't "think" you remember?'

'Well . . . I remember the day in the garden you mentioned. You asked me about a boy, no, you asked me about a child and I told you it was a boy? Well, it's like that. You're asking me about something that is like a dream I had, but it's so vague, or long ago, and maybe it's just what you're telling me that is forming the idea of a memory? I'm sure that all sounds very confusing.'

'That's all right,' I said and patted his hand, his arm had stiffened. 'If you don't remember, you don't remember. I could say some things in an attempt to prompt you, but as you say I might just be instilling the idea that you remember something.'

'Would you mind if we turn back? I'm not really used to so much walking, though I very much appreciate you getting me out of that place for a little while.'

'Sure, not a problem. Do you want to sit for a minute?'

I led him to a nearby bench and we took in the view, the sun was high and Martin raised his face to it. His eyes closed. 'I don't mind you asking whatever it is you need to. It seems there's something important.'

I looked at him, his eyes remained closed, there was a smile on his face.

'A man was murdered, sometime after the evening I mentioned. The circumstances can very vaguely be associated to what you were saying to the staff in the home that night. In particular you make mention of "hearing" and the injuries have been described as a frenzied attack to both sides of the head, in and around the ears.'

'This man was a priest? Or vicar?'

He said this so matter-of-factly that I was dumbfounded. Adrenalin surged to my heart and it was a minute before I could speak. 'You remember something?'

Eyes still closed he shrugged. 'Probably as I described. You made mention of "God" . . . I'm most likely putting two and two together. Or perhaps I've read something in a paper? I suppose it has been in the paper?'

'Yes, it has.'

'Probably that then,' he said and now looked at me. 'But when you mentioned what it was, I was saying that evening, I did picture a priest. Have you discovered why he was killed?' He held out his arm and I stood and helped him to his feet. We started back.

'It's not my case. If Aly . . . If my colleague knew I was asking you about this, she would probably be less than pleased. It's a sensitive case, so I'd be grateful if you didn't discuss anything I've mentioned today?'

'Of course.'

'But between you and me, I don't think they've established a motive.'

'Well I'm no lover of organised religion. It's my belief

that the Church has been responsible for all sorts of atrocities, vindicated by whatever doctrine best suits. Sins of the father, or fathers. Still, murder is murder. Just awful. May I ask, why are you so interested in whatever nonsense I've been muttering when . . . I'm not quite myself?'

I let out a small laugh. This was a question I'd been asking myself. 'I'm not, not really. It's just that I'm not fond of coincidences I suppose. As a cop I'm prone to scepticism when I come across one. Besides, I'm a community police officer, Martin, which means I have too much time on my hands.'

'Do you think it might be all right?'

I wasn't sure as to what he was referring at first, then I realised he was looking at the ice-cream van parked at the end of the path. A small queue had formed at its window.

'Oh, I think Michelle wouldn't mind.'


Martin didn't say much on the journey back to Pennywell and I suspected I was losing him. Certainly, by the time Michelle took him from me and I thanked him for his time, I only received a small wave in goodbye.

'What's that policeman been feeding you, Martin?' Michelle chuckled. She dabbed at his chin where I'd failed to spot a trail left by his cone.

'She's just upset we didn't bring her a ninety-nine, Martin,' I called after them as they started up the stairs.

I made my way down the hall, passing the office as I did. I glanced through and saw that shift change was happening, staff taking off and putting on coats. I stopped to say a quick hello to Vicky. I chapped on the open door to get attention and the various conversations halted. Vicky turned as she was removing her arm from a sleeve and immediately looked away. The other faces in the room grew sullen. 'Uh, would you mind very much if I have a quick word with Vicky?' I said, and the other staff members quickly shuffled from the room. I closed the door and tried to find the right words to begin, but before I got there Vicky began talking, still facing away from me.

'It's not what it looks like,' she said.

I kept my voice low and calm. 'What *does* it look like?'

She didn't reply. Her hands were on her hips as she looked out of the window.

'Are you going to tell me it's been another accident with a resident? I've spent quite a bit of time here now and so far, I haven't seen these marks on anyone else.'

There was a long pause. One hand remained on a hip while another moved around to her face. I could hear her crying. I let her compose herself. When she finally turned around, I could see what I got a glimpse of. Her lip was badly swollen and there were a few sutures crossing an angry black line that ran down the middle. She wiped at her eyes and let out a heavy breath before taking a seat at her desk.

'I don't want you to get involved. It would only make things worse,' she said in a cracked voice.

I wheeled a chair over beside her. 'That sort of puts me in an awkward position, morally speaking. It's not easy to watch someone have to deal with that, but more so, the law is very clear on this sort of thing. If I got a call here with someone concerned about domestic abuse, I would have no choice but to file a report, irrespective of the wishes of the victim.'

'Don, nobody called you. So please.'

It was heartbreaking to look at her. If one of my officers had come to me with this dilemma my advice would have been easy: report it. But in the face of this lady I had come to know, even just a little, it wasn't that simple. 'Your colleagues. They know what's going on, you realise that?'

'Course. But we've all got our stuff and we know when or if to speak up.' She dabbed a tear from her cheek.

There was the growl of an exhaust from outside. I stood to have a look and Vicky stepped in front of me, her hands on my shoulders. 'Please. Just don't.'

It was the blue Subaru.

'Your partner?'

'He just dropped me off. I promise you it's not always like this. He can be such—Don, no, please.'

I was already heading for the door. Vicky called after me again and I pushed past the congregation of staff members in the hall. She caught hold of my arm just as I reached the front door. 'I'm just going to have a word with him, Vicky. Don't worry.' I shook her off and stepped up to the Subaru, the driver was just putting the car in gear when I rapped a knuckle on the side window which seemed to startle him. He squinted through the window at me before reapplying the handbrake and switching off the engine. The window slid down with an electric whine.

'Afternoon,' I said to the man. He was around my age, maybe a few years older, judging by a little grey at his temples. There was a strange caramel or butterscotch smell from the interior. There was a vape-pen sitting on the passenger seat and I wondered if that was the source. 'We haven't been introduced. I'm Sergeant Colyear, I work out of Drylaw.'

'Uh-huh,' he said. He gave me a good look and then moved his eyes to the windscreen.

'And you are?'

He breathed a sigh, which ended with 'Darren'.

'Darren what?'

'Does it matter?' he said and looked at me again before returning his eyes forward.

'So, you're Vicky's other half then?'

'Uh-huh.'

'What do you do for a living, Darren?'

'I've got a garage. What's this about? I need to get to work.'

I stepped away from the window and walked to the front of car. 'Control from three-four with a vehicle check, over.'

'Go ahead with your check, over,' came the reply from the radio.

I gave over the registration and my location and was told to stand-by. Meanwhile I returned to Darren's window. 'Garage, aye? You're a mechanic? That explains the fancy motor then. Bet she's no cheap to run.'

'Uh-huh.'

'Three-four with your check, over.'

'Go ahead.'

'Roger. Blue Subaru Impreza. Registered and insured to a Darren Henderson. No reports. Do you need a licence check done on Henderson, over?'

191

'I looked in through the window. Mr Henderson was looking impatient. 'Negative. That's all received. Thanks.' I placed the elbow of my arm on the sill of his window and tried to get some eye contact with him, but he was having none of it. He gripped his wheel like he might tear it from the dash and beat me with it. His eyes remained on the screen. 'You asked what this was about, Darren, well it's about me getting to see the man who lives with Vicky. She's a nice lady, been helping me with an inquiry I have down here. She might have mentioned it? You might even say we've become friends. Anyway. Friends, they watch out for one another, that's how it's supposed to work, right?'

He cleared his throat by way of a response.

'See, I've noticed Vicky's been coming to work with the odd injury. She tells me they happen when she moving residents around and I can see how that might happen, occasionally. Only it seems to me like she's got a fresh one every week. Now if Vicky insists that's how she comes by them, then I'm not about to call her a liar. But at the same time, it's my job, as a friend, to make sure she's all right. Then it's my job as a police officer to step in if she's not all right. You understand?'

There was another throaty grunt.

'So, I thought it best to highlight this to you. It's also your job, as her partner, to make sure she's all right, so I thought by bringing it to your attention we can both keep an eye out. All right?' There was no response. I stood and tapped the top of the car. The engine roared into life. I was stepping away when he leaned out of the window.

'Can I ask you, officer. Did she report anything to

you? Make any sort of complaint?'

'No, but she—'

'No, I thought not. Until she does you can go ahead and keep your fucking nose out of things that don't concern you,' he snarled. I only just caught what he said over the noise as he drove off.

Alyson yawned and stretched, checking her watch at the same time. She'd knock off in an hour or so, but she liked this time, this calm period that always felt like the warm-down after a long run. It was a chance to look at things without the distracting buzz of the office – especially without the stress that came off DCI Templeton like steam, which was difficult not to breathe in.

The DCI left twenty minutes ago. Alyson could safely leave at any time now that she was gone. It wasn't presenteeism that had her here after most, if not all, had left. Although it probably didn't do her career any harm to hear the DCI saying goodnight most days. She stayed because if she was going to figure this out, it would only happen with a bit of quiet.

The first floor at Leith Police Station had steadily filled. It wasn't as crazy as things had been at the beginning of the Bradley case, but it was getting there. Her own role had changed, and that was a good thing. Before, she felt like an office junior, and now she was part of the core team. Duncan's advice had been sound: 'Stay involved'. There were four new members of the enquiry team, pulled from a pro-active unit who worked out of Fettes, whose only job was to trawl through city CCTV now that they had a more accurate description of the van that may or may not have been involved. DCI Templeton had been happy about that development and Alyson was pleased that Duncan had been sure to let her know Alyson had been responsible for it. The mind-numbing CCTV job might have been hers if she hadn't stayed so close to Duncan and the DCI. It didn't hurt either that she was HOLMES trained. Another reason to keep her from the grunt work.

She recalled when she'd undertaken the training. As interesting as it was, she was also certain as to its futility. They'd used the example of Peter Tobin to show how the system works from a Scottish perspective, but how many Peter Tobins was she likely to encounter in her career? Serial killers were not common in the UK and a rare species indeed in Scotland, yet here she was, using the system she'd been sure she never would. The Home Office Large Major Enquiry System was software designed to take, store, evaluate and crucially link massive amounts of data collated during any large inquiry, its necessity highlighted during the evaluation and review of the Peter Sutcliffe conviction in 1981. West Yorkshire Police had missed several opportunities to link the Yorkshire Ripper to his victims due to the antiquated card-index system they had used.

Still, she'd sat in front of the computer day after day inputting data and running analysis and still no link had been thrown up between a ten-year-old boy and a seventy-one-year-old priest. If you'd started a joke with these two victims, there would have been some grim punchline laying into the Church's deplorable record of child abuse. But these two people, as far as anyone or any piece of software could detect, did not know each other, had never come into contact with one another and there was no person between them, identified thus far, that could bridge the gap. No one, other than the killer.

Alyson sipped her coffee and calmly looked at the information in front of her. Not at the computer screen, but the wall behind the DCI's desk. For all the technology available, this was still the easiest way to think. Three large tack-boards. The one to the left was littered with information on Callum Bradley, the one to the right a little less busy, but still full of information on Father Brian McCauley. The board between them was empty, but for a few scraps of ideas. 'Bible Class?', 'School connection?', 'Takeaway driver?', 'Tradesman?' were a few of the suggestions thrown up there, but nothing yielding a fresh lead. Billy Beattie's fresh description of the van had meant plenty of work for Alyson's Edinburgh-based colleagues who now had the unenviable task of painstakingly going through websites and the Yellow Pages for tradesmen in the central belt, visiting them and taking pictures of vans which might later be shown to Billy. Another shit job she was glad to be avoiding.

*Ten-year-old boy, Catholic priest?* Callum Bradley's parents were not religious, they came from a long line of take-it-or-leave-it Church of Scotland protestants. Their only legacy was to ensure Callum had been a Rangers fan. None of the family had seen the inside of a church in years, except for a cousin who had been married in Bathgate and, again, that was Church of Scotland.

What if there was no connection? What if this truly was

two unrelated random attacks? At a morning meeting a few days ago, Danny Halliday had presented that very idea. The DCI all but took his head off. Everyone around the table sank into their chairs while she berated him, ensuring nobody going forward would utter the idea again in her presence. But alone, here, she could consider it. It was a chilling thought, it made the job of identifying the person responsible much harder, maybe impossible.

The murder of Father McCauley was a fresh opportunity for DCI Templeton and her team. The Bradley enquiry had been reduced, since it was clear some external influence was the only realistic way forward. An anonymous tip, a stroke of luck, a sudden urge for the killer to confess his crime. That same line in the sand was not too far away. The DCI had kept the team relatively small and Alyson was beginning to believe the reason for it was to keep that line as far in the distance as she could.

She perched herself on Templeton's desk, stared at the board and sipped. *Ten-year-old boy and Catholic priest?*

# CHAPTER SEVENTEEN

## Work History

'You look like you need this more than I do,' Alyson said and held out her wine glass. If that was true, I must have looked pretty awful, since Alyson's eyes bore deep, dark circles. She sat at the kitchen table in her work clothes, her ID still hanging from her neck.

'Thanks, but I think I'll stick to the tea.' I clicked on the kettle and checked the clock on the oven. It was a little after 10 p.m. and I'd been watching a movie in the living room, slowly falling asleep in front of it. I'd heard Alyson coming in and the sound of the microwave.

'You had a bad day?' she asked. She sipped from her glass, then exchanged it for a pen.

'Something like that.' She was mistaking my sleepiness for sullenness, but she wasn't wrong.

'Do you want to talk about it?'

'It's nothing. Just when you come across two violent arseholes in one day, it can leave a bad taste. You get what I mean?' I said, then grimaced, realising how that sounded.

Alyson laughed.

'You're planning a late one?' I said, gesturing at the paperwork she'd spread across the kitchen table, scattered around a half-finished bowl of pasta.

'Not really. I just want to get my thoughts together before tomorrow. I'm heading back to Rickerburn, this time to see Callum Bradley's parents.'

'Ouch. That does not sound like fun.' I brought my tea over to the table and sat opposite.

'It's just awful. What do you say to the parents of a murdered child? Especially when all they want to hear from you is that you're close to catching the bastard who did it, and you're not. You can't even tell them you're any closer than the last time you made them live through all this again.'

'What's the purpose of speaking to them?'

'The DCI wants it done. Wants us to ask them further about any link with priests. We had an initial chat that seemed to rule that out, but desperate times and all that. Thing is, we were holding off really pushing this question, not wanting to make the link known outside of the enquiry team, but there's growing pressure from the media on this idea. DCI thinks the media team will have to put out a statement tomorrow. We need to find out if the media might have sussed the link from speaking to the family.'

Alyson dropped her pen onto the pad she'd been scribbling into and leaned back in her chair, stretching and yawning.

'Scale of one to ten, how much do you believe there is a

link to be found?' I said.

'You mean outside for your geriatric mystic?'

'Yes. Other than that.'

'Sorry, I know you're just trying to help. You need to call me out when I'm being a dick. I'm so tired I don't even notice it.'

'All right. Aly, you're being a dick.' I leaned over and chinked her glass with my mug.

She gave me a grin and sipped. 'So, ten being absolute surety that there is a link?'

'Yes. One being certainty that there isn't one.'

'I would say I was a solid three.'

'And your boss?'

'That's tough to answer. From the noises she makes you'd think she was convinced, but really that's just her making sure we turn over every rock. Only *she* knows just how sure she is of a connection.'

'What's the current thinking on it? If you don't mind me asking?'

'It's fine. My boss would probably boot me off the case if she heard us talking like this, but I know I can trust you.'

'Course,' I said, and felt a pang of guilt as I thought about my afternoon with Martin.

'We can't find a direct link between the two victims, so the thinking is this: is there a person between these two, whether that's the killer or just some third-party that connects them?'

'And so far?'

'So far, fuck all. Hence the likes of this awkward chat tomorrow.'

'The family isn't religious then? No link there? His dad wasn't some altar boy somewhere?' I said, thinking about Martin's words, 'sins of the father'.

'No. First thing we looked into.'

'Yeah of course, sorry. Must sound like I'm trying to teach you to suck eggs,' I said.

'It's fine, really. If you've got a suggestion spit it out. I'm not above a little inspiration.'

'OK.' I pulled my mug to my chest and thought. 'Any link at all with the priest and Rickerburn?'

'Not a one.'

'The family and Edinburgh?'

'Nope, beyond a very occasional visit, but nothing obvious there.'

'Priest's family? Any brothers or sisters who might have kids, no wait, grandkids around Callum's age?'

'That's not bad, Colyear. I was a few days in before I checked that out, but no. He had one sister, spinster, deceased.'

'Callum's grandma? Grandpa?'

'What about them?'

'I dunno, just that they must be around ages with Father whatsisname?'

Alyson went searching through her paperwork, draining her glass as she did. I wondered if she took a day off that stuff when she wasn't up to her neck in a murder inquiry. 'Grandma's brown-bread, grandpa is alive. Non-religious, never even been to Edinburgh.'

'Never been to Edinburgh? How do you get to his age and never have visited the capital?'

Alyson's mouth twisted. 'Would you believe that before

this case I'd only been in Edinburgh once?'

'What? How's that possible?'

She shrugged. 'You're either an Edinburgh person or a Glasgow person. I'm balls to bone Weegie. Unlike you, ya turncoat.'

'There's no reason you can't belong to both cities,' I said. Though in my heart I knew she had a point. It would be like supporting two rival football teams.

'How's your day tomorrow?' she asked.

'Day off for me. So long lie and plenty of very little.'

'Lucky bastard.'

'I was thinking about trying to get in touch with that woman from the bar. What do you think?'

'This is the one who told you to call her, but didn't give you her number?'

'That's the one.'

'What's the plan? Stalk her online and send a surprise friend request?'

'No. I mean, that would be creepy, right?'

'Yes, Don. That would be creepy.'

'I was thinking I would just ask Mandy for her number.'

'Still sounds a little crawly and you'd be putting your colleague in an awkward position. I think the best way to approach it might be to ask Mandy to pass your number on to her. If she gets in touch, great and if not, well, message received.'

'That's good. Yeah, I'll do that. Night, Aly. Don't stay up too late,' I said.

* * *

Alyson discovered there was a way to walk to Leith from the New Town while avoiding the festival almost entirely. A series of intersecting tracks, collectively referred to as the 'Warriston Paths', had at one time been train lines, connecting the coastal north of the city to its centre. Now abandoned, they had been reconstituted as walking and cycling routes. Long, straight sections of pathways allowed you to follow the river down towards Leith with nothing but the occasional ringing of a bike bell from behind to disturb her podcast – a debate between two American trainers on over-training, what it constitutes and what the dangers of it were. Not something she had to worry about lately. There were lots of things she missed about home, but none more so than her gym. She had found one; a small outfit connected to an office building. It was used by amateurs on amateur apparatus, but was walking distance from the flat and was something of a port in a storm.

Over a wall she caught a glimpse of an old cemetery below, its headstones broken and overrun with ivy, as if the undergrowth were trying to pull the stones back into the earth. Two people stood down there, talking with their dogs on the leads while the dogs tied their legs like maypoles.

A light drizzle fell and there was a feeling that it might get worse, a lot worse. It had been particularly warm the past few days and there was a pressure in the air that was likely to be broken by a downpour.

Alyson made it to the office before the skies fully opened. She checked her watch and saw that she was exactly on time, to the very minute.

'Cunningham's taken a day, so I'll be joining you this

afternoon.' Alyson hadn't seen DCI Templeton coming, her voice just seemed to appear in her ear and now Alyson was half-jogging to catch up to her in the hall.

'Is he all right? Is he sick?'

'Sick? No. Something about his daughter going into labour or some shit. Anyway, rather than pairing you up with someone new, I'll sit in with you.'

'Aw, that's lovely. It's his first.'

The DCI stopped and turned, her face screwed in confusion. 'What?'

'Uh, grandchild. It's Duncan's first.'

Templeton didn't respond. She continued on down the hall and Alyson wasn't sure if she should still be following. 'You have everything you need?' Templeton asked.

'Yes, I think so.'

'Good. As far as I'm concerned, I'm there for corroboration only.'

'Yes, ma'am.'

'Meet me at the car in ten minutes.'

'Yes, ma'am.'

The wipers swung to clear the screen from rain while the blowers fought to keep it clear from misting on the inside. After twenty minutes Alyson was beginning to think the DCI wasn't coming, or that perhaps she had been referring to a different car. She decided to give it another few minutes before giving it up and going back inside. She sent a text to Duncan, wishing him and his daughter all the best. He didn't have a habit of talking about his family, but he had mentioned this impending arrival frequently enough to show how excited he was.

She hurried to push the phone into her pocket as the passenger door was pulled open.

'Cats and fucking dogs,' Templeton said as she pushed her briefcase through the seats into the back. 'How you lot stand to spend all your lives with this as summer, I'll never know. Shall we?'

'Yes, ma'am.'

Alyson was grateful for the satnav. Without it she wouldn't have known to turn left or right at the first junction. 'You get used to it,' she said as she began to relax, stuck as she was in a line of traffic heading roughly towards the city centre.

'The weather? How do you do that exactly? Develop gills?'

'How long have you been in Scotland, ma'am?'

'Would you mind if we cut the "ma'am" shit when it's just the two of us? Kate is fine. Scotland? Let's see, it'll be three years this November.'

She would have considered this as doing Alyson a favour, dropping the authority, but there was safety in the formality, so far as she always knew how to address her in any situation. Now it had been removed it had also taken with it a comfortable detachment, leaving Alyson feeling somehow vulnerable.

According to the screen, they were on Queen Street, heading west, perilously close to city centre celebrations. She couldn't see the festival, other than the endless placards advertising shows and artists that covered every inch of fencing, but Alyson could hear it, perhaps even feel it. A base drum beat somewhere in the distance, the occasional sound of a whistle. She was directed to keep right at Charlotte Square where a large, enclosed garden was filled with white tents and now people swarmed and congregated at lights, umbrellas forming great shields.

'Where did you come from, uh, Kate?' It felt stupid in her mouth. Perhaps she'd just try to avoid addressing her at all.

'The Met, initially. Greater Manchester after promotion. I got my pips there before accepting the DCI position up here. Do you have family?'

'It's just me and Mum. How about you?'

'Husband. Two kids. You know, the whole kit.'

'That's lovely.'

'Yes, they're all right. They can stay.' Alyson was fairly certain that was Kate's attempt at humour, she pushed a smile on to her face. 'Do you mind if I close my eyes for a bit. I find driving frightfully boring.'

'Sure, go ahead,' said Alyson, thinking . . . *None taken.*

Alyson turned on the radio as they entered the limits of Rickerburn. Kate woke with a start and wiped a little drool from the corner of her mouth.

'We'll be there in five minutes,' said Alyson.

'How are you feeling about this?' Kate asked, stretching her arms out over the dash and rolling her head left and right.

'Fine. It's no problem,' she lied.

They pulled up to the house, a semi-detached ex-council number. It was around five minutes on foot to young Billy's

205

place. Alyson ran through the opening lines in her head as they walked up the drive, the sound of stones crunching against the paving slabs under their feet. She reached for the bell and pushed. If it rang inside the house she didn't hear it, so she knocked as well.

The door was answered by Mr Bradley. He gave a wan smile and pushed the door wide.

In the kitchen, Mrs Bradley sat at the table. She didn't look up as they entered. She held a cup of coffee between her hands that had formed a milky film on top, long since gone cold. Mr Bradley slid a hand over her shoulders as he took the seat next to her.

'Please,' he said and gestured at the two chairs opposite. Alyson sat and laid her folder down in front of her. 'Oh sorry, can I get you a tea? Coffee?'

'I'll get that, Mr Bradley. Please,' said Kate.

She really was leaving this to Alyson. Alyson wasn't short of confidence, and when Duncan had left her to it she didn't feel like she couldn't handle things. But in front of Kate, the boss? She felt her cheeks flush.

'How are you both?' Alyson asked, and immediately wished she hadn't. *How the fuck do you think they are?* Bad start, though Mr Bradley did his best to rescue the situation.

'We're doing OK, aren't we, love? We're keeping it together.'

'It always pains me to have the victims of such atrocious matters have to relive any part of it, and so I'm sorry that we need to be here, only there have been some developments that you need to be made aware of.'

As she said this, Mrs Bradley looked up. She was thirty-six, but you could have plausibly reversed those numbers. The lines or her face were deep and dark, and her brown, shoulder-length hair hung limp at her face. Mr Bradley was also drawn around the eyes, and had lost weight since the last time she'd seen him. Alyson had inadvertently made the mistake of triggering a little hope in those tired faces. She hurried to clarify. 'We're no closer to finding the person responsible for what happened to Callum, I need to make that clear, but we are working around the clock.'

Kate brought a cup of tea over to the table and laid it in front of Alyson before sitting. Nothing for herself. 'There's going to be a story run in the newspaper, perhaps as early as tomorrow, that you need to be prepared for,' Kate said and then looked at Alyson, giving the subtlest nod to continue.

'Did you happen to see on the news, a report of a priest murdered in Edinburgh? This is going back a few weeks now.'

'Yes, of course. Shocking,' said Mr Bradley.

'The thing is, we think that case and ours are related.'

Mrs Bradley's trembling left hand sought out Mr Bradley's. 'In . . . what sense?' she said.

'We're all but certain the person who killed Callum also killed this priest. We can't go into the specifics of this, but the press have gotten wind of the connection and are likely, the tabloids at least, to run front-page stories.'

'Probably as harrowing and sensationalised as possible. Have you been contacted by members of the press in recent days?' Kate asked.

'No, not for a while,' Mrs Bradley looked to her

husband, who shook his head.

Kate continued: 'Well, you will. It's up to you, how and if you respond, but if you wanted my advice, you just say "no comment at this time" and direct them to us. Are you still in contact with the lawyer we set you up with?' During the immediate media clamour after Callum's murder, Kate had passed on the details of a good QC, someone who had managed media attention in the past and had done most of the microphone work in those initial weeks.

'Again, not for a while,' said Mr Bradley.

'Give him a call and then you tell him to call me. I'll tell him what I can and he'll keep you right. Now, Alyson here is going to ask you some questions. The most important thing at this time is that we continue with our enquiries, so any help you can give us is vital.' Again, Alyson got the nod.

Over the space of the next hour, she ran thorough some old information, asking if there was anything they could elaborate on, anything they might have missed. There was a break of around ten minutes to let Callum's parents compose themselves as they ran through the events of the day of the murder. There was nothing said that added to their statements in any meaningful way.

She moved the questions on to the pertinency of Father McCauley, but there was no avenue to explore. There was no connection to Edinburgh, to the Catholic faith, to religion in any capacity. At one point, Alyson was almost wishing Kate would step in. 'Is there anything you'd like to add, ma'am?'

Kate looked like she was drifting off. Her arms were

folded and she looked particularly comfortable in her chair. She cleared her throat and straightened up. Her head began to shake. 'All I would say is that if there is anything at all you feel that we should know, however small or seemingly insignificant, you will call us right away?'

'Yes, yes of course,' said Mr Bradley. He and his wife stood, as did Kate, but something had Alyson rummaging back through her file. Something that Don had said last night and was 'seemingly insignificant'.

'Sorry, just very briefly. Let me just find . . . something. Uh, here. Your father, Mr Bradley, is the only living grandparent, is that correct?'

Kate's eyes narrowed for a moment, but she did not interject.

'Yes, that's right. Sadly, Donna's parents never got to meet Callum and my mother passed when he was very young.'

'I'm sorry to hear that. How about any great uncles or aunts?'

'None. None alive, at least,' said Mr Bradley.

'And your father, he lives in town too?'

'Sort of. His place is between here and Harthill.'

'How old is he now?'

'Dad? He's . . . what? Seventy-two?'

'Seventy-three,' Mrs Bradley corrected.

'Do you think he'd mind if we pay him a visit?' said Alyson.

'I . . . I suppose not, but is it necessary?' said Mr Bradley.

'Callum's Papa is not doing well. As hard as it's been on everyone, he took it incredibly badly. He lived for his

209

grandson,' said Mrs Bradley.

'I understand. I certainly don't want to make things any worse, but it would be good just to get a brief chat with him. You should probably warn him in case any reporters come sniffing around anyway. I promise I'll keep it as brief as possible.'

Callum's parents looked at one another. It was clear they wanted to refuse, but didn't really see any way that they could.

'Could I be there?' said Mr Bradley.

'Of course, I'd prefer if you were,' said Alyson.


It was decided that Alyson and Kate would follow Mr Bradley. They pulled in behind his car and tailed him west through the centre of the town. The rain had stopped, though it remained grey overhead.

'You don't mind that we have a quick word with the grandfather, do you?'

Kate was checking her phone and it wasn't clear if she'd heard the question. Mr Bradley turned left out of town.

'The grandfather?' She said, then looked up at Alyson. 'Is there a particular angle here?' Kate said, her tone carried a note of frustration.

'Nothing in particular. I just figure we're here and, well, he's around the same age as our priest. Figured it couldn't hurt.'

'Same age. Couldn't hurt,' Kate parroted back at her before pushing her phone into her pocket. 'Where the fuck are we?'

'Pretty much nowhere,' said Alyson. While this was,

strictly speaking, their beat, nobody but a curious uniform cop would be up here on a professional capacity. They'd passed the bings where Callum's body had been discovered and were heading south along a backroad with little but scrub stretching off in both directions. A copse of wind turbines came into view on the left on a rise and still they followed Mr Bradley's blue Ford Focus. He signalled right, though there didn't seem to be anything to turn onto. And then she saw it, nothing more than a dirt track, not signposted and in terrible condition. If she'd been driving her own car, she'd have been cursing, but she let this pool car . . . what was it, a Peugeot? Something-or-other, bounce over and occasionally crunch into the muddy potholes.

'Fucking hell,' said Kate, bracing herself against the door. A hundred yards of this and the road opened out where a single row of cottages sat to the right and a parking area to the left in which sat a flat-bed pickup alongside a caravan that had the appearance of a rotten tooth. They pulled in next to Mr Bradley. Alyson had to watch where she was placing her feet; the puddles could easily be shin deep if you weren't careful.

'What is this place?' Alyson asked Mr Bradley.

'Foremen's cottages, from back in the old shale-mining days. You'd have three foremen living here, a cottage each, and they'd work a rota. Sort of a perk of the job. My dad picked this place up for pennies in the late eighties when the industry was on its knees. His is at the end.'

The sound of barking dogs came from behind the cottages, unclear as to which home they belonged.

The houses were small, humble, but well built. Probably

destined to outlast the industry by a full century. There was the smell of a coal fire, combined with something like creosote, though again, it was hard to say exactly where it was coming from. They stayed behind Mr Bradley, single file, to keep their feet dry as he walked beyond the front door of the last cottage and down the side through a metal gate. To the rear was a sizeable garden, the back half of it was overgrown, and the front half of it contained a shed and a small patio area with a single chair. Beside the chair was an overflowing ashtray and a whirligig with a few pieces of sodden clothing hanging. Mr Bradley tutted as he squeezed the sleeve of a jumper, sending a trickle of water to splash to the ground.

He stepped up to the back door, knocked twice and entered into the kitchen. Alyson was just following him over the threshold when he turned and said, 'Uh, can you just give me a second,' before moving to the hall saying, 'Dad, go put something on. There's people to see you,' followed by some sleepy-sounding muttering. They stood awkwardly in the kitchen, waiting. There was a rotten smell rising from the open dustbin in the corner. A large pot of soup sat on the stove and a small loaf of bread lay uncovered on a board. Mr Bradley was half explaining and half arguing with his father in an adjacent room. He returned after a few minutes looking embarrassed and harassed.

'He's in the living room. Can I get you something to drink?'

Alyson didn't want anything, but even if she'd been dying of thirst she'd still have politely refused.

They were shown into a tiny living room with one

armchair pointing at a space between a wood burner, smoking away, and a television, perched precariously on a far-too-small table. Various other tables and shelving, all busy with paperwork and knick-knacks, made up the rest of the furniture. In the armchair sat Mr Bradley Senior, who eyed them as they entered. The man was enveloped by the oversized chair. He was still pulling a vest over arms and chest covered in grey hair. He looked thin to the point of fragility.

'Dad, leave that for now,' said Mr Bradley, but he was shooed away as his father lit a hand-rolled cigarette.

'That's OK, it doesn't bother us,' said Alyson.

'Let me go find you a chair,' Mr Bradley Junior offered, but Kate told him it wasn't necessary and that standing would be fine.

Alyson stepped closer to the old man who drew from the cigarette and blew smoke out of the side of his mouth before picking at a stray strand of tobacco on his lip.

'Sir, my name is Alyson Kane. I'm a detective working on the case of your grandson. Can I first say how sorry I am for your—'

'Sorry isn't justice,' he said.

'Dad . . .'

'It's all right,' Alyson reassured him. 'You're right. Sympathy and apologies aren't what you want to hear from us. You want to hear how we caught the person who did this. You want to hear when the court case is so you can look this person in the eye and tell this person—'

'Tell? I'll no tell them anything. Cut his bastard throat so I will. You let me get to within ten feet of him and I'll end the bastard. Forget court, forget police.'

'I'd feel exactly the same if it were my family, Mr Bradley,' Kate said. She stepped into the centre of the little room. 'We're not going to take up much of your time. We simply have a few questions, after which we will go straight back to finding the fucker.'

Kate's language had the old man looking at them properly for the first time. He took a long draw on his cigarette and stubbed out the remainder. 'What is it you want to know?'

'I want to ask you about a connection to the case. I understand you've been asked a few questions already, but I'd just like to go over them if I may,' said Alyson.

'Fine,' the old man said, and starting coughing. A rasping rattle sounded from his chest. He waved a hand at his son who handed him a towel that sat crumpled next to the television. He continued to hack for a few moments, then spat into the towel before throwing it back to its previous spot. His son looked disgusted.

'You're not a religious man, I understand,' said Alyson.

'No, I'm not. If I had been before, what happened to Callum would have had me giving it up. What kind of God . . .' he stopped to cough again, but it was short.

'To your knowledge have you ever come into contact with a Father Brian McCauley?'

'No.'

'How can you be sure?'

'They stick out a bit, they priests. It's the clothes and that daft white thing at their necks. I'd remember.'

'Fair enough. What about Edinburgh?'

214

'What about it?'

'The detective who called you states you've never been to the city. Is that right?'

'Aye, that's right. Too busy and it's just full of foreigners. I've been to Glasgow, but only because I worked there for a while.'

'And you're retired now.'

'Aye. Retired.'

'What is it you used to do?'

He began hacking once more and the hand was again waving, but Bradley Junior didn't move and instead let the old man reach for the manky towel himself.

'He was a welder in the shipyards originally, but when that all ended, he did odd jobs here and there. Some janitorial work,' Bradley Junior explained.

When the coughing ended, Alyson continued. 'Did priests come to the shipyard, Mr Bradley, or were any of the men you worked with particularly religious?'

He took a few needed breaths before replying. 'Religion was a tricky thing in the shipyard. Personally I didn't give a shit, had no interest, but if you did go in for that sort of thing, you kept the side of the line you lived on to yourself.'

'How do you mean?' asked Kate.

'Well, you're either blue or you're green in Glasgow. Except when you're at your work. Everyone wears the same grey overalls and that's how you keep the peace. Even the day after a Celtic–Rangers match, you didn't hear anyone bleating on about who won. So, no. If I did work with someone religious, I wouldn't have known.'

'The janitorial work, then. Was that in Glasgow too?'

'Some. Some in Lanarkshire.'

'What kind of places?'

'I worked at Burroughs in Cumbernauld for a good while then got work at various schools.'

'What schools? No Catholic schools, I take it? I'll need a list Mr Bradley.'

He was lighting another cigarette, taking his time about it. Again, he pulled tobacco from his lip and flicked it to the floor.

'I was at a couple, but not for long.'

Alyson found that her flow had just come to an abrupt end. She looked at Kate, whose palms were upturned, the thought in her head surely, *What the fuck?*

'You worked at Catholic schools?' Alyson continued.

'Well, aye, I mean amongst others.'

'Dad, I didn't know you worked at a Catholic school? I would have said if I'd known.' Bradley Junior was looking as confused as Kate.

'What schools, precisely, Mr Bradley?' said Alyson.

'Schools are schools, what does it matter?' I was just the janny.'

'Well . . .' Alyson began, she clutched at the question. 'Presumably if you'd worked at Catholic schools, there would have been some interaction with Church members? Nuns? Priests? Whatever?'

'I suppose. But I never met a Brian McCauley, I know that. Didn't think it was worth mentioning.'

'Fucking hell,' Kate muttered under her breath. She was dialling her phone as she left the room.

Alyson reached into her coat pocket for her notebook.

'Mr Bradley, I'd like to take a full statement. I need to know every place you've worked and how long for. I'd also like access to your tax information to we can accurately get a picture of your work history. Would that be OK?' she said and then to Bradley Junior, 'If you could find a chair, I'd be grateful.'

# CHAPTER EIGHTEEN

## Something for You

Either she was late, or I was in the wrong place, though I couldn't see how that was possible. The 'bottom' of Cockburn Street must surely be at the lower end of the hill? Who in their right mind would refer to the higher end as such? And yet I was beginning to doubt myself. I checked for a message and there was none. I was busy composing one when I got a tug on the elbow.

'Hey, stranger. Sorry, have you been waiting long?'

I'd been convincing myself that she wouldn't be as attractive as I'd remembered; that in the cold light of day she'd be nothing compared to the woman I'd met at that boozy night out. I was wrong. If anything, the sunlight brought out features I hadn't noticed in the darkness of the bar. Marcella's eyes were green when I'd thought them brown, with a little grey in there too. She was smiling; I'd been caught staring, taking too long to answer.

'No, just a few minutes,' I lied.

'The buses are completely unpredictable in August. They get you there when they get you there. Still, small price to pay for all this.' She waved a hand towards Waverley Bridge, where tourists swarmed and congregated, trying to find a way onto the rows of open-top buses. 'Shall we walk? How much time do you have?' she said.

'Plenty, don't worry. I'm not due to start until three and if I'm late it doesn't matter.'

I'd asked Mandy to pass my number on to Marcella as Alyson had suggested and had then waited four days without hearing anything. I was beginning to wish I hadn't bothered and that I'd only managed to make a bit of a fool of myself, but then late one night, there was the message from an unknown number, breezy and pleasant. I'd resisted asking her out straight away, leaving it to the following day and a dozen or so exchanged messages before suggesting meeting. We began our ascent of the steep and twisting Cockburn Street.

'I was surprised to hear from you,' she said.

'Likewise. I wasn't confident you'd call, message, or whatever.'

'It was a strange night,' she said and stopped to look in a window. I squeezed in next to her to allow the heavy pedestrian traffic to pass us before walking again.

'I wanted to apologise for that night,' I said.

'You already did in your text and there's no need. To be honest, it's probably just as well. I was in a sort of strange place that night.'

'How so?'

'It's not really the done thing to talk about past relationships on a date, if this is a date, but I suppose we got off to a weird start anyway. I'd been exchanging a few angry texts with my ex that day . . . an issue with owed money that I won't bore you with. Anyway, amidst these texts came one from Mandy, asking if I wanted to go out. I probably wouldn't have were it not for that idiot and I certainly wouldn't have had thoughts of going home with anyone. That's not something I do, but I was just sort of lashing out, I suppose.'

'How's that situation now?'

'You sure you want to talk about this stuff?'

'I don't see why not.'

'All right. Well, you remember I mentioned I had a flatmate?'

'"The worst flatmate", I think you said.'

'Right. I wasn't lying, but there's a bit more to it. The flatmate is my ex. Neither one of us could afford to go get another place right away, so we're forced to live under one roof. Not for long I hope, I'm waiting to hear about a flat in Newington. Is that too weird?'

She wrinkled her nose as we walked.

'I don't suppose it's much stranger than living with your dad at thirty-four?'

She laughed. 'How's that going?'

'Better. He sort of moved out, unofficially. He could return at any moment, but I've hardly seen a hair of him since he met this new woman; who you sort of met at the same time I did.'

'So, you're pottering around in that fancy flat on your own?'

'No. My friend Alyson moved in, though just for a while. She unexpectedly found herself working in town and so it made sense.'

'Oh. Are you two . . .?'

'No,' I chuckled. 'Everyone seems to ask that. I didn't realise it would seem so odd to people that members of the opposite sex could live together and not be, you know, sharing a bed.'

'Seems we've more in common than I realised.' She laughed again and hooked an arm through mine as we neared the top of the street, which bent to the right and joined High Street. A wall of colour and noise met us as it came into view.

The crowd moved almost as one, heading downhill and away from the castle. I felt like we were joining a conveyor belt as we merged with the throng. We passed various street artists all vying for a slice of the crowd and a piece of their generosity. Marcella wore a big smile as she pointed out different acts: a ventriloquist, a group of young teens singing opera and a guy dressed as a wizard statue, appearing to hover a foot above the ground, much to the delight of children. He sheepishly tossed coins into his spare hat as the parents muttered between themselves, probably debating the physics at work to explain the illusion.

'Do you fancy a drink?' I said as we left the thick of the action behind us.

'Actually, I'm starving. Would you mind if we find

somewhere for some lunch?'

It took a while to find anywhere that had a spare table, but we eventually found a little burger place; an independent cafe-come-restaurant. They brought us water and we ordered.

Marcella sipped from her glass and something in her face told me she wanted something, some small crease between the eyes maybe. 'So, I told you about my ex. What skeletons are in your closet? Ever been married?'

I smiled. 'If I knew I was headed for this line of questioning, I'd have ordered something stronger than water,' I said. It occurred to me that she hadn't really told me anything about her ex, just that she had one.

'You don't have to tell me anything, I was just curious.'

A waitress was passing and I caught her eye. I ordered a beer and Marcella said she'd have the same.

'Never been married, though I came close once. High school sweethearts, I suppose you'd call it.'

'What happened?'

'Honestly . . .' I paused as the beers arrived. I took a long draw from my glass and continued. 'Honestly, you'd have to ask her.'

'And if I asked her, what do you think she'd tell me?'

*Sneaky*, I thought, but I didn't want to seem evasive, so played along. 'That we drifted apart I suppose, or some other cliché. She'd tell you that she noticed it a long time before I did.'

'So, she broke things off and it came as a surprise?'

'That's putting it mildly, but yes. She'd met someone else and I'd been too busy with work to put the pieces together.

Some investigator, right?'

'Ouch. Well, I've been there – on both sides of it at one time or another. Never easy. So, she broke your heart and left you bitter and sworn off women for life?'

There was another pause as the food arrived.

'Karen is happy, as far as I'm aware. She has a little one now. I loved her at one time and so there's no grudge. I'm happy for her.'

'Liar,' Marcella said through her napkin, her mouth not yet empty and she winked at me. I laughed and started on my own food. 'So, nobody since then? Not even casual?' she asked.

'There was someone last year, bit of a whirlwind thing while I was working up north.'

'Didn't last?'

I shrugged and tried to formulate my thoughts on it. 'Mhairi is a lovely woman and I'm glad I met her but, I don't know, it sort of blew itself out over the space of a few months. Hot and heavy for a while, but then I started to notice that we didn't have an awful lot to talk about.'

'I've been there too,' she said. 'Something you can't know until you've given it a try.'

'Is that what happened with your current ex?'

She pointed the chip she was holding at me. 'Well turned around, Mr Colyear. If I didn't already know you were a cop, I'd have just figured you out. And yes I suppose so, that's part of it, at least. We were together for four years, first three were great. Then he got into a sort of hump. He got made redundant and then didn't work particularly hard trying to find something else. He lost interest in most things, including me. I stuck with it as long as possible, but then I'd had enough. Since he doesn't have a job and nowhere else to go, I didn't feel like I could just put him out of the flat. He says he's figuring something out, but I've heard that too many times.'

'Sounds complicated.'

'You betcha. At least you're informed.'

'I appreciate it,' and I did. I'd be kidding myself if I thought you could get to my age without accumulating a little, or often a lot, of baggage and as things went, this wasn't the worst.

We finished our meal and walked back towards the city centre, the noise and the crowds. A check of my watch told me it was getting close to two. I walked with her to the bottom of the Royal Mile towards the Pleasance. I left her at traffic lights where we hugged and she kissed me. Not like the night we met, but there was enough in it to know I could call her again.

I felt I had a little time to play with, so I continued on past the parliament building, a slightly bonkers construction, but there was something about the intentional avoidance of the austere about it that I liked. Two pairs of armed police patrolled the outside and I felt sorry for them; how boring must that be? Though they'd probably say the same about a community sergeant working out of Drylaw.

Morgan had spent the past two days working with Vikram while I'd been off. He'd chapped at my door before muster, holding a crime report in his hand and looking like a boy about to show his parents the A he'd earned at school.

Vikram stood behind him, a little fatherly pride in his face. They'd tidied up a theft at the local supermarket, having recognised the shoplifter on CCTV as a local scrote. Vikram was quick to point out that Morgan had taken the interview and it had led to an admission, or at least some sense of resignation, from the suspect and he'd accepted his guilt.

'That's good work, Morgan. How did it feel?'

'It was magic. Really felt like I'd done something right.'

I felt a pang of guilt. I realised this was coming from his little error with Colander McStay. I should have made more of an effort to assure him that it really hadn't mattered.

'Two drug possession cases last night too,' said Vikram, sounding more fatherly by the moment.

'That's great. Where did they come from?'

'We went to the chippy last night for our dinner,' Morgan said. 'There's a bunch of lads outside, bold as brass, passing round a joint. A few ran off, but we rounded up four of them and found a decent lump of weed on the two older ones.'

'I showed Morgan how to use the presumptive test kits. We'll write up the reports today.'

'That's great, really. Morgan, I'll see you at muster.' He took the hint and left me with Vikram for a moment. 'Fatherhood must be honing those nurturing skills,' I said as the door was pulled over.

'He just needs showing where to direct that enthusiasm. He's actually good to work with. There's no bravado about him, no swagger like you see with some recruits. Makes him easy to teach.'

'I think you're doing yourself a disservice. Teaching is not an easy skill. Listen, how would you feel if we sort you out as a tutor constable? It looks good on your record if you ever fancy your stripes down the line. There's a bit of training involved, but nothing you can't handle.'

'Yeah. I mean, sure. Though I wasn't angling for anything—'

'I know. Part of my job is to see and develop potential and besides, I've been a bit distracted with a few things lately, I haven't been devoting the time to him I should be. Between the two of us maybe we'll pull him kicking and screaming through his probation. Agreed?'

'Yeah. Agreed.'

For a moment I thought he was going to reach across the table and shake my hand, but instead he shuffled awkwardly from the room saying thanks too many times.

I was printing off the last few days' incident lists to chat through with the team when my door opened. If it was Vikram back with more gratitude I might have withdrawn the offer, but it was Alyson. She looked beyond tired. Her eyes seemed shrunken, as though I'd always seen her with glasses on and now she'd suddenly taken them off.

'What did you just say to that guy to put that kind of smile on his face?' she said.

'Eh?'

'I just passed a guy in the hall, I'm assuming he came from here, doing a decent impression of the Cheshire cat.'

'Oh, nothing. A microscopic promotion of sorts.'

'You can do that?'

'Not exactly, but I can get the ball rolling for him.

Anyway, what are you doing here?'

'Put the kettle on and I'll tell you.'

'I can't, Aly, some of us have work to do. I need to muster the troops.' I stood and gathered the printed sheets.

'Muster? You're going to alert them to another shopping trolley in the river, or how Mrs Jenkins' lawn is being ruined by her neighbour's cat always shitting in it?'

'Well, that cat's not going to arrest itself. I'll be ten minutes, which gives you enough time to find the kettle.'

To my shock and awe, Aly had done just that. A cup of tea sat waiting for me on my desk when I returned, though she was sat in my chair. I perched myself on the edge of the desk and drank.

'Hey, is it tonight you've got that date?' she said.

I hushed her and closed the door over. 'It was earlier today.'

'Why the secrecy? You're embarrassed that your team know you're human?'

'No, it's not that, it's just a little awkward with Morgan . . . and anyway, don't you have a serial killer to catch?'

'Oh, if my boss heard you use that word . . .' she sucked air through her teeth and shook her head.

'Well, it's what the papers are calling it now. It's all over the place.'

'That's sort of why I'm here. I needed a little breather. There were a couple of menial tasks on the action lists and I offered to tidy them up. I just needed to be out of that office.'

'So, you thought you'd come skive with me?'

'Now you're getting it. First thing is real coffee, though. How does anyone drink this shit?' It looked like she'd found Mandy's box of instant-cappuccino sachets. They were better than regular instant coffee, but not much. She pushed the cup away from her and intertwined her fingers like a cartoon nemesis. 'How did the date go?' She even had an evil half-smile for the full effect.

'It went fine. It was just lunch.'

'What did you talk about?'

'You, most of the afternoon.'

'Really?'

'No, you bloody narcissist. Right, come on then, I really do have some work I need to get to, so coffee and then I'm sending you off on your lonesome.'

'Fine,' she said, vacating my chair with a sigh.


'How are you? Really?' I said as we got in the car and pulled out of the station. 'It must be pretty bad for you to need some time out.'

'I'm just tired. If I could take a few days off I'm sure I'd feel a lot better, but it's just not possible right now. Coffee first, then I'll tell you about it.'

Maxine's Cafe was on Silverknowes Road, just a few minutes away. I'd stopped in there a few times and thought the coffee was pretty good, but I was no connoisseur like Aly. I suggested we sit in, but she said she'd prefer to stay in the car.

She lifted the lid on her takeaway cup, gave it a sniff and drank. There were no comments or nose wrinkling, so I guessed it had passed the test. I drove on with no destination in mind.

'I guess the press getting their hands on this connection puts a lot of pressure on?'

'You've no idea. I think Kate's only just holding on by a thread. You should see people in the office hiding from her, it's becoming toxic.'

'I'd guessed things had become difficult. I haven't seen you this past week. I wasn't even sure if you were still staying.'

'Some nights. But others I've just felt like I needed my own bed and there was one where I worked all night and then shut my eyes in my car, only to come round six hours later and go straight back to work. The place is chaos again and Kate's at risk of losing charge – as soon as the news stories broke, the upper tier started asking a lot of questions, like why the fuck were we working out of a few small rooms in Leith. They threw bodies at it. Staff Kate didn't want. The official line is the enquiry team is based at Fettes Headquarters, but really that's just where Kate has sent anyone who's come in lately and gave them all the shite tasks. As it stands, we still have a relatively small team at Leith, but she'll only get away with that as long as she has something to report back.'

'You need to look after yourself, Aly. Any breakthroughs?'

'We thought we had – thanks to you, actually – but we're not so sure now.'

'Me? What do you mean?'

'That chat we had. I'd been thinking about it and I decided to go interview the Bradley boy's grandfather. It threw up a link to priests. We crunched the info for days but there's nothing we can find to link to our particular priest.

Kate went from ecstatic to dejected and is now verging on homicidal.'

'Sounds tough, but I tell you, I'd love to be working that case.'

'No, you only think you do, trust me.'

'Maybe. Anyway, I can't really take credit for that lead, even if it does turn out to be a dead end. I think I got the idea from our man at the nursing home.'

'Nonsense, it was your chain of thought, not some spooky old man.'

'Shit,' I said. I looked around, not quite sure where we currently were.

'What?'

'Our spooky old man, I think today's his birthday.'

'So?'

'His eightieth birthday.'

'Yeah, he's old.'

'Oh, come on, eightieth! That's a big deal. I promised myself I'd go see him when it came around.'

'You're talking about going now, aren't you?' Her head rolled on her shoulder towards me, one eyebrow raised.

'In and out in ten minutes. Promise.'

'Uh-huh,' she said, rolling her head back to the window.

I stopped at a Co-op for a bottle of whisky. I didn't know if he drank it, or whether the staff would let him have it if he did, but it seemed appropriate. I don't know much about the stuff but recognised one bottle with a good reputation. When the guy behind the till rang up the Glenmorangie, I nearly fell over. I wasn't too proud to ask for a cheaper option.

\* \* \*

There was an ambulance parked at the rear of the care home so I stopped on the street. At the door Vicky and Michelle were helping Mimi out the ambulance and into a wheelchair, but she was having none of it. 'Buckin-noway-bastard-chair-fucknasos-buck-basas.'

'OK fine then, Mimi, but take Michelle's arm and go get yourself some cake, hen.'

'Everything all right?' I said.

'Hi, yes. Mimi had a fall in the shower this morning. I didn't think anything was broken, but we sent her down to the hospital to get her arm checked anyway. That's her just getting dropped back. Thanks guys,' Vicky said to the two paramedics. They closed over the back door of the ambulance and gave her a wave before reversing out.

'You mentioned cake. Is that for Martin? Am I right in thinking it's his birthday?' I said.

'It *is* his birthday. You've stopped by to see him?'

'I have. I just wanted to drop a little something in for him, if that's OK?' I suddenly realised I'd left the bottle in the car, but Alyson appeared just then, holding it.

The news pushed a grin onto Vicky's, still painful looking, face. Her lip was healing, but a substantial scab still remained. There didn't appear to be any fresh injuries. 'Come on in,' she said and took the bottle from Alyson as she pushed it out to her.

'You remember Al— eh, DC Kane?'

'Sure, I do. Come on in. He'll be fair chuffed to see you. Now, we don't normally allow residents the hard stuff, but I'm sure I can sneak him a wee snifter at some point.'

Most of the residents were gathered in the day room. A

few wore paper hats and the television was turned to some music channel playing hits from the sixties.

'Martin's by the window, why don't you go sit with him. There's spare chairs behind the door. Can I bring you something to drink?'

'We're fine, thanks, Vicky. We're in and out in ten minutes I'm afraid,' said Alyson, though she was looking at me. We each took a plastic chair and made our way across the room.

'What happened to her?' Alyson asked.

'It's, eh . . . I'll tell you later,' I said and drew my chair up to Martin's leg. I could tell immediately that the lights were on, but nobody was at home. His face hung in that way I saw the first time I met him. His paper hat sat at an angle on his white hair and the elastic looked a little tight under his chin. His eyes stared off to some spot in the middle of the room.

I patted his hand and spoke to him nonetheless. 'Happy birthday, Martin. Can I help you with that?' a slice of cake sat on the windowsill by his head, half eaten, and a plastic fork jammed straight up in its centre. I removed the hat and nudged the loaded fork at his bottom lip. He opened his mouth. 'It looks pretty good, chocolate and what is that? Raspberry?' he chewed. Alyson sat staring at her phone.

Vicky appeared with two more paper plates with cake and plastic forks. I accepted mine, but Alyson muttered a 'no thanks' without even glancing up.

'How has he been?' I asked.

She smiled, though it was thin. 'He's OK. Aren't you, Martin? He's lost a bit of weight lately but there's nothing obviously wrong. Just the dementia progressing, I suppose. Your Alan called this morning, didn't he? We arranged a video call and he at least got to wish his dad a happy birthday.'

'Well, that's something. Martin, I brought you a bottle of something, perhaps later Vicky will let you have a little. Anyway, I hope you enjoy the rest of your birthday,' I said and laid down the cake he was no longer interested in. 'We better get going,' I said to Vicky, but she wasn't listening. Her eyes were to the window. I became increasingly aware of the sound of a growling exhaust from outside.

Michelle came into the room at something of a jog, her face dark with concern. 'Vic,' she said.

'It's OK, Michelle. Eh, thanks for popping in,' she said to Alyson and myself. Aly had put down her phone, aware of the tension forming.

'Vic, if you don't tell them I will. I'm sorry, but something needs to be done,' said Michelle.

'Vicky, what's going on?' I said.

'It's nothing. It's fine,' she said and as her mouth stretched and her eyes closed it was clear it was far from fine. Tears started to roll down her cheeks.

I took her shoulders gently. 'I'm guessing that's Darren outside. Have there been more incidents?' I asked.

Vicky couldn't talk, but Michelle could. 'That's him all right. After the last time she broke it off, went to stay at her mum's. Since then he's been coming around here, trying to speak to her. Sometimes he just sits out there for hours. Vic won't let me call the police, but I tell you what, I'm glad you're here. This has to stop, Vic. You know that.'

Alyson was now on her feet, her fists on her hips. 'So, this is what? An ex-husband, boyfriend, whatever, outside – harassing you? And he did this to your face?'

'Not just that,' said Michelle. 'It's been going on a few years. Barely a week goes by when she's not coming to work with some new cut or bruise.'

'Oh, no. No, no, no,' said Alyson.

'Aly, where you going? Hey, wait a minute,' I said, but she was striding for the door.

'No, please don't, he can be . . .' said Vicky though the tears. Alyson was already gone.

I let go of Vicky and went to the window. 'Oh shit,' I whispered and started running.

'Oh God. Has he hurt her?' said Vicky, but that wasn't the concern, not in slightest.

I fumbled at the entrance as I looked for the button to release the door. When I wrenched it open, I had a close-up view of what I'd seen from the window.

Alyson was raining punches through the driver window. Her elbow shot back and forth like a piston and she was snarling 'fucker!' through clenched teeth with each blow. I sprinted outside and grabbed her by the shoulder. She got one more strike in before I could prise her away from the blue Subaru. Blue on the outside, but now red inside. The window started to squeak its way up, but not before I got a good look at a stunned Darren. His nose was a mess across his already swollen face. Streaks of blood covered his white T-shirt and I could even see spots on the windshield. He stared at me with wide eyes for a moment before putting the car in gear and skidding out of the carpark.

'Jesus, Aly! What the fuck? Shit, look at your hand.'

Alyson's face was stone. She spat on the ground and then examined her knuckles, flexing her fingers open and closed. 'Don't worry, I think it's all him,' she said, wiping at the blood and panting a little.

Faces stared from the office and at the far side there was a commotion at the window of the day room. 'We'll need to get our stories straight,' I said and led her back inside.

'There won't be a complaint. Pricks like that are nothing but cowards. Trust me, I know. Later he'll be too embarrassed to have been beaten by a woman to mention this to a soul.'

I took her to the kitchen area and ran the cold tap. She hissed with pain as she pushed her hand under the stream. Most of the blood ran off, but there were some cuts and swelling.

'I'll find you a towel and some ice,' I said. There was nothing obvious to hand, so I went looking for a staff member for a little help. As I made my way back along the corridor, the noise from the dayroom was getting louder. They must have been watching the violence and got upset, I thought, but all the noise was coming from Martin. The other residents were being moved clear by Michelle while Vicky struggled to restrain him.

I moved to help her. Placing my hands on Martin's shoulders to try to stop him getting to his feet. His face was furious and he was yelling, over and over, 'Bastard, cut out her tongue, cut out her tongue. Bastard, cut out her tongue . . .'

# CHAPTER NINETEEN

## Wise Monkeys

'Do you want to talk about what just happened?'

'The old fella having a fit?' Alyson said. She was running her left hand over the raw knuckles of her right as I drove. Her head rested against the side window. She hadn't said a word in five minutes, but then again, neither had I. My head was still repeating Martin's words, but it was the image of the blood-spattered interior of the Subaru that I was trying to address. 'You're going to try to make a big deal about it, but don't. Sorry, but I don't want to hear it.'

'Hold on, are you talking about Martin, or are we now talking about the assault?'

'Assault? You know that in the definition of "assault" there is the defence of *self*-defence and that it can used by a third-party protecting a victim.'

'You *are* worried he's going to make a complaint. This is

what you've been thinking about.'

She looked at me for a second, there was worry there. 'Maybe I got a bit carried away.' She wiped at her face, pushed the palm of her healthy hand into each eye and yawned.

'You're sleep deprived and stressed out. Aly, I've never seen you do anything like that.'

There was a minute of silence before she spoke again. 'Do you think he'll go to the police? I could lose my job.' Her voice was unsteady, her eyes were beginning to shine.

'I think it's like you said. He won't want anyone to know what happened to him. And if he does, well, you and me will sit down and figure out what really happened a long time before professional standards get involved.'

'I wouldn't involve you.'

'I was there, so that's not a choice. Look, just forget about it until there's something to worry about. Try to put it out of your mind. But what was going through your mind when you approached the car?'

The fingers of her hand touched her brow and then gestured out in front of her, baffled. 'I think I was going out there to scream in his face. Then, as I left the building, he saw me and his window started lowering. He had this smug look on his face and the next thing I knew my fingers were digging into my palm. I planted one hand on the door and then I just wanted to slam that look off his face. And then I wanted to do it again and again.'

'Even before that though, the second you found out what had been going on, you were furious. I've rarely seen rage like it. In case you didn't know, I'm a cop – I'm used to angry people.'

We reached the station. I pulled into the rear yard and turned off the engine. I removed my belt and had just opened my door when I felt Alyson's hand on my forearm. I closed it back over.

'I had this boyfriend when I was at uni. Real prick. I met him when I was in first year. He was in third, was a few years older and had sort of figured the whole uni thing out. We ended up moving in together. At the time I didn't see things developing, though looking back now it's perfectly clear. All the little controlling behaviours. So, when he hit me for the first time, it didn't really come as a shock. I'll save you all the details, but it took nearly a year and a deep fucking depression to get shot of him. I started going to the gym, mostly to fight the depression, but I think it also had to do with finding a way to never feel that vulnerable again. Anyway, something snapped in that old place. Something that has been in a box for a very long time. There, now I've told you and we don't have to talk about it again. OK?'

Her hand was still on my arm. I patted it and she pulled away, wincing.

'Ah, shit, sorry.' I then started laughing, and soon she was laughing too. She punched me on the shoulder and I got a very small, but nonetheless painful, insight into what that fucker's face took.

Alyson left to complete her tasks before heading back to Leith. The tasks that I had set out for myself had gone completely out of my mind. I sat down at my desk, took a single sheet of paper from the printer tray and wrote:

*'Bastard cut out her tongue!'*

I stared at it for a long time. Exactly how long, I didn't

know. It wasn't until Vikram knocked my door and asked if I wanted something picked up for my dinner that I realised how late it was getting. I thanked him but refused; my stomach was not in a good way. When I was alone again, I took my notebook from my pocket and scoured for the passages I had written after seeing Martin. Above the line I had written on the sheet, I added a statement. I flicked back further and added another line, then put down my pen and looked at what I had:

*'What kind of a monster could cut his eyes out?'*
*'How can he hear the word of God?'*
*'Bastard cut out her tongue!'*

After a few minutes, I lifted the pen once more and at the bottom wrote three more lines.

*See No Evil*
*Hear No Evil*
*Speak No Evil*

I left a little early, heading home before 10 p.m. with the day's events still rattling around in my head. For once I found a space near to the flat. There was still some light in the sky; not much, but a purple glow underlit thin clouds. As hard as Scottish winters could be, this was the payoff – long summer days. I'd heard that they play a midnight golf tournament on Shetland and I could believe it.

As I descended to the basement flat, I could see that there was a light on in the hall. I assumed Alyson had done herself a favour after the earlier drama and come home at a reasonable hour, but no.

'What are *you* doing here?' I said, dropping my bag in the hall.

Dad looked at me like I'd asked the most absurd question. 'This is still my flat, last I checked,' he said. He was holding a bundle of clothes and I followed him through to the living room where a suitcase was lying open on the sofa.

'Of course. I just meant . . . well, I just didn't expect to see you.'

'I came to gather some things. Heading back to Heather's later.'

'It's going well, then?'

'Aye, it's going well. How are you? I was just about to put the kettle on.'

He pushed a handful of boxer shorts down the side of the larger bundle in the middle of the case and wrestled the zip shut.

'Actually, I think I'll need something stronger tonight,' I said and rubbed at my face, trying to awaken tired muscles.

'One of those days?' he said and then paused, his eyes searching the ceiling in thought. 'You fancy going to the pub?'

'Oh, I don't know, Faither, it's been a really long day.'

'All the more reason. You get changed, even with a coat on, it's clear yer fuzz, and I'll call the missus.'

'"The Missus", aye?' I said, my voice trailing higher at the end than was kind. 'Fine, I suppose a few pints wouldn't hurt.'

I came back to the hall as Dad was finishing his call. 'All right, love. I have a key, aye.' There was a brief pause and his eyes shot to me, before he turned his back and said, as quietly as he thought he might get away with it, 'Love you too.'

I stifled a smile. 'Ready?'

Dad turned left at the top of the stairs, which meant we were going to go to the Cumberland bar, as opposed to the St Vincent.

'It's a braw evening, do you want to sit outside?' he said as we approached the bar.

'With that lot? No danger.' A large crowd of student types dominated much of the beer garden seating area. One of them showed the group something on his phone, which prompted an eruption of raucous laughter. My head ached just looking at them.

Inside was much more civilised. Busy, but not so busy we wouldn't be able to sit. The bar stretched back to a restaurant section, but we took a table by the window with our pints.

'How is Alyson liking the flat?' he asked.

'Fine, when she's here. Been missing her own bed lately and this case she's working on has her in the office most of the time. We barely see one another.'

'What case is that?'

'*The* case, Dad.'

'Oh, you mean the, the thing with the boy and the—'

'Yes, that one.'

'Oh, I see. Are they close to catching the bastard?' he whispered, though there was no real need. Three out of the four tables in our area were occupied, but they were all having fairly robust conversations of their own, having been in the pub a good while longer than us.

'I'm not sure. I don't think so. Besides, I can't really talk about it.'

'How?' he said. This always made me wince. Some areas of Scotland where the word was used instead of 'why'.

'You know *why*. All this stuff is highly confidential.'

'But *you're* no working on it, are you?'

The question caught me a bit by surprise. I thought again of the piece of paper on my desk at work, of Martin and of Alyson. 'I've had some involvement, just a little.'

Dad shifted in his chair opposite me. He looked excited. 'I didn't know that. I thought you were community police, or whatever.'

'I am, but when you have a major inquiry like this, resources get pulled in from all over. Seems everyone has a part to play.' Dad said something, but I missed it. *Everyone has a part to play*, I'd just said. Alyson had no time for this thing with Martin and likely she was right, but I couldn't shake it. I was trying to remember how long between these strange incidents at the care home and something happening. What was it? Twenty-two and twenty-three days?

'Oy,' Dad said and nudged my arm. I looked up from wherever I was. 'I said are you having another?'

'Aye, sure. Thanks.'

He got up and took our empties with him, grumbling about getting better conversation from the barmaid.

I had three choices. One, I let this thing go, assuming it was nonsense and take comfort in the fact that those dealing with the case know what they're doing. Two, I try again to convince Alyson, though that seemed even more far-fetched than these coincidences actually meaning something. Or, there was option three.

There was a small thump as Dad laid down my glass in front of me. 'What is it you're daydreaming about?'

'I'm just thinking about some work I need to do, starting tomorrow,' I said.

# CHAPTER TWENTY

## Pushing Forward

*I have to make more of an effort*, Alyson thought, only now seeing Don's text from last night.

GOING TO THE PUB WITH DAD. SURE YOU'LL BE TOO BUSY, BUT IF YOU GET OFF EARLY ENOUGH, COME JOIN US FOR A BEER. X

She made a mental note to respond later and slid her phone discreetly back into her pocket under the desk. She'd do it now, but she couldn't risk what kind of mood Kate might be in. A week ago they'd been waiting for her to arrive for the morning meeting, just like this, and Adrian was checking whatever on his phone. She'd chewed him up and left him red-faced and bewildered. It was only luck that it hadn't been her, she'd been on her screen only moments before, as all of them had done on any number of occasions when Kate came in previously, and she hadn't uttered a word of complaint.

Like Alyson, one or two were risking a glance under the table. Otherwise they all sat in silence, save for the occasional sip from their morning brew of choice. Alyson tried to count everyone. There were eight of them seated around the table with a crowd, two-people thick in places, gathered behind. There were also a few chapping away at terminals, taking the risk of getting some work done before Kate arrived. Alyson estimated nineteen, give or take.

The door crashed against the opposite wall as Kate strode in. There was a dusting of white powder collecting on the carpet underneath where the handle struck the plaster each time she flung open the door. Since every inch of the place was covered in sensitive material, cleaners were not allowed access to the entire floor and it was unlikely any of them would go hunting for a vacuum cleaner anytime soon.

'Talk to me about the van, Duncan,' Kate barked. She laid her coffee down and hung her coat over the back of her chair. She sat and started pulling folders from her bag.

He stood and nervously adjusted his tie. 'There's nothing to report, ma'am. We have a dedicated team physically eyeballing as many vehicles registered in the central belt that have business insurance attached as we can. There were one or two maybes, but they had air-tight alibis and one promising hit, but it went nowhere.'

'Tell me about that.'

'A spark, out by Falkirk. He wasn't able—'

245

'Spark? What the fuck are you on about?'

'Sorry ma'am, an electrician. The graphics on his van included a hammer, but only as a small part of a whole bunch of tools in a bag. You'd have been hard-pressed to pick it out if you weren't looking for it. Anyway, he had no real alibi to speak of. We looked into it, even seized the van, until he remembered going to a KFC drive-through near Bridge of Allan on the night in question. Bank checks and CCTV confirm. I checked and double-checked the timeline, it's possible to make that journey and make it fit, but you'd need to be doing a solid ninety.'

'You got the van checked by SOCO anyway?'

'Of course, ma'am. There had been no attempt to clean the interior of the vehicle in some time and no hits. There's nothing about this guy that would give rise to suspicion.'

'Phone records?'

'We're checking, yes. He gave permission and has been cooperative at every stage. He's not our guy.'

'Fine, but don't lose sight of him, just in case.'

'Ma'am,' said Duncan in confirmation and sat.

'Cross referencing. Where are we with HOLMES?'

*Fuck*, thought Alyson, and stood. 'Nothing new, ma'am. We've gone through every place victim number two has worked and the same for the grandfather of victim number one. The word "priest" is the only link established. We're gathering more information every day and, of course, I will bring anything new to you the second it comes in.'

Kate looked at her, then down at her notes. Alyson was lowering back into her chair when Kate cleared her throat.

Alyson rose once more. After a short period of silence and with all the eyes in the room switching between the two women, Kate spoke.

'You brought us this lead, DC Kane. I can't tell you how impressed I was that day when it landed on us. But you're not going to go and disappoint me now, are you?'

'Uh, no, ma'am. I'm on it. I promise—'

'CCTV. Talk to me.'

Alyson sat awkwardly as the DS from the CCTV team stood and began delivering a similarly impotent update. Duncan looked like he wanted to say something to her, but daren't. Instead he widened his eyes at her. She returned the gesture and tried to settle her pulse.

I looked at the date I'd circled on the calendar hanging on the kitchen wall: the tenth of September. If Alyson asked why I'd circled it, I decided it was my mum's birthday. The fact that her birthday was the twenty-second of January was neither here nor there. I'd counted twenty-one days from Martin's latest outburst, this being the shortest of the two periods between an episode and an attack. I'd circled it last night with a sense of purpose and determination. However, in the cold light of day it felt silly. What were the chances of there being anything to this theory? And if I *did* do what I was thinking about doing, what would that mean for my career?

'What the fuck are you doing?' I said aloud and fell into a chair with my tea clutched to my chest. I looked at the green circle, twenty days and counting. 'Counting to what?' *Counting to some poor bastard having their tongue cut out.* 'Are you really going to risk your job because some old man's been having bad dreams?' I put down the tea, being careful where to lay it. Alyson's paperwork was still spread all over the table. *But what if you do nothing? What if you do nothing and it's another child?*

I drained the remainder of the tea and climbed on top of the chair, so I could get the whole table surface into the camera of the phone. *It must look exactly like this after you're done. She'd kill you if she knew anything about this.*

There was no particular order to anything and what was there was likely to be just a fraction of the case material at Leith, but there was absolutely no chance I could get to any of that, so I'd just need to use what I could find. Alyson herself could be in some deep trouble if anyone got wind that she had this stuff here. I guessed a mixture of tiredness and desperation had resulted in her failure to follow protocol. Besides, the way she'd described her boss, it was likely you'd find a similar scene in her home, too.

There was a recent statement taken from the grandfather. I took a photo of it, as well as some notes on addresses on a final sheet. There was a whole bunch of statements bundled together from Father McCauley's congregation, tethered by a large, red elastic band. There was a post-it note on the front in Alyson's handwriting that read 'Waste of time'. Given my own limited time, I decided to trust her judgement and left it alone. There were DVLA printouts, but no real explanation why. There was a file marked 'Fr McCauley work history'. Not much in there, but it's likely this was an important avenue to explore and I imagined there would be much more of it in the office. I photographed what was there. There were technical notes on the locus at Rickerburn and at the church in Leith; I snapped them along with the initial statements from the witnesses who discovered the bodies in both murders. There were also statements from the immediate family and friends of Callum Bradley, as well as another combined pile of statements from classmates and teachers. It was all too much to go through and Aly would have mentioned something if there was anything to see, so I let it go too. What I had would have to do. I returned the documents as well as I could remember and then checked the picture I'd taken to make the final few adjustments. If Alyson noticed that anything was out of place, well, she'd left them on the kitchen table, nothing that couldn't be explained away.

When I got to work, there had been another report of cowboy workmen; something the uniform shift had left for us under the flimsy excuse that we were already dealing with something similar. Morgan hadn't seemed bothered – quite the opposite. He saw it as an opportunity to gather more evidence on his own case, and perhaps it was. Vikram had been given the go-ahead to train as a tutor constable and I left Morgan in his hands. Mandy had her own thing on and so I was left alone to read through everything I'd captured earlier. If there was any part of me that had hoped to find some glaring hole in a well-trained and well-run major investigation team's efforts, it was quickly disappointed. Even from the scant details I could gather from the kitchen table, everything had been scrutinised time and time again. I didn't know where to start. Even if I did, should I?

*Fuck it*, I thought. *Let's just kick the tires and see what happens.* I ran through the pictures on my phone and stopped at a statement that was taken from close by. Close by, but dangerously close to the Leith office.

I parked down a side street and walked the short distance to Elm Place, one of these colony-style back-to-back streets that were common in the capital. The houses were packed tightly together with small front gardens. The address was a particularly well-kept example, even sporting a tiny greenhouse on the mowed patch of lawn. I rang the bell and was met with an older lady, who smiled warmly.

'Josephine Wilson?' I asked.

'That's right.'

'I'm sorry to bother you, and I hope I haven't come at a bad time. I was wondering if I might have a chat with you?'

'Is this about Father McCauley?'

'Yes. I appreciate you've been spoken to before—'

'Three times now,' she interjected, but not unkindly. I actually had no idea how many times she'd been called on, all I had was her initial statement. This really was looking more and more like a fool's errand.

'It's just a few follow-up questions, Mrs Wilson. It wouldn't take long.'

'Call me Nan. Go through to the kitchen, it's on the right,' she said and pushed the door wide. I wiped my feet and entered. There was a young girl sitting on a stool by the countertop.

'Hello,' I said. She looked bashful. There was a smile, but then she went back to eating her scone and jam.

'This is Poppy,' said Nan. The granddaughter, I deduced, as Nan came in behind me to fill the kettle at the sink.

'Nice to meet you, Poppy. How old are you?'

'You can answer him, love. What does this man do for a living?'

'A policeman,' Poppy said.

'How do you know he's a policeman?' said Nan.

''Cause of the clothes,' the girl said. She was staring at the items on my belt.

'Do you want to try this on?' I said and took off my hat.

Poppy looked to Nan for confirmation and then nodded. I placed it on her head, it came down over one eye. She giggled and straightened it.

'Poppy is six. Her mum's due to pick her up any minute, then we can chat.'

By the time I was nearing the bottom of my cup of tea, Poppy had come out of her shell, telling me all about her school and how a policewoman had come to her class with a sniffer dog one day. 'We weren't allowed to pet him, 'cause he's not a pet,' she said.

'That's right. They've got an important job to do, don't they,' I said.

Her mother arrived and froze when she entered the kitchen. 'It's nothing to worry about,' I assured her. 'It's a couple of follow-up questions for your mum.'

Poppy was full of smiles as she waved goodbye. I could hear Nan's daughter whispering in the hall, asking if she was OK and if she should stay. She was soon shooed out.

'Another cup before we begin?' Nan said.

'No, thank you. I really won't keep you long.' She gestured at the table and we sat. As we did, I thought about where to begin.

'That must have been a hell of a shock, finding Father McCauley?'

Nan was using her hand to sweep together a few crumbs from the table surface. 'I was a nurse, a long time ago, I've seen my share of blood, but I can't say it prepared me for that.'

'I'm sorry that you had to see it. We're working very hard to catch the person responsible.'

'Is it true it's the same person that killed that child?'

There was no point in denying it, she'd read it in any one of a dozen newspapers. 'I'm afraid that appears to be the case. So, as you can imagine, we're throwing every resource at this.'

'Is that why you're here and not one of the detectives?'

'Yes,' I lied, and was glad she'd given me a plausible explanation herself. 'Can you think of a reason anyone would want to do this to Father McCauley?' It was broad brush question, and unlikely to yield anything useful; its purpose was simply to get the conversation started.

'Not one. He was a gentle man. I said as much to your colleagues. I don't remember him ever having an argument with a living soul, a falling out of any kind.'

I thought about the statement I'd read, and about the two I hadn't, trying to find some angle that hadn't been covered. 'Is it possible he had any personal debts he was hiding?'

'As I said to the detective who was here last time, I can't tell you for certain, I guess everyone has a secret, even priests, but no, there was nothing about his behaviour that gave me that impression. Aren't you going to write this down?' she said.

'No, I thought we'd just keep this fairly informal this time, if that's OK?'

'Yes, this is already going so much quicker. Having to stop to let the person write down every word is tedious. But I know this is important,' she said and pulled the gathered crumbs off the table and into her hand before leaning over and dropping them into the bin.

'No, I get that. It's not great having to do the writing down either, trust me. Is there anything you weren't asked, that you feel maybe should have been? Anything you feel we ought to know?' This was a little desperate on my part, but I was already running out of ideas.

'I can't think of anything. I feel like I've been asked so much, even a lot of uncomfortable stuff. I'm hoping we don't have to go through that again.'

'Such as?'

'This stuff about kids. "Is it possible Father McCauley was involved is some sort of . . ." well, you know.'

'So, you discount that entirely?'

'Entirely. While I didn't know him all that well, I'd be horrified to hear of any sort of connection like that.

I wouldn't believe it. I've never seen him with a child beyond saying hello after service. Never.'

'Who did he consort with? Who were his friends?'

'He didn't have much of a life outside of the Church. He'd get the occasional visitor. He played bridge on a Thursday evening with another priest and a few of the church elders.'

'Were you able to give the names of these people to the detectives who were here before?'

'Yes.'

'Anyone else? Did he even mention someone in passing you weren't familiar with?'

She thought on this, pursing her lips and staring out the window, but then shook her head.

'Any other visitors to the manse, other than this bridge club? Anyone at all?'

'Well, yes, but nobody regular. I mean he's the priest, he gets visitors. The odd member of the congregation and there was the odd visit from other priests, all the stuff you'd expect.'

'Again, were you able to give details of these visitors?' Her eyebrows creased for a second and I suddenly felt I'd been found out. I'd know this stuff if I'd read all of the statements. 'I know I'm repeating previous work, but we're just trying to be as thorough as we can.'

'I couldn't be specific about the congregation, I wasn't introduced to anybody really, so I couldn't help there, but I tried to describe anyone I could remember.' I thought about the large pile of statements marked as uninteresting by Alyson. 'The priests he'd usually introduce me to and

I have a good memory for names, so I was able to pass that on.'

It had all been asked. I don't know why I thought I'd get more, but at least I tried. And if anything did happen, I hoped I could take some comfort in that.

'Nan, thank you very much for your time, and for the tea. I know it's not pleasant having to think about this stuff over and over, so I really do appreciate it.' I stood and looked around for my hat, unsure where Poppy had laid it. I found it sitting jauntily on a melon.

'It's fine. I really do hope you catch this person soon and so I'm only happy to be of help, though I doubt I've been that, really.'

'At this stage all information is useful.'

She stood too, using the back of the chair for leverage and breathing out hard. I held out my hand and she took it, leaning on me to get straight.

'I wouldn't recommend it,' she said.

'What's that?'

'Getting old. If someone offers it to you, you tell them no.'

I laughed. 'I'll do that. Just before I leave, I think you just said that when Father McCauley had priests at the house, he *usually* introduced you.'

'Did I? Well, yes.'

'Usually, but not always?'

'What was I thinking when I said that?' She scratched at an ear. 'Well, yes, there was one time when he didn't, or at least one time that I can remember.' I'd just popped in with some shopping and he had a guest. I never caught his name.'

'What do you remember about him?'

'Blonde, he was. Like really blonde. Bit younger than Father McCauley, but not young, and it was maybe that he only looked younger with all that blonde hair. He seemed nice enough.'

'Why do you think he didn't introduce you?'

'I don't know. I mean I was only planning to pop in for a second, I was just passing with some heavy bags and I didn't fancy taking them all the way home only to heave them back the following day. I surprised him, I suppose. It was a Monday you see, and Sunday and Monday I don't go in. Not normally.'

'How did Father McCauley seem?'

'Surprised, like I said. Maybe a wee bit embarrassed, he was in his usual half-dressed way. But don't go reading anything into that. More often than not he'd be searching for his trousers when I appear in the morning. I'd had words with him about it.'

'Sorry to ask, but nothing, you know, hanging out or—'

'No, no. Nothing like that.'

'So, it was normal for you to see him half-dressed when you pop round, as you did most days pretty early. But if he had a visitor, did you ever see him like that? Not fully clothed?'

Again, her eyes went to the window. 'No, I suppose not.'

'And what sort of time was it this particular day when you popped in? Still really early?'

'Not on a Monday. I meet a few ladies for coffee after I drop Poppy at school. It was before midday probably, but around that time.'

'And you've never seen this blonde priest before or since that day?'

'No. I'd have remembered that hair. Lovely it was.'

'How much of this did you mention to the detectives before?'

'I think maybe I mentioned it. I can't be sure, I'm sorry. But you'll have all that back at the police station?'

'Yes, of course. Thanks again for your time, Nan.'

# CHAPTER TWENTY-ONE

## Hangover

I wasn't quite sure what to expect from Ethiopian food. Having grown up watching the plight of the country on television through fundraising events and concerts, I'd failed to ever think about their customs and what the cuisine might be like. In fact, when Marcella had suggested dinner over text and I'd asked what sort of place she might like to go to, I thought for a second her reply was some kind of a joke in the poorest taste; that maybe I'd misjudged her as a liberal and compassionate person. In fact, the restaurant on Morrison Street was quite lovely.

I'd left the ordering to her since she'd been there before and soon an enormous flat bread that reminded me of a dosa but on an epic scale, was laid between us. Upon the flatbread was various pastes, dips and salad. Our drinks sat precariously at the very edge of the table.

'You're into the new flat then?' I said, ripping a corner from the bread and scooping up one of the dips.

'Yes, thank God. It's costing a fortune with renting this flat and paying the mortgage on the other, but it's worth it to be out of that place.' There was a definite lift in her mood. Not that the previous times we'd met she'd been morose or melancholy, but there was a brightness about her now, as if she'd had the first good sleep in a long time.

'How about you? Your dad still living with this new woman?'

'Yeah. Looks to be going well. I was worried that they'd taken this step bizarrely early, but it seems to be working out. Besides, I don't know how long they were seeing one another before he told me about it, could have been months. Perhaps it's not so strange.' I tore more bread and tried another paste, this one green and fresh.

'And what about work? You know I asked Mandy what it was your job entails. I hope you don't mind, it's just that you don't ever seem to want to talk about it. She said she doesn't really know what you get up to.'

*What I get up to?* I thought about the chat with Nan and the trip I'd arranged for tomorrow. 'There's not much to tell. The life of a community cop isn't particularly exciting, I'm sure Mandy's told you that?'

'I think it's a matter of perspective. She tells me about initiatives she gets involved in, the arrests and the car chases . . . it all sounds pretty exciting to me. She says the same thing you do, that it's mundane, but she doesn't seem to know what you do day-to-day.'

'Similar to what Mandy does, really, but with more paperwork.'

'That's it?'

'You thought dating a cop would be more interesting?'

She raised her glass to her lips and said 'Is that what we're doing? Dating?' She watched me carefully as she drank.

'It's probably the word I'd use.'

'Does that mean you're coming to see my new place after this?'

'Uh, I don't know. I thought you wanted to take things slow?'

'Well, there's slow and then there's *slow*. I thought maybe we might move things forward. But you're not sure?'

'I mean I would, it's just . . . I've got a lot on my plate right now with work and—'

'You mean the boring, mundane community cop job that's not very exciting?' She was smiling, but I felt I was perilously close to a cliff edge.

'OK,' I said and took a large gulp from my glass. 'There's some stuff going on at work, some stuff I can't talk about, I wish I could. It's constantly swimming around in my head and I think maybe it would be a bad time to, *move things forward*, as you say. Though I would like to at some point, believe me.'

She placed her elbows on the table, interlaced her fingers and rested her chin on top. 'I can't quite work you out.'

'How do you mean?'

'I get the feeling there's a lot I don't know about you. If I hadn't already been to your place, I'd be thinking maybe you were married, or at least seeing someone, but I don't think that's it.' Her eyes were slits, scrutinising me.

'No, I'm not seeing anyone. I'm sorry if I seem guarded or whatever.'

'Well, I won't press on it for now, but you can talk to me if you want to.'

I reached forward and took one of her hands. 'I know. Thanks.'

We moved on to breezier topics and shared a dessert before settling up.

Her flat in Newington was entirely the wrong direction for me, but I insisted on walking with her, deciding I'd flag down a taxi on the way back. I felt I'd taken something of a backward step with her and thought the gesture couldn't hurt. While we walked, we talked about movies we loved when we were kids, about holidays we'd taken and the conversation again circled around to her ex, and I was pretty sure I hadn't prompted it. Then we were at her door and kissing. We were soon inside, which I hadn't intended, and then I stayed the night, which I really hadn't intended.

I woke early with a start, not quite sure where I was for a moment. My view from the mattress on the floor soon reminded me. The sun spilled in through the curtainless window to shine on boxes stacked around the room; a bedside lamp perched on one next to Marcella's bare shoulder. I reached for my jeans, dragging them toward me with a foot. I fished my phone from the pocket and checked the time, five-thirty. I still felt a little drunk, having come in for one drink and staying for the rest of the bottle and half of a further one, but I knew I wasn't getting back to sleep. There was a niggling tension at my temples, the promise of a later headache. I stood up to pull up my jeans and stubbed my toe on an open suitcase which was spilling over with clothes. Marcella stirred, but didn't wake.

I finished dressing in the kitchen while the kettle boiled and I prepared two cups. I drank my tea and then brought Marcella's to the bedroom. I knelt, laid her cup next to the lamp on top of her bedside box and kissed her shoulder.

She jerked awake, her head rising and then crashing back to the pillow. 'Hey,' she said, her voice thick with sleep.

'Morning. I brought you some tea.'

'You're leaving?'

'Yeah, I have to get to work.'

She rolled onto her back and rubbed at her eyes with a yawn. 'Sorry about the morning breath, but . . .' she pulled me in for a kiss.

'I'll call you later,' I said.

'Much later.' She rolled back over and pulled the duvet around her.


I had a quick shower at home and tried to eat something, thinking about how much trouble I might already be in, not to mention the possibility of being stopped and breathalysed. I wasn't rostered on for today, but nobody at Drylaw station batted an eyelid when I showed up. I tried not to breathe on anyone while I changed into uniform and took a car from the yard.

It took forty minutes to reach the outskirts of Rickerburn. I had a vague recollection of having driven through the town once, though I couldn't recall why. The satnav took me in one end of the place and out the other. I was beginning to think something had gone wrong with the app before I was directed to turn off to the right. Had I not been prompted I would never have been aware this road existed. I bounced along the pockmarked surface and was told I had reached my destination.

A man carrying a binbag had spotted me and he watched me park and exit the car.

'I'm looking for Mr Bradley,' I said.

'Aye?' he replied unhelpfully.

'Would that be you?'

'Uh-huh,' he said, a cigarette hanging from his lip.

I was about to introduce myself, something of a habit, and then remembered the reason for getting into uniform for this job. If he asked me my name, I would give it, but I was banking on the uniform being enough for him. 'I was hoping to have a quick word, Mr Bradley.' The man wore pyjama bottoms and sandals. His vest had been white when he'd bought it, but was now grey and there was a yellow stain at the collar.

He opened the lid of the metal bin next to a crumbling caravan and tossed in the binbag. 'I don't know why you lot have decided I'm needing talked to all of a sudden. Shouldn't you be doing more useful things?'

'It's just a few questions. I promise it won't take long.'

He didn't agree or protest, he just turned and walked towards the last of the little cottages. I followed him to a garden area where he sat himself into a tired-looking folding chair and transferred the cigarette from his mouth to an ashtray.

'I'm a bit busy today, but you can have ten minutes. After that, I'm done. Fed up with you lot,' he said and began coughing. When he was done, he spat at the floor. I almost took a step back it was so close to my foot.

He reached under the chair and produced a glass and a tin of extra strong lager. He poured and placed the tin back in the shade of his backside. His skin was sun-darkened and blistered red at the shoulders. There were some scabs on his arms, a few of them wet and angry that might have been midge or cleg bites.

'I'll get straight to it then, Mr Bradley,' I began and looked around for somewhere to sit, but there was nothing. 'You're aware that we're looking for some connection between the death of your grandson and that of a priest in Edinburgh.'

'You make it sound like an accident or something. A "death"? Let's just call it what it is, you don't need to sugar-coat it.'

'All right. These *murders*, we believe, were perpetrated by the same individual and we need to know why the two victims were selected. I won't lie to you, Mr Bradley, we're still searching for the answer to that question and that's what brings me here.'

'I already told the lesbian detective everything I know.'

Lesbian detective? Jesus, is this what Alyson has to put up with?

'I just wanted to go back over a few points, that's all. These two schools that you worked at—'

'I worked at more than two.'

'Right, but the two Catholic schools you worked at,

264

one was a standard, Catholic primary school . . .' I pulled my notebook from my pocket and went to the page I'd prepared. '. . . St Ninian's. And the other was a residential school for boys, St Cuthbert's. Why did your employment end with them?'

Mr Bradley screwed up his face, whether in irritation or in reaction to the beaming of the sun, I wasn't sure. 'St Ninian's was a bastard of a commute. It was on the south side of Glasgow and at the time I didn't drive. I only took the job because I was desperate. I was there six months or so.'

Eight months according to Alyson's notes, but fine.

He continued, 'The St Cuthbert's job lasted a few years and I was happy there, but they were in the process of closing the place down. That sort of school had gone out of fashion and the funding wasn't there.'

'What did you do after that?'

'Dole for a while, then another janny position came up at the high school in Shotts. I worked there 'til I retired. I telt all this to the—'

'To my colleague, yes. I'm sorry to be going over it again, but it's just for clarification, and it gives you a chance to have a think about anything we might have missed. At St Ninian's, were there many priests involved at the school?'

'I don't think so, not really. I'm not sure how it works, but I think they tie in with the local church and the priests visit the school and the kids go to the chapel. I don't know, you'd need to ask them. But I don't remember this priest I was asked about.'

There was nothing in the notes about further enquiries

at this school, but I had no doubt that it would have been looked into. Still, I might need to go back over this point myself, I thought.

'St Cuthbert's, on the other hand, must have had priests involved?'

He coughed again, using the back of one hand to cover his mouth and the other to refill his glass. The smell of the alcohol was turning my stomach. 'Aye, of course. The priests did some of the teaching, some nuns too. They had proper teachers for some subjects though.'

There was some information in Alyson's notes for this school. Thorough checks on any connection with the second victim. Work histories compared for registered employees, though the records were not great. The school shut down some twenty years ago and the building was now used as a headquarters for an animal charity. There had been an attempt to talk to those who were in charge of the school back in the day, but things were not going well, as one was ten years dead and the other, a nun from County Cork, now doing missionary work in Bolivia.

'Apart from the usual day-to-day staff at the school, were there many visitors that you can recall? Is it possible this priest came, just unofficially?'

'I dunno. I suppose.'

'Are you aware if they kept a logbook of some kind, for visitors?'

'I don't remember ever seeing one. Look, I cleaned up piss when the weans were too stupid or too lazy to hit the bowl, fixed door handles and occasionally did a bit of gardening. I can't answer these questions.'

'What about a blonde priest?'

'A blonde priest?'

'At either school. Do you remember seeing one? Either working there or visiting?'

'What? I don't know. Some priests are brown, some are blonde and most are either grey or bald. What does it matter?'

'It's just something that came up. Apparently, this blonde hair is striking for some reason. It doesn't ring any bells?'

'You suggesting I'm some sort of poofter or something? Why would I find some priest's hair *striking*?'

He began hacking again, even placing his glass down while he coughed furiously into the crook of his arm and it somehow felt like karma.

'Never mind, Mr Bradley. I'll see myself out.'

# CHAPTER TWENTY-TWO

## Old Habits

'OK, what do you have?' Kate Templeton stood at the front of the gathered crowd who were all facing the big screen in the office. The shorter ones peered around shoulders, but Alyson had a perfect view, towering as she was over the DC in front of her. There was an air of anticipation. It reminded Alyson of going to the cinema as a child, the sense of something magical about to appear.

'We've edited this down, ma'am, so you can see clearly what we're focusing on. OK, go ahead,' one of the CCTV team said to another.

'The city centre CCTV doesn't cover the route we're about to show, so the composite video is put together with private footage, except for the first and last shots, which are taken from the bus station. The camera looks onto the exit to Elder Street. When I press play, you'll see a bunch of people disembarking from a coach which set out from North Berwick.' Alyson wasn't sure of the guy's name, maybe Brian? He clicked on the remote and the video ran. The quality wasn't bad. Sure enough the screen showed a line of people, viewed from above and to the side, leaving a yellow coach. Then it was paused. 'This is our focus. This guy here with the red cap on. The time is eighteen-thirty-two hours on the day in question.' He played on and Alyson watched as the guy in the cap hopped down from the step. He was carrying a dark rucksack. 'Now, I won't lie, there's massive holes in the following footage as we track this guy through the city centre, but we're confident that every image you'll see is the same person.' He played on and the screen switched, an interior of an office. 'In a moment you'll see this figure pass by the window, it only lasts a second, coming . . . now.'

This footage was far less clear, but a figure in a cap carrying a bag walked swiftly across the screen.

'Where is this?' said Kate.

'York Place, ma'am. An architect's office. The next images are from various stores on Leith Walk.' The video rolled on and a series of black and white footage played. You had to use your imagination a little, but the stream was well put together and seemed to follow this person who walked at a determined pace. 'This one is from Tesco Express and is the best image we've found.' The screen switched to colour and automatic doors of the supermarket came into view. 'You'll see the figure pass by and then you'll see another slowed version straight after.'

The figure came into view from the left and slowed for

a moment before continuing on, but it was still fast. Then the replay came in slow motion and as the figure reached the middle of the screen, he looked towards the camera and then the footage paused. By some clever use of the software, this image was pulled to the corner of the screen and would stay there for the remainder of the presentation. There was one more clip from a grocery shop before the DC addressed the room again.

'From train station to this point on Leith Walk, nineteen minutes have passed. We've obtained no further footage on this outward journey. The location of the last footage to the locus is four-hundred and eighty metres and can be walked in under five minutes. There is a gap now of twenty-one minutes and then we see this.'

He pressed the remote and there was our cap-wearing, bag-carrying figure, but very small, the camera recording from a distance.

'What are we looking at here?' said Kate.

'This is still Leith Walk. The camera is on the East side, the side our man walks down, but now he's on his way back on the west side.'

'Back towards the station?'

'Yes, ma'am.'

'Wait, play that part back again. There, see? He stops briefly outside that shop. Has it been checked?'

'Yes, ma'am. They do have CCTV and you can see a dark shape approach the window, but nothing more.'

'Bugger. Play it on.'

A series of clips showed the blurry, but reasonably convincing figure's journey back up Leith Walk.

'This clip, from the Sainsbury's door, is the last image before a gap of twenty-three minutes. Then this final clip.'

The recording showed the figure back within the bus station in an image similar to the first, but from a different bay. On the rear of the bus was again a sign for 'North Berwick'. The figure enters suddenly from the left, not a great view of him this time, and he's quickly on the bus which rolls out six minutes later. The screen goes black except for the image from Tesco.

'We think these twenty minutes may have been our guy waiting until the last moment to enter the station and board the bus to ensure minimum capture from CCTV. From arrival at Elder Street to departure, just one hour and nine minutes have passed. Now, our guy could have a legitimate reason for his bizarrely swift visit to the capital, but we think this is significant.'

'Fucking good work. Even if he was avoiding the camera before he departed, it's still pretty brazen. Presumably it wouldn't be difficult to enter the city, even by bus, get off at an earlier stop and take a more secluded path to the locus and return without hitting any cameras at all?'

'Yes, ma'am. Very possible.'

Kate walked forward to the screen and stared at the captured figure. 'But then you've never given a shit about hiding, have you?' she said to blurred man. 'There was no CCTV on the bus itself, or you would have said,' she went on.

'That's correct, ma'am.'

'The bus terminated in North Berwick. Talk to me.'

'Uh, yes, ma'am. It does a loop of the town before

returning to Edinburgh. We've been checking CCTV in the area and have the occasional capture of the bus itself, but not of any disembarking. We've made arrangements to interview the driver. He's out of the country, but returning from holiday tomorrow and we'll ask him to come in next week.'

'No, fuck that. Alyson, I want you talking to this driver the minute his feet hit terra firma.'

'Yes, ma'am.'

For some people it's clowns that send a shock of fear and repulsion down their spines. And while I don't really get the point of them, their red noses, makeup and oversized shoes (is it supposed to be funny?), I don't find them to be creepy or unsettling, except perhaps when you consider the person behind that makeup has made this their career of choice, that *is* a little unsettling. No, for me, it's nuns; always has been.

So, it was unsurprising that I could feel sweat on my palms and neck as I turned into the drive for the Dumbarton Carmel. The road had a steady climb and I kept to a low gear as the tyres crunched the stone-chip surface beneath them. St Ninian's had been a bust. None of the teachers at the school were in post when Mr Bradley had been the janitor and so they were unaware of him and had already been spoken to by a DC, and no link to Father McCauley had been established. I had no plans to re-interview schoolteachers and students or Father McCauley's congregation, it was a small miracle I had been able to look into so much already without ringing an alarm bell somewhere. So, this looked to be the last roll of the dice. *Roll of the dice*, I thought and sniggered. *What goes black-white, black-white, black-white? A nun rolling down a—*

'Ah . . . shit,' I said as a gaggle of them came into view. That sweat on my hands now seemed cold and clammy.

They smiled at me as I passed and I waved through the open window. Three of them were heading down the road, perhaps out for a walk towards town. Then the building came into view and I was surprised to find myself disappointed. There was a small parking area with no vehicles and I pulled up, watched by two more of them who were sitting on chairs in front of the modern building which made me think of the Pennywell Care Home, as it was such a similar interior structure: brown and beige and unremarkable.

'Good afternoon, eh, sisters,' I said and hoped that was the correct way to address them. Though I'd been brought up Catholic, I'd had mercifully little contact with nuns.

They squinted up at me, shielding their faces from the sun with their hands.

'Hello, can I help you?' one of them said, smiling. They might have been sisters, actual sisters, so alike they were in their brown habits and wimples, though I suppose that is the point of it. White, wispy hair was visible to the front of her habit, which was a relief as it removed the austere image I had in my head of the tight outfit with only a scowl visible on a pasty-white face – no doubt instilled by too many movies.

'Hi, I'm so sorry to stop by unannounced. I was just hoping I might speak with someone who I think, uh, works here?' Again, I wasn't sure if 'work' was an appropriate term, probably not.

'You're looking to speak to Sister Catherine?' the other nun said.

'Yes, that's right.' This was a disappointing insight. It meant I wasn't the first police officer here and so in turn meant all relevant information had already been extracted.

'You best wait here. I'll go fetch Sister Gladys.'

The first nun remained seated, smiling up at me. I kept my hands in my pockets to control my nervous twitching. The other nun returned with something closer to my nightmare image. She was younger than the other two, but instantly there was far more authority about her. She strode across the stones of the drive, the nun fetching her struggling to keep up. More wimples were appearing at the windows.

'Can I help you, officer?' Sister Gladys said, her accent Irish, her voice high.

I almost took a step back, in fact, part of me wanted to run for the car. Her face was part questioning and part furious.

'I'm so sorry to disturb you. I just wondered if I might have a quick word with Sister Catherine. If it's a bad time, I can come back.' I had absolutely no intentions of returning. If she had told me to do just that, it would be the end of these enquiries.

She hesitated a moment, her eyes going from me to the building.

'It's just a little . . . inconvenient. I don't mean to be unaccommodating or unwelcoming, but you must understand, this is a closed order and while we can certainly have guests, just turning up out of the blue is not encouraged.'

'I'm sorry, I really should have called—'

'Not at all. But since you're here I suppose you can speak to her. Only I'll ask you to keep it brief, the sisters must have time for quiet prayer and contemplation and your presence here is, well . . .' she jabbed a thumb at the building and as she did the wimples all ducked like whack-a-moles, 'distracting.'

'I, uh, yes. I'll keep it brief. Thank you.'

'You better come inside then,' she said, her features seeming to relax.

I followed her up the drive feeling like a chastised schoolboy. 'How many of you live here, Sister?'

'Sixteen of us,' she said and pulled the door, urging me to step inside. There was a group of them standing and smiling in the hall. 'I think you're making up for the disappointment last week,' Sister Gladys said.

'Sorry, I don't understand.'

I followed her up the hall. 'Your colleague, who, by the way, was good enough to call ahead of time, caused a bit of a stir. The sisters were quite excited to receive a policeman, only to discover it was one of those who wears a suit and drives an ordinary car. I suspect you're far more what they had in mind.'

I slowed as we passed a small chapel and again was struck by just how similar this place was to the care home, if you traded the day room for the altar and pews. There was even a similar smell. Certainly all of the nuns, with the exception of Sister Gladys who might have been in her fifties, could be descried as elderly.

'Are you mother superior to the sisters?' I asked.

'There are no superiors here. We are all of us equal,' she said, though it was clearly not true. 'I'll show you to our dining hall and bring Sister Catherine to you.'

We took a left and entered a wide room. One large table sat at its centre, the walls adorned by visions of saints and Christ. One nun sat at the far end, reading. Sister Gladys cleared her throat, causing the nun to look up and quickly gather herself and leave.

Sister Gladys gestured to a chair and I sat. She made to leave, but turned back, 'You're not after tea or food or anything, are you?'

'No, no, I'm fine, thanks,' I said, taking the not-too-subtle hint.

I was left alone for nearly ten minutes being looked down upon by these saints I couldn't name, some depicted in humble garb, others grandly adorned by crowns floating above their heads and great beams of light shining out from the back of their heads.

There was a knock at the door and a smiling nun entered with Sister Gladys expressionless at her back. 'Brief, you understand. We're keeping Sister Catherine from her prayer time.'

'Yes, of course. I'm sure I'll be far quicker than my colleague,' I said, standing and urging Sister Catherine to sit.

Sister Gladys hovered by the door for a moment, but when it was clear that I wasn't going to start before she left, she let it close behind her.

'Thank you for seeing me, Sister. I really won't take up too much of your time. Before we start, I wondered if I could ask about this place?'

'Of course you can. What would you like to know?'

'I didn't get a chance to look into your order before coming here, so I don't really know what it's about. You refer to yourselves as a Carmelite order?' This was a question I'd have asked Sister Gladys but was afraid to. This lady in front of me, though, was far less intimidating, except for, you know, the whole nun thing. She wore small, dark framed glasses and was around seventy years old. I knew of her only from an entry in Alyson's notes.

'The name derives from Mount Carmel in Palestine. I have to say I like the name, it always puts me in mind of caramel which I love dearly,' she said with a small laugh. Her accent was thick Glaswegian. 'Some pilgrims in the thirteenth century founded the order when they settled in Palestine. We devote our lives to prayer and to our little community, taking time each day to practise silence and solitude for reflection before coming back together as a collective.'

'So, it's not a new order then? It's just that this building is . . .'

'Modern, yes. Well, if you like I can give you directions to where we used to live. We had a proper monastery, it's not too far from here. But our order is small and grows a little smaller every year. It seemed decadent and unnecessary for us to be rattling around in that grand old building and so we moved here around twenty years ago, I think.'

'You've been with the order how long?'

'I joined after they closed St Cuthbert's in nineteen-ninety-eight.'

'I understand you spoke to my colleague?'

'Last week, yes. Detective, but I forget his name. He did leave me a card if you need it?'

'No, that's OK. I just had a few follow-up questions.' Alyson had jotted down details of this nun as one of the few staff members from the school it was possible to speak to, but had not left any indication if she'd given a statement or if that statement was of any interest. 'I'm guessing he asked you about your time at the school, about the other staff members?'

'That's right, though I'm afraid I wasn't much help. He asked about a Father McCauley and I gave it a great deal of thought, I really did, but I'm almost certain I never met the man. What a sin that was, God rest his soul.' She made the sign of the cross, and I almost did the same.

'He would have asked you about the janitor at that time too, I imagine.'

'Yes, he did. But again, I couldn't tell him anything really. I was aware of a janitor, but if I ever talked to him, I've long since forgotten.'

'Is there anything he asked you about that has since occurred to you, anything that came back to you?'

'No, I'm sorry.'

'That's OK. It's important that we're thorough. A lot of these investigations are largely speaking to people to close doors, rather than open them. Did he also ask you about a blonde priest?'

'A blonde priest?'

'Yes. Perhaps another member of staff at the school that might have been blonde?'

She thought on this, her head shaking, her eyes searching the table surface. 'Your colleague didn't ask, but no, no, I can't think of a member of staff who was blonde. Unless? No, but he wasn't really a staff member.'

'Please. If there's something you remember,' I said and gestured with my hand, encouraging her to finish her thought.

'Well, ach, and now I don't even remember his name. Anyway, none of the staff were particularly good with mathematics and we tried to give those boys a decent grounding in education, but someone knew someone, a young priest – young at the time at least – who had been a graduate in something to do with maths before devoting himself to the Church. Anyway, he'd come in, as a sort of favour, to run a class, maybe once a week. Oh, heavens, what was his name? He had this thick blonde hair, great-looking fella. D'you know, maybe Sister Phoebe will remember.'

'Sister Phoebe?'

'Yes, we both joined here from St Cuthbert's. Your colleague spoke to her as well. I can go and get her if you like?'

'Uh, yes. Please. If you think Sister Gladys won't mind?'

'She probably will, but this is police work and between us, Sister Phoebe would never forgive me if I didn't bring her in on this. Gimme a moment.'

She was gone no more than a minute before she returned with another grinning nun.

'Hi, Sister Phoebe?'

'That's right,' she said, clearly excited.

'Come in, please.'

'Should I wait outside? Sister Catherine said.

'No, it's fine. I'll need you to prompt Sister Phoebe here about the person we discussed. Sister Phoebe, my colleague spoke to you last week?'

'He did. A detective,' she said. Her toothy grin was infectious.

'You also worked at St Cuthbert's?'

'For about a year yes, until it closed.' The notes Alyson had left in the kitchen were clearly from an early gathering, before they'd become aware of Sister Phoebe.

'Were you able to tell him anything?'

'Not really. We discussed this didn't we, Sister Catherine, how we were sorry we were a bit useless.'

'Please don't worry. Just one thing, then. Sister Catherine mentioned as priest who worked, well not worked, but helped out there?' I looked at Sister Catherine whose nodding told me I'd picked this up correctly. 'A blonde priest who helped the boys with their maths?'

'You remember him, Sister Phoebe. Young man, head full of thick, blonde curls?'

'Yeah, I do. Livingston, wasn't that his name?'

'Do you know what, I think you're right,' said Sister Catherine, sitting next to the other nun, gripping her arm in delight.

'Father *Stephen* Livingston, I think,' said Sister Phoebe.

'That's it. What a memory you have, Sister Phoebe.' Her arm was now being tapped on in a congratulatory manner.

'Is he important?' asked Sister Phoebe.

'I'm sure not. It's just something that came up. Would you happen to know what happened to him after St Cuthbert's?'

They looked at one another, but shook their heads.

'No matter. Thank you, sisters. You've been most helpful,' I said.

I felt like a mother duck, leaving the place with a line of shuffling nuns following me out to the car.

# CHAPTER TWENTY-THREE

## Confessions

I woke to the smell of toast and the faint sound of dishes. I threw on some clothes and wandered into the kitchen, yawning and stretching.

'Shit, did I wake you?' Alyson said. She was already dressed for work in her grey suit.

I looked at the clock on the oven – 7.30 a.m. 'No, don't worry. I didn't want to miss this chance to say hello. I feel like it's been weeks since I saw you.'

'I know. I was thinking the same the other day.' She pulled two slices from the toaster and held them up, raising her eyebrows at me. I nodded and she took an extra plate from the cupboard. I poured myself some tea and joined her at the table, which had been cleared of her paperwork.

'You seem . . . perkier?' I said. 'Have you been sleeping better?'

'Not really, but we've had a bit of a breakthrough in the past few days, so maybe it's that.'

I felt my pulse quicken a little. 'Can you elaborate?' I said.

'Officially, no. But between you and me, we think we've seen the face of the person responsible.'

'Really? How?' I buttered my slice and passed Alyson the knife.

'CCTV. It's not concrete, but it looks good. There's not much to back it up at this stage, phone use in the area hasn't yielded anything, but I'm speaking to someone today who might help push us forward.'

'That's fantastic. So, what does our killer look like?'

'Blurry.'

'That's it?'

She shrugged and bit into her toast.

'Male? Female?'

'If it *is* our killer, it's a he. Late thirties to early forties at a guess. Pretty short. We did some analysis of a capture from the doorway of a supermarket and we estimate about five-foot-six.'

'Sounds promising. Who are you speaking to?'

'A bus driver. Our person of interest got on a coach headed for North Berwick, but got off somewhere before it terminated. We're hoping he remembers our guy.'

'An arrest isn't likely any time soon then?'

'Hey, it's progress. You want me back in a mood?

'No, I was just hoping for a little more.'

'Yeah, well, I can tell you there's been a big lift of morale in the office.'

I bit down on my toast. I thought about where this investigation was at and about that date I'd calculated from Martin's meltdown. What was it now? About two weeks?

'I thought you said you wanted to see me?'

'Huh?' I said.

'"Didn't want to miss you", you said and yet you're sitting there daydreaming. I asked you what you were up to?'

'Me? Oh, nothing really. Helping our probationer with a complicated fraud case most likely.' I hated lying to her. Really hated it.

'Exciting stuff. How are things going with your lady friend?'

'Marcella? Yeah, pretty good actually. It's not been easy to find time to see one another, but we're getting together on Friday. See the festival go out with a bang.'

'It's ending? Oh, thank Christ,' she said and stood, taking our empty plates to the dishwasher.

'There's a massive fireworks display to mark the closing every year. You can join us if you like.'

'And be what? A third Catherine wheel? Hard pass. Wish me luck today – we could do with it.'

'Good luck.' I said. She mussed my hair as she pulled her coat from the back of my chair and left.

It seemed everyone was excited about progress they'd been making. I passed Vikram and Morgan in the hall. They were hurrying out of the door, asking if it was all right to skip muster.

'It's fine. What's going on?' I asked.

'Another VIPER parade. We have a witness, describes Colander McStay to a tee. I'm confident we'll get a positive result this time,' said Morgan.

'I'll update you on the result, Sarge,' said Vikram.

'Yeah, do that,' I said, though I'm not sure they heard me with the door clanging shut behind them. With that, most of my team were gone and so I asked Mandy if she could brief herself, telling her I had an enquiry that would take me most of the shift. I made a flask of tea for my journey and set out.

I thought about making an appointment, Sister Gladys' admonishment still fresh, but there is something about catching people off guard that I quite like. My tutor John had taught me this in my second year. *Calling ahead is giving time to prepare and a badly prepared lie is easy to spot*, he'd said, or something to that effect.

I'd never been to Dunbar. In fact, almost all of East Lothian was a mystery to me. In my mind it's where the wealthy Edinburgh commuters lived, with those less fortunate moving west out of the city, though I was certain East Lothian had its rougher spots too.

The road out was less interesting than I'd hoped. My phone suggested sticking to the City Bypass almost the whole way, so views of the coast were going to be avoided. I ignored it and took a turn off to Longniddry. Although I found myself amongst heavy traffic, the scenery was far more what I had in mind. The coastal route took me through the quaint towns of Aberlady, Gullane and Dirleton, the Firth of Forth glinting frequently in the distance. The road turned inland once more and I was soon entering Dunbar.

The streets grew narrower as I neared the town centre. The line of cars in front of me slowed to a crawl as the road was barely wide enough to allow two lines of traffic, before it suddenly opened up again as I reached the very centre of town. I passed a grand-looking church before reaching my destination, which was a much more humble affair.

Our Lady of the Waves Catholic Church, the sign read, confirming I was in the right place. I thought about the locus in Leith, St Mary Star of the Sea Church, and the nautical theme that linked both. *Links*, I thought.

The building was old, its heavy stones a slightly ominous dark red, darker at the bottom than at the top, as if the church were soaking up some sanguine deposit from the earth. The front door was closed but unlocked.

I entered into a familiar scene. A desk with Church literature to one side, a font of holy water on the wall of the other. Either out of respect or muscle memory, I dabbed the middle finger of my right hand in the water, then touched my forehead, breast and each shoulder before pushing the inner door and stepping into the aisle.

My childhood came rushing back. My mother in a dress, holding my hand, my father in a tie, trying to look like he wanted to be there. I walked down between the pews; this lucky congregation were provided with small cushions. I remember the bare pews I sat on as a child, comfortable enough for around ten minutes before you ended up shifting between bum cheeks to keep them from dying against the solid wood. At the bottom-right of the altar and next to the ornate tabernacle was the board displaying the hymn numbers. That board, or one similar, was like a clock to me. As the service trundled on, your progress could be tracked as you ticked off these numbers, my soul ironically lifting as you reached the second to last. The last didn't count as it was sung as the doors were unchained and you were permitted to leave.

'Hello, officer. Are you here for confession?'

I couldn't help a small laugh. 'Only if there's something criminal you need to get off your chest,' I said to the tall, thin man. I looked immediately to his hair, more grey than blonde and thin to the point of visible scalp. He laughed and I asked him, 'Father Stephen Livingston?'

'No. I'm a deacon here. Father Livingston is in the back. Do you want to come through?'

I followed the deacon to a door at the far end which led to a few stairs and down through to an annex, some extension that felt newer than the rest of the building. A small communal seating area that might be used for Bible study sat before a small kitchen area. At the kettle was a man in a black shirt and yes, his hair was magnificent, particularly as he was maybe late sixties at least. Blonde curls, a little grey in there too, but it would have been the envy of a man half his age. He looked up at us entering and had a sort of double take as he took in my uniform.

'Officer,' he said. 'Your timing could not be better. I'm preparing a fresh pot of coffee, real coffee, none of the instant nonsense. Will you have a cup?'

'Sure. Thank you,' I said. It did smell good.

'I don't believe we've met, forgive me if we have. But I know Sergeant Williams and a few of the constables from the Dunbar office. Are you new?'

'I'm from the city, actually. No, we haven't met.'

'Milk? Sugar?'

'Just some milk, thanks.'

He handed a cup to the deacon who brought it over to me. I took in a nose-full before taking a sip. Damn good coffee.

'What's brought you all the way out here?' he asked as he handed the deacon another cup before pouring his own and stepping towards the seated area.

'You, actually, Father.'

'Oh.' His eyebrows raised and he abandoned the sip he was about to take. 'Something I can help you with? Is it serious?'

'Perhaps nothing, Father, don't worry. It's just an enquiry I'm working on, but it is of a serious nature.'

'Please, sit,' he said and gestured to the round table and low chairs.

He joined me, but the deacon left with his coffee.

'I'm not quite sure where to begin,' I said, and I meant it. 'Your name came up as a staff member at the old St Cuthbert's residential school in Lanarkshire. We're just trying to speak to anyone we can from that time.'

'I see, but I wasn't a staff member at the school. I helped out now and again, but it was all sort of unofficial.'

'Yes, I was told that. You're something of a maths whizz?'

He smiled and shook his head. 'I was one of those kids that could never quite figure out what I wanted to do. My faith was always there, but in the background. I thought

288

maybe an engineer, but I wasn't great with the practical application. Mathematics, though, came pretty easily and so that was my degree. By my fourth year I knew I wanted to join the cloth, but I've always been a believer in seeing things through, so I completed my degree before making the switch.'

'Who brought you in to the school? Who was aware of this skill for numbers?'

'Father Reid. We attended seminary together in Spain. It's part of the training for priesthood, where you begin your journey in priestly formation, as it's termed. We got friendly and kept in touch.'

'Father Reid. Am I right in thinking he passed some time ago?'

'Yes, sadly. He battled cancer for a few years, but we lost him nearly ten years ago now.'

'I'm sorry. How long did you teach at the school?'

'About a year or so, maybe a bit longer.'

'Were there any gifted students?'

'In maths? No, not really. It's a bit of a dry subject for most. We did manage to squeeze a few of the boys through their Standard Grade though, I was happy about that.'

'I can imagine. You knew the other priests and the nuns there well?'

'I don't know about well. As I said, I wasn't part of the staff.'

'What about the janitor?'

'The janitor?'

'Yes. Mr Bradley.'

'Mr Bradley,' he said, smiling again. 'Yes, I knew Mr

Bradley. We were the only two who smoked. Well – the only two adults that is, there were plenty of the boys smoked when they could get hold of it. We'd shoot the breeze over a cigarette. I haven't thought about Mr Bradley in a very long time.'

'You haven't asked me why I'm here, Father. Why is that?'

He put down his coffee, wiped his hands on his trousers. 'I'm assuming you're getting to that,' he said and smiled once more.

'Mr Bradley's grandson was murdered in April. You may have seen it on the news?'

'Dear God,' he said and blessed himself. The colour drained from his face. He took a moment to compose himself, rubbing his hands and looking at the table in front of him. 'I . . . I do remember seeing that. And Bradley, you know, I never made the connection. That's beyond awful.'

'There's no reason why you'd make the connection, Father. I'm sorry to be the one to make you aware.'

'I don't understand, you think Mr Bradley might be involved?'

'No, nothing like that. The reason for my visit is because we're trying to establish commonality between the murder of Callum Bradley and Father Brian McCauley. You knew him pretty well,' I said. I raised my cup and drank. Really good coffee.

'I'm sorry?' he said. He looked genuinely confused but his neck, right around his collar, was as red as the bricks of his church.

'Father McCauley. Brutally slain in his own church.

That must have been very hard on you?'

'I, I don't understand.' He laid an arm across his knees and leaned forward as if he was mishearing me. I drank again, really taking my time over it. He continued without prompting. 'Oh, the horrible business with the priest in Edinburgh. I read about that. Of course, we said a prayer for him, just awful. You know I did a whole sermon on . . .'

He drifted off as I lifted the phone I'd just taken from my pocket and took a picture of him.

'Sorry, you were saying, Father. You did a whole sermon?'

'I .. we . . . did a . . . Sorry, why did you just . . .?'

'The picture? Sorry, I should have mentioned. You were easy enough to find online. The church has its own website and you were listed as the parish priest, but no pictures. I'd have preferred to have shown a picture to Mrs Wilson prior to coming here. Mrs Wilson was Father McCauley's cleaner, she bumped into you one morning, rather unexpectedly at the manse. I can use this to confirm that to be the case. But, I'm just wondering why a priest, of all people, is lying to the police? What is it you don't . . .'

The man was weeping into his hands. Great sobs from deep in his chest. It took me by surprise. There was no break in it for minutes. The deacon, having heard the crying from wherever he'd gone, pushed his head around the door.

'It's OK. I just had to deliver some sad news, that's all,' I told him. Father Livingston, now aware of the company tried to pull himself together. I waved the deacon away and after another thirty seconds I could finally continue. 'Father. What's going on? Did you have something to do with the death of Father McCauley?'

This sobered him up instantly. 'Oh, no. Lord no. Absolutely not.' He wiped at his face and began searching his pockets for something to wipe his nose. I took some kitchen paper from next to the kettle and passed it to him. 'Thank you,' he said.

'Take your time, Father.'

He blew his nose and dabbed at his eyes. 'I did know Brian, but I swear to you, I swear to Lord God that I could never have harmed a hair on his head.'

'I believe you. How did you know him?'

This prompted more crying, but he managed an answer. 'We were . . . friends . . . for a very long time we've been friends. When I found out about his murder, I just didn't know what to do with myself. I couldn't grieve properly. God forgive me, I wasn't even at his funeral.'

I thought about how to form the next question. 'Father, I don't need to know exactly what your relationship with Father McCauley was. Frankly I don't care, that's between you and him as far as I'm concerned. But would it be fair to say it was beyond friendship?'

He hesitated a moment, then nodded and brought the paper back to his eyes.

'When was the last time you saw him?'

He took a deep breath, trying to push the grief out of his chest. 'Uh, it was a few weeks before his death.'

'And where was this?'

'At the manse. His manse.'

'It would have been a Monday?'

He nodded.

'Because Mrs Wilson doesn't work on a Monday?'

He nodded again.

'When did you meet him?'

He cleared his throat. 'It's funny that I mentioned seminary earlier, it's where I met Brian, too. He was a confirmed priest at that time and was there on a religious retreat while I was studying.'

'How long ago are we talking?'

'Oh, forty-something years.' The tears were rolling again. 'Please tell me you'll catch the person who did this.'

'I'm trying, believe me. Father, the only thing that links Father McCauley's death with that of Callum Bradley is you. You, Mr Bradley and the school. Is there anything you think I need to know at this stage?'

'I – I can't think of anything.'

'At some point, I will need you to come in to provide elimination prints. We can do it discreetly, but it will be necessary.'

'I understand. Yes, of course.'

I felt a sense of guilt, looking at this man in the black shirt. He was no killer. He'd lost the dearest thing in the world to him and couldn't talk about it to a living soul.

*The dearest thing in the world to him*, I thought.

# CHAPTER TWENTY-FOUR

## No Comment

There was a car parked at the rear of Mr Bradley's place. A blue Ford Focus. I stopped and thought for a moment. Was this a detective visiting in an unmarked car? A Focus was just the kind of model you might expect for a pool car. The sensible thing to do would be to reverse back up the drive and do this another time. Yet I was stationary, engine running, just staring at the side of this car. My mind had been racing all the way from Dunbar and so had I, a steady ninety along the M8. I parked and went to have a look, thinking about what I'd say if a suited officer were to suddenly appear. I couldn't think of one plausible reason for being here but the truth.

A look at the registration put me at ease. It told me the car was eight years old and so extremely unlikely to still be part of the Force fleet. Inside I could see CDs pushed into the door storage, definitely not police. CID. Still, the old man had company and that wasn't ideal.

Assuming nobody used the front door, I retraced my path around the side and into the garden as per my last visit. I entered the garden and there was Mr Bradley in his chair, in a vest despite the fact that it was now early evening. Four of his extra-strength lager tins lay crushed at his feet. He appeared to be sleeping, his arms folded across his chest.

'Mr Bradley? Hello?' I said, not wanting to touch the man.

'Hello?' came a voice from inside. A man stepped through the open back door. He was drying a cup with a dishtowel.

'Hi. I'm sorry to bother you. I was just hoping to have a word with your, um, with Mr Bradley.'

'Dad. There's someone here to see you. Dad.'

He tapped at his father's shoulder with the back of his hand. The old man's hands shot out as if her were falling.

'Jesus,' he mumbled. The old man wiped at his mouth and then his eyes.

'Dad. There's a police officer here to see you.'

The man looked around, then saw me. 'Oh no. I'm not talking to any more police. No, you've had it. I'm done.' He stood and had to grab the arm of the chair to stop from falling back into it.

'Dad, sit down. Behave yourself.' Mr Bradley's son tried to lever him back into the chair, but he was having none of it. He disappeared into the house. 'I'm sorry. He can be a bit like this when he's had a few. I'll talk to him. Give me a minute.'

The man followed his father into the house. An argument raged for five minutes and I grew impatient. I ventured into a kitchen the son had been doing his best to clean but was unlikely to make any real progress on, such was the grime at every corner.

In the living room the father was simultaneously coughing and trying to light the cigarette in his mouth.

'I'm sorry. I've never seen him quite this bad,' the son said. 'He's adamant he doesn't want to talk to any more police. Maybe it's something I can help you with?'

'Thank you, but it really is your father I need to speak to. Some things have come to light that I need him to talk to me about?'

'What sort of things?'

I stepped further into the room, leaning against a wall where I could see the father's face and he could see mine. 'I was here a few days ago to speak to your father. We talked about a lot of things, but particularly about the St Cuthbert's School. Well, I've been doing some digging and a few things don't add up. So, I'm here to just clarify a few points,' I said to the son, but my eyes were on his dad.

'I thought DC Kane was dealing with that?' Bradley Junior looked from me to his father and back.

'She is, but there's a lot to cover in an inquiry like this, so I'm helping out.'

His face was one of confusion, but he seemed to accept my explanation. 'Dad, whatever it is, will you please just talk to the man. It might be important.'

The old man stared out of the window from his armchair. His teeth were grinding under his lips. 'I don't need to talk to them. It's my right not to answer questions.'

'What are you talking about, Dad? Anything the police need to know, we tell them. You don't know what little thing might—'

'My lawyer says I don't need to speak to them. I don't have to.'

Bradley Junior laughed, though out of confusion. 'What the hell are you talking about? Lawyer. Don't be so stupid. You don't have a lawyer.'

'I do so have a lawyer. I have his . . .' A coughing fit interrupted him. He was on his feet again and launching spittle about the place, not bothering to cover his mouth as he searched through papers and drawers. 'Here,' he managed, before grabbing a filthy looking towel and continuing to cough into it. He'd thrust a business card into his son's hand. Bradley Junior looked at it, confusion returning to his face, then he handed it to me. 'Alexander Aitchison & Co', and an address in Motherwell.

'When did you speak to a lawyer?' he asked.

'My question would be *why* did you speak to a lawyer, Mr Bradley. What made you feel then need to seek legal advice?'

From the son's face, this question had just superseded his own. He walked to his father and lowered to his haunches in front of him, placing his hands on the old man's knees. 'Dad. What's going on?'

The old man pushed his son away. 'I just don't want keep talking about it, that's all. The lawyer says I don't need to speak to any more police if I don't want to.'

'That's perfectly true, Mr Bradley, but I'm sure you were

well aware of that already. You only had to tell me, or one of my colleagues that you no longer wanted to assist with our enquiries and we would have respected that. So, why a lawyer?'

'I just . . . I just want to be left alone.'

'What is it you don't want to discuss, exactly, Mr Bradley? Does it have something to do with Father Stephen Livingston?' I studied the man's face as I released the name into the air. There was a momentary drift of the eyes in my direction, then they snapped back to the window.

'The lawyer says if you come round and start harassing me, I've to call him. So, you better get out.'

'Dad, for God's sake, nobody's harassing you. Who's Stephen Livingston?' Bradley's son said, partly to his father and partly to me.

'He's someone I spoke to this morning who knows your father pretty well. He also worked at St. Cuthbert's. Used to sneak away for a cigarette with your dad. Only, when I spoke to your father the other day and pretty much described this man, your dad knew nothing about him.'

'I don't. I don't know whoever it is,' the old man snapped, sending him into another coughing fit.

I addressed Bradley Junior. 'Look, I don't know what's going on here, I really don't, but one thing is clear: the link between your son's murder and that of the priest in Edinburgh has something to do with your father. Your father and this other priest, Livingston. The mere mention of Father Livingston's description has had your dad running off to a lawyer.'

'Get out. Get out my house!'

'Dad, stop this nonsense. Stop it right now. Look, sit down.' The old man was wrestling with his son, but he was soon planted back in his chair. 'Dad, you start answering this man's questions and no more shite about a lawyer. This is important. This is for Callum.'

Bradley Senior pushed his hands into his face, his knuckles white, balled into fists.

'This couldn't be more important, Mr Bradley,' I said, forcing my voice to a calm and even tone. 'Thing is, I'm beginning to think that the target of these attacks was not your grandson and the priest in Edinburgh, but rather your old friend Father Stephen Livingston and you, Mr Bradley. Rather than attack you directly, he's taken away the things you both love most in the world. Now, who would do such a thing? Mr Bradley please—'

'I don't know!' he yelled, his eyes wide, his fists beating the arms of the chair. 'Don't you think if I knew who killed my grandson, I'd fucking tell you?'

'Dad—'

'It's OK. Let him speak,' I said.

'Maybe I remember this priest from the school. But I don't know anything. I don't know anything.' The tears were flowing and the coughing had returned.

'Did you see something at that school? Something involving Father Livingston?' I asked. I thought about that poor boy, his eyes cut from his head. There was no response from the old man.

Bradley Junior was prodding at the old man, trying to make his father look at him. 'Dad, if you can help the police, you need to say something.'

'I'll level with you, Mr Bradley. I don't think these attacks are finished and I think another one is coming soon. If you don't help me, I'm going to be powerless to stop it. What if it's another child? What if it's someone else's grandson or granddaughter? Could you live with that?'

'Dad. What did you see? Speak to this man for God's—'

'Maybe,' the old man muttered, suddenly calm. He took the ragged towel and wiped his eyes with it.

'Maybe what?' I said.

'Maybe I saw something. I'm not sure.'

'Tell me. Please,' I said.

'Look, I don't know, all right. But there was this one afternoon I was putting away some things, cleaning things and there's this area, a sort of storage area, utility room sort of thing. Anyway, I got a fright when I opened the door, because I wasn't expecting to see anyone, but aye, this priest was there and, well, he was there with one of the boys.'

'What was he doing with the boy?' I asked.

'I don't know. Not really. The boy was upset. He ran off when he saw me.'

'Mr Bradley. If you know more than that, you need to tell me.'

'I swear. I mean, the priest was sort of doing himself up I suppose, but I didn't see anything, not really.'

'You think the priest was abusing that boy?'

'I don't know.'

I folded my arms and exhaled in frustration. 'I think you do know, Mr Bradley. I think you know more than you're saying. I think this is exactly why you went for legal advice.

Look, right now all I want to do is stop anyone else from getting hurt. I'll ask one more time. Did you see this boy being assaulted by Father Livingston?'

There was a pause. The old man looked at me, to his son and then out of the window again.

'Dad . . .'

'Maybe. Maybe that's what I saw, all right. I don't know for sure, but maybe.'

I wasn't going to get any more than that out of him. I changed the question. 'Do you know which boy it was? Do you know his name?'

He slowly lit another cigarette, his hands shaking. 'Aye,' he said after his first draw. 'I think so. Small for his age he was. Other kids called him Micky Halfpint, that's how I remember, see, it was quite funny. His real name was Halfpenny.'

For a moment, I thought she'd taken the news well. She sat in the passenger seat, nodding as I tried my best to explain what I'd been up to and why. I must have apologised a dozen times through the telling. From trawling through her personal notes to the questions in Dumbarton and Dunbar, to here in Portobello, she'd listened and not uttered a word. Then she did.

'Tell me this is some kind of sick fucking joke.'

'Aly, I'm sorry. I felt like I had no choice.'

'At any point in that sequence you could have spoken to me. And, you're just dropping this on me? Jesus fucking Christ. I feel fucking dizzy, Don. You've just ambushed me with this fucking betrayal . . . Again. I don't know what the fuck to say. Oh wait, yes I do, what the fuck are we doing in Portobello?' I remembered the look on her face as she rained punches in through the window of the Subaru. This was similar and I was nervous.

'Aly, I wanted to say, but I didn't even know what I had and I'm still not certain of anything. But, that house there,' I said, nodding at my side window at the little terraced house in Portobello's Great Cannon Bank, 'is the registered address of a Michael Halfpenny. The only Michael Halfpenny in the central belt, according to Voter's Roll.'

By the time I'd got home after speaking to Mr Bradley, it was late. I'd run the information through my head over and over on that drive back and I knew it was time to speak to Alyson, that I'd taken things as far as I could without doing some real damage, if I hadn't done so already. She wasn't home so I stayed up, nervously listening for the front door. But by 1 a.m., I'd gone to bed, exhausted from the weight of it all.

This morning she'd greeted me with a cup of tea and smile, which I'd returned but she could see in my face that something was wrong. She'd assumed I'd broken up with Marcella, or that I'd had a fight with my father, and when I'd asked her if she could spare a few hours for a drive and a chat, she'd become particularly concerned. I'd waited until we were reaching the outskirts of town before I'd gotten into it, perhaps because in my head it meant she was less likely to pull the handbrake and walk off, never to speak to me again.

'Uh-huh. So, what? You want to go and arrest this guy?

Don, there are fucking procedures and—'

'I know, Aly. Of course I know, but I just wanted to be sure that we have something. I want to hand this over to you so you can do it right, but I had to see for myself, at least this far. Look, I thought we'd knock on his door, have a bit of a chat, get a feel of him. There's no direct evidence stopping us treating him as a potential witness at this time. Aly, I need you to tell me if I'm right, then I'm out, I swear, and I will never do anything like this to you again. I promise.'

She laughed, but not because she was in the slightest part amused. 'You've made promises like this in the past and still you keep leaving me in deep shit, Don.' She sat silent for a moment, her head shaking slowly. She was considering this. Though her face was flushed with anger, she was about to agree, I could see it.

I wrung the steering wheel in my hands nervously.

'Fuck sake, Don. I don't think you quite appreciate what you've done, and how much trouble you've probably landed us in, but . . . Right,' she said, turning to meet my eye. 'I'm doing the talking. If I want your input I'll ask, otherwise you stay in the background and try not to ruin my fucking career. Understand?'

'Thanks, Aly.'

She threw open her door and was on her phone when I joined her in the street.

She was calling Control, giving her number and location. I hadn't even thought about that, hadn't brought a radio. The car was my own and I stood in my jeans. From my wallet I fished out my warrant card and pulled a lanyard from the glove box. Between us, we just about could pass for police.

Alyson hung up and said, 'Remember—'

'You're doing all the talking. Got it.'

As we walked towards the front door, my stomach knotted. Alyson didn't seem to notice me grip my abdomen. I tried to keep up, but another burst of pain shot into my gut.

She was at the door.

'Aly.'

She knocked at the glass panel, four raps of a knuckle.

'Aly, wait!'

She rang the bell.

My stomach pitched and I wretched once, a dry surge that pained my throat.

'Alyson, don't,' I said and this time she heard me.

'What the hell's wrong with you?'

'Something's wrong. Just stop.'

'This was your fucking idea,' she said, she was clasping a hand to the glass, trying to see inside. She reached for the handle.

'DON'T!' I yelled and fell to my knees. A blaze of white light filled my eyes as the pain became too much. When I managed to catch my breath and see once more, she was standing over me, her hand on my shoulder.

'Are you all right? What's happened?'

Now that she was away from the door, the pain subsided. I was sweating from every pore in my body.

'I think something is really wrong here. Just don't try to open that door.'

'I don't get it, Don. Like I said, this was your idea. What's wrong with you? Get up.'

'Here,' I said and held out my hand.

She took it and pushed a hand under my arm and I was back on my feet. There was a single window to the right of the door. I wiped my hands down the legs of my jeans and approached the glass. It was a kitchen, tidy. The door to the hall was open. 'What does that look like to you?' I said and let Alyson peer in.

'Where?'

'In the hall. What's that blue thing?'

'Not sure. Looks like a sort of barrel or something. Hold on.'

She returned to the door.

'Alyson, don't.'

'Relax. I'm just looking.' She lifted the letterbox and quickly drew her face away. 'Jesus,' she said.

'What?'

'The smell. It stinks of petrol or something.' She returned her face to the slot. 'Fucking hell,' she said and lowered the hinge gently and stepped away, pushing her hand into my chest and urging me away from the door too.

'What is it?'

'Wires. There's wires sticking out of that blue barrel. Fuck, we need to evacuate the entire . . . Shit, I've got to call this in. Her eyes searched the pavement as if she'd dropped something. 'Don, you need to get out of here. I can't explain to my boss why you're here. I'll think of some way to connect the dots, but as soon as I make this call this place will be swarming and you can't be here.'

I wanted to protest, but she was right. I ran to the car and got the engine running. As I turned the car away from the house I watched her in the mirror, standing in the street, one hand on her head, the other with the phone to her ear.

# CHAPTER TWENTY-FIVE

## Concussion

I drove straight home and turned on the news, expecting a breaking story, but there was nothing yet. I watched for an hour, waiting for the red banner scrolling at the bottom of the screen to turn yellow, but by the time I had to leave for work, nothing had appeared.

I checked my phone as I arrived at the station, again after I got changed and once more before I put it away prior to muster. Nothing.

With Vikram off on annual leave, I briefed Mandy and Morgan, distracted the whole time, Mandy pointing out to me that I'd repeated something. I suggested they work together so I could keep an eye on developments.

'Actually Sarge, Morgan has someone coming in for interview and I've had no involvement in this case,' she said.

'Who's coming in?'

'Colander McStay. Me and Vikram went to his place to arrest him last week, but he was nowhere to be seen. We later got a call from his lawyer that he would make himself available today. I'm sorry, Sarge, I'd have waited until Vikram's back, but we didn't really have any say,' said Morgan.

'You had the evidence to arrest?' I said.

'Aye. We had a witness successfully pick him out at VIPER. Maybe not quite enough to charge at this stage, but enough to get him here.'

'But he's coming with his brief?'

'His what?'

'His lawyer,' Mandy explained.

'Aye. They're due any minute actually.'

'OK. Mandy, I'll handle this with Morgan. I suspect it won't take long. If he's got his lawyer with him, you can look forward to half an hour of "no comment" and we'll have to give it up.'

I told Morgan to chap my door when Colander arrived, meanwhile I stared at my phone and the news app. Still nothing. Maybe I was wrong, maybe there was some innocent explanation. But petrol smell, barrel and wires?

It took all of two minutes before the knock came. I sighed and threw the phone into my drawer.

'The time is fourteen-twenty on Friday the twenty-eighth of August. I am Police Sergeant Donald Colyear of Police Scotland. We are in interview room one of Drylaw Police Station in Edinburgh. I will ask the others present to identify themselves.'

'Eh, Constable Morgan Finney.'

I nodded my head at the huge man sitting across the table from me, somehow even more menacing in a shirt and tie. 'Colin Christopher McStay,' he said enunciating every syllable with spite.

'I am Sarah Halliday QC, representing Mr McStay from Actioners Solicitors.'

Fucking hell, I thought. A QC? We should just stop the tape now, let him go before she finds a way to turn this into a grievance against us.

'Thank you,' I said. 'And thank you for coming in today to see us, Mr McStay.'

'Not like I had much choice . . .' he began, but then there was a hand on his forearm from the lawyer. He sat back in his chair and folded his arms across his massive chest. Sitting across from him, I was in danger of losing an eye from the shirt buttons straining to contain him.

I looked at Morgan, raised my eyebrows in a gesture of *are you ready?* He looked nervous, but he cleared his throat and sifted through the folder in front of him.

'We're investigating a series of incidents involving bogus workmen. A number of crimes have been committed by what we believe to be a single team of individuals. These crimes include but are not limited to fraud, theft and threats, which have seen several elderly members of the community fleeced out of large sums of money they can scarcely afford to lose. Mr McStay, it is our belief that not only are you involved in these crimes, but you are, in fact, the organising force behind the criminal set-up.'

'If you have a question for my client, constable, now

would be the time to ask it. Diatribes such as this waste your time and mine.' Halliday already looked bored.

Morgan looked at me. I nodded, urging him to continue. His cheeks were beginning to flush. I'd have taken over, but I didn't have time to acquaint myself with the case. He was going to have to do this.

Again, he cleared his throat. 'Isn't it the case that you are the leader of an organisation involved in a fraudulent landscaping enterprise designed to con old men and women out of their savings, Mr McStay?'

The man across from him smirked. He rocked back on his chair a little. 'No, comment,' he said, still enunciating crisply and aggressively, the final 't' almost a spit.

'I've personally spoken to several Edinburgh residents who describe you as being present when they've been forced to hand over exorbitant amounts of cash for substandard work, at times requesting ten times the amount agreed at the outset for small jobs.'

'No, comment.'

'I think you see a pattern arising here, gentlemen. Shall we just come to an understanding that my client has been advised to say nothing other than to confirm his particulars, as is his only requirement under law in these circumstances. To continue this interview would be an exercise in futility,' Halliday said. She closed over her own folder, perhaps hoping she could bully the lad into stopping.

'I'm going to show you a series of stills from CCTV footage and I'd like you to comment on each one as I present them,' Morgan continued, belligerently. This was going nowhere, but I was proud of him.

The better part of an hour passed and there didn't really seem to be any strategy to Morgan's interview other than to piss off the bear at the other side of the table, and in that endeavour, he was doing a great job. The 'no comments' were coming with a bored and frustrated tone. McStay even diverted from script a few times with a sarcastic comment, but that hand from Halliday was always there to pull him back in line. I drifted off a few times and wished I could look at my phone, turn on a radio, perhaps even risk calling Alyson. What if something happened and she got hurt? It would be my fault. How could I live with that? Even if she didn't, how does she explain how she came to be there?

'I really am going to have to insist that we bring this interview to a close, gentlemen. We're repeating a sequence now that is borderline badgering and I'm sure you know the regulations in regard to interview protocol. Unless you have something novel to ask, I think we're done.'

Halliday was on her feet. She had a good point. We *were* in danger of stepping over a line.

Morgan continued, relentless, and this time I was paying full attention. 'You can leave, Mr McStay. I can even give you a lift home, because that's where we're going next.'

This comment had both me and the lawyer sitting forward in our chairs.

'Fuck you talking about?' McStay barked. The guiding hand returned, but he slid his arm out from under it.

'Your wife, Colin. I'll be bringing her in for questioning too.'

'You even try to speak to my wife and I'll fucking . . .' Halliday's gentle tap had become a slap.

'You'll what, Colin? Frogmarch me to a cashpoint and steal my pension? Or is it only frail, old people you target for that? Real hardman.'

I almost laughed. I couldn't quite believe what was coming out of Morgan's mouth. Part of me wanted to reign him in, but the greater portion just had to see where this went.

'If this was out in the street and you weren't hiding behind that uniform, I'd snap you in two, ya skinny little prick.'

'For the sake of the tape, Mr McStay is referring to Constable Finney,' I said. There must have been a smile on my face.

'There's not a single vehicle registered under your name, Colin. I found that strange. It certainly doesn't fit with the idea of you running a bogus landscape business, after all – such an outfit would require vans, wouldn't it, Colin?' This repeated use of his Christian name was wearing on the brute like sandpaper. 'So, I went ahead and had a good look at your wife. In fact, a bunch of us had a good old look at your wife.'

Jesus, I thought, where did this kid find the balls?

'Eight vehicles registered to an A and M Landscaping and the name on the insurance document to cover the fleet was? Can you guess?'

'You fucking leave her out of this, or I swear to— Would you fucking quit that!' he snarled, snapping his arm away and narrowly missing Halliday's face.

'Gladly, Colin. We both know she's nothing to do with this, but the paperwork says otherwise. Unless you man

312

up, I'm going to go to your house, arrest your wife, pursue a charge relating to organised crime and thereafter take action under the Proceeds of Crime Act to confiscate every vehicle, every piece of machinery, and everything of value in that big house of yours.'

I had no words. And if I wasn't sufficiently stunned, I watched and listened over the following twenty minutes as this huge man climbed down off of his ego and accepted several charges from a boy half his age and weight while his expensive lawyer sat and shook her head. *Well done, Morgan*, I thought as I left him processing Colander at the charge bar. I'd tell him as much at some point, but there were more important things right now.

I half ran to my office, but before I got there, a shout of 'Sarge!' sounded from the canteen as I passed. I grunted and considered ignoring it, but dipped my head around the corner.

'Have you seen this?' said Mandy, pointing at the television. And there it was, the house in Portobello just as I'd been looking at it a few hours ago except from a distance, a camera zoomed in. As it pulled back, a line of cars, tape and uniforms restricted anyone from getting close.

'Turn it up,' I said.

'. . . have yet to comment on whether they are considering this terrorist-related activity. Neighbours I have spoken to, who have been evacuated from their homes, have been informed by police that some kind of improvised device has been identified within the property in this quiet street on the outskirts of Edinburgh. A disposal team has been brought

313

in from the armed forces, who are on scene as we speak.'

'Terrorists in Edinburgh? Do you think they're lost?' said Mandy, turning down the volume.

I forced a chuckle. 'Listen, I'm not feeling great, I think I'll head home.'

'You do look pretty pale, Sarge. Don't worry, if Morgan needs any help writing his case up, I'll give him a hand. You feel better.'

'Thanks Mandy,' I said and fetched my phone from the office. Only one message and it was from Marcella, confirming details for the fireworks tonight. I considered sending a message to Alyson. I needed to know what was going on, but it would not have been a good idea. If she had anything she wanted to tell me, she'd get in touch.

I tried to put it out of my mind, and for a while I did. I'd considered cancelling the evening with Marcella, thinking there was no way I'd be any kind of company at all. But in the end, I decided it might distract me. I was right.

Rather than pay for tickets to watch the fireworks officially from Princess Street Gardens, Marcella took me to a spot on the Mound you could watch for free. After all, there was barely a spot in the whole of the city you couldn't watch from. She brought two blankets, one to sit on and another to huddle under. We sat on the small steps outside of the New College university building and shared a bottle of wine she'd brought, along with plastic tumblers. I was grateful for the distraction, the wine and the blanket. Summer in Edinburgh ends abruptly at the close of August.

I stopped checking my phone after Marcella had given

me a bit of a frown when I should have been watching the incredible display above my head. It had only just gone dark when they'd started the performance, but now fully night-time as it drew to a dramatic close. The concussion of explosions reverberated off the buildings around us and sent a physical pressure through your ribcage. The display built and built to a great crescendo and we were left clapping with several others who had stopped in their travels to watch. From our elevated position, you could just about see the crowd gathered in the gardens, but you could certainly hear them, roaring and clapping like a football crowd. We finished our wine and headed to my place.

I thought about what I'd say if Alyson was at home, but the place was in darkness as we entered. I began making us something to eat in the kitchen, but after a long kiss, it was abandoned and we went straight to bed.

I dreamt about a church I couldn't find the exit to. Two nuns huddled together on one of the pews, gripping each other's arms and laughing at my failure to escape the place. The hymn board grew an extra number every time I looked at it. As I grew more and more anxious and frustrated, the nuns became more excited. They were clapping and banging their hands off the backrest of the pew in front of them. They were banging harder and harder and there were fireworks going off outside, exploding at the same point the nun's hands crashed into the pew, over and over.

'Don. Don, wake up!'

I was being shaken hard and sat up in a panic. Marcella looked terrified. Then I heard why – great thuds sounded from the front door in groups of three. It wasn't clear if it was knocking or someone trying to force their way in. I jumped out of bed before realising I was naked and doubled back to tangle my way into my jeans as the door crashed and crashed. I jogged down the hall, trying to secure the buttons of the jeans. I paused at the door but the three bangs rang out again, I twisted the snib and pulled the door wide.

I was half-expecting to be rushed at after all the frantic banging, but three large men stood calmly outside.

'Donald Colyear?' the middle one asked.

'Uh, yes. That's right.'

'You're to come with us.'

'What?' I asked, trying to judge the time by the light outside. All I knew was that it was early.

I squinted as the middle one held out his warrant card. DC Richmond. The other two had their cards on lanyards around their necks. All of them looked gravely serious.

'What's this? I mean, I'm not, under arrest or anything?'

'Only if you show resistance. So, if I were you, I'd find some shoes, sharpish.'

'Uh, fine. I'll need a minute. I need to find a shirt.' *Fuck, fuck, fuck*, I thought as I went back inside, the three detectives following behind.

'Don, what's going on?' Marcella said, wrapped in one of my shirts, pulling at the bottom to cover herself.

I circled around her and grabbed a T-shirt from the floor of the bedroom and rooted around for another sock that matched the one I was holding. 'It's OK. It's just a work thing. I'll need to head out.'

'We need to go, right now,' said one of the other two suits in the hall.

I pulled on trainers and kissed Marcella's concerned cheek. 'Don't worry. Everything will be fine,' I lied.

I sat in the back of the unmarked car with DC Richmond who stared rigidly forward. I thought about asking what this was about, but who was I kidding? The driver pulled onto Dundas street, almost at a skid and punched the accelerator, cutting through a light that had gone red a few seconds before. The blast of a horn sounded behind us.

I didn't know where we were going or who awaited me at the end of this journey, but I was going nowhere good and I would be speaking to nobody friendly. I suddenly realised that I didn't have my phone. I had no keys, no wallet. I felt the desperation of the many criminals I'd arrested over the years. You can see it their faces; the options available to them seeming to disappear one by one. On a fair few occasions, this would result in tears from men who considered themselves hard, seasoned. I felt something like grief rising in my chest.

Leith. We were heading down Easter Road, going to Leith.

'Come on, fuck sake,' the driver muttered as a long line of traffic was queueing in front of us. He revved the engine a few times and then cut onto the opposite carriage, overtaking the line and pulling in as a car braked hard, with lights flashing and horn blaring.

'Jesus. What's the rush?' I said, but nobody spoke.

We arrived at Leith station a minute later. My door was

opened by the driver and I stepped out.

'This way,' Richmond said and I walked behind him, the other two following close behind.

'Dead man walking,' I said under my breath.

Inside, the station smelled as they all do, musty with the hanging notes of detergent. We walked straight past the charge bar, a duty officer scribbling into a book at the desk and barely lifting his eyes. Then we were climbing stairs and pushing through a swing door before Richmond stopped. He nodded at the door in front of me now which had a printed sheet of A4 taped to it.

INCIDENT ROOM

AUTHORISED ENTRY ONLY

I took a breath, pushed and stepped into a room far bigger than I'd expected. I stopped in my tracks. There must have been twenty people, all of them silent, having just stopped whatever task they had been performing to look at me. The first person to move was a lady from the back: tall, angular and pissed-off.

'Sergeant Colyear?'

'Yes, ma'am,' I said. I didn't know her rank, but it was a safe assumption and the safe choice.

'Get the fuck over here and start explaining yourself.'

It was at that moment I saw Alyson, standing slightly behind this woman. She was the only person in the room not looking at me.

# CHAPTER TWENTY-SIX

## Your Call

There was a large monitor on one wall. The screen showed an image of a man from the shoulders up. It was a capture from some kind of work identification card. His name was printed underneath, 'Michael Halfpenny'. Beside it was a CCTV still, a slightly blurry image, of a figure that could be anyone, except next to this ID card, it was a convincing match.

DCI Kate Templeton looked me up and down as I walked towards her. She wore no identification and there was no marker on her desk, but I had no doubt this was Alyson's boss. She was tall, sharply dressed and entirely terrifying. Her eyes were wide, her jaw tense. She stood with her weight on one hip, arms folded at her chest. I felt every eye in the room on me.

'You two, sit,' she said pointing at a couple of chairs at

her desk directing Alyson and myself to them. 'And the rest of you get back to fucking work,' she yelled. There was an immediate break in the atmosphere, which I was grateful for.

Kate sat on the desk and checked her watch. I had the briefest eye exchange with Alyson as I lowered myself into my chair and tried to hide the shaking of my hands. There must have been a window open somewhere as a cool breeze caught the sweat on the back of my neck.

'You're a community sergeant here in Edinburgh?' Kate asked. Her voice was calm, but this felt like a feint before a right hook.

'That's right, ma'am. I work out of Drylaw.'

'And you know Alyson from the training college.'

This was a statement, but I confirmed it to be correct.

'And for some time now you've taken it upon yourself to be trampling shit-covered footprints all over my investigation.'

There was the hook. I said nothing.

Kate checked her watch again. 'I've had one version of events from DC Kane, but I want to hear it from you. At what point did she become aware of your interference?'

'Yesterday, ma'am. I'd stumbled across a few things while I was—'

'Fucking around with my double-murder investigation.'

'. . . and I felt it was, way beyond time to come clean and explain things to Alyson. I swear she knew nothing about it until moments before we arrived at the address in Portobello.'

I looked at Alyson, she stared straight ahead. I wondered

how much trouble she was in. I looked around the room and it was clear every one of these people were mechanically approximating work and were instead listening intently.

Again, Kate looked at her watch. 'Why?'

'Ma'am?'

'Why did you decide to start interfering in a CID investigation? I mean, you must have realised you'd be found out at some stage? And that when you were found out you would be looking at dismissal at the very least, but most likely, facing criminal charges? I started making a list while we were waiting for you to arrive – the charges you're facing. Everything from interfering with witnesses and neglect of duty to perverting the course of justice. So, why?'

'I . . .' I started, but nothing was coming. Alyson was looking at me now. She was probably thinking don't mention the old man, don't you fucking do it. 'I had the feeling that whoever was responsible wasn't finished. I had a theory that the killings were somehow a message. The first with the eyes, then the ears. Like the three wise monkeys.'

'You think that didn't occur to us? You thought that the team looking into these killings were what? Inept? That without Sergeant Donald Colyear they couldn't possibly hope to identify the killer?'

Her voice was ramping up now. She had taken my actions as a personal sleight and I had to be very careful now.

'No, ma'am. Not at all. It's just—'

'It's just what, Sergeant? Come on, fucking spit it out, we haven't got long.' She checked her watch again.

'I felt like another killing was imminent, ma'am, and that if there was even the tiniest possibility that I could help, that I was morally obligated to do just that. Yes, I knew I was putting my job at risk and I also knew what a shitty thing I was doing to Alyson, but if another child ended up—'

'Oh, you thought you were helping?' she said with a small laugh. 'Do you—do you have any idea of what's involved with investigating a major crime? Do you understand the legal framework that exists around the collection of evidence?'

As much trouble as I was in, some anger rose into my face. 'I do have some experience with—'

'I know what experience you have, Sergeant. Unlike you, I don't run around shooting from the hip. I looked you up and I'm aware of that cluster-fuck you got yourself wrapped up in last year. As I understand it, a team of detectives had to pick that whole thing apart in the Highlands, cleaning up your mess.'

This was unfair. I knew I was done here and it took a lot of strength to just sit here and take it. Why should I if I was fucked anyway?

'How many of my witnesses did you speak to?'

I took a deep breath and released it. 'I'm not sure, four or five.'

'Can I see the statements you took?'

'I . . . I didn't exactly take statements.'

'No? So where is your evidence? Where is your legal chain to show how you ended up at that address in Portobello? At least you had some corroboration? Someone

322

to testify that these voluntary outbursts you collected were fairly obtained? That they said what you might claim in court they did?'

Again, I released a breath. 'No, ma'am.'

'"No, ma'am." No, of course fucking not.' She stood and scratched at her head with both hands. 'Right, you listen to me very carefully. I intend to throw the book at you, the whole fucking shelf, but right now, as much as it *fucking* pains me, we need your . . . cooperation.'

I looked at Alyson, she was nodding.

'What does that mean? Cooperation?'

'It means for the time being you are still an officer of Police Scotland and you'll do as you're fucking told,' Kate snapped. She was beckoning someone over from behind me. 'Are we all set up?'

'Yes ma'am. Good to go,' the man said. He was wearing headphones.

'I make it exactly half-past. What do you have?'

'Same,' he said. Then the phone on Kate's desk began ringing.

'OK everyone, this is it. I want absolute silence. Are you ready, Alyson?'

'Yes, ma'am,' she said and sat forward in her chair.

Kate pressed the button to activate the speaker and then answered. 'DCI Templeton,' she said.

'Ma'am, I have your call,' the voice on the line said.

'Thank you, put it through.'

There was a crackle from the speaker and then the faint sound of breathing.

'Is that Mr Halfpenny?'

'What the hell,' I breathed and looked at Alyson. She nodded once.

There followed a few seconds of the breathing through the speaker and then the reply came.

'First, I should point out that it's pointless to trace this call, though I know it won't stop you trying. I have it looped through a dozen VPNs and even if you did untangle it, it's a burner phone that will be in pieces seconds after we end this call. Now, are the officers there?' The voice was low and cracked, as if the man talking was suffering a sore throat.

'They are, they're listening now,' said Kate. She looked down at the phone, her arms still folded.

'If I'm lied to once more, I'll know and I will hang up immediately.'

'I understand that, Michael. I already gave you my word. You just caught us a little unaware this morning. The two officers who attended your house are here.'

There was another pause and then: 'To whom am I speaking?' Michael Halfpenny said.

Kate nodded at Alyson.

'This is DC Alyson Kane.'

'You are the female officer who came to my door yesterday?'

'That's right.'

'And who was with you?'

I felt my pulse spike, everyone listening to what I was going to say. 'Uh, Sergeant Don Colyear,' I said.

'Well DC Kane and Sergeant Colyear, I trust the surprise I left for you didn't work out?'

'If you mean the device we had dismantled, then yes, I'm sorry to tell you we spotted it in time,' Alyson said.

'More's the pity. My question to you is this: how did you come to be at my door?'

Alyson looked to Kate, but she was simply urged to respond by a wave of the hand. She leaned forward to the speaker and said, 'Diligent police work, Mr Halfpenny.'

There was a muffled laugh from the speaker.

'What was it, specifically, that brought you to my door?'

Now Kate was waving a hand at me.

'I had an interesting conversation with an ex-janitor,' I said.

'Interesting, how?'

'I asked him about a blonde priest. He wasn't keen to talk, but I was . . . persuasive.'

'And what did this janitor tell you?'

I didn't want to lay the events out on the table, it went against how I'd normally treat a suspect, but Kate was turning her hand over and over.

'He told me about something he saw, or may have. This priest and a little boy.'

'Explain, "may have".'

'His story went something along the lines of: one afternoon he was returning to his storage cupboard. There he saw a priest, not fully dressed, and a little boy who seemed very frightened. He said he couldn't be sure but—'

The laughing from the speaker made us all sit up a little straighter. It was as if it were coming from a different person. It was high-pitched, maniacal.

'Is that the story he told?' he said through the laugh.

There was a short pause and then he was back, completely composed once more. 'I suppose there's some truth to it. Shall I tell you what actually happened?'

Kate was nodding.

'Please do, Michael,' I said.

There was the sound of him drinking something and some crackling and breathing. I had the impression he was settling himself down to sit.

'That wasn't the first time Father Stephen Livingston molested me. No, there were maybe half a dozen previous incidents. But this was the first time someone witnessed it. You know, I once tried to tell one of the nuns at the school, and was beaten to within an inch of my life for my "seditious lies". When I saw that man standing in the open door, I knew that it was over. I knew that the beast couldn't hurt me anymore.

'Two things happened in that moment. First, Father Livingston stopped, for a moment, shocked that he'd been discovered. Second, the janitor closed the door over and the attack continued. It was like drowning and then seeing a hand reached out to save you, only to discover that hand was a piece of seaweed floating on the surface of the water. He watched, Sergeant Colyear. He watched until the priest was finished. And can you guess what happened the next time Father Livingston pulled me into that small room?'

It was hard to hear, for so many reasons. I was struggling to believe I was in this situation. 'I'm guessing Mr Bradley had a front row seat,' I said.

There was more rustling, and again the sound of him sipping on something. 'I've never quite understood what he got out of it. The janitor, I mean, not the priest. He never touched me. Shit, he never even touched himself, as far as I know. Every time it happened – and it happened many times, Sergeant Colyear – he stood there and watched. What do you think of that?'

Alyson looked at me and shrugged.

'I think you were the victim of a couple of seriously sick fuckers, Mr Halfpenny. But what I'm wondering is how this very unfortunate sequence of events leads to the murder of a child?'

There was a long pause, more buffeting sounds coming through the speaker. Perhaps this question had upset him? He seemed to be moving around. 'You said you saw Mr Bradley recently, Sergeant Colyear?'

'Yes.'

'How would you describe him?'

'Uh, I don't know. Ill? Pathetic? Sad?'

'And if I'd cut *his* eyes out, all he would be was dead. You said it yourself, I'm the victim here.' There was a snap in his voice, angry and impatient. Kate was pushing the palms of her hands out urging me to ease up.

'If it's justice you're looking for, I can help with that. I can make sure they pay for what they did.'

There was the laughter again. A cackle, it could only be described as. I could feel my skin tighten, retract all over my body. 'Oh, where were you all those years ago, Sergeant? No, you can't help me. The police can't help me, and the truth is, I don't need any help. But you don't need to worry. There will be one more and then it will all be over. That I promise you. When the time comes, I will post a letter.

In that letter will be my thoughts and, most importantly, where you can find me. I won't cause you any problems, I'll already be dead and this will all be over.'

The line cut off as soon as he spoke his last word. The dead tone whined out of the speaker until Kate reached over and cut it off with the touch of a button. The room erupted into a dozen conversations.

'All right, people, settle down. I want you at your jobs, briefing in ten minutes. Scott?' she called over my head. I turned to see the officer with headphones shaking his head. 'Thought as much.' She turned her eyes to me. 'He called this morning. At first, we didn't know if it was legit or some fucking crackpot, but he insisted on talking to the officers who had gone to his house. We sat Alyson down and when he asked where the other officer was and she replied that she'd been on her own, he claimed that we were lying and that he would call back at this specific time and that any more lies would not be good for us. He had a camera by the kitchen window you see. Motion triggered and quite untraceable. That is when your name came forward, Sergeant. Reluctantly,' she said and lowered her eyes at the chastened Alyson. 'Who do you report to?'

'Inspector Reynolds, ma'am. He oversees Community Division in the East.'

'I'll get in contact with him today. I'm going to tell him you've been seconded to this investigation, but be under no illusion that this is actually the case. I want you on a lead in case our man gets back in touch and he wants to speak you, and so you can't fuck with my investigation any further, that's all. You will stay by Alison's side and you will be available at a moment's notice. When we have Michael Halfpenny in custody you will be handed over to professional standards. Is any of that in the slightest part fuzzy? Unclear? Ambiguous?'

'No, ma'am,' I said.

'Good. Now off you fuck, the pair of you. Scott, over here with me.'

We vacated Kate's desk and Alyson led me over to her own, blissfully out of earshot of the boss.

'I'm sorry,' she whispered. 'I had no choice.'

'I know you didn't. Don't apologise, I've only myself to blame,' I said. I sat, breathing hard, trying to get my head around everything that had just happened, but feeling dizzy and a little sick. 'Do you really think she's going to have me fired and hit with criminal charges?'

The look on Alyson's face was not what I was hoping for. 'I've never known her to mince her words. If she says she's going to do something . . .' she gave a shrug and patted my knee. 'End of the day, it's up to professional standards to make a case against you, not her. Try not to think about it just now. Although I think it's unfair. If you hadn't interfered, we would be weeks behind this guy. I think she's more embarrassed than anything else.'

The meeting opened with Kate giving everything they had so far on the suspect, if he should even be referred to as such, given the overwhelming amount of evidence against him. Even though I was told to stick to Alyson, I felt like an intruder. Some of the looks I was getting from the suits told me they felt the same, especially since the majority of those in the room were standing around Kate's desk while I was sat in a chair.

She stood and addressed the room. 'Michael Halfpenny. Forty-two years old. Father unknown, mother died when he was an infant and was then placed in the care of the Church until he turned sixteen. Then there is a big fucking gap which I want filled. Cut to today he works for a small computer repairs outfit in Gorgie. Those of you who came in later may be unaware that we attended this address this morning with a warrant only to be told he hasn't been seen by staff in many months, with the assumption that he quit. While we were there, what we did find parked up on the street outside was a white van emblazoned with the company logo: a broken computer next to a bag of tools. It's being turned over by SOCO as we speak but I'd bet my left testicle that it's our vehicle. After we're done here, I'm meeting with top brass and we're circulating this force wide.

'We have a suspect who has informed us he has one more target. I want ideas on who that might be as well as where our suspect might be found, and it needs to happen seriously fucking fast. I'm expecting pressure for us to release this to the press but will resist as long as I can, otherwise all we'll be dealing with will be false sightings and I want this manhunt led from the inside out, not the other way around.'

Kate then broke the investigation team into two parts. One, to look at the suspect himself – this included Alyson. The second was to work on the next victim, with the team looking most specifically at staff at the school and those close to them, the feeling being Michael Halfpenny's sick tactic of going after someone by attacking someone they loved would continue.

Sitting at this table I had the strangest sensation. I was clearly on my way out of the police, and I would have to consider everything that came with that. Yet, working on this case, I had never felt more firmly inside. As worried as I was about what came after, to be at the beating heart of such an investigation was no less intoxicating.

# CHAPTER TWENTY-SEVEN

## Command and Control

The shop was called Tynecastle Technology, taking its name from the stadium a few hundred yards away, home of Heart of Midlothian FC.

The maroon façade of the shop was tired, the boxes of graphics cards and desktop units in the window filmed with dust. The place would have been unremarkable but for the blue and white police tape cordoning the entire building off.

I felt like a spare wheel as I entered behind Alyson and her colleague DS Cunningham who'd had very little to say to me on the journey to the west of the city. It didn't help that I was still in jeans and T-shirt, behind these suits, albeit Cunningham looked like he'd slept in his suit, as ill-fitting and wrinkled as it was.

'We're looking for the owner, Mr Dumitru,' Cunningham said to the man behind the counter. The door was open and

I'd followed into the dimly lit store, sparsely stocked with computer components and accessories. I guessed the main business was the repair side of things. It was hard to see the man we were here to speak to. My eyes needed to adjust from brightness of the street to the gloom in here. What little light there was in the shop seemed to clouded by dust hanging in the air.

'That's me. Hey, when can I re-open? That tape outside is killing my business,' the man had an accent, Eastern European, but there was enough Edinburgh in there too to suggest he'd been in the city for many years.

'Any minute now, Mr Dumitru. I'm just waiting for clearance. Scenes of crime are all done, so we'll get you back open soon. Meantime I just had a few questions, if you don't mind?' the DS said.

SOCO would have been called in to corroborate prints taken from Halfpenny's house and the crime scenes. Perhaps also to see if there was any evidence that might link the device at Halfpenny's home to the shop. *Unlikely*, I thought.

'I don't mind. You know I got a call from the newspaper, they're asking why the police have closed my shop.'

'What did you tell them?' said Alyson.

'Just what I was told to. That they should speak to you.'

'That's good. Thank you. And if there are any more calls, please continue to say that – at least for now,' said Cunningham.

'You mean don't mention Mick?'

'Yes. It's very important we speak to Michael, Mick, and interest from the papers doesn't help at this stage,' Cunningham continued.

'This is to do with the thing they found in Portobello, huh? I saw the news.'

'Is there anything you can tell us about that?' said Alyson.

'No, nothing. I only mention because I know Mick lives out there somewhere and then you come here asking about him.'

'We need to speak to Mick urgently. When my colleague came here this morning and collected his identification card from you, you said you would check to see if you could find any more information. Did you have any luck?' said Cunningham.

'No, I did look. All I have is the phone number I already gave. I'll admit, his employment here is a bit . . . unofficial. Will that mean I could be in trouble?' I could see the man better now. He was bald, but at the same time fuzzy – that is to say, his dark beard and chest hair, sticking out through a shirt unbuttoned much too far, were making up for the lack on top.

'No, Mr Dumitru. We're not interested in that at all. Just in finding Mick urgently. Are you aware of any friends he had? Did he ever mention anyone at all?'

'No. Not that I remember. I really don't know too much about him.'

'How did he come to work here in the first place?' said Alyson.

'I put a card in the window and a message on our website. He was a customer before, used to come in to buy components, RAM upgrades, and I did him a deal on a motherboard and CPU. He spotted the card and I knew already that he was building his own system so must know computers pretty well.'

'The van we took this morning. He drove it often?' asked Cunningham.

'I don't know about often. Sometimes we get calls for repairs in people's houses and any online orders in the Edinburgh area I'd ask him to deliver. Sometimes he took the van home. I didn't mind.'

'Again, Mr Dumitru, you're not in any trouble, but according to our records he doesn't hold a driving licence. Did you ever check with him about that?' said Alyson.

Despite the preceding reassurance, Mr Dumitru looked embarrassed. He thought about his answer before giving it: 'You know, I never asked to see his licence. I'm very sorry. I asked him if he drove and he said yes. I never thought to check.'

'Don't worry. But does he have access to any other vehicles? How did he get to work?' asked Alyson.

'Bus. And no, I don't remember seeing him drive anything else.'

'How long had he been working here?' asked Cunningham.

'On and off for five or six years.'

'On and off?' said Alyson.

The man shrugged, 'Business is good and then it is not good and then picks up again. He understood I couldn't always use him.'

'What did he do when he wasn't picking up hours here?'

'I don't know for sure. I think he just scraped by with whatever work he could find, but I don't know where. He wasn't the easiest to work with, but he's excellent with computers.' There was a ping and a clunk as he opened his till.

'He wasn't easy to work with? What does that mean, Mr Dumitru?'

'He's always arguing. Always he has something to say about something.' The man screwed his face as he said this, counting notes from the drawers of the till.

'About anything in particular? What did he argue about?' said Alyson.

Mr Dumitru snickered. 'He'd argue about what time of day it was. Anything at all. Football, politics, religion, immigration, bloody Brexit. You name it, he would have something to say. More than once I told him, don't come back. My brother, he also works with the computers, hates him. Told me not to give him more work. But, Mick, he was so good with the tech and so I would call him back and he'd return as if nothing had ever been said.'

'What did he have to say about religion?' asked Alyson.

'What didn't he say? Hates religion. Last time I saw him he was shouting at my brother. We had been talking about my nephew's first communion. We were going to have a celebration and Mick, he loses it. Talking about pushing religion on children. He got really nasty and I told him, get out.'

'How long ago was this?' said the DS.

'Ages. Like six months maybe.'

'Can you be sure?' said Alyson.

'I can make a call to my brother?'

'Would you please?' asked Alyson.

Mr Dumitru disappeared into the back, a conversation could be heard, but I didn't understand a word.

The shop owner returned, holding his phone with one hand and covering the screen with the other. 'My brother says middle of March. His boy had his communion in April, and the argument was a few weeks before.'

I thought back to the call Martin made that had pulled me into this thing. That was middle of March. Seventeenth I think.

'Does your brother remember what day of the week this argument took place?' I asked. The man looked at me as if he'd only just noticed I was there. DS Cunningham looked less than impressed.

Mr Dumitru went back to the phone, not having hung up yet. They talked for nearly a minute, appearing to be debating. 'Tuesday. Definitely a Tuesday. We're closed on a Monday and so we're always busy catching up with things and I remember, now that we're talking about it, that I wished Mick had stormed out on a less busy day,' he called in our direction. He then said a few more words to his brother then hung up the call.

'And you haven't spoken to him since?' said the DS.

The man shook his head. 'I called him a few times. There was plenty work, but first time the phone rang out and second time it didn't connect at all. I figured he'd come back when enough time had passed.'

The DS clapped his hands together in a gesture of completion. 'Thanks for your time, Mr Dumitru. A colleague will need to take a statement at some point over the next few days. And I'll make a call to my boss just now, see if we can't get this place opened up this afternoon.'

'What are you thinking?' Alyson asked me as we stopped for coffee. DS Cunningham waited in the car while we went inside. It was already feeling like a long day, despite it only being just after three.

'About what?'

'The day of the week question.'

I laughed. 'You don't want to know.'

'Creepy old man stuff?'

I nodded. 'Yeah. I was just thinking about the point at which Michael Halfpenny decides to go on his spree. Was this conversation at work enough to send him over the edge? Was that the moment these vile thoughts became action? I just thought it might be interesting if that's the point we get the phone call. Do me a favour, check the calendar in your phone. Was the seventeenth of March a Tuesday?'

She rolled her eyes, but checked anyway. 'Yes,' she said in a tired tone. 'Coincidence.' We shuffled forward in the queue.

'Almost certainly. Hey, tell me about what happened when I left you outside that house?'

There was a pause in the conversation as she placed our order. We took our place over by the collection point to wait.

'It was a shitshow. First Kate turned up and I wasn't sure what to say to her. I cobbled together some nonsense about how I came to this guy's house. I point out the suspicious stuff in the hall. She takes one look and calls someone, I don't know who, and within an hour the whole street is cordoned off, incident tent, the lot. And the fucking army are there. Bomb disposal guys are shooing us out of the place and then we're standing around for hours before they disarm what was apparently a pretty crude set-up. The door was locked, but a trigger goes off if the door is forced and, you know . . .'

'Boom.'

'Right. Anyone going in there would have been hit with a homemade incendiary device. There was enough petrol stored in the barrel to have burnt down the homes either side. We get the all-clear and by then we have a warrant, based entirely on my bullshit, and we go in. The place is all but empty. I mean the tv is there, dishes in the cupboards, but the bed is bare, no clothes to be found. Neighbours hadn't seen him in months— thanks,' she said as we were handed our drinks.

'Then you get this phone call?'

'I was starting to think I'd gotten away with it. With all the drama and confusion, I'm thinking there might be a way to pull this off, that a hunch or whatever led me there. Between you and me, I'm even thinking how fucking great this might be for my career. And then, yes, there's this call and I'm being rushed to Kate's desk, and shortly after that I'm confessing like she's the headmistress and I'm in front of the whole school. I've never been so scared and embarrassed in my life.'

'Maybe if I'd spoken to you a while back, we could still have gotten to this point, but without all the mess.'

'Don, there is no fucking *maybe* about it. Now come on.'

The DS was tapping impatiently on the steering wheel as I climbed into the back. Alyson handed her colleague his coffee, which he squeezed into a cup holder without a sip or a thank you.

'What's with you?' said Alyson as she buckled up.

He started the car and pulled out. 'Nothing's up, but in case you weren't paying attention we've got a psychopath on the loose and no idea where he is and who he's after. Coffee's hardly a priority.' He slammed through the gears. He had a point, but to me this looked more personal. Just as Aly had been more hurt than furious that I'd gone behind her back, I was guessing this was a similar situation. He must have thought that Aly and I had been secretly working together.

'I've had some ideas about that,' I said as I gave up trying to drink coffee while this guy was throwing the car around.

'No offence, Sergeant,' he began, so I settled myself in on the back seat for some offence. 'Your role is to stay quiet. Templeton made that quite clear. You're not here to assist in enquiries. You're here so that you can't try to assist in enquiries.'

'Duncan, give him a break. His balls are already in a sling and if you stop tripping over your bottom lip for a second and be honest with yourself, you'll admit he pulled this investigation forward on his own.'

Cunningham opened his mouth to respond, then thought better of it and shook his head. A silence settled between us until Alyson turned in her seat.

'Let's hear it then,' she said.

I risked a sip now that Cunningham had relaxed his grip on the wheel a little.

'I was thinking how much he dislikes the police.'

340

'Fascinating. Especially since everyone else loves the police,' said Cunningham in a drone.

'Point taken. But that incendiary device was set up to go off if someone forced their way in. That's what you said, Aly?'

'Uh-huh.'

'So, it was specifically targeting the police, in the off-chance we figured out who this guy was before he'd finished his . . . work. Also, it was the way he spoke to me on the phone. It didn't strike me as odd until later. "Where were you all those years ago?". It made me think he'd been let down maybe? Had there been an investigation at the home?'

'Do you not think we looked into that? Of course we did, and no. There was none. The Scottish Child Abuse Enquiry was set up in 2015 and St Cuthbert's was not investigated. Despite what he said on the phone, there were no records or reports of abuse at the school. Police have never been involved,' said the DS, he sounded almost triumphant.

'Do you believe what he said about this priest and the janitor?' asked Alyson.

'I do. I don't see why he does all this otherwise.'

'It'll be looked at. But not until we get hold of this guy, and that's where we need to be concentrating,' said Cunningham. He pulled up to Leith station.

'What about calls?' I said, just as he opened his door. He stopped, one foot on the pavement.

'What do you mean?'

'Calls from the home to the police? Or, maybe once he was out of the place, did he make a complaint to the police?'

'I doubt there are any kept records of calls. It would

have been what? Mid-to-late nineties? Call logs wouldn't have been kept that far back,' he said.

Alyson let me out the back, the child locks on as standard. He was already in the building when I stepped out.

'Never mind him. He's actually one of the good ones. I promise.'

The station was alive as I entered, pipped and crowned shoulders everywhere. I probably looked to them like a suspect Alyson had just brought in, and it occurred to me, that I sort of was.

DS Cunningham was on the stairwell calling for Alyson's attention.

'Another briefing in an hour, upstairs,' Alyson gave him a thumb and he disappeared among the throng of suits and uniforms.

It was heavily overcast outside, but warm for late August. Add to that the bunching of bodies and it was unbearable. I motioned to Alyson at the door and she nodded her agreement.

We finished our coffees with a walk through the Leith Links.

'Maybe I could get into teaching?' I said.

'Stop that. You're still a cop, and a good one at that.'

'Thanks Aly, but I really need to start thinking about what happens next. If they do charge me with offences, it could make my next step very difficult. With some luck they'll let me resign instead. Less embarrassing for both parties.' I could see she wanted to say something reassuring, but came up with nothing. She put her arm around my neck and we walked without saying much.

It was a struggle to get back into the incident room. It was unclear if all these people had been invited or they'd just turned up.

We managed to find a spot by the window and we waited for Kate Templeton to address the room. She held one arm up and eventually the crowd fell silent.

'As you can see, we're a bit tight for space, so apologies if you're struggling to see or hear anything. We're joined this afternoon by members of various departments. The uncertainty surrounding the next target of our suspect means we are drafting in the assistance of every available resource. We are, just now, finalising plans for the supervision of places of Catholic worship, as well as the home addresses of priests, nuns – anyone attached to the Church. The families of any living member of staff from the St Cuthbert's School are being contacted and, where possible, we will be posting officers to those addresses.

'We're working with a broad brush until intelligence can narrow our field of vision. On the matter of our suspect himself, we are turning over every stone, however, not a great deal is known about him. Anyone not connected to the victim side of this investigation should be working around the clock to establish his whereabouts. We applied for banking information on him and that has just been returned. So, I can confirm the following: on the seventh of April Michael Halfpenny had a little over £7,000 in his bank account. More than half of it was withdrawn, leaving £3,100. This would equate to five months' rent. No activity on his account since. It's clear that he was serious about bringing this to an end, one way or another, so we are dealing with a very desperate man at this point. Speed is absolutely of the essence at this stage. Any new information should be brought to my attention the moment it is received.

'That's what we're working with. At this stage, if anyone has any other ideas about where or what we should be looking at, let's hear it. I'm not afraid to admit that we're feeling around in the dark here and so there are no stupid suggestions. No?'

Everyone in the room was looking around at everyone else. Then one solitary hand stretched slowly towards the ceiling.

'Yes, Duncan.'

DS Cunningham stood and cleared his throat. 'Ma'am, I was thinking about this, about where else we might be looking. This detail that he left enough money to cover his rent while he executed his plan only serves to back up a sort of hunch. He didn't want his landlord breaking down his door – hence the rent. No, if someone was going in there to trigger the device, he wanted it to be a cop. Anyway, on this hunch,' he paused to clear his throat again and there was a glance towards myself and Alyson.

'I asked the area control room to run a historical search of the old Command and Control system for any calls logged from the St Cuthbert's School. This is going back to the initial implementation of the digital system in the mid-nineties. Information back that far isn't great, but I did get a report that confirms there were three calls from around the period we know the suspect to be resident at the school. Two of these calls were from staff complaining of petty vandalisms, but one was from a resident complaining of assault.'

Alyson gripped my hand.

'What does the log detail?'

'There's not much. It was written off as a false complaint.'

'Do we know who made the call?'

'No, ma'am. Either the officer attending didn't provide much information, or the call handlers didn't note it. It was a brand-new system at that time.'

'Do we at least know who the officer attending was?'

'A shoulder number, ma'am, but I can get personnel to retrieve the details, I'm sure.'

'All right, get on it, Duncan, and keep me informed.'

'Ma'am.'

'I'll now see heads of departments downstairs. Thank you.'

# CHAPTER TWENTY-EIGHT

## Micky Halfpint

There was no apology for hijacking my idea, but I didn't need one. If it meant this guy trusted me a little more and might let me take a swing at then' occasional ball, then it was a good trade.

There were no unmarked pool cars to be had. A lot of officers were following leads around the city on foot, or jumping on maroon buses. We *had* managed to secure a response vehicle and DS Cunningham was putting it to good use, doing a hundred-and-ten on the outside lane of the M8.

'What did he say on the phone?' I asked Alyson.

'That he's not sure if he remembers. He's been retired seventeen years.'

'It's a long shot,' Cunningham said. 'I don't even remember calls I attended last year.'

He cut the flashing lights and slowed to eighty to take the slip road. He put them on again with the siren and we were suddenly entering Bellshill.

'Third right along here, Duncan, then go to the end of the road and it's a left,' said Alyson, studying her phone.

Minutes later we were entering a housing estate and cancelling the emergency functions. The street could have been anywhere in the UK. A mix of detached and semis, all remarkably similar.

'What number are we looking for?' I said.

'Sixty-seven. There, I think,' Cunningham said and pulled to the kerb.

A large man was standing in the doorway when I stepped out. The sky was a bruise of purple as the sun was dipping.

'Ian? Ian Telfer?' Cunningham said.

The man nodded and looked around at the street.

'Yeah, I'm sorry about the marked car. It's all we could get hold of,' said Cunningham.

'It's all right. Come on in,' the man replied.

We stepped into the living room. I stood while the other three settled into the only available chairs. The retired officer, Ian, sat in an armchair by the window opposite the large television. Alyson and Cunningham sat on a green leather sofa that had seen better days. There was a smell of polish in the air and I suspected this man had tried to make the place presentable before our arrival.

'Just to confirm, you're Ian Telfer, retired from Strathclyde police in 2003, and your shoulder number was Q743?' Cunningham asked.

'Aye, that's right.'

'So, that tells me you retired as a constable?'

'Aye. I wasnae the most ambitious of cops.'

Ian Telfer sat forward in his chair, hands clasped, elbows on his knees. He would have been a powerful man in his day judging by those shoulders, though time had relaxed everything else. His hair was shaved short, almost military in appearance, grey at the temples, salt and pepper on top.

'Again, I'm sorry for having to come here, but we're dealing with something quite urgent and I thought it best if we chat face to face, see if we can't jog your memory. Where would you have been working in March ninety-seven?'

Ian rubbed at the back of his neck as he thought. 'I would have been the community man for Strathaven. Saw out my last five years there.'

'That makes sense,' said the DS. He produced a sheet of paper from his folder. 'This is the log from the call handling system. It's now a system called STORM, but in your day it was called Command and Control.'

'Aye, that's right.'

'This says you attended a call to St Cuthbert's boarding school. Do you remember the place?'

'I've been thinking about that since you called. I think so. Priest-run place?'

'And nuns, yes.'

'Aye. Had its windows put in a few times. Probably Rangers supporters, you know?'

'On this occasion, the log says a resident had called, making a complaint of assault against a staff member. Do you remember this one?'

'God, now you're asking. It does ring a vague bell. Look,

348

before we go any further, should I be worried? This isn't some professional standards thing is it?'

'No, not at all. We just need your help, that's all,' said Alyson.

Ian's fingernails rasped against his stubbled chin and cheek as he tried to recall. 'All right. Well, I might be confusing this with something else, but I do remember going to that school, or maybe one like it. A call's been made and the staff don't know anything about it. I explain I can't leave until I bottom it out and they don't like that. Anyway, they start rounding up the kids and there's this big fuss with one of them. He's shouting and screaming. We get him in a room but he's not making a lot of sense. He's complaining about the staff being "beasts". I try to calm him down and I don't remember exactly what was said, but he ends up spitting at me.'

'How was the call completed?' I said.

Ian blew air out the side of his mouth and raised his palms. 'I don't remember.'

'The log says it was finalised as a false complaint?'

'Maybe, aye. I mean if I couldn't get any sense out of him, then maybe, aye.'

'Would there have been any follow-up?' Alyson asked.

'I imagine so. I'm sure I would have done a child referral for the reporter for the children's panel.'

'There's no mention of that on the log,' Cunningham said. 'Nowadays that would have to be logged.'

'Honestly, I don't know.'

'Is it possible you forgot to put one in? I mean the digital system was brand new. If you forgot and the call was written off without looking for one, it's possible right?' said Alyson.

'I suppose so.'

'I know it's asking a lot, but you wouldn't happen to remember the boy's name, would you?' Cunningham asked.

Ian shook his head.

'Michael Halfpenny?'

'I'm sorry, I really have no idea.'

'The other kids called him Micky Halfpint,' I said.

Ian's eyes narrowed. 'Halfpint?' He planted his elbows back on his knees and wrung his hands, his head shaking a little. 'It was a long time ago, but maybe. There was a point where this boy's throwing his arms and legs and we're getting him into a room. There's all these other boys on the stairs getting a good look and laughing and shouting . . . Halfpint? Aye, maybe. What's this about? Are you able to tell me?'

Cunningham looked over at me and Alyson. 'I think I have to, Ian,' he said.

Ian sat and listened, occasionally his big paw rubbed the back of his neck.

'Do you have any family?' Alyson said, when the Cunningham had finished.

'Two sons. Both grown up.'

'Do they have children?'

'No, no grandkids as yet.'

'I think it's best if you give me their addresses. I'll make sure we get a car round, just in case.'

'Do you really think that's necessary?'

Alyson's face was solemn as she nodded.

Ian went to the hall and came back with an address

book. Alyson noted details and went outside to call it in.

'Have you seen anyone hanging around? Male, around five-six, early forties?' asked Cunningham.

Ian shook his head. 'No. I like to think I'd have spotted someone if they were creeping around. Those old instincts don't die.'

'Do we know how this guy selects the target? I mean, how does he decide which loved one to go after?' I said. I was thinking about the fact that this man had two sons and what it was Martin had been wailing: 'Bastard cut out *her* tongue!' Though I had to concede that it was equally likely that the thing with Martin had been a string of coincidences, or that Ian here was the wrong target.

'We're not sure,' said Cunningham. 'We haven't had the time to bottom that out. The priest's relationship with the second target was a closely kept secret so there must have been some tailing involved. As for the janitor, again it's not clear. He could have been watching the house, he had regular visits from his grandson.'

'How about social media? Maybe not the priest, but the old man?' I said.

'I don't know. We never considered the janitor to be the target until very recently. I'll check it in,' said Cunningham. He lifted his phone.

'How about you, Ian? Are you active online? Do you have much personal stuff out there?'

'No, not at all. I don't do any of that anymore.'

'Anymore? So, you *have* had an online presence at one time?'

'Aye, ages ago. Facebook, I mean who hasn't? But I

351

haven't touched it in forever.'

'I called my boss. There will be a car round at both addresses within minutes. What's going on?' said Alyson, thumbing at Cunningham, who was now in conversation with someone on his phone.

'We're just checking something. We're wondering if social media might be a tool the suspect has been using to identify who to go after, but Ian's not active. Not for a long time,' I said.

'Did you deactivate your account? Or just stop using it?' asked Alyson.

'I don't know. Probably the latter. I don't remember deleting it.'

'Do you have a home computer?' I asked.

'Uh, yes. A laptop. Hold on.'

'What do you think?' I said to Alyson as Ian left the room.

She shrugged. 'I don't know. It's certainly worth covering.'

'It feels right to me,' I said. 'I can't explain it, but I feel like we're on to something here.'

Ian returned and set the computer down on the coffee table. It took forever to boot up. Cunningham was still on his phone in the hall, pacing, but not talking, like he was waiting for something.

Ian brought up a browser and Facebook's homepage slowly loaded. He clicked on the login icon, entered his email address and then his eyes went to the ceiling.

'I don't know if I can remember the password. It's been years.'

'You can just reset it if you need to,' said Alyson. 'Or we can even view it from my phone, unless you have it set to private?'

'Oh, definitely private. But hold on, let me try something.'

He tapped at the keys, but was informed that the email and password didn't match. 'Ach, I'll just reset it.' The cursor hovered over the reset request, but then returned to the password box. 'I just thought of something,' Ian said and typed. He hit return and we were in.

'Who's this?' I said as his profile picture appeared on screen. A wedding photograph by the look of it. Ian, fit, with dark hair, half smiling, half kissing a joyful blonde with a bouquet in the hand around Ian's neck.

'That's Lyndsay. Ex-wife. Like I said, I've not touched this for years,' he said.

I suddenly felt a little dizzy. 'Can you cycle through your other pictures?' I said.

He did, and with each new frame that appeared the more a sense of dread rose in my stomach and chest. Wedding pictures, then honeymoon pictures all on beautiful, white, sandy beaches.

'This is Cancun, two-thousand-five,' Ian said.

'So, not your sons' mother?' I said, making a quick count in my head.

'No, second marriage. Went tits up within six years.'

The screen was a celebration of her, of them. The last post was from 2007, birthday wishes for Ian and lots of kisses from Lyndsay and others.

'Where is she now?' I said.

'Uh, out Lanark way with her new husband. Poor bastard.

They have a farmhouse but I don't have the address.'

'You have a number?' I said.

'I do,' he replied and went back to the hall.

'You think it's her?' Alyson whispered. The picture on the screen was Lyndsay with a cocktail in her hand, grinning at the camera, a yellow flower in her hair.

I didn't have a chance to answer as Cunningham returned. 'The old man's on Facebook. Full of pictures of the grandson. What are you looking at?'

Alyson was already moving for the door.

# CHAPTER TWENTY-NINE

## Tinto

'It's going straight to voicemail,' Alyson said, moving the phone from her face and then returning it. 'Mrs Watson, this is Detective Constable Alyson Kane. If you get this message would you please call me back, either on this number or by dialling one-oh-one and ask to be put through. It *is* urgent. Thank you.'

'Keep trying,' I said.

'We need an address,' Cunningham said. He was heading south in the general direction of Lanark, lights and siren blaring.

'Three-four from control.'

'Go ahead,' I said into the radio Alyson had thrown into the back seat for me as we spun out of Ian's street.

'Roger, I have your check. Two Lyndsay Watsons in the Lanark area on Voter's Roll.'

'Roger, does either of them have an address that might sound like a farmhouse, rather than a street? Over.'

'Affirmative. One of them is twenty-seven Kirkfield Gardens, but the other has a name, Tinto View. Over.'

'That sounds likely. Can you pass me the postcode? Over.'

Alyson took Cunningham's phone from him and entered the details into satnav while she continued to call the number Ian had given us.

'If his account was set up as private, how would Halfpenny get access?' Cunningham yelled over the noise from the roof.

'I asked Ian what the password was. It's his ex-wife's name and then the date of their marriage. If Halfpenny managed to get just a bit of information on him, he might have figured it out. I bet it will be the same with Bradley Senior. God knows how long he's been planning this,' I yelled back.

'Still nothing,' said Alyson and put her phone away to concentrate on the other screen. She held it up to the dashboard so Cunningham could follow the directions.

It was dusk and light rain was falling. Cunningham was forced to slow as vision grew difficult. The screen stated we were five minutes away and the siren was cut as well as the lights. We left the town of Lanark, heading southward into the countryside. A few miles on and we traded tarmac for dirt on a private road.

I gave our location to control while Alyson was doing the same on the phone to Kate Templeton. In other circumstances I might have asked for a unit to start heading to our location, but with resources stretched to the limit, it was pointless without some kind of confirmation.

The farmhouse came into view, still just about lit by the ever-deepening purple of the evening sky. One main house and a couple of outbuildings made up 'Tinto View', well titled, with a hill of the same name an obvious feature in the distance behind the home.

'One vehicle parked outside,' said Alyson. It was a black Land Rover, new and fitting with the sort of wealth required to own a property like this.

Cunningham rolled the car on to the verge and turned off the engine. 'It looks quiet enough. I don't want to scare her. Alyson and I will go to the front door, you go around back. Take the radio,' he said.

I nodded in agreement and stepped out onto the gravel drive. The rain fell against my bare arms and neck, cold and uncomfortable. The summer was over.

At the corner of the white-painted house I cut left, leaving the others to approach the front door. I followed the line of the garden fence, which stretched back a fair way and then along the back edge until I found a gate. I could hear the doorbell ringing and then three deep beats of the door. I pushed through into a well-kept garden. The soft trill of an aeration system sounded from the large pond to my right, orange shapes moving below the surface.

Small solar-powered lamps lined a path through the lawn to a large patio. The rear of the property was made up of large glass panels, the type I'd seen could be folded away. Again the doorbell and the thuds.

Through the first of the three large glass panels I could

see the kitchen. The light was off but a glow could be seen from the oven door. I worked my way along to the next panel and I had a pull of the handle there, but it was locked tight. Through here was a living room. I cupped my hands to the glass. There was a lamp lit on a sideboard, though nothing else to suggest any life. Behind the last panel was an office. A laptop on a desk lit the chair behind it. The doorbell rang again, four beats of the door.

I cupped my hands again to the glass. A tumbler sat next to the laptop; amber liquid glowed from the light of the screen. To the back of the room I could see the door was open. It led to the hall. I tried to block out as much light as I could to see through. The shapes of Alyson and DS Cunningham moved against the glass of the front door. The bell and the banging again. And then I saw it. A figure shifted to the left of the front door. Not figure, figures. A hand was pressed against the mouth of the figure in front and something was being pressed to their neck.

I pulled away from the glass and fumbled with the radio, my hands shaking. I pressed down on the emergency button, opening my broadcast to the whole channel.

I whisper-yelled into the handset: 'From three-four, the suspect Michael Halfpenny is at my location. Tinto View, a few miles south of Lanark. He is within the property and has the householder at knife point. That is confirmation that he is here and is armed. I am with DC Kane and DS Cunningham. Backup urgently requested.'

Control was responding, but I was busy looking for my phone, realising I had the only radio and, *fuck*, no phone thanks to those goons practically dragging me out of the house this morning. I turned the radio volume down and placed it on the seat of some patio furniture.

I returned to the glass panel and pulled at the handle and was surprised to feel it give. It slid away with a soft brush sound. I entered the office; more thudding from the door and three blasts of the bell. I moved around the desk and walked slowly to the door. From here I could see Halfpenny clearly, his left hand across the mouth of Lyndsay Watson, his right gripping a blade. It looked like a fishing knife, one that could be folded, but also locked in place. The tip made a soft divot in Lyndsay's neck. My stomach churned and water was flooding my mouth. I swallowed it back, resisting the urge to vomit.

I considered rushing him, but there was a good fifteen feet between us and, in a panic, that knife was going in only one direction.

The bell again. The fist again. Halfpenny rocked back and Lyndsay's cry was muted by Halfpenny's hand. Tears streamed down her cheek. She was in purple silk pyjamas, her hands were pushed to her sides, fingers splayed.

I reached forward and turned on the ceiling light of the office. The pair of them stumbled against the flight of stairs they were standing at the base of. I extended my hands reassuringly.

'Take it easy, Michael.'

The hand with the knife went to the steps behind him for a second to regain his balance and then the blade was back at her throat. He stood on the second step; Lyndsay had one foot on the first.

'Who are you?' he asked. I moved forward a little, but

then stopped as I saw the tip of the blade make a larger dimple. Lyndsay's eyes were on me, pleading.

'We spoke earlier today. I'm Sergeant Colyear.'

His head was shaved and had been done in a rush. Small scabs dotted his scalp where he'd roughly dragged a safety razor. I guessed he'd anticipated his image being broadcast by the media.

'You shouldn't have come here. I told you, one more and I'm done. If you try to stop me, or take me in, I have no problem with adding one more, or several,' he said, motioning at the door where the thudding and chiming had stopped. The letterbox flap was open and I watched it lower slowly back over Alyson's eyes.

'You've made a mistake, Michael. Easy,' I said. He'd been trying to pull Lyndsay up the stairs with him, but he was small, while she was tall. He was unsteady and fell back, his backside coming to land on a step and Lyndsay lying backwards on top of him. She came to rest between his knees, still sobbing into his hand. Her left arm was flat against the wall, the other on the step. She was heaving wet breaths in through her running nose, unable to get any air through her mouth.

I then heard footsteps from the office.

'It's all right. I was just explaining to Michael how he'd made a mistake, that he's come to the wrong house,' I put my hands out to stop Cunningham and Alyson getting any closer. I exchanged a glance with both, there was small nod from Alyson, urging I continue. Cunningham stepped back into the office, tapping at his phone.

'I'm right where I should be,' said Michael. He was

looking nervous now, his eyes switching between those present.

'You're where you *think* you should be, but please listen to me. Hurting her is pointless.'

I could hear the DS giving updates into his phone, I wished he'd take it outside.

'That cop left me in that place. You have no idea the beating I got that night when he left me there. You don't know how many times after that I was dragged into that room?'

'It wasn't his fault. There was some kind of breakdown in communication. There should have been a follow-up, Michael, but it wasn't his fault,' I said.

'If he'd done his job, he wouldn't have left me there, don't tell me otherwise.'

There was acid in his voice, the knife turned a little in his hand.

'OK, maybe you're right. He shouldn't have left you there, but please listen, I promise you, hurting her is no form of revenge.'

He tried again to move her up a step, but they were tangled together.

'He's right, Michael, listen to him. Please,' said Alyson.

'You're the female detective who was at my house?'

'That's right. Please listen to him.'

'Look, talk to me,' I said. 'When did you get out of that school?'

'No, I think I'd rather just cut her throat and be on my way.'

'If you hurt her, you know there's no way out. Please.

When did you get out of there?'

He was looking around, maybe assessing his options.

'Sixteen, I guess? Then you could leave? Where did you go?' I said.

'Go? Where was I going to go? I was fifteen. I ran away and I knew it was close enough to my birthday that they wouldn't come after me. I was on the street after that.'

'Did the attacks continue up until then?'

'What does it matter?'

'It matters, Michael, because when we're done here I'm going after him, and the janitor. I don't even care if you make a complaint or provide a statement, nobody gets away with that.'

He scoffed and adjusted his legs, took a little of the pressure off Lyndsay's neck.

'Please st—' she managed, but his hand was back over her mouth.

'The attacks stopped about a year before I left. I guess I looked too grown up by then.'

'Why didn't you approach the police after that? There would have been an investigation,' Alyson said.

'Like there was investigation the first time I called you? Fuck off. I knew some day I'd deal with it myself.'

'It was a long time before you did. You had a whole life in between. What happened?'

'Who cares? Who fucking cares?' he yelled.

'Shit,' I said and held my hands out again. There was a trickle of blood coming from Lyndsay's neck.

'I had to eat, didn't I? Got sick of begging, got into emergency housing and went to college. Fixed computers for pricks I didn't like. There, real Cinderella stuff.'

'Was it this conversation about a first communion that sent you over the edge?' I said. I wanted to communicate with Alyson, form some idea of how to get at him, but all I could do was keep him talking.

He laughed, that high-pitched cackle. He threw his head back as the laugh came out like barks. 'Maybe, aye, maybe. But I think it had more to do with coming face to face with Father Stephen Livingston a few months before that.'

'Face to face? How?' I asked.

It was a moment before he answered. He seemed to relax a little. The knife was still at Lyndsay's throat as she continued to suck in air through her nose, but the tip was visible, no dimple.

He took in a few deep breaths, resting his head on the step behind him.

'I was driving to a call in Leith. Traffic was at a standstill with the tram-works, everything backed up at Great Junction Street. I've got the window open, radio on. I just happen to look in my side mirror and right there on the pavement two priests are walking, approaching where I am. They're laughing and patting one another on the shoulder. You can't miss that hair. I froze for a second – you'll never know the fear that shot through me. But despite that, before I know it, I'm out of the van. I'm standing in the road with my hand on the open door. He's no more than five feet away from me. The car behind me hits his horn because the traffic is moving again. Father Livingston gets a fright, I suppose, and looks at the road, looks at me. Right at me. Our eyes locked for a full few seconds. Then he goes on walking and goes on laughing. He didn't recognise me. Despite how close that bastard was to me over years, the things he did, he didn't know me to look at. Just another face in the street. I think that's when I decided, Sergeant Colyear. That's when I found out where he was, where he went. That's when I found out why he visited Edinburgh on a Monday. That's when I knew that to really hurt him, I'd have to make him live with pain, not suffer it for a few moments.'

'Like Lyndsay? You think that making her suffer for a few moments will leave that police officer to live with pain the rest of his days? Because you're wrong. That's what I was trying to tell you. Yes, they were married, but that was years ago. Jesus, you should hear the way he talks about her now. He couldn't care less about this woman you have terrorised and left bleeding. Look at her neck for God's sake,' I said.

He did, for a moment, but then the knife was back.

'You're wrong,' he said.

'Look, you were right about the priest and the janitor. You couldn't have hurt them more. But you're dead wrong here, I promise. Maybe you got a bit lazy with your research by then. Wait, go easy.'

It was a stupid choice of words. His teeth bared, he pushed again and Lyndsay let out a cry. More blood ran from her neck.

'I just mean that you, what? Looked at Facebook, saw this police officer, madly in love with this woman. Yeah, that's old news, Michael. They divorced a long time ago. You'll be hurting plenty of people by killing her, no argument, but this police officer is not one of them. Please, let her go.'

He heaved a breath and laid his head back on the step behind him. I felt Alyson move beside me and I grabbed her wrist. She might have been right, but it felt too risky.

Michael was softly banging the back of his head off the step, the knife remained trained to Lyndsay's neck. They stayed like that for a few minutes. I repeated the sentiment that he had the wrong person, again pleaded with him. This time he just listened. He lay on the stairs, silent. Then, his arm dropped. He still held the knife, but he now pushed Lyndsay's back with his free hand and suddenly she was getting to her feet. I let go of Alyson's wrist and she went to her. Great bellows of grief were coming from Lyndsay as Alyson gently placed an arm around her and led her back through the office.

They may have been there for a while, but I was only now hearing the distant cry of sirens.

'What now, Michael?' I said.

He remained on his back, tapping the tip of the knife on the step.

'They're three minutes out, armed response,' Cunningham whispered into my ear. I nodded and he stepped back, allowing me to lead.

'Time's wearing thin, Michael. This place is going to be crawling with cops very soon; the serious kind. I'd like to be able to tell them to stand down, that you're no threat, but we'd need to see you drop that blade first.'

I watched as he lifted the knife and began tapping his forehead with the tip, not gently.

'There's still time to undo some of this,' I lied, 'but we have to have that knife on the floor. How about it?' I could hear the first of the vehicles arriving, the siren being cut, the tyres on the drive.

His head rolled to the right and he looked at me. There was a dash of blood in the centre of that forehead. His head rolled back and he arched his neck, pushing his chin to the ceiling and I suddenly saw what was to happen next.

'NO!' I yelled and started towards him. The blade went to his left ear. There was a moment's pause and he dragged it across his throat to his right ear.

I ran up the first few steps and swatted at his right hand, knocking the knife from his grip, sending it sliding along the hall. I looked at his neck and for a full second there was nothing, like it was some empty threat. His eyes locked with mine and there was something like a smile on his face. Relief threatened to blossom and then, the line. A dark red line appeared.

'Shit,' I hissed. Cunningham gasped. I clasped my hands around Michael's neck as if I was throttling the life out of him, rather than attempting to hold it in. Blood began to ooze between my fingers.

'If there isn't already an ambulance on the way, get one here. And bring me something for this,' I said.

He lay there blinking, looking off into distance as I held the dishcloth to his neck. There was no attempt to fight me off, he just remained on the stairs, waiting to leave.

# CHAPTER THIRTY

## Hanging Up the Uniform

'You're going into work?' Alyson said, seeing me in half uniform.

I shrugged and accepted the hot mug from her. 'I'm still a police officer for the next . . . seven hours and eighteen minutes,' I said, getting the time from the oven clock.

'She can't fire you after all of this.' Alyson put her own mug down and put her arms around me, not giving me a chance to put my own down, so the tea sat between us in the hug.

'We'll find out at three, though technically she won't be doing the firing, just handing me over to professional standards.'

'What exactly did she say to you?' Alyson released me and I sat at the table.

'Nothing, really. Just that she wanted me in her office this afternoon.'

'That could mean anything.'

'I think we both know what it means, Aly, but don't worry. I've come to terms with it. I just hope there's no charges.'

'If there are, you go straight to the newspapers. I'd like to see the look on her face when the article comes out explaining how we'd have a dead accused and one more victim, were it not for you.'

I laughed and sipped at my mug. 'No thanks. I'd no sooner pick a fight with her than you. I'm surprised you're packing up the Edinburgh incident room so quickly. There must still be work to do?'

She clicked her tongue. 'Tons of work to do, but we don't need to be here to do it. There'll still be a team in Edinburgh, but we'll prepare the case from back over the border.'

'So, no longer roomies? How do you feel about getting back to your own place?'

Alyson's bags were stacked in the hall.

'Who'd have thought I'd want to get back out Glasgow way for a rest? This city's supposed to be all civilised and dripping with culture,' she laughed. 'I am looking forward to getting back to what I know, and to my own bed. Listen, I've left a bottle and a card for your dad. Will you make sure he gets them?'

'Of course. Though he's all but moved in with Heather. There's almost nothing left in his room.'

'Good for him.'

'Aye, good for him. I just hope he doesn't suddenly realise how much money he could be making by renting this place out.'

'He wouldn't do that to you.'

'Don't bet on it,' I laughed.

I helped Alyson pack her car up and she gave me another hug. I felt a stone settle in my throat and fought back a tear. I hadn't come to terms with losing my job at all, and this felt more than just a goodbye to my friend.

I was late getting into the office after a longer than anticipated telephone call to Marcella. No amount of 'Everything's fine, really' was going to convince her, so we'd arranged to meet tonight and I'd talk her through everything. I wouldn't be in the mood, but it was probably best, if I was honest with myself. The team had already prepared themselves. Morgan, Mandy and Vikram were sharing a joke in the canteen as they made out their notebooks. I joined them briefly. I could see they were dying to ask me about yesterday's events, but all that was said was a discreet enquiry from Mandy as to whether I was OK.

I wanted to take my office apart, pack everything away, but there was no way of doing that without the others noticing and prompting questions. I did remove everything personal to my car, in case I was stripped of my position later there and then and refused future entry.

With the others headed out to their various tasks and enquiries, I took out my uniform coat for the first time in months. I made a mental note of my belt, how much it weighed, how my cuffs were set for quick release into my dominant hand, how my baton sat on the opposite side to allow a slashing draw if I needed it.

I stepped out onto the street and started my foot patrol.

A group of kids on bikes, too far away to identify, had one look at me and took flight, which drew a smile from two old couples standing outside a bakery. I heard one remark how young the police looked these days. Seeing them put a thought in my mind and had me changing direction towards Muirhouse.

It took twenty minutes to reach Pennywell Care Home.

Michelle met me at the door, her usual beaming smile was infectious. 'Wasn't sure we'd be seeing you again,' she said. 'How's that young colleague of yours?'

'He's doing just fine. Thanks for asking.'

'I saw all that stuff on the news. I don't suppose you were involved in any of that?'

'Me? No. I'm just a uniform cop, Michelle. We've got far more important things to be dealing with.'

She laughed and I followed her down the hall to the office.

'I'll fetch you a tea,' she said.

Vicky was on the phone as I entered. Her face also lit up as she saw me. She held a finger in the air and I nodded, settling myself into a chair. I tried not to stare, but the difference in her was remarkable. It was difficult to articulate exactly, but there was a glow and an energy about her that I'd never remembered seeing. She'd put on a little weight and looked all the healthier for it. There was a haircut too, but it was more about the way she held herself. She hung up and faced me, hands on hips.

'I thought we'd seen the last of you. I'm glad you're back.'

'That's what Michelle said. This may well be the last time though.'

'Oh? Off to pastures new?'

'Yes. A transfer,' I said, and hoped there was enough truth in it to disqualify it from being a complete lie. 'You're looking really well. How's the situation with, uh . . .'

'He's gone. And gone for good. I'm back in with my mum for a wee while, but I'm looking for a place. Bit pathetic, eh? Grown woman living with her mum?'

I didn't mean to laugh, but one escaped me. 'Sorry, no, not at all. I've been living with my dad until recently. It's a tricky thing.'

'Tell me about it. I love her to bits, but if she leaves dishes in the sink one more time, they'll be calling you lot.'

I chuckled. 'How's our fella? Keeping OK?'

The sun set on Vicky's face. Her right hand moved from her hip to her mouth. 'I'm really sorry, Don, but he passed. Just a few days ago. I thought about getting in touch, but didn't know if that was appropriate.'

The hollow feeling in my chest seemed to plumb new depths. 'I'm sorry too, Vicky. That was awfully sudden?'

'It happens. Sometimes without too much notice. His son should arrive today. But he left you something, that's why I was thinking about calling. Hold on a minute.'

She began rummaging through a drawer and then a shelf.

'Michelle, where's that letter Martin left for Sergeant Colyear?'

'Oh, aye. Has she just told you the news?' she asked and handed me my tea. I nodded. 'So sad. Check beside the computer, Vic.'

Vicky found the envelope and handed it to me. 'I thought

maybe I'd just post it through the door at the station. We'll give you a minute.'

The ladies left and I turned the cream envelope over. On the front it read 'Sgt Donald Colyear'. I sighed and opened it.

*Dear Donald,*

*I wanted to write to you for a few reasons. First, I wanted to thank you for coming to see me more times in the past few months than I care to remember (yes, that is dementia humour).*

*It was a pleasure to talk to you and be in your company for a time. I don't get many visitors and I'd forgotten how important it is to properly converse with other humans. We are all of us social beings, after all. I'm writing this down now, because if you are kind enough to pop by again, I may not be in a position to thank you in person. Please forgive me if that is the case.*

*The second reason I wanted to write this letter was to tell you about a dream I had. Only a silly nightmare, but you'd become so concerned about these dreams of mine and since this one was about you, I thought you might like to know. Again, I may not be capable of the telling when we next see one another.*

*In this dream, and much of it was unclear, you were looking for someone, only you didn't know it, but he was looking for you too. He was like you, though I'm not very sure what that means, but there was a strong sense of him being very like you in all sorts of ways and in the dream that was important. Except, while you were a whitish colour in this dream, he was dark. And not just dark, but devoid of colour. He was getting closer and closer to you and you couldn't see it. I called out to you many times, but you could not hear my voice.*

*A silly dream, but I woke this morning with a palpable sense of dread. I knew that you were in very serious danger.*

*Now that I see it written down, I feel a little silly. Therefore, feel free to ignore the dream section, but do please accept the part of my thanks, and look after yourself.*

*Your friend,*

*Martin Simmons*

I read it over once more while I finished my tea and returned the sheet to the envelope, placing it in my coat pocket. I sat for a minute and thought about Martin, about his dreams – or were they visions? I thought about how absurd it sounded when you put it all together. I knew it was something I would be thinking about for a long time to come, if there was anything in it, or if it was just a set of coincidences that set me along a path I simply forged for myself.

I found the ladies to thank them and asked Vicky if she'd let me know the arrangements for the funeral.

I walked instead of taking the car to Leith station for my meeting with Templeton. Why not? It was a hell of trek, but what was I going to do in the office? At least there was Edinburgh to distract myself with. I walked to the very end of Ferry Road and continued on to the shore. There was a market on and the smell of various cuisines from stalls mingled.

Despite the colder weather starting to arrive, there were still plenty of customers at the seafood restaurants further along the shore, willing to dine al fresco. You had to love the Scottish belligerence, clawing on to summer to the bitter end.

I checked my watch and blew out a resigned sigh. I now took a more direct route to the station, knowing that making Kate Templeton wait around would do me no favours.

The station was still busy, though nothing like it had been the day before. I told myself it was pointless to be nervous, but was nervous nonetheless. On the first floor I passed various suits heaving boxes. The doors to the incident room were wedged open.

I entered and saw Kate at the far end, unpinning items from a board. I felt an instant flush of fear. A few officers were still chapping away at keyboards, otherwise it looked like they were taking the place apart.

'Ma'am,' I said. She gave a startled jump and turned from the board. *Great start*, I thought.

She checked her watch. 'Is it that time already? All right. Sit down, Colyear. Can we have the room please,' she called out to two at keyboards and one filling a box. I sat before her desk. She took her own seat and looked out over the room. One of the suits was still typing away. 'Adrian,' she called out.

The typing detective looked up, so engrossed in his screen that he hadn't heard her. 'Ma'am?'

'Fuck off.'

'Ma'am.' He stood, pulled his coat from the back of the chair and scuttled through the doors, pulling them closed behind him.

Kate Templeton typed something into her own computer, the keystrokes now echoing in the silent room. I waited. She was chewing on gum and humming some tune under her breath.

'That was a decent outcome yesterday. You've done your operational statement?' she said.

'Yes, ma'am. I completed it before I went off duty. I thought it was best since . . .'

'Yes. Probably best.'

'Can I ask, how is Halfpenny?'

She raised her eyebrows and there was a loud snap from the gum in her mouth. 'He's stable. Thanks to a combination of first aid and being a bit shit with the knife. Didn't really cut deep enough. Not like it is in the movies, Colyear. If you're going to do it, you need to really commit,' she said, making a fist and giving it a short swing.

'I'll, uh, bear that in mind.'

'Between you and me, I'd be surprised if we get him inside a courtroom.'

'Oh?'

'He really has nothing left and while he made a bit of a tit of cutting his throat, it's not easy to keep someone from topping themselves if they're fully determined. He might make it to prison, but there there'll ample opportunity there to end it, if he still feels the same.'

'I was also wondering about—'

'The priest and the janitor,' she said correctly pre-empting me and snapping her gum again. 'That'll come. Don't worry about that. But that's not who we're here to discuss.'

'No, ma'am.'

She typed again for a moment, then pushed her screen to the side.

'Do you have anything outstanding? Any enquiries that might need to be handed on?'

'No, ma'am, but someone will need to be assigned to my officers' workbaskets. Also, I have a probationer who's doing well, I'm hoping someone will ensure he successfully pushes through his confirmation.'

'I'll see it done,' she said as she removed the gum from her mouth with a tissue, then laid her elbows on the desk. She was looking at me very strangely across interlaced fingers. 'How does it feel to be hanging up the uniform?'

I was stupefied by the cruelty of the question. A small laugh came unbidden. 'I, uh. I suppose I've come to terms.' The same lie twice in one day. I could feel anger rising and I no longer cared if it came spilling out.

'Good. Not everyone is quite ready for the transition to CID,' she said and swung her screen back to resume typing.

Ten seconds might have passed, fifteen perhaps. I felt like I would have to reach down my own throat for something to say. The anger in my chest was replaced by a cocktail of confusion and hope.

'Ma'am? I – uh. Sorry, I'm not quite sure I understand.'

'Of course you do, you're not a fuckwit.'

'You're saying I'm not fired?'

'I could still be talked into it, but I thought we could make better use of you.'

'And CID? Ma'am, I'm flattered and, fuck, I can't begin to tell you how relived I am, but I've never harboured any ambition for CID. Ma'am, if it's all the same, I'd like to return to my own post. Stay with uniform.'

The typing stopped and she slowly pushed the screen away.

'Oh, I'm sorry. Did I make the mistake of suggesting there was some kind of decision to be made here? That you had some say in this?' She laughed and shook her head for a moment. 'I suppose there is a choice, in a way.' She looked around and then pulled the telephone from the edge of the desk to sit in front of her. 'Here's that choice, Sergeant Colyear. In one minute, I'm going to make one of two telephone calls. Either I'm calling the ACC to instigate full disciplinary proceedings with professional standards, or I'm calling the police training college to organise your detective course. Which is it to be?'

It took only five seconds to find a response this time.

'I guess I should go shopping for more suits.'

# ACKNOWLEDGEMENTS

My mother passed away a few years ago and this book is dedicated to her. In her final year, I spent many hours in the care home where she was looked after. The idea for this story was formed during my visits. During this time, I got to know the staff there and witnessed the seemingly endless patience of the care team. I marvelled at the respect, dignity, compassion and endless good humour with which they went about their duties. This book, then, is also dedicated to them, and all care workers our country and our society fails to suitably appreciate.

Thanks go to Sanny Blair and Scott Pollock for their procedural advice. I am very lucky to have ex-colleagues I can call in favours from and I am very grateful for their input.

STUART JOHNSTONE is a former police officer who, since turning his hand to writing, has been selected as an emerging writer by the Edinburgh UNESCO City of Literature Trust, and published in an anthology curated by Stephen King. Johnstone lives in Scotland.

storystuart.com     @story_stuart

If you enjoyed *Into the Dark*, look out for more books by
Stuart Johnstone . . .

To discover more great fiction and to place an order visit
our website
**www.allisonandbusby.com**
or call us on
020 3950 7834